In Guilt and in Glory

DAVID HANLY

Hutchinson of London

Hutchinson & Co. (Publishers) Ltd
3 Fitzroy Square, London W1P 6JD

London Melbourne Sydney Auckland
Wellington Johannesburg and agencies
throughout the world

First published 1979
© David Hanly 1979

Set in Monotype Baskerville

Printed in Great Britain by
The Anchor Press Ltd and bound by
Wm Brendon & Son Ltd, both of
Tiptree, Essex

British Library Cataloguing in Publication Data
Hanly David
   In guilt and in glory.
   I. Title
   823'.9'1F   PR6058.A56/

ISBN 0 09 136690 9

In Guilt and in Glory

'All me life I have been lived among them but now they are becoming lothed to me. And I am lothing their little warm tricks. And lothing their mean cosy turns. And all the greedy gushes out through their small souls. And all the lazy leaks down over their brash bodies. How small it's all! And me letting on to meself always. And lilting on all the time. I thought you were all glittering with the noblest of carriage. You're only a bumpkin. I thought you the great in all things, in guilt and in glory. You're but a puny. Home! My people were not their sort out beyond there so far as I can.'

JAMES JOYCE, *Finnegans Wake*

Acknowledgements

Grateful acknowledgement is made to Faber and Faber, Limited, London for permission to quote from 'Autumn Journal' by Louis MacNeice from *The Collected Poems of Louis MacNeice*, edited by E. R. Dodds, copyright © The Estate of Louis MacNeice 1966; to A. P. Watt Limited, for permission to quote four lines from 'Leda and the Swan' and four lines from 'Under Ben Bulben', both from W. B. Yeats's *Selected Poetry*, edited by A. Norman Jeffares, copyright © A. Norman Jeffares and Macmillan and Co. Ltd 1962; and to the Society of Authors on behalf of the Estate of James Joyce for permission to quote from *Finnegans Wake* by James Joyce.

I

Stephen Crossan, on the morning of his thirtieth birthday, awoke staring straight out front, his eyes unnaturally bright, his mind clear. He enjoyed the first thirty seconds of consciousness more than any other moment of the day. They were silent proof to him that his mind worked in strange ways, was a wild thing, a law unto itself, seemingly indifferent to the ravages of alcohol.

He was familiar with the rubrics of the hangover as practised by Flaherty and King in the office: the deep sighing sounds, the pallid faces and staring eyes, toned and adjusted to provoke sympathy and concern in colleagues. Crossan pandered to their noisy misery, murmuring words of great unintelligibility; he drew their work unto himself, easing the burden, softening the horror.

He felt he was not one of them.

His mind was clearer and sharper after a night's drinking than at any other time. It was brittle with good language, bright with new ideas, hysterical with imagination. His body was light. He felt that his libido must surge in waves through the walls and crawl up the skin of Alacoque and Patricia and Helen in Room 301, that they could hear his vitals thrumming and feel his thoughts upon them.

King, once, had explained it all.

'Blood pressure,' he had said, looking sagely into his pint. 'There's no mystery. Mind you, I don't suffer the same way myself, more's the pity. As for having no hangover, you wouldn't want to get too uppity in yourself about that. We're all different. There's some as gets it in the head and others in the belly. If your head's all right, your belly can't be happy.'

The previous night they had drained the Bankers' Club of Paddy, and King was right: Crossan's stomach was a ravaged field and shortly he would have to sidle from the room and loose the first searing squib: a thistle being pulled slowly from the anus. And sincere promises never to touch another drop of whiskey. Or at least not more than a couple of glasses.

Now, lying bright awake in bed, he stared at the picture in the book propped on the bedside table. It was Beardsley's 'Lysistrata Haranguing the Athenian Women' and he wondered what antic impulse had made him prop it there the previous night before falling on his drunken bed. He disliked Beardsley's peekaboo prurience, but could have tolerated it without the phantasms, without the feyness; a little Hogarthian vigour would have been welcome. But then the exquisite Aubrey's life was in every way far removed from Hogarth's.

To hell with Beardsley. Another who turned 'church' when the blinds were coming down.

The book belonged to Monica Whiting in the garden flat below, a tiny, black-eyed woman in her thirties whose hair was cut to within half an inch of her skull and who always wore skin-tight black trousers, Her husband, Francis, wore dark glasses day and night, and kept unusual hours. Crossan found Monica stimulating, her birdlike movements catching his eye as she tidied the flat. And she praised him.

He had taken to dropping in on the Whitings, initially only when he knew Francis was in. He always brought a book with him, usually poetry.

When Monica had first called on him – to ask if he knew anything about electric cookers – she had been astonished at the number of books on the walls. 'One a week, over the years,' Crossan had said, 'you don't feel them building up.' He said it casually, as though talking about handyman's tools.

Later he told her wryly about sacrifices, the weeks of fried bread to purchase the dictionary. She invited him for snacks. She cooked well. She had no children. 'We said we'd wait.' He passed into another stage with her, establishing himself in her eyes as a genuine literary type, whose knowledge of books and authors was casually intense and different from her own, which was bred in fad and fancy, without discipline or direction.

8

It was a penny admiring tuppence. She was desperate to be well read, and among her peers – in Booterstown and Glenageary and Dundrum – she would flaunt what little she knew. 'I like Beardsley's boldness.'

But with Crossan she was a child, suppliant and absorbed, a pupil.

She was, in other words, another potential victim, as he could not help but think of those women to whose beds he cut a path, beating down the shrubbery of reluctance with tiny essays on Waugh and Isherwood and Joyce and Fitzgerald – 'Imagine poor Scott dying, thinking Hemingway was a better writer' – and Yeats, always Yeats. But he was not a careless lover when he reached the glade. Take care to take care, he adjured himself; when, afterwards, his partner fell prey to regret or shame, he came into his own, caressing with words gentle and understanding, the right words, the proper words, the simple, straight and ordinary words, conjured into a mosaic of love, for love, he realized early in his stealthy peregrinations, was unavoidable, and love was easier to give when you did not have it to give: all you needed was the vocabulary.

Beardsley's flatulent symmetries brought his mind back to the present. He could not remember visiting the night before, but this did not faze him: he knew his form in drink. He became soft-spoken and dreamy and more often than not morose. He was never obstreperous, never *physical*.

If he had visited the previous night, he knew he had nothing to fear. If Francis had been there they had probably talked about the horrors of herbaceous borders, or the coldness of tulips – 'as flowers', Francis was fond of saying.

If Monica had been alone, then Crossan thought he had probably let her know he wanted her, but this would have been done in such a gently elliptical manner that it could be brushed aside without damage or rancour.

He rose and showered and dressed, took the Beardsley book from the table and tripped down to the garden flat.

Monica said, 'Well, well,' and he went in past her, alarmed once again by the tidiness of the flat. She had nothing else to do. No wonder she liked Beardsley: no sloppy finishing, no rough edges.

'I brought your book back. Strange young man.'

'You surely haven't finished it by now.'

'I didn't read it,' he said honestly. That was another lesson he had learned: tell as much of the truth as possible. 'I looked at the pictures. I read writers.'

She said that she supposed he was right. She plugged in the kettle. He watched her movements. A small, attractive, vulnerable young woman.

'I don't think you like Beardsley,' she said, finding that tone that grandmothers find for children who will not eat wholesome food.

'True, true,' he said, in seeming sorrow. And then he told her, in simple sentences, why he did not. She poured the coffee and sipped. He filled his mouth and drank it down. It was not as good as tea: nothing killed thirst like tea. He gave a long 'Aaah' and replaced the cup. 'A long day yesterday and a long night last night.'

'Not last night. You were fidgety. Anxious to go.'

'Conscience. I have to meet some Americans tonight and take them to a ball. I'll probably fall asleep at the table, before those chinless wonders start to go mad.'

'You have an exciting life. I envy you.'

'Nothing to envy . . .'

'All those people . . .'

'That's the worst part. I've never met any of them before. One of them will turn out to be a perfect shit' – he took care to drop judicious profanities into his sentences: they opened small gates – 'and I will end up hating him, and he me, before the fortnight is up. And, of course, I'll return exhausted and hoping never to lay eyes on another American again.'

The jeremiad was familiar to him for the frequency with which he uttered it. He resented the envy which his job provoked, principally because at the end of a week travelling with writers or cameramen or VIPs he *was* exhausted, and wanted nothing more than to sleep and wake and read and sleep again for several days. The exhaustion was caused by the number of hours he put into his job on these junkets: his charges should never lack entertainment, should never be bored. He told himself that the greatest sin was to bore, next to giving in to boredom. The heavy spiritual ennui which had descended some years before had had the paradoxical effect of making him determined to fill every moment of his life with people and ideas and stimulation of every kind, and when these were not readily available, to have in his pocket a book which would provide them.

Now he took from his pocket the *Selected Yeats* – 'Norman Jeffares's handy little manual,' as J. J. Haslam called it – the paper evening-brown and spattered with curry and Bolognese sauce, the meals after drink.

'Would you like to hear some before I go?'

'In a rush again? It must be my company.' A proper dash of coyness.

'I would stay all day if I could. Was I offensive last night?'

'Anything but. I was very flattered.'

'I meant it. Every word.'

She stayed silent on the settee, looking at him.

He opened the book and riffled through the pages. 'I'm going to make myself comfortable.' He slid off the settee on to the floor, so that his head was level with her thigh, his temple just touching it.

He began to read.

> 'A sudden blow: the great wings beating still
> Above the staggering girl, her thighs caressed
> By the dark webs, her nape caught in his bill,
> He holds her helpless breast upon his breast.'

He read on.

Her hand came softly down on his shoulder and then up, so that it lay on the crown of his head, her fingers brushing back the fine fair hair.

He finished the poem, reading the last verse slowly and barely audibly. He closed the book and put it down, raising his arm and taking her hand in his. He could not see her face, but her open palm he brought to his mouth and slowly licked it, covering her fingers to their tips with his saliva.

Then he closed his hand upon hers and leaned back, looking into her face and seeing a familiar torment.

Everything from now on was bathos, to a greater or lesser degree.

He said, 'You know what we are doing?'

She nodded, her eyes never leaving his, and he talked slowly and with sour self-depreciation, comparing himself to a careless, barely sentient animal who trundled into other people's lives bearing bright and shiny gift boxes. He damaged lives and left to ply his slithery trade elsewhere.

The monologue, during which Monica's hand stayed tangled in his, was perfectly pitched to show the depths of his rancour, a symphony of self-hatred.

'Stop saying bad things about yourself.' She leaned over and put her lips to his head. 'Say nice things about me instead.'

He lifted his head, held her chin in his hand, and kissed her deep and long. Then slowly he pulled away from her, holding her hands in his.

He shook his head abruptly. 'I am going.'

'Please stay. Please, Stephen.'

'No. Not today. But the next time' – he touched her palm with his tongue – 'the next time I'll stay until you throw me out.'

He stood up and slipped the book into his pocket. Monica stayed on the settee, her eyes on the floor, the crown of her head making a perfect black round ball, hiding the desolation beneath.

He moved to the door and turned. 'You are lovely, and I want you very much. But I am a bad, bad man.'

He left before she could protest, the image of her black, tormented eyes staying with him into the street.

The air was clean and good in Leeson Park, and Crossan's light step belied his feelings. The specious self-hatred which he had glibly summoned for Monica was displaced by the authentic: true disenchantment lodged heavy and sodden on his mind, and as he passed over Leeson Street Bridge he felt shabby and bitter and hopeless, mutely railing against the awful vulnerability of people who were such quick and willing victims.

He was predatory and cavalier, and he knew he had made a deep hole in Monica's day, in her week.

The remedy, though, was unchanging. In the morning, or next month, he would visit her again, and probably read some more Yeats and they would make love. And at some stage he would tell her that he loved her, and she would protest that he didn't, that he need not feel that he had to say it. But her heart would bump when he said it, and the familiar sourness would roll over him again.

It was a piquant scenario, one he had shuffled through many times before. Bootless to let it agitate him now.

He went into his office.

2

Oliver Mulligan gazed disconsolately from his bus window out on the Royal Canal and wished with familiar fervour that he had never chosen to live on the north side of Dublin.

Once a noble causeway, navigable and beautiful along its banks, the Royal Canal had suffered the fate of other canals at the ill-timed birth of the railway, but it had suffered more malignantly, loved by nobody.

For miles out of Dublin it was a fetid creek, a cemetery of contemporary jetsam, prams, mattresses, beds, sad metal detritus and, in latter years, bright immortal plastic.

He was trying to conjure the canal into a metaphor for his own life, but without success. For one thing, the canal was irretrievably dead – so the experts averred – but he himself was alive and, he believed, with the best years of his life still before him. No man was dead at forty-eight. Forty-eight. It was a sturdy age. He remembered looking out of his study window in Maynooth Seminary, savouring the mauve twilights, wondering where and what he would be thirty years later. Now he knew: Publicity Chief of the Irish Board of Welcomes.

Life in the seminary, of course, had had a formal momentum and it seemed that the future would run on fairly rigid tracks. A teen-age promise made to his mother, and utterly believed by himself, had brought him to Maynooth, and three years had passed before the first prickly questions touched his mind.

After that it had been briefly agonizing, but he knew that his first doubt was all he needed, was what he had been wishing for. The promise had been impulsive, uninformed. It was unfair of adults to allow people so young to decide so momentously.

Not that he had been subjected to any overt pressure, but the tacit assumption that his decision was irrevocable had grown irritating, and finally caused him to think of himself as a victim.

That was the seed of his self-pity, and he nurtured it carefully against charges of cowardice, charges which no one made but himself, and were therefore all the more insidious.

Cutting away the trappings of his vocation was less painful than he had imagined it would be, and he found immediate employment in a South Dublin school, nondenominational, described by its secular board of governors as 'an honest experiment'. They had made Mulligan headmaster within four years, and he had impressed both management and staff with his enthusiasm and charm.

But mostly with his charm.

As his admiration for the 'honest experiment' waned, he found himself increasingly dependent on his charm to ferry him over the spiky confrontations with 'new ideas' put to him with wide-eyed enthusiasm by his newer staff members, those who wanted to break completely with what they regarded as rigid and outmoded teaching principles. They used the word 'heuristic' a lot.

Even as he made his name and reputation as a 'progressive', a 'humanitarian' who regularly found forum for his opinions in the *Irish Times* and was once profiled in the *New Statesman* under the heading 'Eire's Future?', Mulligan lost interest in education, lost patience with those new ideas that produced what he found himself thinking of as 'happy dunces'.

He lost heart, and increasingly felt that his particular gifts were ill used and underused in his job.

Then Angela Madigan arrived. She was buxom and energetic, and she was a gift from heaven for the governors, who were desperate for a housekeeper. But for Mulligan her outstanding quality was an innocence which was transparent as spring water, an unknowingness, an artlessness which gave her every utterance a simple wisdom. This was in sharp counterpoint to the wordy pretentiousness of his staff – and himself – and drew him quickly towards her, causing him to shed the prudence which would ordinarily have governed his behaviour towards a woman in her position.

His absences from his room became frequent and remarkable. Whenever Angela's duties required a car, he drove her. 'There will be no caste in my school,' he told himself. Later, when confronted, he told the same to the staff, managing to convince himself that motoring the housekeeper from shop to shop, collecting the laundry, and posting her letters home to Mayo were proper errands for a headmaster who would brook no class distinctions in his school.

He even believed that the board would see it thus.

But there were limits, even to honest experiment.

When the letter came – the ill-written, eight-point letter – his fury was almost real.

But all that came after the Dalkey Drama Festival, which had been moribund for a decade but which Mulligan took over in 1958 and brought to the front pages of the newspapers.

It was a strange and potentially disastrous idea to put on six different plays in one week. But it was a huge success. Dalkey had never seen anything like it, neither had Dublin, and the Dalkey Drama Festival was the talk of the capital for a long while afterward.

It was at the opening of the festival that Mulligan made his famous 'Small is Wonderful' speech, catching the ear of Gerald Craig, recently appointed chief executive of the Board of Welcomes. Craig had been searching for someone with the grit and gumption and personality to convince an apathetic populace that they had the wherewithal to make Ireland what Craig called 'the playground of Europe'. Mulligan sounded right. They spent several hours together. Craig offered the job. Mulligan said he would need time to think.

Almost simultaneously, the governors' patience with his behaviour exhausted itself. The letter was sent, categorically listing the grounds for their disaffection.

His meeting with the governors was tempestuous and one-sided: they were showing their true colours, he raved; the letter amounted to a slander; if they thought they could push him out at their whim they had another think coming; no amount of money would make up for the insult contained in the letter.

The governors understood. They asked him to resign with a 'consideration' and he promptly did so.

He immediately wrote to Craig, accepting his offer 'after careful thought and conscious of the fact that I shall be leaving a vocation for a job, but equally mindful of the need for sacrifice

16

on everybody's part if our beloved country is to achieve maturity and prosperity'.

He married Angela, and seven months later she gave birth to twin girls, Siobhan and Sinead. His life was turned upside down in a year. He took to his new job with relish, attending every reception, every opening, every concert. His was one of the first faces seen on the screen when RTE, the national television station opened, in 1961.

Within two years he had made Gerald Craig's name known in every household in Ireland, and his own known in those places where he deemed it right and proper that it should be. It was annoying to have one of the Dublin columnists describe him as 'the Board of Welcomes barker' and label him, acronymically, 'BOW-wow'. The name Bow-wow Mulligan stuck, and he hated it, but he reasoned that it was part of the price to be paid for the kind of attention he got: better to be known as Bow-wow than not to be known at all.

Anyway, his friends never called him that, and he now had many friends, in every possible part of Irish life.

Ireland was blossoming. It was the early sixties. The government's new economic plans were in action, the hopelessness and apathy of the forties and fifties were fading. Ireland was on the move, and Oliver Mulligan was in the eye of the movement. Tourism brought millions of pounds into the country, and Mulligan was confident that his ideas were substantially responsible for much of the increase in the number of free-spending visitors. He travelled the country, cajoling and convincing local committees, presenting prizes, giving speeches, exhorting the people to clean up their towns and villages, to start festivals, to *act*. He accompanied Craig everywhere, never allowing him to say a word which he had not first scrutinized and sharpened and toned for the particular audience. His life was hectic, colourful and rewarding. He had at last found his métier.

But there was a worm in the apple.

His home life, such as it was, began to disintegrate within a year of his marriage. It had begun to disintegrate, he later felt, on the first day of his marriage, when he was lying on the hotel bed in the Isle of Man, reading the paper and drinking a celebratory glass of champagne. Angela had gone into the bathroom and after two minutes he heard a great bellowing fart which shocked him so much he hardly heard her say 'Whoops' with that artlessness which he so liked.

He put down the paper and stared at the ceiling, unable to shut out the noises which followed the first, and the tinkling laughter and 'Oh, dear me' which followed each one.

He realized with sudden pain that he had married an unsophisticated girl, a girl without guile, a girl who would never hide anything from him. And he realized that he had made a terrible mistake. He should have loved her innocence from afar, as something alien and lovely and unsullied, but also as something with which he could not spend too much time, not to mention the rest of his life.

For dissimulation was by then as necessary to Mulligan as breathing, and whoever would live with him would have to appreciate that fact and accept it. Angela did not even know what the word dissimulation meant. 'You're the brains, love. I know enough for my own simple needs.'

But she did not know enough for his needs, as became achingly obvious as the months wore on. He unconsciously began to ledger her faults: her skittishness and timidity whenever he deviated from the missionary position – nervous laughter which robbed him of erection and excitement as surely as if an ice bucket had been emptied over his member; her inability to pursue any conversation which was not utterly commonplace; her inane chats with the unborn twins and her endless lists of the perfect names for them – she sent away for three books of names; her constant interruptions at those times when he most desired repose; her purblind loyalty to radio soap opera and women's magazines; her fatuous 'news of the day' bulletins on those evenings when he was at home for dinner.

Daily it was borne in on him that he had been totally blind in his courtship, seeing only what he most admired; worse, in his new role, his wife should have been much more than a domestic appendage. What he needed was a social accomplice. What he wanted, desperately, at the countless functions and dinners which he attended, was a woman who would be an object of admiration, a witty, stimulating companion, graceful and elegant, and with such an abundance of presence that all who met her would find her as remarkable and enjoyable as, he felt sure, they found him.

18

Far from this ideal, he realized, he had taken unto himself a plough horse, socially inept, a platitudinous presence who drove him over the years through horror, irritation, anger and finally grim self-pity.

The artlessness which he formerly admired he now found grating. Her lack of interest in intellectual discourse – 'You and your *Neetsy*' – had become a burden. The stolid, pragmatic acceptance of things which had earlier been such an attractive counterpoint to his own impatience was now a dragging anchor on his wild flights.

Angela was burdensome, Angela was a bore.

But all of these things, he felt, he could have tolerated, since he spent so little time in her presence. What he could not abide was her neglect of what he considered basic wifely duties, Quite soon after they got married he found that he had to go two days in the same shirt. 'I can't fit them all in. Other men go two days. My father went a week and not a word out of him.'

She began to send the shirts to the laundry. White and soft, they turned grey and stiff. Soon, everything was being sent to the laundry, and he often thought of his mother bent over the ironing cloth on a Saturday night, smiling and listening to Sean O Murchu's 'Ceili House'.

One evening, when the twins were still in nappies he had got a distinct odour in the house, hot and stuffy, familiar from his days visiting tenements as a concerned member of the Society of St Vincent de Paul; nappies half-washed and put in clammy closets before they were fully dry. Clothes unironed. 'You're turning this into a slum house.'

No reply. A sigh and a sad shaking of the head. Humour him. It was profoundly irritating. She plodded on. He resigned himself to the fact that he had married an irredeemable sloven. He was untouched by the irony that he had met her because she was a housekeeper.

On another occasion, when the twins were seven or eight years old, he had come home unexpectedly one afternoon to find Angela and the children sitting on the carpet in front of the television set, eating lunch – a large bowl of cereal and chocolate ice cream. He was distracted.

So it had gone. The twins were now sixteen, enormously fat, constantly bickering, and the victims of frequent and savage fits of envy and jealousy. Angela, too, had grown fat and rarely dressed in anything but floppy black slacks, shiny and stained, the top not fastening, her laddered pantyhose and grey rubber girdle showing above the waist.

He looked after his own laundry, got his own breakfast when he could eat one, rarely appeared in his own home before the early hours. Communication atrophied into irritated mono-syllables. He never brought home friend or stranger, and to questions about his domestic life he replied with a long-suffering sigh, implying problems vast and unsharable.

But questions about his home life rarely arose, for he had become a very public person, almost a public property. There was little about Ireland that he could not talk about cogently, wittily and often brilliantly, and his contributions on tele-vision and on public platforms were sparkling and original. He danced ahead of the contemporary vocabulary, and long before they were on the tongue of everyone in communications, Mulligan used the words 'Christian', 'human', concern', and 'decent' with facile spontaneity. Ireland loved a talker, and cared more for the shape than the substance of what he said. Mulligan was born to satisfy this appetite, for he never let his private doubts and griefs obtrude themselves except in very intimate company. As the public charm drew its admirers, so did the private melancholy draw its sympathizers: the grief was carefully ladled out to seduce a number of women in the Board of Welcomes, and countless others, Irish and foreign, who crossed his path.

In the beginning this had been a stimulating diversion, and very flattering, for he had never thought of himself as a Lothario. When his experiments with a sniggering Angela left him feeling frustrated and betrayed, he had fallen easily and comfortably into his first affair – Gerald Craig's secretary, a young redhead of infinite guilelessness. She was followed by others, and gradually he began to think of himself as a prac-tised and successful philanderer, but with a weakness – which he could not master – for women who were innocent and vulner-able and young and caring.

Now, as his bus reached the city centre – it was a matter of quaint pride to him, and of frequent anger to his friends, that he had abandoned motoring – he thought of the forthcoming lunch with Stephen Crossan and J. J. Haslam and Alice Foley.

He was determined on this trip to seduce Alice, whatever it

cost him in lost dignity. She was such a distant creature, and seemingly attached to that crazy Teddy French in Oxford, a madman if ever there was one. It was common knowledge that Teddy plunged his spike into every woman who crossed his ken. Common knowledge to everyone, that is, but Alice, the serene archaeologist, who demurely but firmly turned down all offers with a reference to her lover in Oxford. He would try again at lunch. He had a fortnight to bed her. But then Haslam and Crossan probably had the same thought, and Haslam's reputation as a swordsman was notorious. He was a novelist of course. A curse on novelists. Why did women find them so attractive? Haslam was sixty if he was a day, and no Adonis, but he still worked the oracle.

And Crossan. Mulligan had tried for years to make himself like the young man. He listed his virtues: he was young, handsome, intelligent, with a sometimes pawky and unpredictable sense of humour and an attractive dustbin of knowledge. He had been generous to Mulligan in the past and had filled in for him when necessary. But virtues in a person you disliked became faults, and Mulligan hated Crossan's youth, his handsomeness, his insulting ease with woman. Latterly, too, Mulligan noticed an unseemly impatience and irritability in Crossan which was unbecoming in one so young. Not to say arrogant.

He got off the bus and hurried into Bowes of Fleet Street for an early morning snifter.

3

Sean Flaherty sat before Crossan's desk, his legs uncomfortably crossed, a pad resting on his knee and fountain pen poised. His index finger was blue-inked up to the second joint.

He told of the arrival that morning of the NBS television crew from the United States. 'They are all in bed now. Sleeping off the jet-lag.'

'And the booze,' Crossan said.

'I don't think so, old son,' Crossan's deputy said in his infuriating way. 'I may be wrong, but they don't look like a boozy group to me. You may have your hands full.'

Crossan drew his hand across his face to banish the implication. A crowd of drunkards he could handle, but if they did not imbibe . . . He said nothing, bringing his mind back to simmer.

Then he asked, 'What about the ball tonight?'

'Everything okay. Dress suits in the rooms. Pete Ober, the producer, brought his own along. Something in tartan or sky blue, I shouldn't be surprised.'

He talked about the press reception at six o'clock in the Shelbourne. Crossan would be host, though the cost would be shared by the Board of Welcomes. Crossan would make a speech. 'Oliver Mulligan rang and offered to say a few words, if you wished.'

'I'm sure he did.'

'All of this he'll tell you himself at lunch today. Half past twelve at Snaffles. Alice Foley and J. J. Haslam have confirmed that they will be there.'

'What time is it now?'

'You have an hour.'

Crossan sighed. It would be a long day. 'I'm going to take a walk. Get some air into my lungs for this evening. I presume the women in this outfit are all right?'

'One of them was wondering about a partner for the ball.'

'Which one was that?'

'Virginia Green.'

'The reporter?'

'The very one. She's the tough one that Gogarty told us about.'

'We are a gallant race. She'll not want. I'll take her myself.'

He went to the door, wanting out of the office and the stacks of beige files. He turned to Flaherty.

'Did you speak to her?'

'I did that.'

'Will she be trouble?'

'She seems to be very efficient, businesslike.'

'I see.' Then, casually, 'What does she look like?'

'Bloody attractive. Tall. Leggy. Well built.'

'Then I will certainly take her myself.'

'She's black, old son.'

4

'*You humpy-backed pig-faced snot-nosed fuck pig of a shitty-arsed miser cunt fucker ballocks ballocks ballocks cunt.*'

The note was barely legible, done in mauve crayon on the torn-out title page of *Swan of Bright Plumage*.

J. J. Haslam balled the note in his hand and, murmuring 'Hell hath fury,' he threw it to the far end of the bed-sitter. It hit the grill over the gas cooker, settling on the second gas ring and drawing his attention to the cooking pot which sat on top of it. He had not put that there. He got up and walked across in his torn Paisley pyjamas, the string trailing along the scuffed and grimy jute carpet. He looked into the pot and saw two inches of water and a porridge of paper which had yesterday been his last remaining copy of *Swan of Bright Plumage*, his favourite among his own books.

He stood looking into the pot for a long while in silence, smiling at first and then opening himself to loud laughter as the memories of the previous night stitched themselves together in his mind.

He walked back to his window and looked out on Huband Bridge. There she had stood, a witch in mascara, her cigarettes and lighter in her hand and green knee boots on her legs. He knew her face from before. Huband Bridge grew whores as other bridges grew lichen, for as long as anyone could remember. Last night was the fifth time he had taken one up to his room, but the first one he had not paid.

The approach was always the same. Drinking all day, shambling home alone while the others went off to their wives or lovers, inexpressible loneliness in his heart, and then the painted sirens on the bridge. He always, at this time, thought of himself as Dr Johnson: it was an emollient.

'Why aren't you at home in bed at this hour of the night, craythur?'

'Five pounds.'

'It's a shame to have a lovely young girl like yourself . . .'

'Fuck off. There's a car coming.'

'We'll see what we can do.'

And they came trailing up the four flights, and there was nothing he could do except talk to them, and they did not mind talking if he paid them first, and even in his thumping drunkenness he was aware that J. J. Haslam, 'Ireland's foremost raconteur', was paying a whore money to listen to what he had to say.

And last night it had been too much. She sat and stared at his books, swinging one green boot over the other and smoking a cigarette through a holder, her eyes two black holes.

'Do you know who I am?'

'I don't give a fuck who you are, mister. You're wasting my time.'

'Child, I was considered a great man. Before you were born. Still am.'

'You've enough talk.'

'You're just a cheap whore.'

And he had fallen asleep as though to ward off her angry blows. But there were no blows. She had heard it all before, and worse. He felt her going through his pockets, but he knew she could not roll him out of the chair and get at his back pocket where his wallet was.

So she had scrawled the note and put the book in the pot of water. It was a strange revenge. She must have known something.

He felt in his trousers pocket: the wallet was still there, and the money in it. And this morning's post should bring a cheque from *Harper's Bazaar*. The next fortnight would be taken care of by the government. They could never pay him back for what he had suffered.

He had kept the flag of literary Ireland flying, by Christ, while they fumbled in the greasy till. Yeats must be turning in his grave. They would be visiting that very grave, Crossan had said. He wished he were as young as Crossan again. A confident young man, as befitted the mood of the country.

He did not wish he were as young as Crossan again. All the

25

best characters were dead. Each morning a familiar name in the left-hand columns.

But he still had plenty in him. Plenty of life and plenty of stories. It was what kept him going. He had watched Behan stretch his meagre talent on the rack and die. It would not happen to J. J. Haslam. He had served his time, and he had much in him yet. This morning he would finish the story on the matchmaker. It was beautiful. Particularly the ending. Which was not an ending at all but a beginning.

He sat at his desk and picked up his beloved A. T. Cross fine felt black pen. He would be finished in one hour. And then lunch.

5

A few hundred yards from where J. J. Haslam was writing, Crossan sat on Patrick Kavanagh's seat on the Grand Canal, watching the water flowing 'Niagarously' over the fourth lock.

The sound of the water was a balm to his fury at Flaherty, and at himself. For he had been totally spontaneous in his reaction to his deputy's parting information. He wished he had muttered 'I see' or 'Good'; instead, he had stopped still at the door, looking at his informant with silly surprise, his mouth open. Flaherty had just looked straight back at him, his face puckered by his small triumph.

People loved to shock.

The information that Virginia Green was black had been missed in all the telex traffic between New York and Dublin. Or else Gogarty had deliberately withheld it, hoping that some social solecism would result.

Jesus, Crossan thought, what the Irish will do for a story. Here he was sitting in a place of idyllic serenity in Dublin, surrounded by the ghosts of Kavanagh and Behan, trying to decide whether another Irishman, a happy exile, had tried to place him on a spit.

Truth was, he liked Gogarty and Gogarty's ways. The man loved the bounce and venery of New York, but he sorrowfully missed what he called 'the perpetual crack' of Dublin. On his frequent visits he assiduously collected all the latest anecdotes from Grogans and the Bailey and Bowes, stories of money lost, of vomit on carpets, of suicides, of lying and prevarication and loss of face, of shattered dignity, of deadly and astringent gossip wherein solid virtues were sneered at, of squalid affairs and meaningless intrigues. He gulped them all down and glee-fuly reassembled them for his Irish-American cohort.

Kavanagh the poet had been a victim, a turbulent, grace-less ploughboy finding little solace in Dublin. Except maybe in Parson's bookshop, behind where Crossan was sitting. Thousands of red-spined Penguins, and Mary King's head barely visible above the book counter as she read and read and read. What kind of perversion was it to be interested in the goods of your trade? Kavanagh used to shuffle in of a morning, the compleat poet. And Behan in his pyjamas, tousled and belligerent. But never the two together. Didn't they hate each other, like good Irish writers should? And Mary King listened, and May O'Flaherty listened, and the little bookshop on Baggot Street Bridge was an oasis of sanity after the ravaging nights.

Yes, there was solace for Kavanagh and Behan there, for those victims of the transatlantic snigger. But Crossan could think of neither of them as a true victim: they enjoyed being talked about.

He rose and moved down the canal. The first August leaves were already shed and soon the canal bed would have a soft covering of gold and brown and ochre.

To his right, among the red-bricked flats, lived the furious Liam O'Flaherty, gone past his eightieth year. No sign of him this morning, far from his Aran Island, his great handsome head topped by a seaman's cap, yachting shoes on his feet, a simple shopping bag in his hand, his mind full of violence and by his side the New England lady of seraphic amiability.

Down Lad Lane lived the sensible Mary Lavin, stitching together her delicate moving cameos, and a few hundred yards out the Morehampton Road the scholar fabulist Benedict Kiely was no doubt now covering a lined yellow sheet with generous longhand.

Damned city was awash with the living and the memories of the dead, all of them pushed to telling the world about their country and its people.

Was ever a nation so written about?

He turned into Leeson Street again and looked down on the Georgian fenestrations, wondering how long they would last. Wondering, too, whether he really cared. When they were built, no doubt there were people, vocal and righteous, who found them boring, predictable and painfully functional.

Now they were all that Dublin had, its red-bricked heart, and they were falling fast to shiny-faced developers.

He crossed the street and stepped down into the cool gloom of Snaffles.

John Nolan opened the door, an immaculate relict of the Red Bank, where you could once get a good cheap meal, and a good expensive one, too. No Red Bank any more: it was now a place of perpetual adoration, run by American priests. That was all Ireland needed: one good restaurant less, one chapel more.

''Mornin', Mr C. Brisk enough for August.'

Crossan looked about the dark room, relieved to find it empty. He sat under the large gilt mirror, looking at the heavy brown tables of old mahogany and the salmon in the painting opposite, lying dead and cold and awkward against the furry brown background. Horses and greyhounds, their bodies made rigid by the painter's brush: no life, no movement.

He ordered a carafe of white wine and wondered again about Alice Foley and how her presence would affect the caravan for the next fortnight.

She had been a last-minute replacement for another archae-ologist, Harry Tynan. He had told Crossan not to worry: 'She will fill the gap admirably.'

'As I remember, she is not a very clubbable woman.'

'My dear Stephen, considering you'll have J.J. and Oliver along, I should have thought that was a virtue. She's not a termagant, you know. She's in love with Teddy, you know Teddy French?'

'Slightly.'

'Would someone like Teddy saddle himself with a bird who won't put up with an awful lot?'

But Crossan was still uneasy. He had met Alice Foley three times previously and each time she had treated him as a total stranger, allowing herself to be introduced with some protocol. He resented the pretence, but could do nothing about it: one did not advance oneself in the Department by making enemies. Dublin was, when all was said and done, a tiny place, and Alice was not the only one who played that particular game.

She was a tall, austere-looking woman with very black hair swept back from her forehead. She smoked incessantly and her glasses were rimless, 'in case,' someone had once remarked 'she might miss anything'. She floated on the edge of Oliver Mulligan's social circus. She appeared often enough for people to remember her – especially the men, who admired her lovely, full breasts – but when she was absent no void was felt, no one inquired.

Her refusal to become totally immersed in Mulligan's world – receptions, parties, lunches, dinners, all-day boozing sessions – and her dalliance with the untameable Teddy French gave her a certain aura: she was at once resented and admired. Most of the admiration came from the men, the resentment from the women, who saw in her a threat: she lived alone in Dublin, dipping into their lives, holding fast to an exile capstan, Teddy French, the distant lover. The women wished she would do something. But Alice did nothing.

Now she was coming into Crossan's life for a fortnight, and he wondered about the strength of his amiability. He did not like women to have mystery about them, and felt no challenge in their company. At any rate she did not seem to like him, and that was a challenge he withered from.

At times, such as the present, sitting alone over a glass of wine, he reflected on the strange, unreal nature of his work. He had spent twelve years being agreeable to people, having come straight from high school to the department at a time when it was considered a triumph to do so. His benign concern during those years had been rewarded, and the letters flowing back from those whom he had tended left their soft impression. He was now Head of Information Section, Department of Foreign Affairs, with responsibility for overseas publicity. He was paid an adequate salary for a man living alone in the very provincial capital of a small country. But his work demanded a high prudent tolerance of the foibles, the shabby hauteurs, of visiting people, those judged valuable 'publicists' by the government. They were rarely as important as they believed themselves to be. Some of them were profoundly ignorant, insensitive and demanding; the more ignorant, the more demanding. A few were gifted, and wore their gifts lightly. They were journalists of all kinds, writers on politics and economics, current-affairs writers, travel writers and colour writers, television producers and reporters.

There were also those described in official files as 'leaders of

opinion' – usually trade-union organizers or public function-
aries or company presidents.

There was also that amorphous category known as VIPs,
whose demands on time were almost always social, always more
exhausting; the publicity they generated about Ireland was
always in inverse proportion to the time spent entertaining
them.

All of these people had little in common beyond curiosity
and an unblinking willingness to allow their hosts to pay for
every tittle of hospitality.

Ireland needed their kind words: let Ireland pay for them.

Crossans' job was to become for them a channel to the
'authentic' Ireland, a land without leprechauns or shillelaghs,
a nation moving towards maturity, a country ambivalently
proud of its contribution to English literature, now intent on
making its presence known in more tangible areas of social,
economic and political advancement.

He had given this message – with more or less conviction,
more or less wryness, depending on the audience – to American
and French and German and British and Dutch, and even on
occasion to Russian and Pole. And they had returned to their
countries to write stories which were termed, again in official
files, 'positive'.

In latter years he had gradually and without reluctance
transferred to Flaherty and King most of the responsibility for
all countries except America. King's natural irony was sufficient insulation against endemic British insensitivity, and
Flaherty was too shallow to reflect on national failings in any
depth, thereby escaping much anguish.

Crossan had nurtured an early interest in America, in its legis-
lative system, its incredible energy, its politics, and particularly
its literature. He believed the literary torch had long since
passed from the British: he found their cold mannerisms dated
and intrusive, and their preoccupations becoming increasingly
provincial and bogus – with the noble exception of Fowles.
Isherwood and Auden and Huxley had made for America.
Crossan felt sure he knew why.

The idea of America – the greatest social experiment ever –
at once excited and repelled him. It was not one but fifty
different countries at least. It was, he felt, the only civilization –
yes, yes, civilization – in the history of the world which was at

once adolescent and decadent. All others had the solidity of painful centuries of evolution, which gave certitudes, those inflexible points of purchase in an evolving national psyche. The United States had had two hundred years of massive polyglot immigration, combined with equally massive technological advance, and now its flag purported to fly with disinterest for black, Jew, Eskimo, Puerto Rican, WASP, Amerindian, the obscenely rich and the wretchedly poor, the vast middle class and the maverick, cynical dropout.

How did it work?

For it did, Crossan believed, it did.

Not least among its virtues – in the eyes of his employers – was the fact that every year it poured hundreds of millions of dollars into Ireland, from tourists, from Irish-Americans who retained obligations to their families, from companies who had set up operations in Ireland. That was why his job was important. That was how, listening to the complaints – 'Showers aren't the greatest, huh?' – or bearing mutely with grossly misinformed attitudes to his country and his people, he could close his mind, fix his smile, and live with his job.

J. J. Haslam stood before him, beaming.

He sat, and Crossan poured wine, and they drank a toast to the success of the forthcoming venture. Haslam began to recount a story he had just heard about Freddy Barton, the Minister for Posts and Telegraphs.

Crossan watched the novelist as he talked. His head was completely bald on top, but the sides of his face were covered with generous ginger sideburns which somehow emphasized his masculinity. The point of his nose was the centrifuge of a thousand purple capillaries – one for every drunken week – which spread about his face like the rivers on an ordnance map, his eyebrows were shaggy and lofted, and his grey eyes perpetually alternated between balefulness and detachment. Crossan had seen the face before him on so many occasions, in icy sobriety, in relaxed merriment, and in mean drunkery, yet rarely had he seen it register any but the two masks: the writer was either scornful or interested, depending very often on whether he was talking or listening.

Now he was talking, finishing his story on Freddy Barton, the most reviled man in the country, and the butt of many stories far less amusing, far more cruel and vengeful than the one told by Haslam.

Barton was the scion of a South Wicklow milling family, the only Protestant in the Irish cabinet. His blood was pure Irish for at least three centuries, but like so many others of equally immaculate lineage, his whole affect was un-Irish in the extreme. He had been schooled in England and at Trinity College in Dublin, and he had been half forced into politics by the sudden death of his maternal uncle, one of the Bagnalls of Carnew.

The party had taken to him, initially admiring his energy and conscientiousness and his unaffected willingness to knock on doors. He scraped in on the strength of his dead uncle's popularity at the by-election, but in the following general election he topped the poll. He was quickly rewarded with a parliamentary secretaryship, and later with the first of a number of ministerial portfolios.

Now he was Minister for Posts and Telegraphs, finding that the problems of his department could not be solved by intelligence and hard work. But his mind was on more important matters. While keeping his department ticking over and diligently ignoring the waspish and frustrated letters about the telephone system which crowded the newspaper columns, he appointed himself unofficial government spokesman on the Northern question, usurping the role of the Foreign Minister. Barton believed that his Protestantism gave him an insight into the problems of Northern Ireland – a dimension of sympathy – which was denied his Catholic cabinet colleagues. The media loved him.

He was a tall and exceptionally handsome man, soft-spoken, immensely erudite, and gregarious. In a cabinet that sorely lacked intellectual substance, led by a Prime Minister who was a professed semiliterate, Barton was outstanding, and he made himself constantly available to every reporter, home and foreign, who appeared on his doorstep. He was the only spark in a cabinet that was mean-minded and insular, and to his friends he would bemoan his obligation to play 'on this team of horny-headed bogmen'.

But these were private opinions, expressed only to intimates. He well knew that by accent, affect and background, he was an object of suspicion to the great majority of the Irish people, notwithstanding his consistently good polling record in his constituency. If his accent and demeanour were not enough, his scholarship – which was wide-ranging, solid and deep – would have marked him off as a politician who was therefore not quite trustworthy: there was little respect or trust for Barton's sardonic brand of intellectualism in Ireland.

Such a situation might have deterred a man less wry, less committed, than Barton. But in a fatalistic way he believed in Ireland, and was self-consciously zealous, even to the point of folly, in his efforts to bring about a country without myths, where the jagged history of the little island would be a valuable prop to the future, not a soggy burden on the present.

He put this message to his constituents, and to the people of Ireland, regularly and with force, and in the nature of things he created an army of enemies who resented his scholarship, distrusted his logic, and were infuriated by his intellectual insouciance.

J. J. Haslam was not a uniformed member of that army, sharing, as he did, many of Barton's attitudes and beliefs. But a good story is a good story, and no Irishman was ever inhibited from telling one by mere liking for the victim.

Oliver Mulligan ushered Alice Foley to her seat with verbose flourishes.

Crossan, standing, once again suffered her surprise at a new face. Haslam she acknowledged with that simpering recognition that all women reserved for the novelist, and which he absorbed quietly as his due.

They sat, and Mulligan immediately – verbally and by faint gesture, and to Crossan's heavily veiled irritation – began to act as host, ordering wine, inquiring whether the kidneys were good *today*. It was a chronic habit of Mulligan's to act as host in all things except payment.

They ordered and ate.

Crossan recounted the itinerary. 'Think of yourselves as sturdy native ballast. Ober wants us around in case there's a shambles.'

Mulligan said, 'This man would be of the Hebrew persuasion?'

'So far as I know.'

'Excellent.'

'No anti-Semite, our Oliver,' Haslam said.

34

'They are almost invariably witty and intellectual.'

'Bringing them up to your own level.'

Crossan said, 'The cameraman is Max Maynard. There's a script and continuity girl named Ellen Harbo. And the reporter and presenter is a woman named Virginia Green.'

'Splendid.'

'She's black.'

Haslam sipped his port. 'Nothing to beat the touch of colour in a good story.'

Alice Foley said, 'What do they know about Ireland? Has any of them ever been here before?'

'Not that I know of,' Crossan said. 'They had two researchers here for a fortnight, and they have had several meetings in the consulate in New York. I suppose they have a trusting layman's knowledge of our little country.'

Haslam said, 'A lot of good that will be when they come up against the real thing.'

'That's as may be,' Crossan said. 'Anyway, there's no need for me to impress on anyone here the potential value of this programme in terms of our overall publicity efforts in the United States. NBS consider "The Whole Story" their showcase programme, and it is watched by over ten million people every month. It is vital that Ireland shows up well in this, and we all have a part to play.'

His platitudes went uncensured, and they talked about the coming evening.

Mulligan said, 'I'd be happy to say a few words, if you wish.'

'I'm not bothered about that,' Crossan said. 'It's the ball.'

'Ah, yes, the ball,' Haslam said, looking at Alice. 'I'll have the pleasure of your company, my dear?'

Mulligan said, 'Can't have you cutting out the beautiful women for yourself all the time, J.J. Alice may be spoken for tonight. Is Teddy in town?'

Alice removed her glasses, opened her handbag and covered her face with a handkerchief in what seemed like one movement.

Mulligan's springs of solicitude flowed reflexively. 'What is it, my sweet? What's the matter?'

'Teddy is dead,' she said, barely audibly, into the handkerchief.

The three looked at her, appalled. Snaffles was not the place to announce the death of a vibrant young man.

'He hanged himself in Oxford on Friday.'

The three heads hung silent, Mulligan momentarily speechless.

'I went over on Saturday to take care of the arrangements. The people at Oxford were very nice. They've had to deal with this kind of thing before.' She was staring at the table, and her voice was a monotone, but she had replaced her glasses. She took a note from her bag. 'He left this.'

Mulligan read the note and passed it to Crossan. Haslam read it aloud: ' "Now I know what you'll all find out sooner or later: there's no fucking god. A pox on everything." ' There was no signature.

Alice said, 'He always said he wanted to be buried at Lough Conn.' She looked at Mulligan. 'We'll be passing there, won't we?'

'So far as I know, but . . .'

'Then we can all bury him.'

She took from her handbag a small blue porcelain urn and placed it on the table. The modest and unlikely cynosure held them for a moment. Haslam and Crossan were silent. Mulligan was restless, pregnant with eulogy. He took Alice's hand between his two and slowly began to massage it as he spoke.

'What is a body to say? I'm a coffin man myself, with maybe an old-fashioned regard for the rituals of burial. But what is more sacred than a man's last wish?' His alabaster face was heavy and lugubriously solemn as he coughed and leaned forward, looking at all in turn.

'I know – we all know – people whose company we cherish. Nevertheless there are times when even the dearest friends wear one's patience. One of the great tests of friendship is whether a man can remain constant in the face of his friend's foibles. With Teddy, well, there was never any test. He was never a man you had to *tolerate*.' He gave a low groan, looking gravely at the urn while he paused. Then he looked sadly up at Alice and said, 'Teddy was a *human being*.'

With bathos came relief. Mulligan's portmanteau of superlatives had been abused and exhausted of its rich variety over twenty years of occasions, grave and pleasant, public and private, and latterly he had reverted to the sharp and simple.

The vocabulary of his praise had become so convoluted that words like 'intelligent' and 'nice' now dripped from his lips as bile.

He had paid the dead Teddy the supreme compliment. Another onerous task completed by the maestro. But not quite. He moved his hands to her face.

'Teddy was a friend to us all. None of us was privileged to know him as well as Alice, but we appreciated his great mind, his free and independent mind – and God knows there aren't many of them around nowadays – and also, and this cannot go without mentioning, his *sense of humour*. Many was the occasion made unhappy by circumstances and Teddy would cut through our grief by insisting on ordering another . . .'

'There's no need,' Alice interrupted.

Mulligan put his fat hand on hers. 'He would have wanted us to do it. Wherever he is now – and far be it from any of us to be the judge of that – I know he would want us to have one to his memory. A large Cockburn's. I would like everyone to have one. No argument.'

Crossan thought of the price of four large ports as the drink was brought. Alice felt obliged to order another. The company sank into a limbo of happy melancholy, close enough to hysteria. Haslam repeated his invitation to Alice. 'Teddy wouldn't want you in mourning. I'm sure. And anyway, it will be your only opportunity to see me in a monkey suit.'

Mulligan belched. 'No woman could resist an invitation so graciously put.'

Then he insisted on accompanying her back to the college, where she had a three o'clock lecture, and Crossan was left alone with the bill and J. J. Haslam.

The writer said, 'I fancy Oliver would like to comfort Alice.'

'The port should be a help. He has a fortnight to make her forget Teddy.'

'Methinks she has forgotten already.' Haslam nodded at the urn which stood blue and silent and forgotten on the table. Crossan took it and put it in his pocket, smirking mentally. Ashes and poetry.

The pubs of Dublin were shut until half past three: the holy hour. Crossan went back to his office to think about the evening ahead. Haslam said he would go home to rescue a drowned book.

6

Mulligan was in the Constitution Room of the Shelbourne Hotel – where the first Constitution of the Irish Free State had been signed – twenty minutes before the reception was to begin, brushed and tidy in a tuxedo which was beginning to show its years, arranging for a bottle of white wine to be secreted under the serving table so that he could better pace his drinking.

''Evening, Mr Mulligan. A fair turnout tonight, I suppose?'

'When I nod, Barney, fill me a glass of white wine and hand it to me. And if anyone else asks for a glass, tell them you've run out of it.'

'Message received and understood, Mr Mulligan. Them spirits is the devil.'

Haslam arrived with Alice. She looked handsome in a black sheath. Haslam was in tweeds. 'I forgot to collect the bloody monkey suit, after ordering and paying for it.'

'You're not a nice man,' Alice said.

'Will they let me in?'

'Not without the proper apparel, I'm afraid,' Mulligan said.

'I'm getting old,' Haslam said morosely. 'I overslept my nap.'

The room was filling. Crossan arrived and chatted briefly with the group before spotting Toby O'Mara at the door, his notebook and sheaf of invitations flapping in his hand. His photographer was behind him. For twenty years O'Mara had written the 'Townbeat' column in the *Evening Telegraph*, a page of insipid gossip and pictures which purported to reflect the night life of Dublin. O'Mara felt that his true merit had never been acknowledged, while genuine charlatans – like W. B. Yeats – enjoyed undeserved exaltation.

He insisted on having tea at receptions such as this, causing wonder and confusion in the first year of his duty. Later, he began to specify which brand he would like, changing over the years from Halpin's Golden Amber to Lyons' Green Label, from Twinings Nectar to Bewley's Special.

He had his hand on Crossan's lapel. 'Tell me about this thing now. What are they doing here? You don't give enough information in this handout at all. I wish people would do their jobs properly. God knows what the EEC must think of you fellows. Where are they going? And how long will they be here for? Will they be going to Killarney for instance?'

'They probably will be passing . . .'

'Because what nobody knows is that the Baron Munchausen is buried down there. Did you know that, now?'

'Baron Munchausen?'

'I didn't think you would. What's your name, by the way?'

Crossan gave his name, and O'Mara began to write it. 'I suppose a cup of tea would be too much to ask? Dom and myself are gasping. Where are these people anyway? You invite us here to meet them and they don't show up.'

'You're a bit early . . .'

'What about the tea?'

Crossan beckoned to the barman. 'Bring us two cups, my good man,' O'Mara said when he arrived. 'One and a half cubes in mine and no milk. No sugar in Dom's and a tiny drop of milk.' He turned to Crossan. 'Who's paying for this, by the way?'

'You mean the reception?'

'Of course I don't mean the reception, I mean the whole trip. You're not going to tell me that NBS is paying for the whole thing. And what about the Aran Islands, are they going out there?'

'It's very difficult to get . . .'

'Will they be filming Dun Aengus, one of the finest historical monuments in Europe, if not in the world? Synge, O'Flaherty. That's what they should be doing, you know, but of course you fellows will never let them get near the place. Leprechauns and shillelaghs. We'll be the laughingstock of the United States, as if we weren't laughingstock enough already, beating the shit out of each other in the North for what happened three hundred years ago. They're not going up to the North, I take it?'

'It's not on the itinerary.'

'Oh, keep them away from reality. What's this the name of the programme is again? "The Awful Truth"?' He looked among his invitations.

' "The Whole Story",' Crossan said, looking over OMara's head. In the door stood a large mosaic figure with a black beard and thick brown glasses, dressed in Levis and wearing a light meter around his neck.

Crossan went up to him and introduced himself. 'You must be Pete Ober. Can I get you a drink?'

'I don't drink.'

'A mineral, cordial?'

Ober shook his head.

'One of our newspaper columnists would like to meet you, talk to you about the programme and so on. Could you have a few words with him?'

He led Ober to where O'Mara was by now sitting and left them together.

The drink flowed free and freely to a dozen members of the Irish press and half as many from radio and television. Few of them would mention anything about tonight's proceedings, but all of them could be seen any night of the week wherever free drink was available, intent on getting drunk quickly and without expense.

Crossan bumped into a large white-haired man with a huge, pockmarked nose and small brown eyes. He was standing in a corner and looking impatient.

'Are you by any chance Frank Dinneen?'

'Francis J. Dinneen the Third, out of New York via Roscommon and Boston,' the man rattled off, looking over Crossan's shoulder.

Crossan said, 'Ah' and finished his drink. 'Can I fill you?'

'Sure. A large Paddy's on the rocks.'

Crossan went for the whiskey. A Paddy's. No Irishman would ever use the possessive s.

Dinneen was the travelling newspaper journalist with the group, sent by his New York paper to do several 'colour' stories on the making of the programme. He had been to Ireland several times before and professed to despise the directions the country was taking. Crossan remembered Gogarty's memorandum: 'For the purpose of transatlantic communication we'll call him curmudgeonly. He was a sportswriter for thirty years and now has his own column, called "The Fearless Spectator". He loves that title more than his next free scotch, and tries to live up to it in private as well as in print. He is therefore very popular over here.'

'*Slainte*,' Dinneen said, flattening the vowel. 'You're the guy who makes sure they hit the right spots, aye?'

'I'll be along. They chose their own locations.'

'With a little help from you guys.'

'You've seen the itinerary. Bit of this, bit of that.'

'Don't read itineraries. They can do that. Listen. I might split along the way. Do my own thing. See what's real.'

Why don't you take a walking tour of the Irish Sea? Crossan thought. 'That's all right. Just let me know.'

'You'll have them at that medieval shit at Cranmore, right? Well, they don't know any better. That Ober's a kike, you know. And the reporter is a black dyke from Harlem. Know as much about Ireland as I do about Dahomey.'

Crossan looked out over the drinking, noisy crowd.

Here was another who could run the country better than the Irish. There were thousands of them in the Bronx, in Boston, in Chicago and Philadelphia and even in San Francisco. People for whom the Northern flare-up had been a godsend, a chance to *do* something for the homeland. The Israelis had monopolized this kind of thing for long enough. Now it could be shown that the American Irish, by God, would not be found wanting when the siren call of nationalism blared across the globe. Dinneen's righteous voice was regularly heard in his column.

'The smoothies have really taken over here.'

Crossan said, 'You wouldn't want us to sit back and let the world pass us by, would you?'

'Why not?' Dinneen raised his voice, happy to have his sentiments heard by all. 'This place used to be honest. Poor but honest. And damn beautiful, by God. Now what? Look at those hotels. All that's missing is one-armed bandits. The real Irish never got their noses inside a banquet hall. All those painted colleens twanging their harps. What a fucking sellout.'

'Time for me to address the multitude,' Crossan said.

41

'Go ahead. You tell 'em. The noo Ireland. Progress.'

'That's it.'

Crossan bumped into Mulligan as he moved away.

'Who was that?'

'Francis Dinneen the Turd, out of Noo Yawk via Boston and Roscommon,' Crossan sang.

'Oh, no,'

'He says he may go off on his own. To find the *real* Ireland.'

'One of *them*.'

'See if you can get me some attention.'

Mulligan tapped a spoon against a glass. 'Ladies and gentlemen, and, of course, members of the press' – chuckles – 'I want to thank you all for coming here tonight. It is an unusual occasion. Indeed, so far as my experience goes, it is unprecedented. We are about to embark on a journey which should be of great benefit not only to Ireland, but also to millions of Americans, many of whom know little or nothing about our country beyond the fact that it is in the middle of a tragic postcolonial situation. There is, as we Irish know, more to Ireland than what is heard and read and seen in the media each day. We would like people to share this knowledge, and I would here like to say a word of gratitude and commendation to Stephen Crossan, who was responsible in no small measure for persuading the NBS team to come here. Mr Crossan will be guide and mentor for the next fortnight, abetted by our esteemed archaeologist Alice Foley, our equally esteemed, if not yet venerable, novelist J. J. Haslam, not to mention my humble self. Mr Crossan will say a few words.'

Crossan began to speak, conscious that his audience was mostly Irish, and particularly aware of Dinneen's tiny eyes upon him.

Another American had entered the room. Why was it always so easy to spot them? She was a woman of medium height in grey skirt and black sweater with a black delicate pendant in front. He guessed that she was Ellen Harbo. She was near forty, he reckoned, and she looked around the room calmly and made her way without hurry to the bar.

'I add my welcome to Mr Mulligan's. The reputation of "The Whole Story" has preceded it. It is a reputation for honesty and integrity, for an even-tempered and unbiassed approach to its subject, and for absolute professionalism. . . .'

42

He continued. Another American came in, his greying hair carefully combed, in jacket, sweater and loafers, moving to the side of the room and languorously draping himself over the fireplace. Max Maynard, the cameraman.

'. . . the roots of these differences bring us back far into our history, and many people think we do too much of this . . . a thriving cultural centre, indeed *the* cultural centre of Europe for hundreds of years . . . our easterly neighbour spent centuries trying to make our island a wholly owned and wholly ruled province . . . a long and bloody conflict, and ultimately unsuccessful . . . not to mention Ireland's greatly disproportionate contribution to English literature. . . .'

A tall and beautiful black woman had just come in, wearing blue skin-tight velvet pants, high black leather boots and a blue shirt which was open almost to the waist, so that the inner outlines of her breasts were visible. Virginia Green.

Mulligan was already on his way to her.

'. . . no shortage of people in the United States who, for one day, become fervently, publicly and raucously Irish . . . wish our country to remain in aspic . . . talk to a man about the romance of his life in a thatched cottage and you will find an unsympathetic listener: thatch means poverty. . . .'

Dinneen's presence had made Crossan become defensively polemical, and his speech lacked the lightness of tone which he had intended to adopt.

'It is our visitors' intention to do a thorough study of Ireland in all its aspects. It is the hope of our government that what emerges will be simple, honest and direct. We can ask for nothing more. If it doesn't manage to tell the whole story – for who knows that? – it should go some way towards dispelling myths which have dogged us for long enough.'

He smiled shortly at the applause, angry at the way Dinneen's presence had affected him.

Haslam came up and muttered congratulations. There was some small engine in the novelist which made him do these quiet, private things which belied his public reputation, and Crossan was glad of his words.

'I gather from Oliver that we have a Yankee patriot in tow.'

Crossan sighed. 'We can handle him.'

'He won't like the things you said.'

'I said little. Glib ambivalence is the tone for the times.'

'Careful, my boy. You're too young for those sentiments.'

'You're not going to the ball then?'

'I was thinking about it. You know, I have never been to the Meath Hunt Ball, or to any other hunt ball for that matter. And of course I haven't the clothes. But I have an idea.' He smiled. He looked around the room. Dear me. Imagine starting a trip around Ireland at the Meath Hunt Ball. Ah, well, if they are to get the whole story, they might as well begin in the charnel house.'

7

The din in the Horseshoe Bar in the Shelbourne was almost soporific, but the quality of the sounds was quite different from the familiar clamour of Irish pubs late at night. The pitch was more strident, the greetings raucous and unself-conscious. The smoke was from thick, brutish cigars, and it mingled with the smells of expensive perfumes above the small, packed throng.

Crossan sat in the corner, under the dahlias and cinerarias which had been brought that morning by tiny Miss Burke-Drummond in her mini-van. Holding her poodle, Whiskey, in her left arm, she set the flowers with taste around the hotel nooks and was gone.

Virginia Green sat beside Crossan. The reception was long since over and she had showered and changed for the ball. She was staring at the crowd and sucking at a long delicate meer-schaum, holding a Daiquiri in her right hand, the long lines of her body matching Crossan's at every joint. She wore white trousers of sheerest silk, and her white halter, which just covered the front of her breasts, was wrapped around her neck to make a collar, with a bow at the back which trailed down her naked spine.

When she bent forward to knock her pipe in the ashtray, the halter loosened and her breasts hung free.

Crossan said, 'They're feasting on you tonight.'

'You know, they look at me, then they look away, then they look back again. That's the moment I enjoy.' She inhaled. 'Are there many of us in Ireland?'

'About forty. All surgeons.'

'No problems, huh?'

45

'We think of blacks as chubby African babies, or skinny African babies, with fingers in their mouths. For decades they collected for the "black babies" in the schools. Hundreds of thousands of pounds. I think I have shares in most of the prime ministers of Africa. I may own Amin.'

'You're welcome to the asshole. He's undone twenty years of work.'

Crossan asked about the cameraman, whom he had not spoken to yet. 'A handsome fellow. Popular with the ladies, I imagine.'

'Max doesn't go in for ladies.' She stared at a large, grey-haired man, his face suffused with gin, a crease of open wonder on his forehead.

'How about Mr Ober?'

'Straight. Straight and dull. How about you?'

'Same.'

'I tried the other in the sixties. Who didn't? You comfort a sister and the next thing is you have a head on your shoulder. What do you do? It just wasn't my scene. But it was tough splitting. This little lost white kid, on speed. Jesus. Like a little puppydog. I had to get out. And then she OD'd.'

'Merciful hour!'

'What did you say?'

'I said, "Merciful hour." It's a common . . .'

'Beautiful. Just beautiful. Say it again, yeah?'

He looked at her and took the chance.

'Will you sing "The Camptown Races"?'

She looked down at the table, placed the pipe on it and said, slowly, 'I'm sorry.'

Crossan was immensely excited in her presence. He had never before spoken to a black woman, and his mind and body tingled with the thought of a fortnight of surprises. Everything about her was different, and he was determined to make her his own. But his path was strewn with spikes and potholes, and he would have to be a wary traveller.

He said, 'I was in New York one night some years ago. About two o'clock in the morning. I had spent the whole night imbibing with an Irish-American, a diverting raconteur, too, the same fellow. We broke up and I walked back to my hotel.'

'Which one?'

'The Algonquin. That lovely brown lobby.'

He told her the story of how he came upon a sign advertising the Toon and Co. Club, Drinks and Dancing Till Three. Never wishing to pass up an experience, he had gone down into the club and at the foot of the stairs was a tall black man, dressed completely in white, with a large wide-awake hat, who took his three dollars without a word. Crossan ambled into the dance area, getting himself a whiskey and walking to the far side of the dark room, and not looking round until he was seated. There were twenty or so couples dancing and he watched them for almost a quarter of an hour in almost total darkness.

'And then I realized that I was the only white person in that room.'

'So you shifted ass.'

'Well, I moved out. I went up to the man on the door and asked if I was in a black club. He said yes. I asked him why he had let me in and he said, "Your money was good." We got to chatting and he told me his name was Tyrone Toon, and I told him there was a whole county in Ireland named after him. He got a great charge out of that. 'Course I was a bit stocious. And then I went off into the Manhattan night.'

'Wondering why you weren't knifed in the back.'

'Nothing like that. But I haven't told you how I knew I was the only white person in the place.'

'You got eyes.'

'It was almost pitch-dark.'

'So?'

'It was the way the dancers moved. They had a suppleness and grace, a kind of physical confidence that whites just don't have. Now tell me this: if I had gone up to our friend Tyrone and said, "Look, I've been watching those people dancing back there, and because of the sheer physical eloquence of their movements I suddenly realized they were all black," would Tyrone have told me I was a racist?'

'Why should he? It's a compliment.'

'And why is something complimentary about a race never racist, when something derogatory always is? The Jews are often described as the greatest contributors to the musical culture of the US – that's classical and light classical, so to speak – a judgement which I wouldn't fault. I never heard that judgement denounced as racist. But when some buck general accuses them of "running things" there's an almighty hoo-ha.

Isn't it just as racist to call the Dutch industrious as it is to accuse the Irish of being drunkards? Or the blacks of being lazy?'

He slipped the last in quickly, watching her face.

'I never thought about,' she looked at him musingly. He had set her thinking. But not for long.

J. J. Haslam, holding tight the arm of the hotel's assistant manager, was approaching through the crowd.

'Eureka, eureka, my dears,' he exclaimed, as he spotted them. 'I want you to meet Mr Barry Foster, a Christian gentleman, a Samaritan, by God. Barry, my dear man, this is the beautiful Miss Virginia Green from New York. Isn't she very beautiful? What do they say? Black is beautiful. By Jayses, now I know why. Stephen, my good man, what do you notice about Mr Foster here?'

'A patient man,' Crossan gave Foster a smile of sympathy.

'And do you not also notice that he's the same height as yours truly? See?' He stood head to head with his victim. 'And furthermore, not a pick on him. Look at that.' He placed his thumb inside the top of the other's trousers, showing how thin the young man was. 'So. We have solved the problem. Don't you think Mr Foster will look well in these tweeds? And he has consented, like the decent man that he undoubtedly is.'

Foster stood transfixed in Haslam's grip, smiling grittily, his face full of the realization that it was worth his job to cross his famous captor.

But he protested when Haslam began to strip. 'We can change upstairs.'

'My dear boy, haven't you ever seen a rugby match? And some unfortunate loses his drawers after what they describe as overrobust play? How does he get them changed? They rally round, am I right? They rally round. And that's what they're going to do here. All you men.' He raised his voice, addressing the crowd behind him. 'You men rally round here. Cover our nakedness, for we are about the changing of garments.'

In the small space beside the bar, amid much laughter, Haslam pulled and pushed and buffeted until he and Foster disappeared inside a circular wall of bodies. Jim and John and Sean, barmen intrepid and inured, watched the whole charade quietly in one of the huge and beautiful mirrors, and decided that the wisdom of the situation lay in inaction: Horse Show

48

Week had thrown up events far more traumatic than this in the past.

Virginia looked at the contrusion of men, alight with anticipation, watching the walled backs and forgetting her pipe. 'God, I wish Max were here. He would have loved this.'

After many shouts of 'Splendid fit!' and 'Perfect, old boy', the wall broke up and Haslam stood triumphant in the centre, pirouetting gracelessly, his right arm raised in the air. Foster shuffled to the door in his newly acquired suit, forgotten. The picture was near perfect, except for Haslam's brogues and green socks. He sat down by Virginia, panting slightly.

'Have I told you that you are looking absolutely beautiful tonight? And I do not use that word lightly, I can tell you. I have rarely seen a damsel so fair. Well, maybe fair is not quite the right word. I met your friend Mr Ober earlier on and we had a long chat about Irish literature. No. A short chat. What's there to talk about? Isn't Irish literature dying a quick death, with only myself and a few others doggedly trying to keep the flag flying? God knows, not without some little success, even if I say it myself, and I have to say it myself, since there are damn few others will say it for me. You didn't by any chance read my story in *Harper's* in June, "In Her Innocence Bright"? I used to know that girl, you know, and every one of those things happened to her before she was seventeen. I tell you not a word of a lie. She was a small thing, lived beside the edge of Bansha Wood, and her mother was the greatest tramp ever to draw breath in the Glen of Aherlow.'

Crossan pulled back. Haslam had a new audience in thrall, black and strange and beautiful. A new web was being woven, the strangest and most elaborate mating dance in the world.

The clamour had increased, the cigar smoke had thickened, in spite of the air conditioning, of which the hotel was inordinately proud. The high, honking voices demanded attention from the barmen and from companions, and the buzz was frequently eclipsed by blasts of eldritch laughter. Gins and tonics plopped over rims and onto arms, to the floor, thick grey bullets of cigar ash fell on shoulders, faces grew red from drink and laughter, eyes teared, the whole bar was a continuous explosion of industrious gaiety. The unmistakable noises of Horse Show Week.

Through the throng, pushing this way and that, dressed in a

49

maroon tuxedo, his thick black hair plastered down, came big Pete Ober, followed by Max Maynard. Crossan, feeling the bulge uncomfortable in his pocket, placed the urn containing the ashes of Teddy French on the table.

The producer waved his hand behind him in feigned awe as he sat. 'Who are all these people?'

'These, my dear man,' Haslam said, pulling his attention away from a rapt Virginia, 'are the remains of the Irish ascendancy. Look close now, for you will never see their like again. Note the physiognomy: pale, unpimpled skin – that's three hundred years and more of the best food in Ireland. Plenty of thick straight hair, no money worries, you see. And big feet, from tramping on all the rest of us for all that time.'

Maynard laughed. Ober rubbed his nose.

'There's two brothers in Brazil,' the novelist continued, 'what's their name? . . . Boas. The Villas Boas brothers. The very men. Off into the black heart of the Amazon to protect the Indian from the ravages of civilization. Where's the Villas Boas that's going to protect the vanishing Irish ascendancy from the ravages of the Catholic gobhawks of the new Irish Republic? Every copy of the *National Geographic* you pick up, there's fifty pages of some great tribal rite among the savages. Where's the *National Geographic* tonight? Have a drink. You're witnessing a tribal rite. In the flesh.'

Ober asked for a Coca-Cola, turned round, and knocked the urn from the table, managing to push it over the protective brass ring which the hotel thoughtfully provided on every table. The urn smashed into small pieces, the ashes spilling on the floor.

Ober looked down at them, perplexed. 'What the hell was that?'

'That is the late Teddy French,' Haslam said. 'He wasn't the worst.'

He called the barman and spoke to him. Five minutes later the ashes were entombed in a naggin Paddy bottle.

Haslam said, 'He is now where he always wanted to be.'

Alice Foley arrived with Ellen Harbo, and Haslam greeted her loudly. Crossan put the Paddy bottle in his pocket. Ashes, whiskey and poetry. Haslam was getting drunk, and he forced large drinks into Alice, telling her with great invention how it was that he had a monkey suit after all. As he told the story,

Crossan and Virginia – who had witnessed it – were given a privileged glimpse of the writer at work. There was no need for fantasy. The bare bones of a suit exchange in the bar were enough to give the writer a rich and curious tale. He embellished and excised, and he described the assistant manager's rigid demeanour with perfectly chosen words and phrases. Furthermore, he recounted aspects of the drama that it seemed impossible he could have noticed at the time. Crossan wondered whether it was all spontaneous. Surely he could not have been putting it all together in his head while talking to Virginia? Certainly he could. Writers were strange people.

After an hour, Ober left with Maynard to get the camera equipment. Ellen went with them. The crowd had thinned at the bar. The large mirrors – especially the one advertising Liebfraumilch – were more apparent. What scenes they had reflected over the years. If only mirrors were sentient storehouses, what stories they would tell.

Those who were left were in deep drunken conversation, supporting each other, their eyes earnestly on the floor.

The party left the bar and made its way into the ballroom, Alice Foley falling back to apologize to Crossan for leaving the urn behind at Snaffles. He liked the tone in her voice. He patted his pocket and reassured her. He whispered to Teddy that he would at least have a ball at his funeral.

They went into the ballroom, and Mulligan was already at a table in the far end of the room, making a forceful point to Dinneen, who was wearing a green cummerbund.

Tom Clancy and his orchestra were ploughing frozen-faced through 'La Paloma'. The group circled the edge of the dancers, couples locked into each other, or attempting the classical tango movements with greatly exaggerated finesse. Some, as the party passed, squeezed their partners' arms and nodded towards Virginia, their remarks drowned in the blare of music and voices.

Crossan ordered six bottles of champagne and they sat, to the Americans' great surprise, to eat a breakfast of bacon, sausage and egg.

At the next table, smoking a long cheroot, her chin glistening with dribbled wine, sat Lady Fanny Fanshaw, 'the ugliest woman in three provinces', her eyes heavy and apathetic as she half-listened to her husband. Her daughter, Susan, was draped across the shoulder of Paddy Cusack, Minister for Livestock, at thirty-five the youngest member of the Cabinet.

Beside him sat a beautiful young Indian girl in a turquoise sari, listening intently to her partner, the young Lord Bowrawn, his head a mass of jet-black hair, dressed in bright green dress jacket and frilled shirt, into which tiny shamrocks had been embroidered.

The others at the table included a couple in their fifties, the man pulling without interest on a massive wet cigar, the woman sitting beneath a gothic bouffant hairstyle that stood a foot above her head. She seemed sullen and frustrated, and no one addressed a word to her throughout the meal.

The party occasionally bubbled when a familiar arrived, baying greetings. Hands were shaken, congratulations proffered, news swapped. The Irish jumping team had failed again. Damned Germans took it by a whisker. Bloody Glenmacnass always hated water. Missed you at Dickie's last night. Sarah said you'd just gone. You heard about Jilly's ankle. Girl was damned lucky. Roddy is giving a party at Crawtown tomorrow night, if he ever gets back from Julie's place in one piece. Her daughter is turning into a proper little Lolita, don't you think? Break a heart or two one of these days. Harry is still *hors de combat* after Tuesday. Nigel and Sally are back from Rhodesia. Hated the place. Said they might be here tonight but old Fang probably has them cooped. Yes, why not, the woman needs a bit of exercise. Come on, Fanny, show a leg, dammit.

The large room throbbed with noise and movement, the dancing was uninhibited, graceless and frenetic, and the orchestra banged out a vile 1950s medley, their taciturnity oozing from every note.

Half of the men on the floor had abandoned their jackets and opened their shirtfronts, showing chests pink and white; damp grey discolorations appeared under arms which waved wildly or groped for unwilling partners.

Susan Fanshaw, her eyes half-closed, lifted a jug of ice water and, making a sieve of her fingers, emptied the water into her mother's coffee cup. She took out the ice cubes and one by one threw them at chosen targets around the table. Then she began throwing them at random over her shoulder while Paddy Cusack looked on with a nervous smile.

The unhappy woman opposite was attracted by the game and

began to spray the tables with her own cubes, one of them hitting Maynard's forehead just as their eyes met, hers full of malicious fun, his venomous.

'Silly bitch.'

'What did you say?'

'I said you're a silly bitch.'

'Ooh, a party pooper,' the woman said, establishing herself as an American. 'Enjoy yourself, fella.'

'One more of them and I'll slap your stupid face.'

'What a boring old man.'

'Old! Jesus, look who's talking.'

The woman looked at Maynard through unhappy, drunken eyes. 'You are the ugliest person I have ever met in my whole life,' she said slowly.

'You ever look in a mirror, lady?'

The woman rose from the table, picking up an open Coca-Cola bottle and advancing on Maynard, covering the top of the bottle with her thumb and shaking it as she did so. She stopped in front of him, pointed the bottle at him, and lifted her thumb slowly. The liquid sprayed his face and shirt front, and the woman laughed wildly as she weaved back to her table.

Maynard picked up a bottle of champagne – 'Not champagne, Max! She only used Coke!' Virginia cried – and walked to where the woman sat, standing behind her as she smiled triumphantly at the rest of her table.

He poured the champagne slowly over her hair, emptying the bottle so that the great structure, so carefully built a few hours before, sagged and collapsed, and the woman's confidence collapsed with it. She kept her head down, and her tears mingled with the champagne flowing into her lap. Throughout, her husband stared through her, watching the dancers and sucking on his cigar, and the rest of her table companions looked on with amiable interest, wordlessly.

Maynard had returned to his seat.

'No gentleman would do what you've just done.'

The cameraman looked up into the face of a young man with eyes of purest cerulean, his lank blond hair parted just left of centre and combed away over his ears.

'I beg your pardon?' Maynard said, appraising him.

'You heard perfectly well.'

'Did you see what she did to me?'

'The lady is the worse for drink.'

'The bitch is stoned out of her mind. That allows her to throw rocks in my face?'

'I think you should apologize to her.'

Both tables had gone quiet. The confrontation could be heard by all.

'Listen, sonny. I was sitting here enjoying myself, minding my own goddamn business when that tramp threw ice at me. I asked her to stop and she wouldn't.'

'Please do not refer to her in those words, if you don't mind.'

'I'll refer to her in any damn words I like.'

'I think you should apologize, and so do my friends.'

'I think you and your friends should go jump in a lake. And take Madame Defarge with you.'

There was a roar from the dance area. Tom Clancy and his men stopped playing. At the top of the hall, on the raised and carpeted eating area, stood a large silver hunter, snorting and jerking nervously at the bit. On her back was Major Eddie Simpson, his jacket off, a bunch of multicoloured balloons in his left hand. The other held the reins. He swayed drunkenly as he kneed the frightened horse down the steps onto the floor, and then he egged the horse into a trot as the dancers cleared with whoops of applause.

Simpson roared unintelligibly at his audience, increasing the horse's gait, and the applause was deafening as he circled the floor. On the second round the horse's legs slithered on the polished floor and Simpson shot off his back and under Lady Fanshaw's chair, his balloons sailing up to the ceiling.

The blue-eyed boy caught the terrified horse and led him gently out of the hall. Simpson climbed up on a table, waving a champagne bottle, and began to sing. 'By an old Moulmein pagoda. . . .'

The two tables had come together. Maynard had used his camera under Ober's staccato direction. They were both furious that they had missed the Simpson episode. Maynard had graciously listened to and accepted an apology from the blue-eyed boy, whose name was Dick Townes, and had made one in return, and was now sharing champagne with him. Ober was talking to Lord Bowrawn and Lady Fanshaw.

Mulligan, Alice Foley and Ellen Harbo were listening to Haslam sing 'She Lived Beside the Anner'. Dinneen had left.

The American woman's husband had disappeared, too, and Crossan sat down beside her.

She was a handsome woman, with good bones, but her makeup was heavy and some of it had been washed away by the tears and champagne. She had not bothered to replace it. Her hair lay like seaweed on her shoulders and her whole body drooped sadly. She was a picture of misery.

Crossan said, 'I'm very sorry about what happened.'

'Why should you be sorry? It was my own fault. It's always my own fault. That bitch got away with it.' She nodded to Susan Fanshaw. 'They can always get away with it. But not poor old Becky.'

'I'm Stephen Crossan.'

'Hi. I'm Becky Packer. I gather you're all returning home in a fortnight. I wish to God I was going with you. Why we ever left Virginia for this place . . .' She shook her head, looking around.

Crossan did not disabuse her about his provenance. She sought only a listener, and unquestioning sympathy. 'How long have you been living here?'

'Two years. Two long years. And I haven't made one friend, not one. We own the Killeen stud farm and we employ twenty-three people. We give dinner parties every second night. We invite people for week-ends. We spend a fortune being popular. My husband, Freddy, is worth millions. And I mean pounds, not dollars.' She dabbed her face. 'And they hate us.'

Crossan looked across the table to where Bowrawn was talking with Ober. The little Indian girl was now resting on Bowrawn's lap, her hand running through his hair. The American woman followed his eyes. 'And they're the worst,' she said. 'See that guy there? That little leprechaun with the Indian kid? He has his own band. Pipers. Wonder they're not sitting around him now, wailing. You ever hear those pipes? Not the ones you blow through: they're civilized. Well, don't. Oh, God. Lord this and Lady that. I never met a lord or a lady before I came here. I guess I didn't know what they would be like. But I sure didn't think they would be such a bunch of creeps.'

She looked across at Susan Fanshaw. 'Imagine calling that

trollop "Lady"! Lady! God, it sticks in my craw. We're suckers, you know that? Suckers is what we Americans are. First sign of a title and we're slobbering to get a look at it in the flesh, see what it's like in real life. I'll tell you, in forty-eight years in Virginia I never met a single person as revolting as those I've met since I came here. We're royalty compared to them, and they have the cheek to sneer at us. That's what they do. I know it. I've heard them. They're rude, you know? Offensive. I can't even understand what they're saying half the time. And they're supposed to be the gentry. Give me the ordinary Irish any time. At least you know where you are with them. As far as they're concerned if you're American you're just rich, big rich. They just try to rip you off. But you'd expect more from the . . . well, from your own kind, if you know what I mean.'

She drank deep of the champagne and Crossan refilled the glasses. He said, 'Come and dance this waltz. You're supposed to be enjoying yourself.'

They danced slowly round the floor. Her blouse was wet from the champagne, and Crossan's hand stuck to it. She laid her body into him, arousing him, but she was sobbing noiselessly. 'My husband does the right thing. Freddy gets so drunk when he comes to something like this that nothing ever bothers him. He says I'm too loud. Keep my opinions to myself. Loud! God, you should hear *them*. I mean they never talk to each other. Not in a normal way. They always shout, like they were leaning out of a train window saying good-bye. Or talking to a deaf person. I often wonder how they talk to each other in bed.'

She giggled.

'Did you ever try to find out?'

'Once or twice. But I always have to be drunk to make any kind of pass, and by that time they're drunk, too. They're always drunk, seems to me. Wonder they ever manage to reproduce at all.'

They danced on and she moved languorously against Crossan's body, enjoying his attention and silence.

'I'm trying to persuade Freddy to go back, sell out. We were big in Virginia, you know, Here they don't give a damn how much money you have. It's all the same to them. Freddy isn't too keen on going back. But he might change his mind now. This was a great place up to a few years ago. We picked the wrong time to move.'

56

'What happened a few years ago?'

'Socialists. You used to be able to keep what you earned. And believe me that's a lot as far as Freddy is concerned. He's worth millions. And I mean pounds, not dollars. He's in zippers in the States. Now they take it off you. It's not worth your while staying on. They're moving out in droves. And those big houses, really beautiful houses, you know what I mean, with fabulous antiques and works of art, they all have to be sold off. Most of them are, by now. They'll be sorry, though, when they're all gone. Then they'll know what they lost. Damn taxes. And you wouldn't mind if you got something in return. But I swear nothing in this country works. Nothing. Try making a phone call to someone down the road. Takes you an hour. I'm not kidding. That's if you're lucky enough to *get* a phone in the first place. You know how long it took Freddy to get a phone? I mean Freddy, and he has plenty of clout? Seven months! Seven months for one lousy phone, and when we asked for two they had a fit. Another six months.'

'It didn't help that your husband was a namesake of the minister?'

'Don't mention that bastard's name to me. This place is worse than a banana republic. At least you know where you are with the ni— with those people. They don't know any better. But here!' She shook her head wearily. 'Where are you from?'

'Dublin.'

'What! Are you telling me that you're Irish?'

' 'Fraid so,' Crossan said, smiling down at her. 'Don't worry, I'm emancipated.'

'Oh, God. And you had to listen to . . . Oh, my God, why didn't you stop me?'

'I was interested in your opinions. I may even share some of them.'

She was slightly mollified. They started dancing again and she looked over at the table. 'You're not one of them, are you? You don't sound like one of them.'

'I'm just a working stiff, I think is how you people put it.'

'They're the worst, believe me. To be honest, I get on all right with the ordinary Irish. But I've no one to talk to. You can't talk to the grooms, for God's sake. If only those people would open up. I'd settle down here. It really is lovely. And

I've never seen grass like it, and you have real seasons. But those people.'

The orchestra stopped playing, and she dropped her arms slowly, reluctantly. Her hand, on the way down, brushed against the Paddy bottle in his pocket.

'My God. Is that whiskey?'

'That, my dear, is a dead atheist.'

She looked up at him, her face creased in sadness and despair. 'You Irish,' she said. 'You're all mad. Totally mad.' And she walked slowly back to her table.

Cusack was asleep on one side of Susan Fanshaw, Bowrawn on the other. She had her hands on their crotches. 'I think Paddy's is bigger.'

Bowrawn opened his eyes and said, 'Romantic Ireland's dead and gone, it's with O'Leary in the grave,' and fell back to sleep again.

Ober was sitting between Lady Fanshaw and the Indian girl. He was fascinated by the careless vulgarity of this titled lady; she effed and blinded with aplomb, and her conversation was strewn with references so earthy that Ober found himself constantly and nervously adjusting his glasses.

The Haslam group had enlarged and was now singing 'Boolavogue'. Alice Foley, to Crossan's surprise, was singing as loudly as the rest, and Mulligan had his arm around her. Haslam's left hand was resting lightly on Ellen Harbo's shoulder, and she was smiling and tapping the table with a spoon in time to the slow air. Maynard had gone, and so had Dick Townes.

Virginia sat alone and apart, her eyes heavy, a champagne glass tilting in her hand. Crossan sat down beside her, picking up her pipe from the floor.

'It was that fifth Daiquiri . . .'

'And the first, and second, and . . .' Her voice trailed off. Her head was resting sideways on the table.

He bent down and said, 'Can you see me?'

'I can see you well. Toooo well.' Her words fell on each other. 'An' I know wasson your mind.'

Crossan sipped his champagne.

'You wanna ball li'l ole me.'

He pretended surprise. 'Good heavens.'

'Goood hayvens. Lissen to the man. I love it.'

She took his hand in hers, black on white, pink against pink, and laid her head on his shoulder.

'Come on now. Don' be ashamed. You can tell Ginny.' Her voice was incongruously schoolmarmish. 'Ginny sometimes kisses, but nayvuh, *nayvuh* tells.'

He put his arm around her shoulder gingerly, his hand on her bare brown back, the first brown back he had ever touched, and thought about what she had said. No more than the truth. The cruelty of the American language. 'You wanna ball li'l ole me.' Was any language as cruel and crude as American? Or as vibrant?

'Is Mr Ober happy with his filming?'

'Would you be happy to have those freaks on film?'

He said nothing.

'You'll be proud to have this seen in the States?' She waved her arm to the whole drunken scene in the ballroom, spraying the table with champagne.

'It happens every year.'

'Authentic, huh? Part of the whole story? Jesus.' She put her glass down. 'Max has done his job. And now he's doing another one. He's found himself a nice new pink bum. Max's shooting for the rest of the night will be up our blue-eyes' asshole. Good ole Max.'

Crossan looked down at her jet-black head, just below his chin. Her body jerked violently, and she vomited into his lap, champagne, Daiquiri and egg-yolk fragments spreading all over his thighs. She heaved again several times as he brought her head up and gave her his handkerchief. He took several paper tissues from the table and began to clean his trousers.

'Ooooh, sheeit. I am sorry. Oh, God I'm sorry, Stephen. I couldn't move my head in time.'

'It's better to get it all up. Are you feeling better?'

'Lots, thank you. Oh, I'd feel perfect if I had gotten sick in the head rather than over your lovely trousers.'

'They're rented. I'll wash them off with water when I get home.'

'No one to do it for you?'

'No.'

She smiled at him, completely recovered, but light-headed. 'I guess the least I can do is wash them for you, no? They'll dry in a few minutes on the rad in my room.'

They left the ballroom without farewells. The place was almost empty. It was four o'clock.

Crossan led the way through back corridors to the second floor.

'You seem to know your way around here.'

'The porter isn't happy about visitors to rooms at this time of night.'

'I bet Max had no problems.'

'Hotel rules are kind to queers.'

'I've never been so drunk in my life. They all warned me before I came over.' She opened the door and let him into the room. 'You want another drink?'

'No, thank you.'

'Right then. Off with your trousers.' She grinned. 'Ever have that said to you before?'

'It's most unusual.'

'Dig those whiter-than-white legs.'

She went into the bathroom, and he took off his jacket, loosening his tie.

'Are you a natural blond?' she said through the door.

He killed the prematurely familiar reply on his lips. 'Yes.'

'I guess you must have some Scandinavian blood. You look like a Viking in that beard.'

'Probably some Norseman had his devilish way with one of my forebears.'

'You're very attractive.'

'Thank you. You are beautiful.'

'Thank you, kind sir.' She brought his trousers out and laid them on the radiator. She knelt in front of him.

'What shall we do?' She looked straight into his eyes, and he was uncomfortable.

'Would you like to hear some poetry?'

'Poetry? Sure. You know some?'

He sat on the bedside and took the little book from his jacket.

'Come and sit here.'

She sat obediently between his legs, the back of her head against his crotch, causing his penis to unfold itself inside his underpants against her poll. He began to read, moving his hand over her head onto her face.

She sat immobile until he had finished 'Leda and the Swan'.

60

Then she got up and sat on the further bed, facing him. He was still looking down at the poem, as though interested in it. Here, she thought, smiling, was another stud who thought she was an easy lay. Though his approach was most un-New Yorkish. Still, she did not want him to lose interest: the whole thing was as interesting for her as she knew it was for him. But he must be checked.

She said, 'That was lovely. And very sexy.' She was smiling hard at him, and he had looked up from the book. 'You know, I used to know this guy in San Francisco before I joined NBS. Big bastard, common as hell. His name was Wilt, and that,' she chuckled, 'was something he never did. He tried to lay me first date. Drove out to Sausalito, right on the marina over the water. He stopped the car, unzipped, and dropped his cock out on his lap. And then he turns to me and he says, "Would you like that?" Isn't that something?'

Crossan shook his head. Why was she telling him this story?

She stood up. 'You know what I think?'

'What?'

'It's all a matter of style.'

'Style?'

'Yeah. Poor old Wilt flashing his dong. And you flashing your swan. Almost rhymes.'

Her smile was brighter than ever, and Crossan just stared at her, defeated.

'Yoh trousahs ready, suh.'

He put them on.

She said, 'We're having a look round the city tomorrow?'

'Yes.'

'Good. Then we can get to know each other a little better, no? And who knows, at the end of the trip we may know each other very well indeed!'

She kissed him quickly and lightly on the lips and he went out into the dawn.

8

One man sat in Doheny & Nesbitt's pub in Baggot Street when J. J. Haslam pushed in from the sunlit street. A black pint of Guinness stood in front of him, new-poured, the cream overflowing down the sides of the glass into a small pool on the thick wooden counter.

John Kealy stood behind the bar. He was white-haired, from Castlecomer, in Dublin for thirty years, most of them behind the counter in the Princes, before the redhead inherited and sold it off, they said, for a quarter of a million pounds, partitions, brass, mahogany, the lot.

It was almost noon, and the gloom in the bar was welcome, for the sun was high and hot in the streets. Haslam sat at one of the wall tables, black, cast-iron tripod and Kilkenny marble top, and ordered a pint. He liked the bar empty. And he liked the umbral cool on a hot day. And he loved this pub. He reckoned there were no more than two dozen other pubs out of the nearly one thousand licensed premises in Dublin that retained any semblance of their former shoddy grandeur.

In Dublin, and all over the country, owners old and new had succumbed to a crass impulse to toss out the heavy dark counters, the black, brass-topped pint pullers, the worn wooden floors with the knots like little hills – all into the refuse dump – to be replaced by a chilly compendium of Formica and steel, cream and purple and gold, and carpets which flung up a stifling odour after four months on the floor.

But wily Ned Doheny and pragmatic Tom Nesbitt had served their time in New York, watchful exile barmen in the Emerald Stone at Thirty-ninth and Eighth and the Blarney Rose on Fourteenth Street. In the New World, they had seen the virtues of the Old, returning to buy this pub and leave it exactly as it was.

'One pint of the best, Mr H.' John put the drink on the table in front of Haslam, rubbing his hands on his white apron. 'And the best to you, Mr H., God bless you.'

Haslam returned the salutation, thinking that John must be the last barman in Dublin to invoke the deity as a matter of course in his greetings. All gone. A straight translation from the Gaelic, of course, as with most of the English spoken in Ireland. That was the secret of the 'quaintness', those inversions and convolutions that the stranger found so delightful. It was impossible to say hello or good-bye in Irish without calling on God or the Virgin to be a witness. But fifteen years of television had killed all that. The present generation made do with 'Hi' and 'See you'. America.

Crossan came in with the Americans. There were murmurs of exaggerated pain.

'All well this morning,' Haslam said, looking at Ellen, who was unaffected by the very late night.

'You look great,' she said.

'Practice, my dear.'

While they drank, Ober said to Haslam. 'You've been to Glasnevin a lot?'

'More and more, recently.'

Maynard said, 'I guess it's a kind of Arlington.'

'Well, I always had the idea that you reserved Arlington for your heroes. But Glasnevin is in no way discerning about the bodies it takes into itself.'

'Still,' Dinneen said, 'most of our great men are buried in Glasnevin.' He was brazen but uncomfortable in his use of the possessive pronoun.

'Great and bad, known and unknown, monks, and priests and dockers and writers and revolutionaries. They're all lying there equal in the dust, to paraphrase one of your own poets.'

Mulligan's phone rang and he rose and went wearily downstairs.

It was Maggie Porter, public-relations woman for the Industries Development Board, the semigovernmental body which lured foreign industries to Ireland with a twenty-year tax exemption.

'Jesus Christ, Maggie, I thought we had an agreement about week-ends.'

'We do, Oliver, we do. But those Yanks you have in. Phil is worried.'

Phil Madden was the chief executive of the IDB.

'He should be delirious at the opportunity.'

'He is. But that factory is still a hot potato.'

'I'm not surprised. You've done a good job keeping from the Irish just what is happening out there in Killala.'

'For God's sake, Oliver, we're all in the same boat.'

'Not me, dear Maggie. The only thing that enables you to open that place is the invincible ignorance of the Irish. Every week those Japs are getting fifty tons of acronitrile and whatchamacallit . . .'

'I can't pronounce it either,' she said wearily.

'. . . from Alexandra Basin in Dublin all the way across the country to Killala, and you and I know what will happen if there's the tiniest little hitch, don't we? If someone forgets to turn screw B, or lock hatch C?'

'You're worse than the environmentalists.'

'Maggie, you're a bigger liar than I am.'

'I have more to lie about.'

'What do you want?'

'I want to be in Killala.'

'That would be breaking the rules.'

'Whose rules, for Christ's sake! You fellows in the Board of Welcomes give me a dose of the shits, Oliver. You're all so high and mighty. We give jobs, Oliver, *jobs*.'

'And what wonderful jobs they are, too, Maggie, what? Listen. We had an agreement. No interference with the television crew. They're not fools.'

'I will not interfere. I want to help.'

'What's wrong, Maggie? Come on, tell me. What's wrong?'

'Nothing is wrong.' She caught her breath. 'Look, you saw what those Germans wrote last month. They had everyone in Germany thinking that Ireland was taking every dirty industry in the world.'

'Well?'

'You bastard. It's not true.'

'Listen, Maggie. The only reason those Japs came here was that they had been turned down by every other country in the world. They wouldn't even be allowed into Venezuela, for Jayses' sake, and did you ever hear of the Venezuelans turning down *anything*? We're a soft touch, Maggie, little children poisoning ourselves with big, beautiful sweets. Who do you think I am?'

'I'm beginning to wonder. Listen, Oliver, I'm going to be at Killala.'

'Whatever you say. But I'm not the ringmaster in this circus. Why don't you talk to Crossan?'

'I like to talk to *real* people.'

'You're very kind, my dear. But watch him. He can be very nasty. All these young men are, nowadays.'

'To hell with him. I'll be in Killala. He's going to need me.'

'It's nice to be needed.'

'Piss off.'

And she hung up. He shaved and dressed and went in to meet the others.

They had taken two taxis to the cemetery at Glasnevin.

They left the taxis and their drivers at John Kavanagh's pub in Prospect Square and walked up to the cemetery gates.

'This is not really Glasnevin Cemetery,' Haslam said as they went through the gates. 'It is properly called Prospect Cemetery, but proper names are often a problem. My own father insisted on baptizing me John Jameson Haslam, for reasons which I need not go into, so you can see why I steadfastly call myself J.J.'

He led them down to the left to Parnell's grave. The green and gentle mound, and the simple block of granite, with the name PARNELL engraved.

'Lapidary, you could truly call it,' Haslam mused. 'You could compare its modesty with the monstrous tower to O'Connell,' he said, turning to that edifice. 'You might even draw conclusions about the two men from their monuments. But it would be a double folly.'

His musing tone was of no help to the Americans.

Virginia said, 'Was Parnell your greatest patriot?'

'In some people's eyes he was the greatest Irishman that ever lived. For others he was a charlatan. The same can be said of O'Connell. If it came to that, the same could be said of all those men whom we revere.'

Ober wanted a solid bite. 'Was Parnell a great man in your opinion?'

Haslam looked a long time at the granite block, as though he had not heard the question. 'Yes,' he said at last, 'he was a great man.'

Maynard set up the camera, and Virginia, from notes prepared by Ellen Harbo, began to interview Haslam about Parnell and the other names that graced the headstones about the cemetery.

On camera, the novelist's preoccupied musings were transformed into clipped and pungent certainties. Whatever private doubts he harboured about the man beneath the clay, he battened unmercifully, and Mulligan and Crossan marvelled at the unhesitating professionalism of the performance.

Haslam gave a wonderfully concise sketch of the life of Parnell, showing in his phraseology and in the perfectly condensed nature of the biography all the experience he had gained as a radio broadcaster. He told of Parnell's sad end and finished just before Ober called, 'Cut!'

Maynard was hugely impressed both by the performance and by the life of this man Parnell, of whom he had never heard.

'Somehow you never think of an Irish politician losing his job for screwing around.'

Ellen Harbo's face showed genuine dismay. 'He was in *love*, Max!'

'Oh, you're such a romantic, Ellen.'

Haslam shook his head and looked at the ground, smiling.

Mulligan said, 'A tincture, perhaps?' and they trooped out of the cemetery to walk back to Kavanagh's.

In the pub, the two taximen were having half-pints of ale, and the group shuffled in beside them. One of them, Teddy Halpin, said, 'Well, what did ye think of all our dead patriots?'

'Very impressive,' Virginia said.

'They're always very impressive when they're dead, isn't that the truth?'

'Some of them were equally impressive alive,' Mulligan said, but Halpin ignored him, addressing himself again to the Americans.

'That's how to get to be a hero in Ireland, you know. Get yourself shot, or hanged, or starve yourself to death. You saw them all lying in there. Venerated. That's what they are.

Venerated. But only because they are in the clay. There wasn't much veneration floating around when they were alive, no, sir.'

He drank from his glass, and the Irish stayed silent. But Dinneen was perky, and, being American, he could not sniff the menace in Halpin.

'Name me one man who wasn't venerated when he was alive.'

'Out there?'

'Anywhere, for Christ's sake.'

'Well, you passed the General Post Office, right? On the way out . . .'

'Yeah, I remember. I know it.'

'Now do you know what happened there in 1916?'

''Course I do.'

'Well, tell me then.'

'Tell you what?'

'Tell me what happened in the GPO in 1916.' The taximan sat back.

'The Rebellion,' Dinneen said. 'It was what the Irish . . .'

'Aha!' Halpin said, raising his hand. 'Hold it there. Hold it right there, me bucko. You were about to say that the Irish did this or that, doesn't matter what. Let me tell you that the Irish did *nothing* in 1916. The *Irish* did nothing.'

'What the hell are you talking about?'

'I'll tell you what I'm talking about. What I'm talking about is that the Irish didn't want any rising at all. They were quite happy the way they were. A few madmen get together and decide to have a rising, it doesn't mean that the whole Irish nation wanted to have a rising.'

Maynard said, 'But it was successful, wasn't it? I mean the British got out.'

'It was anything but successful, with all due respects, sir. Anything but. It wasn't the Rising that was successful in uniting the Irish against the British, it was what the British did to the men of 1916 that united the Irish. That's the very point I was making to you. If the English hadn't killed all those men there wouldn't have been a titter out of the Irish. And we woulda had Home Rule by the end of the war. Prove me wrong.'

Dinneen said, 'You seem to be saying that the Irish had no time for Patrick Pearse and all those brave men who gave their lives . . .'

67

'I'm saying no such thing. You're not listening to me. I'm saying that the Irish had plenty of time for them. But only *when they gave their lives.*' He gulped down his stout quickly, fearful of interruption. 'But what really gets me is that there was a few thousand more killed in 1916 – and '14, '15, '17 and '18 – and there's never a blessed word about them. A hundred thousand Irishmen were on the Continent fighting for the freedom of small nations. Every little fart who blew his nose in the GPO is commemorated, but never a word for the men on the Somme, or on the Marne. Not a word. Same as if they never existed. And by Jayses they were Irishmen just as good as any patriot in the GPO.'

'They were fighting for England,' Dinneen said, with the blind bravery of ignorance.

'They were not fighting *for* England, my American friend. They were fighting *with* England. Against the Hun.'

Mulligan shot an arrow. 'Mr Halpin, were your family involved in the Great War?'

Halpin put down his glass. 'My father saw his own brother's head shot off within twelve feet of him on the Marne. And my own father lost his left arm. Amputated on the field. But I'll say this much. The British didn't forget him. Not like our own crowd. He got his pension on the nail and the house in Bengal Terrace. The British look after you when you're alive, see. They don't wait till you are dead and it's no good to you.'

Maynard said to Dinneen, 'Looks like you don't know it all, Frank.'

'I know what I'm talking about.'

'I beg your pardon,' Halpin said, 'but you don't know what you're talking about. That's the trouble with you Americans, if you don't mind me saying so. You think you know it all.'

Dinneen's face grew red and he leaned across the table. 'My mother was Irish, and my father was Irish, and I've been visiting this country for fifteen years. I know what I'm talking about.

'Still,' Maynard said, enjoying his chew, 'you're an American, Frank. This man here is Irish.'

Virginia said, 'You wouldn't like Mr Halpin to drop into the Lion's Head and start telling you you were all wrong about 1776, would you?'

'That's a different thing. Nineteen-sixteen was an inspiration to the world. It gave heart to thousands of revolutionaries. Lenin himself said . . .'

'Never have taken you for a crypto, Frank,' Maynard said.

'Will you for Chrissakes shut up? What the hell do you know about Ireland?'

'Not much. But I'm prepared to listen to those who do.'

Dinneen turned back to Halpin. The taximan was enjoying the split he had caused in the alien camp. 'Are you saying that 1916 was a mistake?'

'Stupidity,' Halpin said, encouraged to excess by the passions around him. 'Sheer bloody stupidity.'

'I'd like to hear you stand up and say that in public.'

'I'll shout it from the top of Liberty fucking Hall. What do you think, I'm afraid or something?'

'You could get into a lot of trouble.'

'Jesus, a Yankee Provo. Well, well. Dollars for the dead.'

'Gentlemen, gentlemen,' Mulligan intervened, in soft eirenic voice. 'There's no need for this unseemly bickering. It's too early in the day. Now look. In 1916 a small group of men staged a rebellion, the centre of operations being the GPO.' Afterwards, chuckling at the memory, he would label his *aperçu* Lecture No. 13a. 'As Mr Halpin said, not all of the Irish people were in agreement with their ideals or their methods. But, as Mr Dinneen said, the Rising was an inspiration. Every nation needs, or seems to need, a certain date from which to begin its modern history. America has 1776, France has the Revolution, Russia 1917. Ireland, whether we like it or not, has 1916. But while other countries have had centuries to dig through the myths, in Ireland the re-examination has hardly begun. Ideally, I say *ideally*, there should be academic excavation, followed by debate, followed by gradual acceptance that all was not black and white. That there were vast areas of grey. I mean the Republic is only sixty years old – and not even that, properly speaking – and how can we impartially examine the action when some of the actors are still alive? I mean, we all remember 1966. Now *there* was an orgy of commemoration, and I, for one, was all for it. But several of my friends were highly critical of it, and for what they considered good reasons. Fair enough. But if we want to get at the truth of 1916 it should be done at a time when politics and ideologies don't intrude their passions. The historians should be able to go about their work in stolid.

academic fashion. But they can't. Because events have con-founded the process. The sectarian boil burst in the North, and suddenly we are all forced to think deeply about the responsi-bilities of nationhood. And God knows we are getting no help from either historians or politicians. Now for some people, like Mr Halpin here, 1916 is a great mistake. For others it will always be a great and glorious moment in our history, and the men who took part great and glorious heroes. But it will help nobody, nobody at all, if sixty years later we find in 1916 a cause for insult and antagonism. We have to work together. We have to live together.' He lifted his empty glass. 'And now we have to drink together. An excellent idea.'

Once again showing his mastery of bathos, he left the silent group and ordered another round.

A chastened Halpin said, 'I'm sorry if I spoke out of turn.'

'Not to worry, not to worry,' Mulligan said, patting him on the shoulder, thinking that his exposition had finished the question.

But Maynard had his teeth in Dinneen's tail. 'Tell me, Frank, do you consider yourself Irish or American?'

Dinneen was forcedly nonchalant. 'I'm Irish when I'm in Ireland. I'm American when I'm in America.'

'That's funny. I would have said you were Irish in America and American in Ireland.'

'Who gives a damn what you think?'

'Seriously, though. It really matters to you, doesn't it? I could never understand that about Irish-Americans. They're always jawing about the mother country. They've been in New York for maybe a hundred years, and still they talk about the mother country. America is their mother country, for Chris-sakes.'

'You wouldn't understand.'

'Well, explain it to me then, eh? Explain to me why it matters where the hell your mother or your grandmother came from.'

'If you know where your mother comes from, it matters. In your case it probably doesn't.'

'Now don't go all nasty, my dear.'

Virginia said, 'I'd like to know where my ancestors came from.'

Maynard put his hand to his head. 'Oh, Jesus, Virginia.' An

argument about her origins would have reverberations absent from his challenge to Dinneen. His voice softened. 'Look, honey, I know that blacks are now being encouraged to do this kind of thing. Why? Why? First of all they probably won't be able to find out anything, and even if they do they'll have to admit that what they have now, no matter how bad it is, is better than what their ancestors left.'

Virginia stared around the room, taking in the wooden partitions done in 'modern' stainwork, the hard tables, the small drawers in shelves behind the counter which once held tea and sugar and other domestic sundries in those days when the pub was all things to all families.

'Max, it may not be important to you to know where your ancestors came from. Because it doesn't have to be. Do you understand? You're white . . .'

'Frank is white.'

'He is *Irish*. They suffered, you know, when they came to the US. Same as the blacks.'

'Hardly the same as the blacks, Virginia.'

'It doesn't matter. Their feet were on sand, too, for a long time. You don't care where your people came from. Okay. If you don't understand why it might matter to others, I guess there's no way anyone can explain it to you.'

Maynard turned to Dinneen, half smiling. 'See what you started? This gorgeous broad used to like me.' He turned back to Virginia. 'Listen, do you want to find out that your great-great-great-great grandmother lived in a straw hut in Angola and was dragged off to North Carolina in the eighteenth century and raped forty times on the boat over? What's the point of finding that out? You *know* that's what happened, more than likely. Why put yourself through the misery of confirming it? Everyone knows that the blacks had a raw deal, nothing will ever make up for it. But it's past. It's over. And you know what's happening now? The whole goddamn thing is turned upside down. My own brother – you know Jamie? He couldn't get a job teaching at CUNY because he was white. Right? So where does that get us? You think it's a good thing for Jamie to find out what the blacks went through? It'll make him more sympathetic? My ass. He worked his butt off for four years to get that job, and they give it to a black who hasn't half the qualifications. But fuck that, the board says. He's black and we have to fill our quota or we get no money. Now the black is in the shit, and Jamie is in the shit. And the students? What about the students? Who gives a shit about the students as long as the quota is filled? It's all horseshit, Virginia, horseshit, and you know it. We have to forget about the past for Chrissakes, and start living in now. Now!'

Dinneen was looking at Maynard throughout his outburst. He said, 'I agree with you about that black thing in New York.'

'Of course you would, you asshole. As long as it's blacks. We weren't talking about blacks. I wasn't talking about blacks. I was talking about this horseshit that you were going on with about being Irish. You're American, and that's all there is to it. These guys here are Irish, real Irish. That taximan is an Irishman.'

'He sounds more like an Englishman to me,' Dinneen said.

Halpin had his hand around Dinneen's tie before he had finished the last syllable of his sentence. His right hand cracked twice, back and forth, across Dinneen's face, as though he were hitting a child.

'I don't take that from anyone, my American friend. Now if you don't apologize for calling me an Englishman, I'll fester your hole so that you won't be able to sit down for a fortnight.'

Dinneen, half standing, blurted an apology through his astonishment and rushed out.

Haslam was chuckling quietly. He could see the column taking shape in Dinneen's head. Halpin's rejection of the orthodoxy would be visited on every Irish taximan, on the whole Irish people. The Irish have sold out. A servile bunch of lackeys, still tipping the forelock to John Bull.

Aloud, he said, 'I suppose no day is complete without a vanquishing.'

The taximen excused themselves and went outside.

Maynard said, 'How do you guys put up with these assholes, coming over here and telling you what to think?'

Haslam said, 'Some people seem to be more interested in their origins than others, the Irish more than most. I don't know why. Mostly it's harmless.'

Maynard was pained by the writer's tepidness. 'These guys are sending money to the IRA, supporting them. People are getting killed because of their long memories.'

'We haven't yet reached the stage where we legislate people's memories,' Haslam said slowly. 'No doubt it will come, as it already has elsewhere. But I won't be alive to suffer it. And I cannot imagine your welcoming it.'

'That's not what was on my mind, J.J.,' Maynard said defensively. Haslam's seriousness had wrong-footed him. 'I'm simply saying that Dinneen and his kind are not helping the situation in the North. I can't see that their solution is the best one.'

'There is no solution,' Haslam said.

Ellen said, 'That's very bleak, J.J.'

'Would you have me tell you a lie?'

Ober probed. 'Have you any idea what would solve the problem?'

'None.'

'None at all?'

'None at all.'

There was silence, the silence of unbelief, at the table. The Americans were heavy with disappointment. They were in the communications business, where people every day solved the problems of poverty, overcrowding, racism, big cities, pollution, nuclear threats. They did not, of course, solve them. But for a fee, they would appear on screen and glibly ladle out their three-minute solutions. It was unthinkable that on an NBS current-affairs programme anyone would dare say that there was no solution to a problem.

But Haslam had just said it, leaving them with nothing more to say.

So they returned to the hotel.

9

Later that evening, Mulligan sat with Ellen, Ober and Virginia, flicking through the three sheets of questions that Ellen and the two researchers had put together for the interview with the president of Maynooth College and Seminary on the following day. He had offered to screen them and to mark their cards on any mistakes.

Ober sat in the corner, smoking a chest-warming pipe. His mind was elsewhere.

He had napped after their return from Kavanagh's that afternoon, finding deep slumber after five minutes in bed. His body clock was awry, and it had taken him some seconds, when he awoke, to realize that he was in Ireland, at the beginning of what would be the most important programme of his career with NBS.

Halstead had made that clear after the Tuesday morning conference. 'It's not just a question of editorializing, Pete,' he had said with that harsh drawl that he had brought from Niles, Michigan, and never shed. 'Your ratings on the Denmark programme were lousy and you know it. Same with the Eskimos.'

'The Eskimo story was a good story.'

'I ain't denying that, Pete. But eight thousand feet to get forty minutes? And nine thousand for Chrissakes on the Denmark programme? Come on, Pete. We can't afford it. And that's not all. You'll have to keep the lid on your own opinions. There's more to Denmark than porn shops.'

'There was only ten minutes on porn.'

'Five minutes too much. Six minutes too much. Corry put the goddamn Reeperbahn into eighty seconds and said a helluva lot more. Without voice-over.'

'Send Corry to Ireland then. I never wanted this one anyway.'

'So you said, often enough.'

'Look, Leo. You hired me six years ago *because* I didn't keep the lid on my opinions. You were fed up to the teeth with the pussyfooting film you were getting from the staffers.'

'Come to think of it, that wouldn't have been a bad title for the Denmark programme.'

'What?'

'Pussyfootage.'

'Thanks.'

'Don't mention it.' Halstead lit a cigar. 'Well, pussyfootage is one thing you won't have to worry about where you're going.'

'I'll have enough on my plate.'

'You'll have a great time there, Pete,' he said, waving a generous hand. 'It's only seventy degrees there now and they're calling it a heat wave. Green fields, cows, plenty of jaw. You'll love it.'

Ober looked out on St Stephen's Green. It sure did deserve the name. No cows yet, but plenty of jaw. Ellen had remarked on it on the way in from Glasnevin.

Ober liked Ellen. She was dependable, unfussy. They all were dependable. Max was his favourite cameraman, in spite of his fag's temper, and Virginia was the hottest front woman on American television. There was a bitterness in her which he had often sensed but never probed. He was quite nervous of her. She could be, and he had seen her be, the worst kind of bitch, particularly with guys who made premature passes at her. But she did a good job, and the viewers loved her.

She had got very drunk at the ball. Well, what the hell, it was Ireland. But he would have preferred her to remain sober. Especially with that Crossan guy. He had watched her get sick on Crossan's trousers and the fellow never turned a hair. Ober disliked that kind of self-possession: he did not have it himself, often blowing his top in minor flaps, though he believed that in major crises he was cool. But of course Crossan was paid to stay cool. It was part of his job. And anyway he probably wanted to lay Virginia. Ober had never seen a man in her company who did not want to go to bed with her. Except maybe Dinneen, with his Irish-American bigot's heart. But then even he would probably want to lay her, provided he did not have to live with her – or near her – afterwards. He had taken Ober aside at JFK in the hospitality suite. 'Listen, I got to tell you something. I don't like Jews. Never did. Can't help it. Don't like blacks either.'

'How about gays?'

'You gay, too?'

'Max is.'

'Jesus, what a bunch. The whole echilada.'

'Looks like you're going to have to spend all your time with Ellen.'

Ober had wanted to smash Dinneen's face. But Halstead had warned him about that, too: 'You just play along with that Irish sonovabitch, Pete, and everything will be all right. No bad ink before the show goes out, okay?'

Why, Ober wondered, were all Irish-Americans so predictably boorish? His friends told him otherwise – that there were decent, civilized, urbane and witty Irish-Americans all over the States, and he had to accept that it must be true. But he himself had never met one. He hated Irish-Americans. Those he knew in the newspapers drank too much, and invariably fought when they drank. Why did they do it? He himself could not drink. Not many Jews did. But they got along fine without it. The Irish just drank and drank, and became loudmouthed and personal and righteous and maudlin, usually in that order. St Patrick's Day was the day when it all happened at once, as though by special licence, and their ridiculous parade closed the city down for a day. What the hell was that for? What were they proving? Black men selling green carnations to Chinese, just because the Irish wanted to celebrate. Every bar in Manhattan full, the whole city reeking of specious bonhomie, and those awful songs pervading every street. Songs of the old country. The old country! Max was right. The sheer arrogance of it. What did the old country ever give them to make them love it so much? Many of them had never even seen the place. And who the hell gave a shit anyway?

That was another thing about them: they acted as if the whole world should share their troubles. He had said as much to an Irish-American in Costello's one night. 'Paranoid!' The man had exploded. 'The Irish *paranoid*? Jesus, that's rich, coming from a fucking Jew.'

Ober could not reconcile the drunken, fumbling, vomitous

louts he had met with the great names in literature. That was another of Halstead's baits. 'I've seen your bookshelves, Pete. It's like the Irish Library of Congress. Joyce, O'Casey, Yeats and Synge.' He pronounced them 'Yeets' and 'Singe', making Ober wince. 'Must be *something* over there to produce those guys.'

There must be. Was last night a worthy introduction? He had watched Crossan throughout the night and felt there was little joy in his face. Haslam had bent his ear for an hour before the ball, talking about Irish literature. Ober had wanted to talk about Joyce and Behan – they were the ones he knew most about – but Haslam had been dismissive about Behan, 'a minor talent with a gift of the gab', and was impatient with Joyce. 'Old Shem the penman was inhuman. Remember that, young man. Loved making lists. Forced himself into exile. Exile is a wonderful thing. If you can sponge off half the world. I wouldn't mind a Harriett Weaver myself. Inhuman, yes.'

He showered, and sang as he showered, trying to wash away his angst, slapping himself briskly all over. Just for a moment, he expected Lois to come through the curtains, singing out an invitation. But Lois had gone. Four years of marriage, two of misery. He was, he had decided, happy without her. Playing the field was a lonely business, but the surprises made it worth while.

Virginia had come in with Mulligan and Ellen, and Mulligan had read the questions.

Ober said, 'We don't want to cause any offence. We thought . . .'

'It's not as easy to offend churchmen as it used to be,' Mulligan said. 'They become laminated by the times.'

He found nothing offensive in the questions. Ober was relieved.

Ellen said to Mulligan, 'Would the Irish call you a spoilt priest?'

Mulligan smiled. 'The phrase doesn't have much currency nowadays.'

But there had been a time, not so long ago, when the phrase was a blasting mark. The dream of every Catholic mother: to kneel in front of her own son and receive his blessing. Some mothers had it twice, three times. Whole families of nuns and priests. Letters arriving to Irish towns and villages from the Philippines, Pago Pago, São Paulo, Caracas, Lagos. 'Today I baptized a man who can remember killing and eating his enemies. Now he has joined the army of Jesus. Thanks for the socks.'

Ah, yes. Father Jim will be home in September. Only once every five years, you know. Aren't they wonderful? You must be a proud woman. Others, like Mrs Haslam and Mrs Mulligan had to live through the shame and failure. But there was no shame nowadays.

Ellen said, 'Was it very traumatic? Leaving, I mean?'

'For a while, yes. But we all make mistakes. People swear to be faithful to one partner for the rest of their lives. Two years later they are divorced. These things happen. Promises made in hope and ignorance. Are you divorced?'

'I have never been married.'

Mulligan looked questioningly at Ober and Virginia. They both nodded. Mulligan said, 'They tell me that two out of every three divorces in the US end up in marriage.'

Virginia asked him about his education.

'Christian Brothers. Then straight to Maynooth.'

'Did you have a hard time with the Brothers? I heard they could be very tough.'

'Some of them were. Some of them were gentlemen. It was a lottery. The Brothers have been subsidizing education in this country for over a century, and all they've ever got is abuse.'

'But it meant that education was kept in the hands of the Catholic Church,' Ober said.

'And what's so terribly wrong in that?'

'It hasn't helped things in the North, has it?' Virginia said.

'With all due respect, if I hear one more person blaming the Northern problem on Catholic education I'll go through the ceiling. That aside, though, it was a bloody good job that the Church looked after education. Because the politicians have never faced up to it. I was glad to get any education, and without the Brothers I would have got none at all. And hundreds of thousands like me. The whole country should be on its knees thanking them.'

Ellen said, 'Did they beat you?'

'Yes.'

'Often?'

'Whenever they thought I deserved it. And sometimes, unfortunately, when I didn't.'

Ober said, 'What kind of beating did they give you? I mean, did they punch you?'

'Rarely. More often than not they used a leather strap. Two or four or six of the best, depending on the enormity of your misdemeanour.'

Virginia said, 'They wouldn't beat you just for not knowing something.'

'Indeed they would. If you were supposed to know it, and didn't, you got walloped.'

'Barbaric,' Ober muttered.

The questions made Mulligan impatient. The Americans would never understand what it was like to be taught in an Irish school by Irish Christian Brothers, most of whom came from the same poor background as their pupils. Their only psychology was intimidation: some intimidated by words, others by the strap. They knew no better. And they got the results.

Ellen said, 'Didn't your parents object?'

Mulligan shook his head. 'They never knew. What happened at school stayed at school. Anyway, even if they had known they would have done nothing about it. The worst thing that could happen to any child was that his father – or worse still, his mother – would come down and complain to the teacher.'

'Was this fear of the teacher or fear of ridicule by his peers?'

'A bit of both. You didn't rationalize these things. The teacher was absolute authority, never to be questioned. Any punishment was simply accepted.'

'It must have left terrible marks on the children.'

'Children are resilient.'

They talked on desultorily for another half-hour. The Americans were very tired.

Mulligan, too, was tired, but when he left the hotel he did not turn for home. He thought of Angela sitting before the fire, watching an American serial on the Irish television channel, her women's magazine on her lap, the twins bickering and eating chocolates around her.

He walked down towards Davy Byrne's, passing the two policemen on duty outside the Dail.

He had been tempted to ask the Americans about their education. Probably they had all been to college and post-

79

graduate school, feeding the monstrous American academic industry. Had he been an American in their company he would probably have felt inadequate. They would have felt him so to be, with his miserable bachelor's degree. Consciously or unconsciously they would have felt that their education better prepared them for life.

And there was the nub. For decades, American educationists had painstakingly worked a programme for their children that was supposed to 'prepare them for life'. Anything that impeded this ambition, anything that was felt to be redundant to it, was jettisoned. If it is difficult, make it easy. Children are discouraged by failure, upset by it. Whatever happens, the children must not be discouraged or upset. Therefore, they should not be allowed to fail. Failure, error are negative factors and should not be dwelt upon for fear of causing a 'negative reaction' in the pupil.

So American education – public education, that was, for the private schools did not have to take the slightest notice of this deadly and unjust philosophy – had been gradually democratized downwards. A nation of graduates emerged, and kept on emerging, with a vocabulary as circumscribed but not half as imaginative as an Irish farm worker's, a total inability to reflect, and a nervous ignorance of true intellectual endeavour.

The regime was naturally self-perpetuating. The ignorant taught the ignorant – 'preparing them for life' – and gave them credits and degrees for table manners, skin diving and the history of the Hula-Hoop.

So what's wrong with that? the nervous graduate whines, whining being the passionate sound of American youth. Table manners are part of life. They are important, man. More important than goddamn Horace. What good will Horace be to me in an interview? What's the point in being able to quote Homer at a board meeting? Anyway, I never liked Latin. Or Greek. Nobody I know likes Latin or Greek. Why should I be forced to learn something I don't like? Why should education be drudgery? We got rid of all that nineteenth century shit a long time ago, man. Education should be enjoyable, painless. My education was enjoyable. I wasn't hassled. The teacher didn't push me. He helped me.

He helped you all right, Master Spencer D. Atwater III.

But he did not *teach* you. He did not teach you that *all* learning means work. That most learning implies drilling and drudgery. Learning is *discipline*, you fool. But of course you are not a natural fool. Just a made fool. A victim of the soggy nostrums that rule your educational system.

It would have been bad enough, Mulligan thought, had this appalling system been contained in the United States. But Europe had grasped its most poisonous myths to its bosom – healthy men sucking toxic gas – and foisted them on new generations of helpless templates. The British, sharing the language, fell quickest and most heavily. And now Ireland, as Mulligan so well knew from his teaching days, was being dragged by the nose into this forest of ignorance and anti-intellectualism. The children were becoming the classroom gauleiters. He himself had seen it in Dalkey. The question 'What good is Latin?' could no longer be answered with an avuncular cuff of the ear, or, less directly, with 'You'll find out when you're older and you'll thank me.' Now the teachers had to be sensitive to the child's feelings, to his reactions, to his mental allergies and 'home environment'. They had to smooth the stones on the road to learning, letting the child learn by doing.

Poor Montaigne, poor Rousseau, poor John Dewey himself, how they would cringe if they saw what was being done in their names. Teachers! Passive robots without resource, turning every intellectual endeavour into an 'activity'.

Well, I escaped that, Mulligan thought, as he passed by the Buttery on his way down Dawson Street. But only just. No visits to the Boyne, no cardboard cutouts, no peer-group comparisons, no cross-fertilization of disciplines, no writing away for information for 'projects'. Just learning. Mangan and Ferguson and Yeats, and Homer and Virgil and Horace. Two on the right and two on the left if you didn't know it. Learning six hundred lines of the first book of Virgil *off by heart* and carefully remembering that it contained the only reflexive infinitive in the whole *Aeneid*. Learning to *name*, to *describe*, to *explain*. Learning to do these things clearly and well, in English and Irish and Latin and French.

Drudgery. Pain. Discipline.

And meanwhile my counterpart in Hackensack was immersed in 'social studies', and panoramas, and 'living predicaments', the better to emerge as a 'rounded man' with a good 'general education', knowing a little about everything and nothing about anything.

'How was the game last night, Mr Atwater, with your master's in English from Berkeley?'

'The game? Jeez, that game. What a game. Shit, man. Christ, it was, oh, man. Let me tell you. You should have seen that game.'

'I should have, Mr Atwater, because you are not capable of describing it to me.'

Functional literacy. The art of inarticulateness. But what matter? They could *feel*, couldn't they? Yeah, man, they could feel. An Irishman never knew how he felt but could describe it. An American always knew how he felt but could not.

And was that what was facing Ireland now? The most articulate nation on earth? Were the wonderful, wearying waves of words to give way to mere living? Oh, yes, they were. It was happening right now, in front of his nose. Oh, God.

What, then, is the purpose of education?

The purpose of education, sir, cannot be defined until the word *education* is first defined.

That was it. The Americans will pronounce him educated who has been to the right school: the world's greatest mediocrity is metamorphosed into a genius by the words 'Harvard man'. The Irish still insisted that a man be more than a qualified cipher.

Mulligan remembered Haslam's comment on an acquaintance's indiscretion with his best friend's fifteen-year-old daughter:

'*Penis erectus non conscientiam habet.*'

Had Haslam been whisked from his infant bassinet to the US, would he now have said the same thing?

No.

'Guy was horny, for Chrissakes.'

10

Before leaving for Maynooth, J. J. Haslam had riffled through some books on his shelves, coming across Archbishop Troy's memorial to the Lord Lieutenant in 1794.

May it please Your Excellency, the Clergy have been complimented on many an occasion for assiduously instructing their respective flocks in the sacred precepts of Christianity, and for inculcating obedience to Laws and veneration for His Majesty's Royal Person and Government . . . from these considerations, and considering that piety, learning and subordination would be thereby essentially promoted. . . .

Haslam found the blunt sycophancy difficult to stomach. The Church on its knees, not to God, but to the Lord Lieutenant, The King's Vicar in Ireland. Give us our College and Seminary, your Excellency, and we promise that we'll beat every jot and tittle of nationalism, every taint of republicanism, out of the hides of priests and people. You will have nothing to fear from us. We will do your every bidding. We will bow and we will scrape and we'll make sure that the people do the same, and won't that be a grand relieving thing for the King now?

But even as he was saddened by the memorial's pedantic abasement, he could not help but admire the bishops as men of their times, ready to suffer any ignominy – aside from anything else, surely those signatures contained the names of some republican hearts? – for the great and good Church. So they promised the English to protect their students of Maynooth from contamination 'by the contagion of sedition and infidelity'.

And they found support, though qualified.

Edmund Burke wrote, 'If the founding of a Catholic College is completed as it ought to be, and as it will be, if the hands of the jobbers are kept out of it, I expect more good to come of it than from anything else that has happened in our day.'

And his expectations had been fulfilled, seemingly.

Had not John Henry Cardinal Newman himself come to describe Maynooth as the 'most important ecclesiastical seminary in Catholic Christendom'?

As they passed through the main gate Haslam noted the repellent sphinxes, and the yew tree that Gladstone had admired, under which Silken Thomas Fitzgerald – in the days when his family owned the castle – had played the harp of an evening, before being brought to the Tower and Tyburn to be killed.

Haslam and Mulligan, both prey to nostalgia in the Pugin building, took the group into the dining hall, and they all commingled with the president, the Reverend Thomas Paschal O'Meara and his chosen staff, under the vast painting of St Peter's Square in the Vatican, drinking sherries and whiskeys and other aperitifs. The staff priests – theologians, historians, philosophers, linguists – were interested and interesting, and the Americans – Ober the Jew, Virginia the lapsed black Baptist, Ellen Harbo the New England Episcopalian, Maynard the New York agnostic homosexual, and Frank Dinneen, beady-eyed and uncomfortable – found that their first experience with the Irish Catholic Church in its very engine room was both exciting and stimulating, and they laughed and chatted and became serious and ate heartily and drank well and tried to hide their constant surprise at the ease and erudition with which the twelve men around them spoke of contemporary life and its problems. Later, they would interview the president.

Meanwhile, Stephen Crossan had disengaged himself from the dining party and gone into Stoyte House, the beautifully plastered accommodation building. He made his way to Vincent Keegan's study and knocked on the door.

'Stephen, your presence is a joy. A joy.'

He took Crossan's hand in both of his and shook it well. 'Come into my castle.'

Crossan followed him into the room, an old room with modern furniture, an incomplete acoustical job covering one wall. There were many bookshelves. In the middle of the room was a large walnut desk on which there were more books, neatly piled, and a modern desk lamp cast a crooked, spiny shadow across the typewriter.

Keegan's greeting was a throwback to their youth, when he was often shy and inarticulate in company and found pleasantries difficult. He overcame his social timorousness with elaborate salutations. 'It isn't that I don't like talking to people,' he had once confided to Crossan, 'it's just that I don't like *starting* to talk to them.' He felt he either said too much or too little, and this often led him into premature silence, giving unintended impressions of aloofness or garrulousness. 'One way or the other I never seem to be able to make my companion of the moment easy.'

The years had washed away the timidity, but traces of the early camouflage remained.

Crossan sat down by the fireside and watched his friend pour generous whiskey into heavy Waterford glasses.

'Well, what shall we drink to? A sucessful interview for your Yanks with the Fascist downstairs? A silent wish that Christian humility might triumph over doubletalk?' He looked brightly at Crossan. 'Or to our glorious schooldays?'

'I think that's safer. At least we know the truth about it.'

Keegan sat down. 'I wonder. Have you ever been back?'

'Never.'

'I went back two years ago to see Sweeney . . .'

'I thought of him only yesterday. How is he?'

'He died last February. I thought you might have heard. Cerebral haemorrhage. No pain, they say.'

'Poor old Sweeney.'

'He wasn't that old. Sixty-six. The orders have a tradition of longevity, you know. Sweeney was a comparative youngster. And he wasn't poor. For a Christian Brother, he had almost everything he wanted. Particularly the company of nice young boys.'

Crossan looked up sharply. Keegan sipped and nodded.

Crossan said, 'Good God.'

'We were very innocent then, as was proper for our age and time.'

Crossan said nothing for a while, and then Keegan said, 'Well Stephen? Disenchanted? Has "poor old Sweeney" turned into a dirty old man for you?'

'I'm just a bit surprised.'

'Why?'

Crossan did not answer immediately. His answer might betray instincts which he had spent years trying to conquer. Primitive, irrational reactions without coherence or logic. He had already betrayed himself, he felt, looking across at Keegan in the twilight.

The boy had become a man, a big handsome man, his face almost covered by a blue-black beard, the curls on his head receding slightly.

Crossan remembered the boy who had sat beside him through five school years. He had been fastidious, studious, conscientious, but in none of these things unusual: theirs was the best class in the school, industrious and serious about study; frivolity had been as boring to the students as to the teachers. But what set Keegan apart was the serenity with which he had moved through the years, seemingly untouched by the grubby upsets and disappointments of puberty and adolescence. Examinations had held no terror for him, as they often had for Crossan. He had exuded an inoffensive self-sufficiency which drew the admiration of even the most fractious among pupils and teachers.

He had had, of course, a goal, and that was unusual.

Ollie Collins vowed that he would become a seaman, but nobody believed that. (They believed it years later when his thin young body was crushed between ship and quay in Kuwait.) Diarmuid Walsh would be an artist, and everybody believed that, the evidence of his passion and talent covering every spare inch of his copybooks.

But these ambitions, though not thoroughly worldly, were acceptable. Keegan's simple belief that he would be a priest set him apart, and should have made him the butt of typically cruel adolescent jibing. But that had not happened. He was, it seemed, too likeable, and he was devoid of sanctimony, matching in vocabulary and actions the exaggerated masculine vulgarity of his companions. His marks had placed him, as usual, among the top four in the Leaving Certificate examinations, and he had gone to Maynooth as he had always said he would.

And here, in this building, he had made his mark, choosing the Virgin as his subject. Now, in his thirtieth year, his work in

86

Mariology was a source of pride in the college and had the admiration of theologians right through to Rome.

But the years had changed him. His self-effacing manner had been replaced by a joshing brittleness which did not settle comfortably with Crossan's memory of him.

'I'll tell you why you're surprised,' he said. 'Sweeney, and the memory of Sweeney, are from a part of your life when everything was black and white, when authority was authority. When life, Stephen, was *normal*. And then you came to the big city, and started your voracious reading, and you ran into your first and second and third piece of abnormality. Things began to turn grey. You fucked your first woman . . .'

Crossan blinked.

'Don't wince, Stephen. It's a perfectly valid word. The best I know to describe the act. Unless, of course, you cared deeply about that first woman and your entering her was the consummation of a love and concern that was almost divine. I'm pretty sure it wasn't though, was it? It was probably like most of the rest of them – tentative, messy, nervous and unsatisfactory. And you came too quickly and she said it didn't matter, and you went home and thought a lot about it, and she went home and worried about being pregnant.'

'For a priest . . .'

'I seem to know a lot about it?' He stood to refill the glasses. 'In this place you learn in theory everything the layman learns in practice. In fact you learn an awful lot more. In order to know good, you must first learn all about evil. When I came here first, Sweeney's particular deviation was considered one of the worst abominations. It still is, of course, by Rome, by the bishops, by our smooth friend downstairs.'

'I hope he doesn't get too near the cameraman.'

'One of them, is he? Poor fellow. Tough life.'

'He's a New Yorker. It doesn't bother anyone over there.'

'Bullshit, Stephen. It bothers everyone, everywhere, all the time.'

'Why should it? It's just as normal . . .'

'Not *normal*, Stephen. Never normal. Just *natural*.' He sipped his whiskey briskly. 'Don't feed me any of that chronic liberalism. You've spent the last twelve years accommodating yourself to the knowledge that the world is full of perversions from what you used to consider normal. And in true liberal

87

fashion you berated yourself for having primitive and unsophisticated reactions to these things. You convinced yourself that there's no such thing as perversion. That there are, as your Yanks downstairs would say, different strokes for different folks. Well, to use another quote they would be familiar with, that's a whole lot of crap.'

He rose and went to the window, looking out on the twilit grounds, swishing the whiskey absentmindedly in his glass. His spiritedness was in odd counterpoint to the autumn peace which pervaded the room. The serenity had gone.

'You're a changed man,' Crossan said.

'So are you,' he said, without turning around. 'So are you, if I may say so. Captain of the debating team, leader in the songs, never short of a word. Has the civil service silenced that voice for ever?'

'As you said, things were simpler at school. I thought I knew it all.'

'And now?'

'I don't think I know anything.'

'Join the clan.'

'I mean something more than that.'

'You thought knowledge would bring wisdom?'

'More.'

'What?'

'Faith.'

Keegan came back from the window and poured some more whiskey. He filled and lit his pipe, another action that aged him, and sat down.

He stared at Crossan for a long time as the room gathered in the darkness. He did not turn on the light, as they sat in silence.

Leaving Dublin that afternoon, Crossan had looked forward to meeting a dear school friend with whom he could exchange some hearty reminiscences. There had been no heartiness, and the calm school friend had turned into a man of sharpness and forthright opinions, his remarks full of echoes of dissatisfaction, echoes, too, of Crossan's profound personal disillusion.

Keegan said, 'It's been a long time since we spoke to each other.'

'Yes.'

'We were very close one time.'

'As close as friends could be, I imagine.'

'But we were young friends. We parted and changed. Our experiences have built up walls around us. Even if we didn't want them to.' He knocked out the pipe dottle into an ashtray. 'You may not want to say any more.'

'I don't mind.'

'Is it just God?'

'That's a strange thing for a man of the cloth to say.'

Keegan was silent.

Crossan said, 'I don't believe in anything. I don't believe in God. I don't believe in the ability of humanity to improve itself. I don't believe in love. I don't believe in belief.'

'But you want to?'

'It would make life easier.'

'But it wouldn't make you happier?'

'I don't believe in happiness either.'

'That's very lonely.'

'I make my own distractions.'

They sat in almost total darkness. Keegan's pipe lay dead on the table. He drank the last of the whiskey, and then said quietly, 'Well, as I said, join the clan.'

Meanwhile, Thomas Paschal O'Meara said: 'Much of that, of course, one must take with the proverbial grain of salt, Much of it indeed, it seems to me, is the mere expression of wishful thinking on the part of the media. I wouldn't for the world wish you to misunderstand me here. I hold, and the Hierarchy in general in Ireland hold, the media in the highest regard. And we have nothing but respect for the valuable work which they do every day. Nevertheless, it would seem that certain people in the media are more susceptible to fashion than to facts.

'There is undoubtedly a wave of antireligious feeling abroad – this is not confined to Ireland, of course – and if one were to judge purely by what one read and heard in the media, one could be excused for thinking, as you seem to think, that the whole Church was in disarray and that people were falling away from Catholicism in millions. Well, of course, nothing could be further from the truth. The media claim that they carry out these surveys which show that such-and-such a percentage of young people, or even middle-aged people, are leaving the Church, are turning away from their religion.

Well, with the greatest respect to the people who carry out these surveys – and incidentally, rarely are we given details of the methodology used – we in the Church carry out our own surveys, and what we find directly contradicts what the media say. Of course, we don't have to go from door to door to find out these things. Our proof, and it is ample proof, is to be found in the churches every Sunday. And the churches, the crowds in the churches, prove, no matter what the surveys say, that the faith is still strong and vital in Ireland. In fact, it may even be stronger than it was twenty years ago. The media may claim that fewer people are attending church, and even if we allowed that claim – and I don't for one minute do so – well, obviously their faith was never very strong in the first place, was it? Our methodology, of course – and I say this with the greatest deference to modern sociology – is one which we had handed down by Jesus Christ our Lord Himself. It doesn't deal in percentages and questions in the streets. Our researchers are not housewives in part-time jobs. They are priests, men of God, and believe me, they know better than any part-time researcher what the people of Ireland are thinking. In this respect, I feel obliged to say that the media have been slanted in their reportage of recent happenings within the Church in Ireland, reporting more what they wanted to see and hear than what they actually saw and heard. We must always bear in mind that there are forces at work in the world that are intent on destroying the Church. Just as God works in mysterious ways, so does his enemy. I am not for a moment suggesting that the media are, consciously or unconsciously, agents of Satan. Not for a moment. . . .'

They walked slowly in the college grounds. The air was heavy with the scent of new-mown grass. A gibbous moon hung high and white, and the silence was broken from time to time by the shrieking of an urgent blackbird flitting under the pine branches.

Crossan's shock had subsided and now mingled with a strange ease at having found a like soul. Keegan's revelation had taken his breath away. He had imagined that he would find in his friend the kind of certainty that he himself had lost years before. He had assumed that his loss of faith was an imperative. Living alone, letting his mind travel hitherto forbidden or unknown avenues, shedding adherence to each commandment as it became irksome, gradually finding the whole structure of his religion to be artificial, a manual of convenience, an escape from thinking. It was bound to happen. As the years wore on, as the guilt receded – or changed to other, more abstruse kinds – his philandering, for one instance, became casual and untraumatic. It was typical of his upbringing, and the teaching priorities of the Catholic Church in Ireland, that he should still think of his loss of faith first in terms of sex.

It was so unutterably banal.

But he had been in the world. Keegan had been twelve years in this seminary, shut off from 'temptation' by walls concrete and spiritual. And now he had admitted that he, too, had lost faith. In spite of himself, Crossan was comforted that the ague had struck one so insulated.

Keegan bent and plucked some grass and put it in his mouth. He said, 'Did you wake up this morning and say "I will not serve"?'

Crossan smiled. 'I'm not prone to epiphanies. Unlike young Mr Daedalus.'

'Daedalus was very sure of himself.'

'So we must infer. Mr Joyce is a burden on me.'

'Mr Joyce is a burden on us all.'

Crossan said, 'Would you say that he did, therefore, manage to forge the conscience of our race?'

'His greatest virtue was that he never grew up.'

'Don't go Jesuitical on me.'

They walked through the shadowy gloom, passing under the shuttered window whence, long ago, two seminarians had jumped to death. Had they, too, lost the faith?

Keegan said, 'Still, I wish old Jimmy Joyce were here right now. Some of that certainty might rub off on us. One way or the other.'

'He would be anachronistic. We seem to produce men for our times. Our guru now must be Mr Beckett.'

'Ah.'

'I fear his cockerel's head.'

'He has nothing to say.'

'Excuse me. He has plenty to say, but knows the futility of saying it.'

'Mr Beckett is an evangelical zombie, preaching for years

to an empty church. Then the word gets out, the church fills to overflowing, and when they hear his sermon he is telling them that they shouldn't listen to preachers.'

Crossan smiled. 'A very hard thing to accept.'

'Especially if you're Irish.'

'Do you think of yourself as Irish?'

'It's a useful appellation.'

'Do you think of Mr Beckett as Irish?'

'He's a Protestant of English blood, educated at Trinity, a cricket player who lives in Paris and writes in French. Of course he's Irish.'

'The man should be writing end-of-the-pier farces in Brighton. Why do people with nothing to say insist on telling us that they've nothing to say? What terrible times we live in.'

Keegan said, 'We listen to them. We will listen to anyone nowadays. I will listen to anyone. Just in case.'

After a while, Crossan said, 'Did you have an overnight fall?'

'Much the same as yours. Gradual. Subliminal. I did, one day, in the middle of a lecture to a group of first years, realize that I didn't believe a word of what I was saying. But I also realized that I hadn't believed it for a long while before that.'

'When did that happen?'

'About six months ago.'

'All is not lost.'

'All is lost now.' The priest spat out the chewed grass. 'I am leaving here in a month. I am being laicized. Soon after, I shall marry Katherine Tierney.'

Crossan stopped and looked at his friend, finding no words.

'If everything goes all right, I shall be a father soon after that.' He turned and they walked together. 'You don't have to say anything. Except to wish me luck. It does have its little touch of irony, you know. For eight years people have been calling me father. Some time from now, I shall actually be a father, and no one will call me father at all.'

Crossan said, 'I thought I had problems.'

'Life here is very simple,' Keegan said musingly. 'One is looked after. One doesn't have many responsibilities. Not of a mundane kind. There's a commonplace admiration for the sacrifices that priests make. My admiration runs the other way, for the men and women who rear families, pay bills, run homes. I'll have to come to terms with all of that. I love this woman deeply, and she me. We shall make out, I'm sure. But that, supreme irony, is the biggest problem of all.'

'Making out?'

'Simply getting a job. Who wants to employ a Mariologist? What company is desperately looking for an expert on the Virgin Mary? Even in the Church she is not a favourite person nowadays. She gets in the way of ecumenism. I've wasted eight years of my life?'

Crossan searched for a bromide. 'No experience is wasted.'

Keegan's answer was weary. 'I know. Years of painstaking work and study, discipline, application. What employer could discount those virtues? But it's not like that, and you know it. Twenty years ago a man of my calibre and attainments would find work here through the network. Not now. Jobs are too important. Priests are not so special any more. And the Hierarchy doesn't want to know you. Neither does our friend downstairs. This country is growing secular faster than any in the world: more ground to make up, of course. There isn't the same sympathy abroad. Certainly none at all from Silken Thomas O'Meara.'

Crossan was surprised by his friend's unconcealed and bitter antipathy towards his superior. O'Meara showed a very diplomatic and even-tempered public face. His statements were unhectoring and untainted by that omniscient moralizing tone that had always marked episcopal statements in the past and was still to be heard in the too-frequent utterances of Cro-Magnon bishops such as Lucey and Newman.

Crossan said, 'You certainly went all the way.'

'Worse than that. It was the first time for both of us, and' – he turned smiling to his friend – 'it was messy and nervous and satisfactory.'

'You'll be telling me next that she's a nun.'

'That would be the perfect contemporary picture, wouldn't it? No. But she's a teacher, and that's a good thing. She's employable.'

'I don't know what to say.'

Keegan waved a dismissive arm. 'Your job seems to have its own rewards.'

'Yes, yes, yes. And if I don't soil my bib, some day I shall sit grey-haired and benign in an ambassador's chair, a humble legate in some storeyed capital. But what of it, if I don't believe?' They halted before the door. 'There was I, envying you your certainties. I wonder if anyone is certain about anything any more?'

'There are a few in this building,' Keegan said as they climbed the stairs to his room. 'Though not as many as there used to be. I had three good friends when I came here first. Joe Manifold and Pat Cassidy, who became dogmatic theologians. And Bill Kemmy, who did canon law. Of the four of us, at the end of this year, only Bill will remain. And I'm not sure that he'll remain. Mind you, I'm the only one who has lost the faith. The others were just laicized.'

'All is crumbling.'

'And the number coming in here diminishes by the year. The Church says there's a greater need than ever for priests. The people seem to think otherwise.'

'I suppose it makes some kind of odd sense that the Church should feel the need for priests just when the people don't. The Church is just another ailing industry.'

'. . . Here again I must say, with respect, that you have been misinformed, and again, it would seem, by your colleagues in the media. As a matter of fact, we had two more seminarians this year than last year, and one more than the year before. So you see, it is not true that the number of seminarians is falling away drastically. Naturally, I would have to agree that there had been a falling-off over the past decade, a lull as it were. But I wouldn't immediately ascribe this to a loss of interest. Rather, to an increase in the number of, let us readily admit it, very attractive and lucrative employment opportunities for intelligent young men nowadays, compared to, say, thirty-six years ago when I entered Maynooth. Nor when I say this do I mean to imply that any priest ever entered Maynooth because the priesthood would offer the kind of security and comfort that he might have had difficulty in finding elsewhere. But even if this were true, and I don't admit it for a moment, the necessary corollary is that we are now getting young men who, even if they are fewer in number, are totally committed to the priesthood. Young men who quite obviously would not darken our doorway if they found the life of a layman in any way more rewarding. The Church has been through, and is still going through, I have no hesitation in admitting it, a traumatic time in its history. Much of this trauma, if not indeed all of it, was initiated by our late beloved Holy Father, Pope John the Twenty-third, when he convened Vatican Two. Now maybe it has taken longer in Ireland than elsewhere for the full implications of the Council to be assimilated. It is not easy to overturn the traditions of centuries. But I believe in all honesty that the Irish Church and the Irish people – and let us not forget that the Church *is* the people, and the people *are* the Church – have adapted themselves very well to the new orthodoxies. Many people, again in the media, have accused the Hierarchy of dragging their feet on certain issues, and indeed, it may well seem that way. But, as I said, the Church is the people, and it would benefit nobody if the Hierarchy were to move *ahead* of the people. In many instances around the world, I regret to say that this has happened, and it has been good neither for the people nor the Church. There are many areas where the media would have you believe that the Irish people are crying out for change. Let us say in the matter of divorce and contraception, and even abortion. The people themselves, of course, are doing no such thing. The problem is that these media people have their eyes and ears open, not to the people of Ireland, but to other countries and other people. We are asked to stay silent when some indulgent or permissive article of legislation is mooted. Why *should* we stay silent when we know that such legislation will open the way for further more permissive and more indulgent legislation? I would remind you that *Humanae Vitae* – which, incidentally, too few people have read, especially among those who talk most about it – specifically enjoins us to refuse to countenance contraception and abortion. This is not to suggest that the Church is not sympathetic and understanding. We are aware of the problems. Who could be more aware than the confessor? It is possible that legislation will be passed making contraception freely available in Ireland. As I say, we would prefer that this didn't happen, and we have made our feelings known and will continue to do so. But, to be perfectly frank, and between ourselves, we would prefer the present situation, where contraceptives are quietly available, rather than publicly and freely, as they would be if such legislation were passed. The psychological and sociological implications of publicly available contraceptive devices would be very grave indeed for Ireland. . . .'

Keegan poured some whiskey while Crossan browsed.

Schillebeeckx on marriage. Bonhoeffer on ethics. Oh, the words and titles. Morals, ethics, sexuality, marriage, growth, personality, theology, grace, conscience. Five pale volumes of Aquinas.

And a whole shelf on the Virgin.

Crossan had never thought of her as a subject for a book. She had been such a vague presence – beautiful, ethereal, unsullied, silent – in the religious classes at school.

Lurking modestly amidst the Olympians, all ninety-four pages of it, was Freddy Barton's sharp and lively monograph on Johannes Scotus, aside from George Berkeley, Ireland's only philosopher. It had been written fifteen years before, when Barton was a political neophyte, and it had been almost totally ignored. James Mew, reviewing it in *Studies*, had deplored the neglect by the Irish of this 'brilliant *enfant terrible* of the ninth-century church' and had praised Barton for attempting the monograph. But the book had done little to lift the veil of ignorance and apathy which covered the life of this strange man.

Crossan took it from the shelf and read aloud the opening sentences of Barton's preface.

'Johannes Scotus – or John the Irish – was the most extraordinary Churchman of his time and, in my opinion, the most original thinker between Gregory the Great and St Thomas Aquinas. I am aware of the cries of "chauvinist" that my claim will provoke in certain quarters. But it is not John's Irishness that astounds one. Nor is it his staunch neo-Platonism, which perforce made him a heretic and put his life in danger. Nor even his Greek scholarship, which non-Irish philosophy students and teachers – with culpable ignorance of European philosophical history – still find surprising. Nor his Pantheism, nor his Pelagianism, both of which constituted almost suicidal stances in ninth-century Europe. What astonishes us today is his lifelong and steadfast refusal to set Faith above Reason.'

He closed the book and replaced it on the shelf.

'*Enfant terrible* indeed. Young Mew was right. The Irish should not neglect someone who set reason above faith.'

Keegan said, 'When that man was alive he was the only one in all Europe who could translate the Greek of the pseudo-Dionysius. Did you know that when Pope Nicholas got the translation he nearly choked on the fact that it had been done by a man from this barbarous country?'

'No. I did not know that.'

'Down the road in Glendalough and elsewhere were universities chock-full of students. For hundreds of years, mind you. Civilization had disappeared from Europe. And here it was nourished and fed. To be served up again in Europe when the time was ripe.'

'You sound like a public-relations man.'

'I'm bloody serious.' His voice had become harsh and declamatory. 'Ireland preserved for Europe the classical culture. The monasteries, for all their piety, didn't give a tinker's curse about theological niceties, and couldn't care less about Rome.' He gestured broadly. 'Look at us now. Look at this place. Can't fart without the permission of the Pope, or the say-so of some oily nuncio.'

Keegan was leaning forward, his eyes alight. Crossan stared at the gilt fireguard. Constable's 'The Haywain'. On the black marble mantlepiece, a small Mexican figure made from brass wire strummed his guitar.

Crossan said, 'For one who has lost the faith, the Church still moves you mightily.'

'Ach. Lost the faith. I hate the phrase. What does it mean? I have no patience anymore with Catholic rituals, the choking bureaucracy. And the young Daedalus answered forever any questions about alternatives, and more succinctly than I ever could. But the simple fact is, Stephen, that we Irish Catholics are spancelled for ever by our upbringing. And Mr Joyce, for all his vaunted free-thinking and *non serviams*, was the pluperfect example of it. Wouldn't allow his own son to bring his girlfriend home because they were sleeping together! Now where did he get that from? Your friendly neighbourhood Marxist will tell you that it's bourgeois convention. But we know better, don't we? That man was an Irish Catholic first, last and always, and a lucky man he was, too, for he would never have written a single word without those two things he professed to despise most. Ireland and Catholicism.'

There was silence. Keegan was patently enjoying himself.

His language had become careless, his normal prudence had deserted him.

Crossan said, 'So what are we to do, we poor lost souls?'

'The awful thing is that when you no longer believe, there's not very much you can do. Obviously, you cannot pray, since you have decided – or it has been decided for you – that there is no one to pray to.'

'Your hieratic training should have given you some spiritual ballast for something like this.'

'Plenty.' He let a shade of annoyance infect his voice. He stood up and walked about the room. 'I could sit down before you now and prove to you that I had not lost the faith. That my very insistence that I had lost it was certain proof that I hadn't. Inverted ontological . . . ah, shit on that.' He turned to Crossan. 'I could blind you with the most exquisitely arcane jargon you've ever heard. And I don't mean to sound patronizing. But I'm not going to tumble into that mire of so-called logical imperatives which would leave me back where I started, only more disenchanted than before.' He sat down again. 'You know, when I believed, I could see belief all round me. Now that I've lost the faith, I think I can see that everywhere, too. I don't know whether I've shed an old burden or taken on a new and infinitely more painful one. I don't know whether I'm deliriously happy or terribly sad. If there is a God, then it's damned sly of Him to make happiness contingent on belief of His existence.'

'He would argue, if he were the arguing type . . .'

'Go ahead. Make him Irish.'

'. . . that you are free to believe or disbelieve.'

Keegan drew his hand across his forehead. 'As I said, I'm not going to blind you with jargon. I have all the proof I need that there is a God. But it's no good.' He drank the glass dry. 'It's not proof I need.'

Crossan sighed. 'Let's drink to the late great Johannes Scotus. Willy-nilly, we are now in his camp. But be warned. The man insisted that reason and revelation were both sources of truth, and therefore need never conflict.'

'He also said that if they *seemed* to conflict, reason was your only man.'

'No wonder the Irish abandoned him.'

They drank, and Keegan took from his pocket a small roll

of notes, withdrawing a five-pound note and holding it up to the light.

'They didn't abandon him completely,' he said. On the note was the flat-domed forehead and rounded shoulders of the philosopher, gazing balefully to the west of the bearer. 'What other Catholic country would put a heretic neo-Platonist on a fiver?'

I I

The following morning the train sped to Sligo, crossing the central plain of Ireland to the northwest. At Sligo, the minibus would pick them up and take them thirty-eight miles into County Donegal to Bodmore House, half-way between Donegal Town and the bustling, romantic fishing village of Killybegs.

Mulligan sat by the carriage window, Alice Foley opposite, both of them staring out at the flat fields of Meath to the north. To the south, the equally flat fields of Kildare. This was the bloodstock centre of the world – thousands of gangling awkward yearlings prancing under the beady eyes of the best horse trainers and breeders, fed and found and fattened into the sleek engines of speed that would cause joy and heartbreak, make and break fortunes, at Sandown and Ascot and the Curragh. You could smell the money in the grass.

'I have decided what my affliction is,' Mulligan said, not turning his eyes from the landscape. A cold cup of coffee was in front of him.

Alice said, 'Something terminal, I hope.'

'I suffer from Pinkerton's Syndrome.'

'What are the symptoms?'

'They are various, my dear. Firstly, it is solely a male disease, so worry not about contagion. The male, a man of some station and regard, is irresistibly drawn to a young female of no station and no regard. She does not have to be Japanese, mind you.'

'*That* Pinkerton.'

'She must be innocent, guileless, trusting and wide-eyed.'

'And he?'

'He must be prevaricating, smug, callous and uncaring.'

'And does he always go away and leave her with an heir?'

'He's not that uncaring.'

'And she doesn't have to disembowel herself when she discovers his true nature?'

He turned from the window. 'None has, that I know of. Not, at least, in the physical sense.' He finished the cold coffee in a gulp. 'Dreadful. Something stronger is indicated.' He raised his eyebrows.

Alice said, 'A Campari? Why not?'

He went off to the bar, where some of the others were still finishing breakfast.

Alice watched his large frame disappear through the door. There was something very sad about his whole presence, a sense of great talent wasted or abused, ambition unfulfilled. Alice had known him for years. She loved his big white face, his sad Labrador's eyes, his persistently self-depreciating monologues. But she knew he was a perfect example of the adage that all self-criticism is oblique self-praise, and she also knew him to be a consummate actor, one who would put most professionals to shame. It was part of his job, of course.

He returned with the drinks, and shuffled into his seat, his belly rubbing hard against the table edge.

Alice nodded to the flabbiness. 'One of these days you won't be able to get into that seat.'

Mulligan looked hopelessly down at his straining shirt. 'Too late,' he said. 'It's part of me now. People think of me as jolly, you know. There's no such thing as a jolly thin man. "Jolly" is a fat word.'

'And fat is a jolly word. For me.'

'God bless your kind heart. . . . I think,' he said, 'I will write a book.'

Alice held out her hand. 'A shilling.'

'What for?'

'I said years ago that if I had a shilling for every time I heard someone say that, I would be a rich woman. So now I collect shillings.'

'How many have you?'

'Eighteen.'

'Did you have to give any of them back?'

'Not one.'

The bars of Dublin were laced with great novelists, young

and middle-aged men who could be seen any night in various stages of alcoholic trance and who had, indeed, many of the marks of all great writers: a huge conceit, a desperate need for praise, a fitfully fed drink problem, a longing for fame and acknowledgement, and severe paranoia. All they lacked was the ability to sit down for the countless lonely hours and translate their inspiration into prose.

'You don't believe me, do you? Think I'm another Dublin slob perpetually pregnant with a masterpiece?'

'It's a Dublin disease. And anyway, you like Dublin too much to leave it. And nobody can write in Dublin. Teddy always said that.'

'Yes. By the way, where is . . . ah . . .'

'Stephen Crossan has him in his pocket. Or had.'

'Crossan has us all in his pocket.'

'Not me.'

'You don't like him.'

'I don't think he likes me. I honestly don't know what to make of him.'

'A confident young man.'

'Certainly that.'

'Well, he's only thirty. A little buffeting will shape him. Actually, he's been decent enough to me from time to time. In fact, he's got me out of many a scrape, to be fair. It makes up for his impudence.'

'I thought impudence was the prerogative of the very young.'

'I find *everybody* very young nowadays.'

He drank again and leaned back, once more looking out the window. 'Alice, what in God's name is a man of my age and talent doing here? I'm fed up with being at everybody's beck and call, gobshites who know nothing about my beloved country and couldn't care less.' He was suddenly animated, his big white face angry and furrowed, the shock of red hair seeming to quiver on his head. 'This country was going places once. *I* was going places once.'

'The country is still going places, Oliver. Maybe you don't like the paths.'

'Of course I don't like the paths. We're selling our soul.' He waved back at the television crew.

'That's a nice thing for a Board of Welcomes man to be saying, I must say.'

'We have done good work. Very good work. Made a few mistakes, but overall . . .'

'Overall?'

'I'm not impressing you? A begrudger. Ah, yes. By God, if those tourists stopped coming tomorrow you'd soon find out how right I was. Balance of payments, my dear. The magic words. The country doesn't appreciate us.'

'Lord Bodmore does.'

'Oh, God.' He put his hands over his face and slowly pulled them down, changing from a Labrador to bloodhound. 'The poor bugger is doing his best.'

'The poor bugger should sell out and retire to a semidetached in Clontarf. But that wouldn't be good enough for him.'

'You don't understand, my dear. You just don't understand.'

'I don't understand *you*. I never noticed that you had such time for our erstwhile lords and masters.'

'This is different.'

'It always is.'

Farther down the carriage, sitting alone, J. J. Haslam had been writing in the diary that he had diligently kept for thirty years. Even when the muse was indifferent, he filled a page. He put the journal aside and rose and walked down the carriage to where Virginia and Ober and Ellen were sitting.

Ellen was patting Virginia gently on the hand. 'You were perfectly fine, perfectly fine.'

'I seem to remember that Dorothy Parker used to say that to people who were perfectly obnoxious the night before.'

Haslam sat beside Ellen. It was becoming a habit. 'What is this then? Did Virginia go off and get drunk after Maynooth?'

'Nothing like that,' Ellen said.

Ober said, 'We can't convince her that she did a good interview with the president of the college.'

Haslam took Virginia's hands in his and with a heavy, confessorial air, said, 'What's ailing you, my child?'

'I just don't think I got through.'

'Was it how you expected him to make statements that would have the Pope of Rome down on top of him?'

'Look, J.J., I've done interviews in my time. And I've got them to say things that they've regretted. Kissinger, Carter, even that tight-lipped bastard Scoop Jackson. They all sang.'

'These people would all be in the field of politics, I take it?'

'Yes.'

'Aye,' Haslam said gently, tapping her hands with his fingers. 'And now, tell me, are you going to compare a few tin-pot politicians with a man who may one day become a Prince of the One, Holy, Catholic and Apostolic Church? And an Irishman, to boot? Do you think that this monstrous, magnificent edifice has survived the centuries by appointing blabbermouths and poltroons to its highest offices?'

'Now, J.J., come on, that's a bit much,' Ellen said, laughing.

''Tis as well that this grand girl learn the truth,' he said. 'I'll tell you, my dear, your beloved Capitol itself is only the veriest village council hall compared to the Vatican, and your politicians, the very ablest and most gifted of them, would not hold a candle to the most junior Cardinal. These people, from the very first second they step inside the seminary gates, are groomed for the highest politics of all. And it doesn't matter where they are posted or what position they occupy, they are the supreme professionals, absolutely unbeatable for deviousness, prevarication, dissimulation and holy deceit. And you must remember that all their lives they are preparing for the greatest interview of all. They are not going to be wrong-footed by a mere stripling from the planet earth, now are they?'

Virginia looked pleadingly at the others. 'See? What did I tell you? It was a lousy interview.'

'It was a great interview, Virginia,' Ober said. He was nervous of Haslam since the night of the ball, and could not decide when or whether to take him seriously.

'I'll tell you honestly, child,' Haslam said, 'you did as well as anyone could have. He set out to talk a lot and say nothing, and in this he was successful. But if it's any consolation to you, you got the whole man on your tape.'

'*Gee*, thanks.'

Ellen said, 'You must encourage Virginia, J.J. She's the only reporter we have. And this afternoon she's to interview Lord Bodmore.'

'More of the same, Ellen dear,' Haslam said. 'Another poor hoor trying to face down the changing world.'

After a silence, Ober said, 'Have you ever met him?'

'Never. But they say he's a decent skin.'

Ellen said, 'How do Irish people feel about having lords

living among them? I mean they're not really lords now, are they?'

'Not in the sense that they used to be, no.'

'How do you feel about them?' Ober asked.

'My feelings are mixed.'

'The Irish seem to have mixed feelings about everything.'

'About lords and ladies and the aristocracy in general, their feelings are very mixed indeed. But I imagine you won't blame them for that.'

'Was this Bodmore, I mean his ancestors, were they good or bad?' Ober pursued, tamping his annoyance at the writer's vagueness.

'If there were worse than them, I never heard of them.'

Ober leaned forward: meat at last.

'They were the most vicious, tyrannical landlords that this part of the country ever experienced. Your average Southern plantation owner was a veritable St Francis in comparison. They owned everything – lands, buildings, people – and what they didn't own, they grabbed. They did nothing for the land, and less for the people, and they robbed the unfortunates of everything they possessed. They took their liberty, their crops, their daughters, their pride. And they gave nothing back, except the privilege of working all day every day for the Bodmores' aggrandizement. Most of the time they spent in England while their agent increased the rent to make life bearable for them. If the tenants didn't pay it, they were shovelled out, for there was always another more unfortunate family ready to take their place.'

Haslam paused in thought, and Ober said, 'What was the population of Ireland then?'

'In the heyday of the Bodmores, it was about eight million.'

'Jeez, you'd think they could have taken on those people. I mean . . .'

'I know what you mean,' Haslam said, looking up at the producer. 'I know what you mean. But it isn't easy for a people in subjection to rise up in unison and overthrow their oppressors. As millions of your ancestors would tell you if they were alive today.' Ober stared at the table, and Haslam turned to Virginia and said, 'Or yours, either.'

Ellen it was who eventually broke the heavy silence. 'I guess the Bodmores are not much liked in Donegal, then.'

'Well, if you mean that the people around harbour murderous feelings for them, you'd be wrong. Nowadays they're too busy making new money to be worrying about the past too much. Not that they aren't aware of it, you know, but they don't go around yelling about it, or breaking Bodmore's windows or the like.'

Virginia said, 'I guess that's because Ireland belongs to the Irish people now.'

Haslam gave a short, harsh laugh, shook his head and looked out the window as the train neared Sligo. The gentle unspectacular undulations of the central basin gave way to rolling hills. The Iron Mountains stretched to the north in a triangle from Drumshanbo to Swanlinbar to Belcoo. The rain, too, came down softly, and Haslam noted it and said that he hoped it would be cloudy and overcast when they passed Ben Bulben. 'It's the best way to see this grand mountain. No good in the sunshine. No mystery, no majesty. Ben Bulben should be seen in the rain.'

He talked on, prodded by the others' questions, about the Bodmores and their like, and the fate of the lords in the new Ireland. Their presence on the national scene, he said, was nowadays freakish and selfconscious. They clung together on racecourses and in clubs, where their antique presence was still unremarkable, massaging each other in their shrill, astringent patois for comfort and consolation. The more prescient forefathers had immersed themselves in businesses and investments which had a built-in immunity to the declaration of Irish independence – though many of those ventures were now bleakly circumscribed by independence movements elsewhere. The new Irish government, and all those that had followed independence, were indulgent and without apparent desire for revenge. So the lords, a good many of them, stayed happily and quietly in their great homes, adapted to the new orthodoxies, and still spent most of their time in England or the South of France.

But some, of course, could not adapt. Whatever mighty initiative, whatever courage and resource had spurred their forefathers, had long since been dissipated. The wilier scions of these wasted dynasties, conscious of the cachet of a title, had slid into more pedestrian spheres, becoming reporters, or photographers, or film makers or investment bankers or restaurateurs. But the others, the dispirited and resourceless few, were left flapping helplessly in the dried-up lake of privilege.

Bodmore was one such, pinioned by his inheritance. His past was all he had, Haslam said. 'The future holds nothing for him. He is forced into alliance with the grubby parvenus of the new Republic, and the tourist chiefs will try to forge a livelihood for him out of the shell of his family's history.'

The approach to Bodmore House was over four miles of twisting pitted driveway, following, on the left, the shores of a large still lake, with occasionally a rigid heron grey and mute on the mudbank. On the right were thick drowsy rhododendrons, the bright red flowers long since rotted and gone from the bushes, which were now thick green and silent.

Behind the rhododendrons stretched the acres of woodland, good timber and valuable, though now greatly diminished. For twenty years Bodmore had given care of the woodland to an agent who had sold most of it in small lots and put the money in a bank in Switzerland, where he now lived.

The house was square and grey-black, large rectangular blocks of stone placed one on the other. It was devoid of ornamentation, and was surrounded by large chestnut trees which crowded in upon it, as if coveting its space. The windows were small and functional and the whole place exuded an air of thick gloom.

They halted in front of a massive black door, almost twenty feet high but only five feet wide, showing its dour face between two great stone columns.

Crossan looked around. The driveway was pitted with small holes, filled with water by the recent shower. Ragwort, its flowers perished, its stalks now bronze and dry, grew along the edges. The grass in the small garden in front of the house was patchy and uncared for. A small old Renault car, light blue and rusted, lay in a corner, its back door missing and all the tyres flat. A rocking horse lay sideways on the grass, the straw extruding obscenely from its behind, the glass eyes missing.

Crossan turned in the silence as the others alighted and went up to the door. As he reached up to the knocker, a lion's head of heavy brass now painted a dull black, he saw a torn notice stuck to the door; it was attached by adhesive tape which had become wet and lost its purchase, so that he had to straighten it with his fingers: 'PLEASE USE EAST DOOR. DO NOT PARK IN DRIVEWAY.'

Crossan shouted back to the group, 'Which side is east?'

'The right-hand side,' Maynard shouted back. 'It always is on maps.'

Crossan made his way around to the right-hand side of the house. There was a small glass door at the top of a flight of dangerous-looking iron stairs. He knocked, and after a minute a woman opened the door.

She was tall and angular, in her forties, with prematurely greying hair brushed straight down around her face, which was the colour of semolina, with a nicotine stain on her upper lip. She wore loose black pants and grey sweater, both of which were soiled, and on her feet were yachting shoes through which her two small toes protruded at the sides. She was smoking a cheroot, and her fingers were stained, the nails short and dirty.

'I'm looking for Lord or Lady Bodmore.'

'Ah, yes, you will be the American group. Forty of you, isn't it?'

'Just nine, actually.'

'Oh, dear. The film chappies, of course. Do come in.'

Her voice was high and nervous as she ushered Crossan into the small room, which had once obviously been a utility room but which now served as a dining room with table and chairs, so that there was little room to move about. There was litter everywhere, and on the table the remains of a morning meal.

'We weren't expecting you quite so early. You must excuse this. Our girl let us down again this morning. My husband should be back in a moment. If you can find a place to sit down. Are the rest outside? What part of America are you from?'

Crossan introduced himself, irritated again that his accent had become so bland, but she kept on talking and he reminded himself that certain kinds of people never listen to anyone.

The group filed into the room, filling it, and gradually forcing the still chattering hostess into the farthest corner by the sink.

'He should be here in a jiff. I've been trying to get the silver . . . I wonder if you would hand me the table stuff? We'll just pop it in here until later. P'raps she'll turn up.'

Dinneen, who was by the table, had to clear off the ware and utensils, awkwardly handing the cups and saucers to Virginia Green, who passed them on to Ober, and they eventually reached Lady Bodmore from Max Maynard. She put them all in the sink and filled the kettle. 'Hot-water tank went again yesterday. Third time this year. And of course they will come only if you ring before ten o'clock. Not that that's been possible either for the past week.' She smiled weakly through the cheroot, which dripped ash into the sink. 'The phone is gone again.'

She had the complete attention of the group, none of them being able to move or turn without knocking something over. They stood mute as she rattled on.

Crossan, hunched in a corner, and furious at the cool aristocratic blindness which had them all thus cramped, said, 'Perhaps if we moved farther into the house.'

They slowly left until the room was emptied, following their hostess into another room. She turned and looked over their heads and said, 'Ah, there you are, dear. These are the film people. They've just arrived.'

A tall man came through the door, taking off a pair of worn leather gloves, the tips of the fingers split and ravelled. He was in his forties, with very thick brown hair and blue eyes in a narrow face which was sallow and pointed. He was wearing faded cavalry twill trousers and thick-soled boots, with a brown, polo-necked sweater. His greeting was effusive, stilted and high-pitched and he looked slightly to the right of everyone as he shook hands.

'Glad to have you chaps here. Didn't expect you so early. Well, now.'

The room was large and very cold, with little light from the two small windows. Bookshelves, half-empty, covered two walls, and on the others were huge prints and small originals, mostly hunting scenes from the previous two centuries. Large Chesterfields lounged about and in the centre was a small mahogany table with an inlaid ivory chessboard, badly cracked.

'A drink, what?'

He went to the large cabinet by the door, grimacing fleetingly when the door would not open. He raised his voice. 'Darling? Do you have the key to the . . . a drink for our visitors, what?'

As his wife's approaching footsteps sounded in the hallway, he turned to the company, smiling ruefully. 'Have to keep the stuff locked up, I'm afraid. One or two experiences . . .'

His wife came in and opened the cabinet. Bodmore said, 'Perhaps you'd better leave me the key dear. We probably . . .'

'You always lose it, darling,' she said briskly. 'I'm afraid the stock's gone down a bit.' She looked into the cabinet. 'You can have whisky, – that's scotch – or gin, or,' she looked out at the group, 'that's about it, actually.'

Bodmore sat himself down with a large whisky when everyone had been served.

Ellen said, 'We didn't see you at the Hunt Ball.'

'The Meath? Oh, yes. Used to go up for a week one time. Can't any more. Too much to be done. Height of the tourist season, of course, can't neglect the job, what?'

Virginia said, 'Could you give us a little bit of the history of the house? Maybe something about your family?'

'Ah, of course. And then maybe a tour later, what do you think, dear?' But his wife had gone out again. 'Yes. Only the ground floor, I'm afraid. Lots of renovation upstairs. Place is in rather a mess. But at least it's lively when the workmen are around. I fear I could never reconcile myself to being a mere curator. Like the place to have some life. That's why I've put in the ghost train in the cellars, and of course the caravan park in the back – trailers, I think you call them. Bring life to the place, wouldn't you say?'

'And do you get many visitors?' Maynard asked.

'Good lord, yes. This afternoon a party of forty Americans. Families, you know. Children. They get a kick out of the ghost train.' He filled his glass again. 'Now the history of the house. Yes.'

He rose and opened a drawer in the cabinet, taking out a sheaf of brochures. He leafed through the top one. 'Yes, yes. James Francis Arbuthnot, architect. Only example of his work in Ireland. Now . . .' He handed a brochure to Ober and another to Virginia, putting the rest back in the drawer. 'Don't have enough for you all, I'm sorry. I have a new supply ordered for the past month, but you know how it is at the end of the season. Didn't expect such a heavy demand on them. Ordinarily, we charge ten pence for these. Can't very well charge you people, I suppose.' He laughed, and filled his glass again.

When he had finished that he stood up. 'I must pop down to the cellar. See things are in order. Tell you what.' His eyes suddenly brightened like those of a child about to commit some harmless mischief. 'Don't move, any of you. Back in a jiffy.'

Virginia said, 'If he has another one of those he'll be soused when I talk to him.'

Haslam said, 'The upper classes have a high tolerance of alcohol.'

Dinneen said, 'Practice.'

'I guess he's not very upper-class any more,' Virginia said.

'Poor sonovabitch doesn't know his ass from a hole in the ground, far as I can see,' Maynard said.

Haslam said, 'Chickens have a habit of coming home to roost.'

There was silence again.

Ober read the brochure. ' ". . . a later example of Arbuthnot's austere style. He died before the building was completed, and indeed there is no evidence that he ever visited the site during construction. There are no other surviving examples of his work in Ireland, and only two in England: St Ives's Hospital for the Insane, now known as Lowether Psychiatric Unit, and Cockermouth Prison, both in Northumberland." '

There were steady banging noises from the hallway, and then a figure appeared at the door, dressed in chain mail and all the trappings of a medieval knight, including fluted armour and a helmet with vizor. The figure carried a heavy sword in his right hand, and clomped slowly into the room.

Along the shoulders and down the arms, and also on the helmet and breastplate and down the legs, there were small bulbs, and an electric wire trailed behind, ending in a junction box.

A muffled voice came from inside the helmet. 'Shocked you, what?'

Bodmore lifted the vizor and looked out at his guests, smiling broadly.

'What do you think? Do I make a good ghost?'

'You make a perfect ghost,' Haslam said.

'. . . The important thing is to make a contribution to what we may describe as the emerging Ireland. My wife and I put our heads together, see what we could do. To be perfectly frank, it's not easy these days to keep a house like this going. Help is difficult to find. People don't have the same regard. There isn't the same kind of loyalty, if you know what I mean. When I was a boy I used to spend every holiday here – I was educated in England – and there was such a happy air about the place. Everybody knew his . . . his work. Did an honest day's work. We had a wonderful chauffeur. Old Billy Paxton. Drove my mother around. He was really splendid with her Pomeranians. And Tommy Ahern, the butler. With us since he was sixteen. All dead now, of course. . . .

    '. . . Then I put the ghost train in the cellar. Best idea I ever had. Especially my dressing up as the ghost. Then there are the holiday trailers, fifty of them, completely booked out this year. Rather spoil the view of the lake, but then one can't have everything, what?

    '. . . Oh, dear me, yes. Problems all the time. But one doesn't knuckle under, does one? We could do with a little more help. I was saying early on that there isn't the same sense of loyalty. Ireland now has a welfare system, of course, and indeed that is naturally a wonderful thing. It is not quite as drastic . . . as all-encompassing as the British one, but nevertheless it is substantial. And of course, while it is a wonderful thing, well, it does rather diminish people's incentive to work. It all comes back to what I said at the beginning. One must make a contribution. If only more people would make a contribution. But some, I'm afraid, just take everything they can get and put absolutely nothing back into the country. Ireland is a beautiful place, with tremendous potential, if everyone would just knuckle down and pitch in. One doesn't want to sound carping. . . .'

As they strolled in the grounds, the silence was broken by the sound of the arrival of a large touring bus, followed immediately by the sounds of young American voices, high and demanding.

    'Ahah,' Bodmore said. 'Our young friends have arrived. I think we'll all go into the cellar and you can watch as the ghost train comes through. I'll place you so that you can see me when I appear in the armour.'

    Ober had already decided that they would not shoot film in the cellar. They trooped down the stairs behind Bodmore, and he showed them the miniature tracks and the train, which had four luminously decorated carriages with room for twenty-four small bodies. 'This is where they begin, you see, and they go round these columns and back again twice, and then out at the exit further on.'

He led them towards the exit.

'If you will position yourselves here in about ten minutes I shall come in from the door opposite, and you will not be able to see me. But just before the train goes through the exit, I shall turn on my lights and then watch the children's faces. Gives them a helluva jolt.'

Outside, Lady Bodmore collected the children's coins and handed them tickets which she asked them to return on the way out.

One of the children, a blond boy of about twelve, had bought a shillelagh and was waving it over his head and chanting a school song.

The train moved off and disappeared slowly into the cellars, the children setting up an immediate chorus of cynical shrieks, much to the amusement of their parents, who stood outside in the sunlight in their yellow and blue and green double-knits.

The group stood inside where Bodmore had placed them, so that they would be facing the train at the exit. They would also be able to see Bodmore when he appeared as the ghost. They could hear the train chugging through the cellars, and the shouts of mock horror continued.

As the train reached the exit, Bodmore flicked on his switch, the lights went on all over his suit of armour, and he raised his sword and bleated fearsomely.

There was loud, mocking laughter from the train, and as the engine passed Lord Bodmore by, the young blond crashed his shillelagh with all his strength into the side of the helmet, knocking the man flat on his back.

Crossan stepped quickly across the tracks when the train had passed. Bodmore was unconscious. It was four hours before a blacksmith could be found to prise the helmet off. By that time, Bodmore was conscious again. And smiling.

12

On the road to Sligo late that afternoon, Crossan sat at the back of the minibus between Haslam and Mulligan.

The scene at Bodmore House had left him with a sense of desolation, a desire to pour sympathy on the owners of the house.

But sympathy was more difficult to receive than to give. Certainly, there was no sympathy forthcoming from the blacksmith, or from any others of those whom Bodmore referred to as 'the people'. They had long memories, and they waited, almost without interest, for his demise, monitoring each crack in the plinth, cackling casually in the local pubs at the futility and incongruity of his latest desperate experiment.

Crossan was aware of his own alliance with these people, and he disliked such irrational enjoyment of another's downfall in himself. But there was nothing he could do about it. Bodmore's very voice, the unselfconscious loudness of it, set off an engine of simple, primitive hatred in his belly. There was, to be sure, a great pathos in the image of a craven lord. It was poetic. It was a spectacle to provoke compassion of a classical kind, and Crossan – at that moment when he had bent over Bodmore's helmeted, unconscious head – had tried to summon all the sympathy and understanding he could muster, building images of dinosaurs living beyond their times and environment.

In vain.

The sight of the man lying beneath him, the circumstances of his fall, had excited in him not a poetic compassion but a sly glee that made his guts jump, so that he kept his head down lest his face, even in the darkness, betray his savage satisfaction.

'Why should I have felt like that?' he asked Haslam.

'Atavism, surely.'

'Only that?'

'That, and much else. You were *taught* to hate these people, remember. Think of the shameless bias of your history books.'

'I worked very hard at correcting that.'

'Only in your mind, child.' He looked blandly at the young man beside him. 'I suppose you despise your emotions?'

'When they provoke me to irrational . . .'

'Oh, be quiet, boy. And don't start mixing up what is irrational with what is unrational.'

Mulligan, looking out the window, said, 'The boy asks for an explanation of his feelings, and the elder writer gives him a lesson in semantics.'

Haslam said, parrot-fashion, 'If language is not correct, then what is said is not what is meant. If what is said is not meant, then what ought to be done remains undone. If this remains undone, morals and art will deteriorate, justice will go astray. If justice goes astray, the people will stand about in helpless confusion. Confucius.'

Mulligan said, 'You're a thundering ballocks, J.J.'

'If the same Bodmore had any spark he'd need no sympathy from Stephen or anyone else.'

'A good piece of material for you.'

'Perfect for *Final Twilight*.'

'For God's sakes, J.J., the poor man is trying.'

'Very trying.'

The conversation grew snappy and personal as it touched on the role of Mulligan's organization in giving Bodmore's life a meaning and purpose. Haslam did not hide his scorn for the way government money was being spent, and Mulligan – though privately sharing his feelings – felt constrained to defend the Board of Welcomes, and to bring what he called 'an element of Christianity' into his judgement.

The small quarrel grew loud enough to be heard beyond, and Virginia slipped back to hear it. But the men immediately changed the subject, and Virginia sat silent while they talked about the majesty of Ben Bulben, and the majesty of the man who made it famous. She knew they had changed because of her presence, and she felt angry that they should exclude her. But her own memories were too full of examples of similar situations – with her doing the excluding – for her to voice her anger.

In truth, it was something that everyone on the journey was sensitive to: some of the best conversations went perforce unrecorded; the Irish would not let themselves go in front of camera and microphone, and often enough they were hesitant in front of the Americans. It was not merely that an unspoken tribal loyalty inhibited any comment which might be construed as critical of the home country: there were times when this broke down, and Haslam, particularly – since he was not snaffled by a government salary – said what he wished to say and without fear. There was another impediment: the ironic tone into which the Irish persistently lapsed was a continual baffle to the Americans, who were brought up in and lived in a society where even the intellectuals always said what they meant, often having their chronic honesty mistaken by foreigners for gullibility. Irony had little currency in the New World, and the constant inversions and *louche* remarks of the Irish caused moments of shock and horror which lasted for but a second, but which kept the Americans on a perpetual teeter. As the days passed, each of the visitors learned to look carefully at the speaker's face when he delivered himself of some typically shocking apothegm, finding reassurance only in the lightly lifted lip or the unmistakable smile in the eyes.

Dinneen was most affected by this. Whatever Irish talent for the oblique his parents had taken with them to America had been totally lost, and he, of all the Americans, felt most affronted when one of Haslam's or Mulligan's pellets took some seconds to sink in. It was degrading to find yourself laughing some time after the speaker had passed on to another topic. The situation was made more demeaning for Dinneen by the obvious fact that Virginia Green, for whom he bore a dislike which was only partly ascribable to her colour, seemed to be in tune with the Irish far more than he was, and he had seen Ober smiling fleetingly on occasions when the joke was not at all apparent to him.

All of the group were aware of the gulf that separated them, but none had, as yet, remarked on it. And when Virginia sat in on the conversation in the minibus, it seemed natural to change the topic. Her resentment was short-lived, and she was soon involved in Yeats and Ben Bulben, and the bus sped on into Sligo.

Alice Foley knocked on the door of Crossan's room in the Great Southern Hotel, Sligo, at midnight that night. He was lying naked on one of the twin beds, smoking and reading Louis MacNeice's *Autumn Journal*, marvelling again at the simplicity of tone, the clarity of language, in this personal history in verse of the autumn before the Second World War. Crossan had showered and was feeling well as he read through the poet's pungent, discursive stanzas. He had almost reached the end of stanza XVI when Alice knocked.

'Who is it?'

'It's me, Alice. May I come in?'

'Just a minute.'

He put on a pair of tiny black briefs and covered himself in his dressing gown, wondering what would draw Alice Foley to his room. When he opened the door she smiled at him. 'I hope I am not disturbing you,' she said, as she slid by him into the room.

'I was just finishing something. Sit down and I'll finish it aloud.'

He smiled to himself that he would for once read poetry without motive to a woman. He took up the *Collected MacNeice*. 'The Irish don't read enough of this man.'

'He was a Northern Protestant,' Alice said, settling in her chair. 'I suppose that's part of it.'

'A little more than that, methinks. Too many truths for us to stomach.'

'I'm glad you said "us". I don't like the way you say "the Irish" all the time. As though you didn't belong.'

Crossan began to read:

'Why should I want to go back
To you, Ireland, my Ireland?
The blots on the page are so black
That they cannot be covered in shamrock.
I hate your grandiose airs,
Your sob-stuff, your laugh and your swagger,
Your assumption that everyone cares
Who is the king of your castle.
Castles are out of date,

The tide flows round the children's sandy fancy;
Put up what flag you like, it is too late
To save your soul with bunting.
Odi atque amo:
Shall we cut this name on trees with a rusty dagger?
Her mountains are still blue, her rivers flow
Bubbling over the boulders
She is both a bore and a bitch;
Better close the horizon,
Send her no more fantasy, no more longings which
Are under a fatal tariff.
For common sense is the vogue
And she gives her children neither sense nor money
Who slouch around the world with a gesture and a brogue
And a faggot of useless memories.'

He put the book down and looked up at her.

She was sitting in the easy chair at the foot of the other bed, leaning back. Her legs were crossed, and Crossan noticed that she was wearing stockings: a small triangle of pure white flesh showed under the skirt. She was, as usual, smoking, and she looked at him through glasses which seemed to keep her eyes hidden, though they were neither strong nor thick.

'Take off your coat.'

She stood up, and, as he lifted the coat from her back, she turned slightly, so that her full breasts glanced against the front of his dressing gown. He went to the wardrobe.

She said, 'I'm not staying for a week, you know.'

He hung the coat up. 'How long are you staying for then?' His annoyance with her distant mannerisms, partially subsided, was still sufficient for him to talk to her with a brittleness which he found uncomfortable. He sat and lit another cigarette.

Alice sat and studied him, and half wished she had not come, but dismissed the thought as soon as it was born.

She had something to do.

The young man in front of her was the only one she had ever met who consistently made her feel uncomfortable. She could never tell whether he remembered her or not, and he always made her go through full introductions when they met. She had watched him, on those occasions when they had met previously, surveying rooms of people, and there was a quite unmistakable arrogance in his simplest glance. Her college colleague,

Margaret Nash, had felt the same thing, and confided so to Alice. 'I'm going to pull him down a peg,' she had said, and had tongue-lashed Crossan in company, calling him, among other things, 'a pompous, priggish, arrogant, self-admiring little rat'. Crossan had said, in a deliberately hideous drawl, 'Little, Maggie? But I'm six foot one, my dear.' Margaret's hatred for him doubled, but Alice, to her chagrin, had found herself chuckling. Oh, yes, he was a challenge, and a damned attractive one.

She lit another cigarette from the first and said, 'It's Oliver.'

'He looked all right when I left the pub.'

'J.J. left soon after you. That left just me and Oliver.'

'Splendid deduction.'

She blew smoke between her teeth and plunged. 'Why do you dislike me so much?' Her fingers were trembling slightly.

Crossan sat up and spoke quickly to hide the shock of the sudden intimacy her question had created. 'Alice, it's not a question of my disliking you. *You* are the one who dislikes me. You have consistently treated me as a stranger. It's bad for my ego, surely, but I haven't a trace of masochism in me. Other men like to pursue. I don't.'

She smiled. 'I know.'

'What do you mean, you know?'

'I know that you don't pursue. Everyone knows you don't pursue.'

'Everyone?' Crossan was genuinely shocked.

'A lot of women I know . . .'

He said quickly, 'I'm sure you didn't come here to tell me about my status among the women of Dublin.'

'No.'

She looked down at her hands, and the smile disappeared again. 'I told you. It was Oliver.'

'Yes,' he said, with studied patience. 'But you didn't tell me what it was about Oliver that made you knock on my door. in the middle of the night . . .'

'If I'm that unwelcome,' she said, rising from the chair.

'For God's sake, Alice, will you sit down. Listen, I don't dislike you. I thought you disliked me. That's all there is to it. It happens all the time.' He drew on his cigarette and then, looking at her, he said, 'Do you dislike me?'

'I don't *dislike* you.'

'Well, then, why do you carry on the way you do?'

'Because I don't want it to be obvious, you idiot!' Her voice was very low. 'I've seen them throw themselves at you.' Once again Crossan was shocked. He had never been conscious of any woman throwing herself at him. He had the sudden deflating thought that he must be a very naïve young man. She leaned back in the chair. 'I don't want to do that. Anyway, I can't. I just can't do it.' She pulled hard on her cigarette. 'I'm too bloody shy.'

Crossan lay back on the bed. What she had said seemed unequivocal, but he had the wariness of experience. Or at least what he had *thought* was the wariness of experience – the very caution which had probably blinded him to all those women who were supposed to have thrown themselves at him.

He said, 'What did Oliver do to upset you?'

'He was . . . he was a bit forward.'

'Jesus, Alice, your vocabulary is lodged in the last century.'

'Only when I'm nervous.'

He said, painfully aware of his disingenuousness, 'What the hell are you nervous of?'

'Who else is here, Stephen?'

'Wait, wait,' He put a soothing finger to his lips. 'I didn't know you were nervous of me. But if you say you are nervous of me, then of course I believe you. Merciful hour, my syntax is growing as baroque as yours. If I didn't know you better . . .'

'You don't know me at all.'

'Alice?'

'Yes?'

'What, Alice, did Oliver, Alice, say or do, Alice?'

'Nothing very much,' she said quickly. 'He just wanted to go to bed with me.'

'So?'

'I said no.'

'And?'

'He said he would come to my room tonight. I would have to throw him out.'

'Persistent devil.'

'And arrogant. Like the rest of you.'

Crossan said, 'Oh dear, oh dear.' He did not want to listen to any bitter tirade about the inequality of the sexes.

'Why the hell should Oliver think he can just hop into

bed with me? I mean, I like Oliver. But God, the conceit.'

Crossan swung his legs down over the side of the bed, planting his feet firmly on the floor, elbows on knees, jaw in his left palm.

'Tell me something, Alice. Tell me a few things. Are you offended because someone asked you to go to bed with him? Or because Oliver Mulligan asked you to go to bed with him? If you had wanted to go to bed with him, would you be sitting here now hiding from him? Have you ever slept with a man before? If a man who you wanted to sleep with asked you to go to bed with him, would you say yes?'

She was staring over his shoulder, tautly nervous, her body alert on the chair. His questions had created their own momentum, their own inexorable destination, and he could not have stopped himself from saying what he did next.

'If I told you I wanted you, would you say yes?'

He wanted then to turn away from her eyes and lie back on the bed while she breathed deeply and conjured an answer that would leave her self-respect intact, her own view of herself unviolated. But that would have been cruel, too cruel even for him. More, it would have diminished the power of the question, and robbed him of the enjoyment to be derived from watching her as her mind tried to accommodate what was warring within it.

Her lovely body, her angular, unsullied face, he had seen them before through a disfiguring veil of dislike – for he had indeed disliked her with a protective ill feeling which kept *his* ego intact – and now the veil was drawn away, she had become a human being, lovely and desirable.

She said, '*Do* you want me?'

He rose from the bed, stubbed out the cigarette and knelt beside her chair, taking her face in his hands, gently brushing her hair away behind her ears. He looked long into her eyes, and then he took her glasses off and kissed her eyelids so that she hardly felt his lips, moving down her face to her mouth, which opened to his. Her arms went quickly around his neck, her hands cupping his head, and their tongues moved hurriedly in and out and around each other. He pulled away from her and laid his cheek against hers and said, 'Come, take your clothes off.'

'No,' she said softly. 'I want you to take them off. Please.'

She rose slowly from the chair. 'But I want to see you, all of you, while you do it.'

She opened the belt of his dressing gown, pushing it down from his shoulders and kissing him on the lips. Then she knelt before him and rolled down his briefs, cupping his buttocks in her hands and laying her cheek against his rigid penis. She took his scrotum in her mouth and sucked slowly, and then, holding his penis in her hands, she lightly touched the purple bulb with the tip of her tongue.

He wanted to control, to pace.

He lifted her up, and she came slowly, her tongue leaving a trail of saliva from his navel to his throat. He unbuttoned her blouse, flicking the ends out from her waistband and throwing it on the bed. Her breasts hung in a light-blue brassiere, large brown nipples showing through the flimsy material that held them. He kissed them through their casings and undid the button and zipper on the side of her skirt, while she nuzzled and touched him all over. The skirt dropped to the floor and he saw the long black garters that held her sheer stockings, and black panties, tiny and inadequate covering: curled flecks of black hair peeped out on her thighs and flat white belly.

He stood back from her to take in the full picture of created wantonness. He brought her to him and undid the brassiere, and she hunched her shoulders, dropping it to the floor. Then she straightened up and watched him with some pride as he looked at her breasts, large and round and beautiful, the nipples high and strong. He knelt down and drew down the garter belt and stockings, while she fondled his hair and ears. He pressed his face into the V, getting that delicious tang, and he drew her panties down to her feet. She brought him up to her and held him close, placing his knight between her thighs, moving her hands slowly up and down his back.

He said, 'If you don't lie down, I'll come between your legs.'

She led him to the bed and said, 'You lie down, and close your eyes, and think of nothing.'

He lay on his back and she squatted over him, her buttocks on his thighs, while she massaged her clitoris with his tip. Her eyes were glazed and fixed, and she mumbled softly, and then gently and slowly she guided him into her, making soft noises as he penetrated deeper and deeper. Then she began to move on top of him, her hands flat on his belly, her face contorted in swoon, her breasts swinging freely and rhythmically as she brought herself to climax. She opened her mouth and her breath came in gushes and she fell on top of him, holding him tightly, her nails in his flesh, and she trembled for a long time.

He held her in silence while her shudders dimmed, massaging her whole frame and kissing the top of her head.

He had spent himself before her, but he was still stiff within her and she moved languorously from time to time, murmuring as she did so.

She said, after a while, 'Are you cold?'

'I'm very warm.'

'Please don't come out. Let's sleep like this.'

'That would be very nice.'

'It was wonderful.'

'You did all the work.'

'Next time it's your turn,' she said, and then she slept, and he gently rolled her off him: however desirable it might be to sleep inside her, it was a physical impossibility.

They made love twice later, at dawn and again before they rose. He played gently with her, awakening her with his tongue at her thighs, staying down there until she pulled him on top of her, and she came several times, with the kind of urgent pleasure that implied long and forced abstinence.

He wanted to ask her about it, that following morning, thinking about Teddy French, but he had no desire to damage the harmony of the moment. The breadth and variety of female guilt, he believed, were even more complex than those of the male.

But she mentioned it herself, when she had used his toothbrush and was dressing herself.

'You must be wondering what kind of person I am.'

'I've been wondering that for years.'

'Did you enjoy it?'

'Every minute.'

'Have you got Teddy's ashes with you?'

The question shocked him, following without pause and so tangentially upon the others. He nodded to the suitcase. She rummaged and found the whiskey bottle, taking it out and placing it on the bedside table. She looked at it for a few seconds and then she leaned over and took Crossan's penis in her mouth, sucking lazily until it was erect. Then she turned to the bottle and said, 'Now what will you do, you cheating bastard?'

Crossan lay back, astonished, feeling that he had witnessed something he should never have seen.

Alice rose and went to the bathroom and he heard the toilet flush. She returned and placed the whiskey bottle on the table again. It was empty.

After what seemed like hours, Crossan turned to look at her. She was smiling vacantly.

He said, 'I thought you loved that man.'

'Oh, I did. And he me. There was nothing I wouldn't do for him. And I thought he felt the same.'

'But he didn't?'

'He said he did. Maybe he even believed it. But meanwhile he slept with every woman in Oxford. Lecturers, students, canteen girls, the lot.'

'I don't know what to say.'

'There's nothing to say. I know it all now. I'm not bothered by it any more.'

'He must have been very popular.'

'He was the perfect man for the women there. Wild, anarchic, brilliant, and red-haired. And of course he had the perfect camouflage.'

'What do you mean?'

'He was *Irish*. Nobody in the world ever thinks of Irishmen as stallions. They get away with a lot.'

'Why didn't you join him in Oxford.'

'I couldn't. I had my job. He was to be finished in another year. We were to get married. Ah,' she said, dabbing powder lightly on her face, 'that's enough about me. Why should I burden you?'

'I always thought you were fairly self-sufficient.'

'Don't be ridiculous, Stephen. I'm a woman. And I want a man. I think I have plenty to offer. But all I get is Oliver's paw down the back of my skirt and a drunken invitation to bed.'

Crossan was silent, and then said, 'Nobody ever knows anyone else.'

'It's better that way.' She began to dress. 'I'm sure you don't want to know all about me. I don't want to know all about you. I envy you *your* self-sufficiency. Because, whether you feel that way or not, that's the way you act. And that, Stephen, is because you're a man.' She buttoned her blouse and went to the mirror to brush her hair.

'Rubbish.'

'It's not rubbish. Men are hunters and women are hunted. That's the way it's been, and that's the way it will be for a long time to come.' She rubbed some lipstick on lightly. 'It may all change in a hundred years' time, but I won't be around to enjoy it. I want it now.'

'Hunter and hunted are very strong words. The hunted in this case can simply say no. And the poor hunter has to grin and bear it.'

'I'd be happy to swap roles, if only to see what it was like.'

'No, you wouldn't.'

'Yes, I would. I quite enjoyed my recent expedition. Well, parts of it.' She smiled at him in the mirror. 'You don't believe me, though, do you?' She turned around to look at him. 'May I ask you a personal question? You can tell me to mind my own business.'

'I'll hear your question first.'

'Have you made love to Virginia Green?'

'No.'

'Do you want to?'

'That's two questions.'

'Ach,' she said, and turned back to the mirror.

'Yes, I do.'

'Aha. And maybe you will, before the trip is over. And J.J. and Oliver will look upon you as a successful lover, a good man with the women. You may even bed Ellen Harbo. Another notch on the gun. But supposing I go to bed tonight with Pete Ober, and tomorrow night with J.J., and even with Oliver? What does that make me? A successful lover? Oh, no. Oh, no, no, no. A bloody tramp, right?' She turned and brushed her hair vigorously. 'That's the way it is, and that's the way it will be while I'm alive, and those shrieking lesbians don't speak for me most of the time, but by Christ they're right about that.'

Crossan said, 'You're right.'

'Of course I'm right.'

She got up and came over to him. She was laughing. 'I enjoyed that. Got it off my chest. Poor Stephen. Would you like to hear more?'

'They'll be waiting for us.'

'I don't mean right now.'

'You're learning this hunting business fast.' He smiled and nodded and went into the bathroom. He was under the shower when the telephone rang, and Alice reflexively picked it up.

She said, 'Hello?'

The caller said nothing, and hung up.

13

Frank Dinneen paced up and down in his hotel room dressed in green-silk boxer shorts and woollen undervest. His typewriter was on the dressing table and every so often he sat and wrote a sentence or two and then rose and paced again. His room door was open, he told himself, to let out the cigarette fumes left by the previous occupant, but in truth to let any chance passerby get a privileged view of the great columnist at work.

Pacing helped Dinneen to think; or, more properly, to cut and hone his sentences to the briefest. He believed in brief sentences. And in brief paragraphs. He abominated subclauses. The man who could not say what he meant in one sentence was a fool: commas, hyphens, semicolons were the tools of bush-league writers. His column was the tightest in New York and he was proud of it. He had spent thirty years perfecting his style, and it owed nothing to anyone but himself.

The first sentence of this morning's column read, '*Montaigne said that there is a kind of glory which is to have too good an opinion of our own worth.*'

A friendly night-sub-editor named Larry Weiss had given Dinneen a copy of Montaigne's *Essays* when the columnist was at the height of his career as a sportswriter. It was the spark from heaven. Now, whenever he could, he punched a Montaigne quotation into his column, using it as a dowager uses a lorgnette, at once to see more clearly and to intimidate. He had, he was fond of saying, a love-hate relationship with his readers: 'They love me and I hate them.'

But while Montaigne provided the occasional sprig of

authentic class – even a cursory study of the *Essays* perforce introduced one to Martial, Tacitus, Seneca, Lucretius, Plautus, among others – the sixteenth-century autobiographer was not the most powerful influence in Dinneen's life. From Montaigne, he had, he believed, learned to despise humbug and flimflam, to pursue truth tirelessly. He noted well the essayist's advice to 'use plain words, and display such goodness and purity as we have at the bottom of the pot', and he constantly stirred the bottom of his own pot in public, finding a happy and very Catholic equation between self-flagellation and the search for truth. He never referred to his column, but rather to his 'essay', and he believed that he was the best, if not the only, essayist in the United States since Mencken.

And Mencken was the second powerful influence on Dinneen's life. He had idolized the scold of early twentieth-century America from his teens, rhapsodizing on his style and opinions, convinced that he was one of the 'civilized minority' for whom Mencken declared that he wrote. Apotheosis came in 1945 when Dinneen, visiting Baltimore, noticed Mencken sitting alone in a hotel lounge. He introduced himself, and the great man made him welcome, and later invited him to dine in his club, explaining that he had recently savaged both club and members in print, but it was more convenient than home for entertaining. Dinneen sat rapt while his hero talked about everything from Nietzsche to William Jennings Bryan, poking fun at 'the rube', and about Kipling and economics and Shaw, and finally, with great bitterness, about Roosevelt – 'the milch cow with 125 million teats'.

What had the most profound effect on Dinneen that heady night was the craven adulation with which Mencken was treated by the club members and staff whom he had so lately and viciously denigrated. From that night on, Dinneen worked hard on turning himself into a pathological ingrate, convincing himself that he was ascended to a higher and purer plane of existence.

But the seeds of this disease had already been planted by the third and greatest influence in the columnist's life. His mother, Mary Ellen Dinneen, *née* Hanly, had run away from Boyle, County Roscommon, with the wilful Frank Dinneen in 1915, and they had scarcely settled in a squalid, two-room apartment in Boston when her husband disappeared with her savings, leaving her with nothing but the clothes she stood in and a three-month-old foetus in her belly.

In a few years, the proud, passionate, generous young woman turned into a poisonous, bitter harridan, with an implacable hatred of men and a general misanthropy and suspicion which sentenced her to a lonely life. She took in washing, she stitched and mended, she was a chambermaid and cook, a nanny, a waitress, and finally, with the advent of prohibition, the owner of a small and vulnerable speakeasy in Boston and later in New York. She focused what love she had on her son, protecting him as best she could from the horrific uncouthness of those customers who were bread and butter to mother and child, from the stench and filth of raw New York. But she could not protect him from everything, and his deep child's slumber was often blasted to bits by raiding police.

She made enough money to get him through high school and college, and she fenced in his growing years with a plethora of sanctions, usually couched in the language of the pseudo-adage. She cosseted and protected him, and she was the only purchase he had on life. He revered her with total love and total fear, and when he eventually took a wife, she sundered the liaison in a short time. The wife was the saurian Lady Annabel Shaw, who had been visiting New York and was much taken by the tormented young Irish-American. She took him back to her estate in Wiltshire and showed him as her ancestors once showed blackamoors, and he almost went mad before his mother came and dragged him away. He took nothing from the marriage except the belief that mustard, to be any good, had to be made from powder, and it had to be Colman's powder.

Two other marriages went the same way, barren and useless, and, at fifty, every inch a successful columnist, Dinneen had gone back to live with his mother and had lived with her ever since. Each year, he went to Tijuana for a fortnight and spent a lot of money to sit behind a two-way mirror and watch blacks and Mexicans and Puerto Ricans perform every possible combination of sexual acts, and he returned to New York sated, and ready for another fifty weeks of tight essays and sour comment on the manners and morals of the modern world.

On his way to the top of his profession, he had served for a time as a public-relations man, suffering with tightened heart the quotidian humiliations of that profession. Launching out of it, he set about getting even for the hurt he had suffered, indifferent to the fact that the people who suffered his brutishness, callousness and bile were just another crop of public-relations men.

He was profoundly conscious of being Irish, at first resentfully. He would for many years have given all he owned to be thought WASP – it was at this time that he fell in love with Lady Annabel and Colman's powdered mustard, and while the titled lady was never mentioned in his column, mustard was a regular.

Larry Weiss, the lover of Joyce who had given Dinneen his copy of Montaigne, later, in wry regret, wrote a piece of doggerel which became known to everyone on the newspaper, and ended

> Mother, Mencken, mustard and Montaigne
> These are the loves of fearless Frank Dinnaigne.

But Weiss could have added Ireland. For Dinneen gradually became interested in, and proud of, his mother's home country, and in recent years he found it warming that the eyes of the world were on Ireland, and that he was Irish, and therefore gifted with an understanding of the problem that others were denied. He published his 'insights' frequently, sounding off with blunt righteousness at the British propaganda machine, telling the 'true story' of Protestant barbarity in the North, pointing the finger at the true villains, praising the true heroes. The ordinary people.

Dinneen had a passion for the ordinary people, and he liked to sit in pubs on his visits to Ireland and eavesdrop on farmers and dockers and barmen who did not know that he was the great Frank Dinneen, the Fearless Spectator himself.

He disliked and distrusted people like Mulligan and Crossan – he called them 'buglers' – and he was put off by Haslam's rueful whimsy.

Indeed, he found little to like in the new Ireland, thinking it already heavily tainted by those things that he hated about America. There was a slick self-satisfaction about Crossan which was barely distinguishable, he felt, from that of any young American executive. Mulligan was a blatherer, and in that he was Irish, but he was a moralizing blatherer, and therefore suspect.

And they had all listened to that cabman in John Kavanagh's spouting his John Bullshit, and not one of them had raised his voice in protest. Mulligan had delivered himself of a sermon that would have sounded right from a spinster Quaker, Haslam had smiled through the whole thing, and Crossan had cocked an eyebrow. Wimps, the lot of them, living on the government gravy train.

He sat down and looked at the first sentence.

'Montaigne said that there is a kind of glory which is to have too good an opinion of your own worth.'

Dinneen typed, 'That is not a fault you will find in the present-day Irishman. Let me tell you about the new breed of Irishman . . .'

14

They were at Drumcliff, 'doing five minutes' on Yeats in the cemetery. The sun shone brilliantly in an azure sky, Haslam waved his ashplant like a baton, and Maynard sang 'Somewhere over the Rainbow' in memory of his beloved Judy.

But there was a sour note in Ober's voice when he spoke, having surveyed the poet's grave and headstone for a solid five minutes in silence. 'I was expecting something more . . . effective. Something more worthy of the great epitaph.'

He spoke with a casual irritation that to Haslam's mind betokened unconscionable philistinism.

The novelist recommended darkly that Ober ponder the true meaning of Yeats's words. 'Maybe you expected two vast and trunkless legs of stone, what? Maybe he should have written "Horseman, fuck off"?'

But his ire found other targets when Virginia introduced him on camera as 'Ireland's greatest living writer, and a name to be reckoned with in English literature today.'

For all the fulsomeness of the flattery, the writer soaked it in. As the camera rolled, Maynard esctatic because of the pure quality of the light, Haslam spun a liquid web of words about the man beneath the clay, praising him without caution, and becoming animated and spikily erudite when he spoke of the 'mere insects' who sought now to belittle what Yeats had done.

'It's very easy for these little minds to cast their nervous, pernickety pellets at him now,' he said, with that relish that marked the rehearsed line. 'They would do far better to take the advice he gave them before he wrote the words on this stone here.

Irish poets, learn your trade,
Sing whatever is well made,
Scorn the sort now growing up
All out of shape from toe to top. . . .

It would serve them well to harken to that, and old men like myself, who have done their years' apprenticeship in the forge, might listen to these little minds when they can produce a poem half as good as "Under Ben Bulben".'

Thus he continued, the five minutes becoming fifteen as Ober, happily surprised to mine controversy at this hallowed shrine, insisted that Maynard keep the camera rolling.

Virginia needed to say little, and she stood beside the grave of the poet, the quintessence of contemporary freedoms, her black skin shining, as Haslam rambled exquisitely to the end of his panegyric. They would have gone on longer but Ober feared that the interview would turn into an attack on a lot of unnamed people. 'It might then be incomprehensible to a lot of Americans.'

'It will be incomprehensible to them anyway,' Haslam said.

They came into Ballina by the coast road, cutting out at Dromore for Easkey, and driving down through Kilglass and Enniscrone.

Haslam pointed out to Killala Bay. 'There now is the site of another abortive attempt to lift the English yoke. A thousand Frenchmen landed there in 1798, supposed to be the vanguard of a large contingent that would free Ireland.'

'What happened?' Maynard asked.

'What always happened. They were wiped out. Eventually. Being great fools, they depended on the Irish to help them.'

'And didn't they?'

'After their fashion. They took the guns and the food and the uniforms. And they ate all the food and broke the guns, or killed each other accidentally, or shot off their feet with them. They're still at that kind of thing in our own time. I often feel that all any enemy ever had to do to defeat the Irish was give them plenty of weapons. They will all accidentally kill each other sooner or later.'

The massive new Fujikawa complex came into view at the other side of the bay, and Mulligan roared across the water,

'You're too late. Two hundred years too late.'

Everyone laughed, the Irish heartily, and Crossan, growing easier by the day, endorsed the hysteria of the moment by joining in the scenario into which Mulligan, in appalling imitation of a Japanese accent, immediately plunged, making believe that the thousand men of 1798 had been Japanese, not French.

'Me Crackywacky. Take me to your reader.'

'Would that be *McGuffey's Reader* ye had in mind, now, yer lordship, sir?'

'We tousan' Japanese soldier.'

'Begob, I tought dere was a nip in de air all right.'

'We come to flee Ireland.'

'An' why would ye be wantin' to flee an' ye only afther arriven?'

'Can you brame us?'

'Deed an' I can't, and that's a fact, yer lordship. But shur, you haven't seen the half of it. An how could you, wid your eyes half shut de way dey are. Or is it half open dey are?'

'Japanese soldier hungly.'

'Why don't yer lordship sit down dere an we'll bile ye up a bit of bacon? Tis a grand ting for de jahndice.'

'Japanese no like Irish pig.'

'Bejayses, ye sound as bad as the bloody English.'

The mood lasted to Ballina, the Americans – except for Dinneen – taking turns to try out their Irish accents, which consisted almost entirely of sentences studded with *afthers*, and ending in *bejabers* and *begorrah*, two words never heard on Irish lips, except when they are imitating the Americans imitating the Irish.

The factory complex lay sparkling and anachronistic against the green mountain, like an electric organ outside a mud hut, and was soon out of sight.

Maggie Porter, true to her word, greeted them outside the Four Elms Hotel in Ballina, bristling with intent to succour. Mulligan made the introductions with an air that implied that the Americans should have known she would be along to help. Ober's face screwed into a characteristic frown, but she charmed him, as she did everyone else, with a mixture of apparent omniscience and schoolgirlish self-depreciation, the perfect mixture to beguile.

She had another virtue, tacit and inherent; she was shapeless and plain, so that no sexual frisson ever marred the professional air of her presence. She knew that beauty frightens as many men as it attracts, and she exploited this knowledge. She was proud of her prowess in a profession dominated at the top by men, hardy ex-journalists, but she kept her pride to herself, sensibly.

She took the group to the factory, Mulligan giving a reassuring wink to the suspicious Crossan, who stayed behind with Haslam and repaired with him to the bar of the Four Elms.

The writer's bitter tones of the morning had been displaced by a jaded disenchantment.

'Oh, what a bore it is to be Irish,' he said, plonking his pint of Guinness on the Formica table. 'I mean, does any nation have to carry the burdens that we have to bear? All that history, all that tradition, all those writers, all those emigrants, all that endless talk?'

'There's a lot would envy us our burdens,' Crossan said.

'The young Africans?'

'The young Americans.'

Haslam took a long draught. 'America is the spoilt brat of the world.'

'That spoilt brat runs the Western household.'

'More's the pity. He needs a good whipping.'

'We were happy to have him resolve our little fights.'

Haslam scratched his sideburns and his face became almost winsome. 'It all happened too quickly,' he said.

'Everything happens too quickly nowadays.'

'Nobility, that's what's missing. Nobility is dead. It died in my lifetime. And do you know where it died?'

'Tell me.'

'Nobility, my dear young man, died in Singapore in February 1942.'

'Of course.'

'I'm right, by Christ. The British Empire was the greatest loss since the Romans, and Singapore was the beginning of the end.'

Crossan's feigned alarm prodded the writer.

'And we could have prevented it.'

'The mere Irish?'

'The mere Irish, boy. I'll tell you –' he leaned across the

table, as though to impart some horrific intelligence – 'before ever Percival got to Singapore he was stationed in Cork, and there was an order out to kill him. But for some reason the boys didn't manage it. If they had killed that moron there would have been someone else in Singapore when those little men came cycling out of the trees, someone who had a proper sense of his job, someone who knew what depended on it. He wouldn't have handed the British flag to a mob of little yellow pedal-cyclists! He would have given them a cup of tea and told them to fuck off back into the jungle where they belonged. And the Empire would have been saved. The Empire is the thing, I tell you. Any empire! Any empire is preferable to the shitty mess of anarchy we have now, little paper men of every colour setting up their ridiculous little nations. Nations! Jesus save us from those little nations.'

'And where are you leaving Ireland, J.J.?'

The writer waved his arm with an impatience that was near anger. 'Don't compare us with them, my good man. Remember that we had universities – and plenty of them – before ever Oxford was founded! We've been around a long time, boy, and for all the damage done by the English, by God we profited by them in the end.'

'Imperialist lackey.'

Haslam waved a minatory finger in Crossan's face. 'Mark it well, young man. The Western world is finished. No backbone. No strength. It is led by America, and America is too young to lead anyone. As De Madariaga so rightly said, it's the land where boys refuse to grow up. I'm glad I'm going into my sixtieth year, and not into my first. At least I knew a time when there was order, when there were standards. Where are the standards today? "All out of shape from toe to top", old W.B. said. And he was right. Where's your art today? Eh? Mr Henry Moore? Mr Calder? Mr Rothko? Mr . . . Mr . . .' He sought a name in anguish. 'Who's that whey-faced albino in New York?'

'Andy Warhol.'

'Mr Warhole,' he shouted. 'Mr Arsehole. Thousands of years putting a civilization together and little gobshites like him bring it to its knees.'

'Maybe it is spent. Worn out.'

'It is spent all right. Thousands of years . . .'

136

Crossan got two further pints.

'And nowhere is it disappearing faster than in Ireland. Look at all those young men streaming into that Japanese monstrosity. Their fathers stood behind horse-drawn ploughs.'

'You're an incorrigible romantic.'

'Don't you denigrate that, my boy, because you're caught, too. I know it.' He drank. 'Anyway, what's wrong with being a romantic? I'm not ashamed to admit that I'm a romantic. And Ireland used to be the country for people like me. But I have been robbed.'

His voice went soft. He lost his anger, and he laid his glass heavily on the table, as he spoke, very slowly, his sentences punctuated by long pauses.

'I'm a writer, you know? I never wanted to be anything else. Those years in Maynooth were an aberration. Though they were useful, God knows. Discipline. For forty years, more or less, I've plied my trade. An Irish writer. Do you know what I mean, Stephen? An *Irish* writer. All you had to do was live and observe in this country and the whole world wanted to hear what you had to say and the way you said it. . . . The props remained unchanged. The scenery of your stories deferred to nothing but the seasons. Boreens and cattle, green fields and hedges, hills and mountains and streams, and people deep and devious and deferential, with an unholy love of words. They were the immutables. All the research you ever needed, all the vocabulary you ever wanted, was in your own life. You could sit in your dark room for years and never venture out, knowing that Healy's pub was still there at Toomglen crossroads, that the diamond-shaped fields of Ballylaghey were still there on Mac's Mountain, that the worries and fights and disagreements were still as small and local and muddled as they had been the day you were born. But now, aah, look at this.' He waved a weary arm at the modern room, taking in the Formica-topped tables, the tubular steel chairs, the bright carpeting, the empty hole where the fire used to be, the white central-heating radiators. 'I knew this place when Annie Furlong had it, and she would match you every glass, and fill in the news till the early hours, and the sergeant would slip in the back door and have a few with you, too. She was a poet in her own way, Annie, and her father before her. Not now.' He leaned forward again, his eyes sad and brimming. 'Do you know, Stephen, I don't know my country any more. I try to pretend that my writing is still catching the essence. But the essence has changed, and I haven't the heart to go searching for it, to start all over again. I cannot write about Ireland now. It has passed me by.' He leaned back and stared into the distance. 'I haven't the vocabulary.'

Sympathy and sadness welled in Crossan. He was looking at an artist who had had the tools of his trade stolen from him, not by a sly nocturnal thief, but by an inexorable historical impulse which had swept over his country and changed those immutables which were the cornerstones of his writing life, changed them casually and carelessly and arbitrarily and brutally, and with such speed that he could never hope to catch up.

He was right. He did not have the vocabulary for the new Ireland. His tales were now written in aspic, and he would continue to his death to write them in the pretence that there was no Fujikawa factory spread over the Bay of Killala, that Annie Furlong and her kind were still sipping and swapping tales in the inns of Ireland, that the breadth of his own experience incorporated the experience of his nation. The pretence gnawed at him, as was evident in his confession, but he would be saved by the power of his memory, his hidden compassion, and the habits of a lifetime.

Without a change in style or technique, his role had been metamorphosed from that of gifted and astute reporter to that of historian, subtle repository of the soul and features of old Ireland.

J.J. the writer was now J.J. the remembrancer.

They left the pub and walked through the town, and the young man listened with silent pleasure to the writer's reminiscences, which ambled down avenues of experience over forty years of travelling his country. They were tales without a beginning or an end, for he disliked neatness in stories about human beings, and when one memory intruded upon another, he allowed it to take him by the hand, and he followed it until another memory led him elsewhere. His monologue was spontaneous and unhurried, without moral or profundity, as simple and complex as human experience. His stories, too, were without wit, though suffused with humour, for he disliked anything that might seem forced.

He was a droll man, and in the sunshine of the streets of Ballina, Crossan wished that they could stroll together for the rest of their lives, while the writer was free from the bitterness which frequently marked his presence. But in the pub that they found, Haslam became silent again, and after half an hour, Crossan decided to return to the hotel.

'I'm worried about that factory.'

'Well, I'm not, dear boy. Off you go about the country's business, I'll sit here and have a bit of a think for myself.'

15

Crossan's worry was well placed, but the drama had been played out by the time he reached the hotel.

Ellen Harbo was coming out the door. She said, 'Well, you missed all that.'

'What happened?'

'A tiny contretemps. Oliver will tell you all about it. He handled it all. I'm going for a walk.'

Crossan found Mulligan sitting in the hotel bar. 'I gather there was trouble.'

'Nothing that couldn't be handled. The old dog for the hard road.'

'What happened?'

'There was a picket on the factory.'

'Merciful Jesus. What did you do?'

'I didn't have to do anything. Maggie did it all.'

'All what?'

'She went to the picket, talked to the fellow in front for about five minutes. He talked to his friends and hey presto! No picket.'

'We should make that woman Minister for Labour.'

'She could hardly do worse than the present incumbent.'

'How did the Americans react?'

'They carried on. They interviewed the assistant manager or whoever, and he was a veritable angel as far as we are concerned. I thought the whole thing was over until we got back to the hotel.'

'And what happened then?'

'I'll tell you, dear boy.'

Ellen Harbo and Pete Ober had gone straight to Ober's room on their return, asking Mulligan if he would join them. Maynard and Virginia took off around the town with Alice Foley.

'We'll have to go back to that factory tomorrow,' Ober said without preamble when Mulligan entered. 'When that woman is gone.'

'You mean Maggie?'

Ober nodded impatiently. 'We had an understanding.'

'Maggie is okay,' Mulligan said. 'She can be a bit overbearing sometimes.' He mixed loyalty to a colleague with a cautious admission of her faults. This peddling of words, verbal massage, was a habit which Mulligan felt was surely monopolized by the Irish. Another Irishman would have intuited that he was tacking gently around the shortcomings of a colleague, and would have played the game out, knowing the proper dance steps.

But not Pete Ober, or Ellen Harbo, or any other American. For they were reared to believe in the importance of time, and in the purely functional role of talk as a means of communication. What they found quaint one moment – the circumlocutions, the tautologies, the punned clichés – they later, in the heat of business, found tiresome and out of place.

Ober said, 'We agreed that there would be no interference with our interviews, and that your role would be simply to help us.'

'We've tried to stay within that brief.'

'Not this woman.' Ober found it difficult to use Maggie's name. 'She took over out there today, Oliver, and that's just not good enough.'

'She was only doing her job. Trying to help.'

'Help who?'

'Help us all, really. I mean there was a picket on that factory.'

'That's right. And we could have interviewed those people and found out what the trouble was. But this woman gets to them first and they vanish into thin air.'

'It was a fine piece of work, you must admit.'

'At any other time, fine. Then she lines up the Japanese spokesman. Jesus, the guy sounded like a government PR man. Everything was perfect. The Irish were the greatest workers in the world. They were punctual, dependable, fantastic workers. He sounded like a machine.'

'Maybe he meant it . . .'

'Come on, Oliver. The Irish the greatest workers in the world?'

The statement-question was insensitive and Mulligan, in spite of himself, glared at the producer with belligerence and hurt.

'Okay, okay,' Ober said, in reluctant amelioration, 'don't misunderstand me. You know what I mean. The guy was giving us a handout. It's not that we want to paint a bad picture, but, well . . . no one will believe it.'

Mulligan rose and walked to the window. 'Pete,' he said, without turning around, 'this country is new to industry. The industrial revolution passed us by, and many, myself included, would say thank God. *Real* industry is a comparatively new phenomenon, and there have been problems in the past twenty years. Problems which have given people the impression that the Irish are lazy, undependable, shiftless. Words with which Virginia Green would be familiar.'

Both Americans looked up in shock at the last phrase, but Mulligan continued to stare out the window, denying them a look at his face. 'If the Irish are as useless as some people make out, how did they become the hardest workers in the US and Britain? Backbreaking work in all weathers, for a pittance. Now industry, *big* industry, is foisted on people who have never seen a factory bigger than a creamery. And there are problems. Of course there will be problems. What happened everywhere else over the past hundred and fifty years is happening here in two decades, and the people are supposed to adapt to it without bother. Is it any wonder there'd be trouble?'

Ellen and Ober looked at the fat man in slight surprise. They were both taken aback by the passion and commitment in his voice, ill-fitting his roly-poly presence.

'What *are* you looking for out at Fujikawa?' he continued, turning at last from the window and facing them, half sitting on the radiator. 'You want to present a balanced picture. You want to bring back a film that will show Ireland warts and everything. I suppose the picket was an attractive wart.'

Ober said, 'Tomorrow we go out and interview the picket leaders.'

Mulligan sat down again, sensitive to the resolution in Ober's quiet statement.

The Americans had been offended by Maggie's intervention.

Possibly they were goaded to retrace their tracks more by that than by a great desire to present a balanced report. So Mulligan thought. And he was right. Ober, who had not intended to film the picket, was furious when the I D B woman went ahead of them and caused the picket to vanish. She had undermined him, and he would not have it. Tomorrow they would go out and interview the picketers.

'I wish you wouldn't do that,' Mulligan said.

'Why not?'

'For many reasons. But for one simple one. It may harm my country.' Mulligan looked straight into the producer's eyes as he spoke, and he hardly blinked through what followed. 'I don't know why the pickets are on out there, but I do know they will be gone in a few days. The problem will be cleared up, the men will be back at work, the factory will resume production, wage packets will be brought home, unemployment will be averted. But you will return to the US with your "balanced report", which may show workers who are seemingly intransigent and troublesome. No matter that these troubles are simply teething pains. The programme may be seen by people who may be thinking, at that very moment, of investing a lot of money in a new factory here in the West, where it is badly needed. They may see your programme and decide to go elsewhere. So we lose it. One hundred, two hundred, five hundred people remain on the dole, or depart the country to find work. But they can't do that now, because there is no place for them to go. Your country won't let them in, Britain has no work for them. They have no Continental languages. So they stay here and rot. That's why I ask you not to go out there tomorrow morning. If you would measure the good your balanced report will do for you against the damage it might do to a lot of Irish people, then you might come some way towards seeing my point. Ireland, modern Ireland, is a very young and very vulnerable country, and it does not have the resources that your country has. Anyone with grit and a willingness to work can find employment in the United States. Here, that is not true. Things are bad enough already. Your programme might make them worse. That's all I have to say.'

There was a long silence before the producer spoke. He had been listening carefully throughout Mulligan's plea for the slightest note of flimflam, but he could find none. His years in his business had laid scepticism over him like a protective shroud, but Mulligan had been very simple, very direct, and very convincing. At length, he said, 'I'll think about it,' and Mulligan knew he had won.

Ober's problem, Mulligan thought happily, was that he had a heart. People in Ober's kind of job almost always did. No businessman would have given a moment's notice to his plea. People in communications had a soft centre. They cared. That's what made them go into communications in the first place: concern and vanity, and sometimes one tripped up the other. But it made them ideal sieves. They believed in the public's right to know. What a ridiculous idea. Haslam would chortle at it. But he was in the middle of it, too, a soft-centred story man who loved human beings and found humanity tiresome.

Mulligan rose with a theatrical sigh. 'I'm grateful to you both.'

Ober rose, too, brusque and selfconscious. Mulligan wanted to put an arm around his shoulders and tell him to think of his seeming weakness as magnanimity. But he did not.

16

On her walk through the town Ellen Harbo had been spotted by Haslam as she walked past the door of O'Brien's pub. He had brought her in and bought her a drink and listened to her somewhat awed account of Mulligan's performance back at the hotel.

There were only three other men in the pub, each of them dressed in white shirts, dark ties, dark suits, the uniform of the Western man come to town for the day. No colour for the Irish – their clothes were as drab as their words were wild and bright. The men talked to each other in bursts, sitting hunched far back in their barstools, the sides of their mouths stained with the cream of many pints, caps lying far back on their heads, pints on the counter, their faces full of weather.

'Good old Oliver,' Haslam said when Ellen got to the end of the story.

'He was so convincing,' Ellen said. 'I almost believed him.'

'And why would you not believe him, Ellen?'

'He's a PR man, J.J., a seasoned campaigner. I've been watching him since I came. He's not exactly the soul of spontaneity.'

'He tries to be.'

'I don't think he could believe all that he said back there.'

'Such scepticism, my dear Ellen, ill becomes a beautiful woman like yourself.'

'Thank you,' Ellen said, smiling.

After a short silence, Haslam said, 'Tell me, do you love your country?'

She hesitated, as he knew she would, and he did not give her time to answer. 'No quick and simple yes? Why not? Fifty years ago we would have been able to say "Of course I do" without as much as a thought. Twenty years ago, maybe a slight twinge. Now we hedge about. Love of one's country is not fashionable any more. There's a taint of jingoism about it. If a man stands up and says, quite simply, "I love my country," he's put down as a lunatic patriot, a dangerous chauvinist.'

'You're lecturing me, J.J.'

'Not at all. Far be it from me to do such a thing. I'm just pointing out that it's eminently possible that Oliver does actually love his country. I *know* he does. I know that I do. I even know that Stephen Crossan does, although being a young man he would probably think it unsophisticated to admit it. And anyway, even if Oliver didn't believe what he said, he got Pete Ober to believe it, didn't he? So all you're doing is accusing him of doing his job well. Eh? Now that's a most un-American thing to do, isn't it?'

She ran her hand over her hair, which was tied at the back with an expensive scarf, a muted silk, and for Haslam the gesture held infinite grace and beauty. She always dressed so well: so many Americans did.

The sun came in through the front half-window of O'Brien's, an early evening orange sun, gentle and rich, sinking reluctantly out beyond Achill Head into the Atlantic, and throwing light on Ellen's fine-boned face. Tomorrow they would go down through Connemara, and Haslam's heart bumped at the prospect of seeing those mountains and hills, their reds and greens and browns and blues and startling yellows, colours and shapes of a richness and variety that no painter, no writer, had ever captured in their awesome authenticity. The beautiful, poor West. Why did scenic beauty and poverty so often run together?

But now, as you turned corners in Connemara and Mayo, in Clare and in Kerry, the great and wonderful sweep was rudely splotched by new buildings – houses, factories, shops, service stations, hotels – garish and intrusive. They were few yet, but their numbers would increase, welcomed by the locals, deplored by the metropolitan middle classes and the writers and artists and tourists who all wished the countryside to remain unchanged, so that they could paint it or write about it or visit it for a fortnight each year.

'Do you think,' Haslam said aloud, 'did anyone object to

146

the building of the Acropolis because it spoiled the skyline?'

Ellen laughed.

'Wait till you see Connemara tomorrow,' he said, with an uncharacteristic enthusiasm which charmed her with its suddenness. 'I've been a visitor every year, sometimes several times a year, and I am still a slave to its beauty. I find something new and surprising every time. It has something to do with the clouds. If there are plenty of soft clouds moving slowly ahead of the breeze, you can see the mountains in a dozen different colours in half an hour.'

He went on to describe the beauty of Kylemore, the majesty of The Twelve Pins, the spartan magnificence of the valley of Maam, letting the adjectives flow freely and without prudence.

Ellen watched him as he talked, in thrall to the words and the naked love they revealed. The sun's light held a million motes in a shaft that stretched from the half-window to the back door. Then men at the bar were murmuring, on their sixth or seventh round, their bodies sunken farther back on their stools, their caps lower on their polls. Owner Fonnsie O'Brien leaned on the worn counter, an authoritative centre-piece in the placid tableau, occasionally dropping a dollop of publican's wisdom into the conversation. It was a summer's evening in the West of Ireland – where summer came late – in a bar that was private and quiet and infinitely peaceful, and Ellen Harbo was as far away from the mercenary turbulence of Sixth Avenue as she would ever be again.

In such mood she looked at the life-scarred face of the man before her as he reached the end of his unrestrained love song. The sun caught half of her face, making her squint appealingly and showing all of her forty years – lines of early laughter, fine down on her upper lip, her lined left hand to her forehead, a shield. Haslam saw them all in her face, and she read correctly looking into his eyes, that his love song had not been sung without motive. She smiled at him, and he at her, and he placed his thin hand on hers, stroking it gently as he talked into the dying day.

Back at the Four Elms, Crossan and Mulligan had been joined by the others, and Mulligan was answering, harshly, Virginia's question.

'No. I do not want a factory there. But my opinion doesn't matter a damn when set against the reason why the factory *is* there.' He ran his hand back through his flaming hair. 'I don't want it there because it's polluting the countryside around the bay. Its very presence . . .'

'You bet your sweet ass it is,' Dinneen said.

Mulligan ignored him. 'It's very presence is pollution, and each day it pollutes the waters around it. But which is worse? A polluted bay or two, or three hundred men on the dole?'

Dinneen said, 'That's too goddamn simplistic.'

Maynard said, 'Frank, would you for Christ's sake let us hear what these people have to say? We didn't come all the way over here to hear what *you* think. We can read that fucking junk any day of the week in New York.'

Mulligan was shaking his head, impatient with the interrupters: the subject moved him terribly. 'Try deploring pollution to a man who has lost his whole family to emigration. Try telling *him* that a new factory would be a bad thing because it would spoil the beauty of the locality or ruin the river for foreign anglers.'

Dinneen said, 'Listen, why do you have to have *monstrosities*, for God's sake. They're all right for America and Germany: let them do what they like, they're ruined already anyway. But why do you let them in here?'

Crossan came in to relieve a very agitated Mulligan. 'Maybe we take them because nobody else will, and damn glad to get them. Maybe we are so grateful for a factory, *any* factory, that we push our environmental conceits to one side. Anyway, if the truth be told, the worst polluters of all are the farmers. Pig farming has done for dozens of lakes and rivers. Creameries the same. Fertilizers the same.'

Crossan's varnished urbanity had cracked. The Americans were allowed to see into him for the first time, as he went on to give them his thoughts on pollution and what was happening around his country. His imprudence would have shocked Mulligan but he hardly heard. He was biting hard on the fact that he agreed wholeheartedly with Frank Dinneen. He had a constant dream: thousands of small local factories, intrinsic parts of each community, producing small, exquisite, high-class goods for the international market, everyone interested, everyone in love with his work, everyone proud of his finished product.

It would never happen now. Instead of adapting the demands of international commerce to the peculiar faults and talents of the people, it was the people who were being forced to adapt. Mulligan went up to the bar and ordered another round very loudly, thinking to banish the anger and sadness from his mind.

'You don't drink much,' Haslam said.

They were still sitting in the bar, reluctant to leave, both aware that a message had passed between them – barely enunciated, barely acknowledged – and they both wished to continue while the spice of uncertainty remained.

'Not as much as the Irish do,' Ellen said. 'Those men up there must have consumed a lot.'

'They have as much alcohol in them as your average American after his second martini.'

'Everywhere we go, no matter what time of day, there are people in pubs.'

'You wouldn't want to infer from that that the Irish drink more than anyone else. The difference is, you see, that when the Irish drink everyone knows about it, because they do it in public. Apart from the working alcoholic, there are very few solitary drinkers here. The conversation is the thing. Chat. People are drawn to pubs by the presence of other people. That's why we love our lingering black pints. There's more time to talk. Maybe the talk is more therapeutic than the jar.'

'You like to drink.'

'I love it. It makes life tolerable. Mr Joyce was right: it helps a man to think.'

'Is life all that intolerable?'

'On the midnight pillow, sometimes. Devil time. No drink, no words. Black thoughts. Hopelessness. Futility.'

'I've had that myself.'

'We don't monopolize it, to be sure.'

She watched his face as he spoke. All the black nights of devil time were etched in it. He had a strange habit of looking away into the distance when he spoke to her, as though unable to look into her eyes, but when she spoke he gazed intently into her eyes, and she was forced to look away herself. It was disconcerting, but pleasantly so. There was a beaten air about the writer, a sadness, which she found sympathetic, and when he had placed his hands on hers earlier she had felt not the usual urge to recoil, but rather a simple pleasure that he should do so.

He said, 'Do you ever get lonely?'

'Like everyone else who lives alone.'

'You've never been married at all?'

She shook her head. 'Have you?'

'Yes. I married once. A beautiful young woman. That's what I miss most. To turn round in the mornings and look at a sleeping face. Ah, yes, she was a beautiful, beautiful young woman. And I wasn't a bad-looking young man, even if I say so myself. We would be together forever.' He laughed suddenly, mirthlessly. 'And then she ran off with a magician, leaving me with the boy. She couldn't stand my fantasies, she told me. I was too wild. Can you imagine that?'

'It must have been a blow to your ego.'

'That was bad enough. Who likes to be thrown over for a professional trickster? But that wasn't what had attracted her at all. He had a steady income, and I didn't. When he wasn't pulling rabbits out of hats, he liked to smoke his pipe and read his paper.'

She smiled and said, 'Maybe you should have bought a pipe.'

He shook his head. 'It wouldn't have done. The big problem was that she couldn't get into my mind. I suppose this isn't fit talk in front of a woman, but sure, what about it? Women want to know you, and that's why writers should never get married. They're unknowable, do you see. Most of their time is spent thinking about their work. As far as the wives are concerned that's the same as thinking about themselves. And what wife likes to know that she's not the most important thing in her husband's life? Most wives worry about their husbands finding another woman. A writer's wife worries about his starting another book. My wife could handle her magician because he had no imagination. Just tricks. I had no tricks. So off she went. And I had to rear the boy on my own.' He drank. 'If only I could have liked him. But he was a pathological liar. So much for heredity.' He smiled glumly down at the table, his eyebrows raised as though at some sudden surprising thought. 'I haven't seen him for ten years. My own flesh and blood. He changed his name. Couldn't abide being called J. J. Haslam's son. Small blame to him for that, God knows. I had to send him away to school and he hated that. But what could I do? I couldn't afford to go on hiring housekeepers. And then I'd arrive home maybe a bit jarred, and aah . . .'

He drank again and shook his head.

After a silence, Ellen said, 'Maybe it's not that writers are unknowable. Just that they don't want to reveal themselves.'

'It's a thought,' he said, happy at the vibrations he divined in her musing. 'But wasn't it Havelock who said that every artist writes his own autobiography?' He smiled suddenly. 'Most of the writers I know are revealing themselves every day of the week. Some of them are even exposing themselves.'

She laughed, and he said, 'Are you a Catholic?'

'Episcopalian. From Connecticut. Not any more. Just groping.'

'Like the rest of us.'

'I had a very happy childhood. I feel deprived in certain company.'

'Would you be referring to Virginia, now?'

'No. I think Virginia was okay. Her father was a successful businessman in Alabama. She went to Brandeis. I guess she was protected from the more awful side of growing up black.'

'Where did you go to college?'

'Smith, in Massachusetts. My father was a professor of English there.'

'Was he, faith?'

The reminiscences flowed easily, helped by more drink.

'He was a nice man, in an old-fashioned way. He loved the English language, the sounds, the words. But he should have been a fisherman. We had a small house in a place called Noank near Mystic, and he spent all summer there with us, fishing, messing about, collecting coal from an abandoned mine on one of the islands. I fell in love with a little boy named Stephen Jones, who was beautiful and mystical and very literary. But he threw me over. My father organized little carnival days, when everyone had to dress up in the role he or she would most like to play in life. They were lovely days.'

He wished that she would continue this story so strangely different from that of his own childhood. 'What did you dress up as?'

'Virginia Woolf.'

'Virginia Woolf!'

She laughed at the memory, and at the writer's surprise.

'Now you know. I wanted to be a writer. I didn't want to *write*, but I wanted to be a writer, to have written the books, to have people point me out as "Ellen Harbo the writer". I used to raid my aunt's attic and dress in Victorian flimsies and long necklaces, as I thought Virginia Woolf did, and I'd suck in my cheeks and pout my lips and sit all day long on the window seat trying to look hopelessly suicidal.'

'Did they know whom you were impersonating?'

'Oh, yes. I had a placard hanging from my neck with VIRGINIA WOOLF written on it. I wasn't taking any chances.'

He laughed. 'Has your ambition died?'

'I'd still like to be a writer. Not to write. But to be a writer.'

'Irreconcilable ambitions, I'm afraid. Though one or two of your countrymen seem to have managed it.' He smiled again. People were coming into the bar. The three men had gone.

'I should have been born in Ireland,' Ellen said. 'Everyone here is a writer.'

'There's a few of them around all right. That's a fact.'

'Why is it?' she said, looking closely at him. 'This country has produced more writers per square inch than any other country in the world. Why is it?'

Haslam grimaced slightly, and shook his head. 'I don't know,' he said slowly. 'Tradition. Religion. Conflict. They are very helpful basic ingredients, I suppose. And we had them all in abundance. And Irish people love to talk, as I said. Some of them like to put it down on paper. They like to be praised. They like to be loved. These longings produce writers.'

'Then I should have no trouble. I have those longings myself.'

'Well,' he said, putting his glass back on the table, 'they're easily satisfied. You're a very attractive woman and sweet, and damned nice company.'

Ellen smiled fully at him, one lock of her hair covering one eye. 'It's very nice of you to say so.'

'I'm sure you hear it often enough.'

'At my age you can't hear it often enough.'

'You could hear it as often as you like tonight,' he said, now looking down at the table, then looking up, and there was silence between them for a full minute, their eyes locked.

'We hardly know each other, J.J.,' she said.

'Well enough.'

'Would you like to see my heart? Badly burned in several places.'

'It's a wee bit early for you to be showing your heart. I wouldn't burn it for all the tea in China.'

'You wouldn't mean to.'

His eyes wavered from hers, and he said quietly, 'Should I forget about it for ever?'

'No. I don't think you should.'

17

The sun shone down on the hard grey sand of the beach at Carna, its million reflections shooting up from the Atlantic. The group had arrived just after lunch after the morning drive from Ballina.

Throughout the drive, Mulligan disgorged gobbets of history and information, occasionally personal: as the days went by, Crossan and Mulligan were gradually and supportively shedding the muzzling blandness of the government persona, though Dinneen's presence still inhibited. They went down through Castlebar – 'Frank O'Connor thought this was a boring place: the town reeks of history, but O'Connor had sharply defined dislikes' – and into Westport, a well-laid out town of gentry, split by a slow-moving river and its tree-lined mall. Past Croaghpatrick – 'a place of yearly pilgrimage: thousands climb it in their bare feet, believing that St Patrick – one of the St Patricks – did the same'. Past Louisburgh – 'there was a suggestion that one thousand holiday chalets be built here, but we managed to scotch that, thanks be to God'. Through Delphi – 'Delphi!' Ellen cried. Through Leenane and out past Kylemore, stone mansion quiet and serene over the lake, the nuns serving hot tea and wholesome biscuits, through Letterfrack and out to Renvyle House, which Mulligan pointed out was once the summer home of Oliver St John Gogarty, 'who as you all know was the model for stately, plump, Buck Mulligan in *Ulysses*'.

After sandwiches in Gogarty's former home, now a hotel full of the *nouveau riche* from Dublin and Cork, they took off again on the road through Clifden, capital of Connemara, and Mulligan pointed it out as resembling a 'charming Swiss village', keeping his mouth firmly shut as the minibus passed the charming village's most eye-catching attribute: a stinking roadside dump acrawl with rats, and the carcase of a sheep about to explode its entrails all over the road.

Down through Ballyconneely they went and into the untouched village of Roundstone. Throughout the trip, the minibus stopped many times, with both Ober and Maynard almost singing in ecstasy at the colours and shapes that confronted them at every turn of the road.

They drove through Toombeola and Cashel and Gowla and Glinsk, and the minibus brought them as near as possible to the strand at Carna.

The beach was covered with people, a fair number in black or grey suits and white shirts, but there was plenty of colour in the clothes of the young, milling raucously and with a proprietorial air along the beach.

Race day had brought them to fill this empty place, and the four currachs lay upside down on the sand, vulnerable black pods of wood and canvas, their prows to America. The racing oarsmen had not yet appeared, but were probably milling in the crowd.

Prowling among them, his machine perched on his shoulder, Ober at his elbow, was Maynard, nosing his lens this way and that, provoking in his subjects sniggering selfconsciousness and occasional peacockery. The cameraman was elated by the clear white skin, cerise cheeks and violent red hair that bobbed and weaved in front of him.

From a distant rock, her chin in her hands, Virginia Green watched the throng through heavy shades. She was in denim shirt and slacks, and on her head she wore a stark white tressure. The soles of her feet massaged the thousands of tiny limpets on the rock.

Stephen Crossan, in turn, watched Virginia, black and incongruous against this white, white background, and saw the side glances and open stares that her presence provoked, the first sighting by one of a giggling few, the whispered intelligence, the gradual frank interest of the whole group. Most of them had never seen a black woman in the flesh before. Were their thoughts the same as his own? Virginia writhing in the sand, her buttocks heaving and twisting under him, making perfect round indentations, the perspiration on her chocolate shoulders forming in salt bubbles to be licked off, the fine mist of sweat on her eyelids to be sucked into his mouth while she murmured a litany of profanities – black, strange, unheard-of profanities – sweet blasphemous music in his ear.

He looked away from her siren figure and down on the crowd.

He felt immediate revulsion.

Youth was to the fore, carrying six-packs of lager, wearing big sunglasses which they constantly fingered, uneasily attired for the sunshine in ill-fitting, long-sleeved shirts and grossly flared trousers. Girls and boys wore blocky, awkward platform shoes, their hair, unkempt, grew long in crass uniformity, in styles that were themselves screeching rejections of elegance or even neatness. They had, in a miniscule span of time, and under a decade of bludgeoning television, jettisoned the simple, rugged garb of centuries, and adopted a cheap and tatty mélange of the sartorial fads of Liverpool and London and Los Angeles. Some carried transistor radios held to their ears, and gyrated gracelessly to private impulses, puffing on cigarettes. Some sprawled on the sand or the rocks, heckling each other in a formless, bastard patois, the vulgarities of their favourite American television series superimposed on the rich native idiom.

'Listen to the Seamus McKojaks,' Haslam said, sitting down on the rock beside Crossan. Ellen was with him. 'They don't know how to dress and they don't know how to talk.'

They sat apart from and above the clamour below them, and Crossan felt moved to defend those who were nearer his generation. But he was a poor advocate.

'Stasis is death, J.J.'

'Anything is better than this.'

'Might as well try to hold back the waves.'

Haslam said, with a grimace of disgust, 'Here we are in the heart of the Gaeltacht. Probably every boy and girl of them born and reared to glorious natural Gaelic, and now listen to them spewing out that dreadful goo that they pick up every night on the TV. If the British had had TV in the seventeenth century they wouldn't have had to send a single soldier to Ireland.' He looked down in disgust on the scene below them. 'They can't shed their culture fast enough.'

'Culture, J.J.?' Crossan said. 'What is culture?'

'If you don't know what culture is, my boy, then I'm not going to waste precious time telling you. I would remind you of what Thomas Davis said. This country of ours is no sandbank thrown up by some recent caprice of earth. It is an ancient land, honoured in the archives of civilization. The man was right. This country had a culture, by God, and they don't even know it down there.'

He plucked some grass and chewed it.

Crossan said, 'They know what they know. And what they know is that what you call culture never put a penny in their pockets. Would you want them to be human museums, open all week, half-day Saturdays, so that we could all come and watch them?'

'Will you give over with that penny-in-your-pocket nonsense? There's no pricing culture.'

Small crowds had gathered around the currachs, and from their vantage seat they watched the four hulls appear above the throng and move down to the sea, seemingly under their own power, the legs of the men underneath hidden by the accompanying crowds.

The boats reached the water and were upturned, and the men clambered in, four to each boat, grabbing the thin, unlikely wooden blades and pushing the craft backwards and outwards from the land. They would row a mile to the south and turn at the red buoy, and return to pass the land point they called Joyce's Rock. First past the rock would be the winner. The race had taken place at this spot for as long as anyone could remember.

Crossan said, 'Would you say we are about to witness a cultural event?'

'We are witnessing a cultural event,' Haslam said, looking at the boats bobbing into position at the starting line. 'It isn't exactly Cowes, but it would qualify as far as Eliot was concerned. Derby Day, a Cup Final, Wensleydale cheese, the music of Elgar. That was how he defined English culture.'

'He was from Missouri, of course. No Englishman would have made out such a list.'

'I suppose no man is best judge of his own culture.'

'I beg your pardon, but weren't you a moment ago so sure of what ours is that you declined even to define it for me?'

'I was merely pointing out the fact, dear boy, that culture

is not an easily defined thing. That is not to say that it is not easily *understood*. I haven't used the word once in all that I have written, but every paragraph of mine is about Irish culture.'

Crossan noticed that Ellen watched Haslam all the time he spoke, a light smile around her mouth, her eyes interested. The distanced mien of earlier had been discarded, and there was now an ease about her presence which made her even more attractive.

A white flag was raised on the beach and the small black boats surged forward as the crowd roared encouragement. It was a gentle day, with but a few solitary cirrus to disturb the blue; and the currachs had easy passage over the tiny rills. The crowd moved down the long strand to keep pace with them, and would follow them all the way to the buoy and back again.

Crossan said, 'Would you like that crowd down there to speak nothing but Gaelic?'

'Today, yes. To speak it proudly and happily.'

'I'm at a loss. Yesterday you bewailed the fall of the British Empire. Didn't the British do their best to kill the Gaelic language with methods foul and cruel, and didn't they all but succeed? Aren't there only about thirty thousand people speaking it natively now? And they're all over here in the poor western ghetto.'

Haslam did not take his eyes from the boats. 'If the British were still ruling this country, I'd lay my life that the Gaelic language today would be healthier now than it is after fifty years of nursing by the Irish themselves.'

'That's a queer thing now.'

'Look at the Welsh, dear boy. There's more time given to the Welsh language on British television than to the Irish language on Irish television.'

Ellen said to Crossan, 'Do you speak Irish?'

Haslam said, 'Of course he does. You have to, to get a government job. Another piece of chicanery.' He chewed more grass and said meditatively. 'Of course the secret is to make the language the "in thing". If those gobshites down there could be convinced that the Irish language was *cool* – I think that's the word – you'd never shut them up.'

'Too late,' Crossan said. 'Irish and poverty go hand in hand.

It's taken a few hundred years to bring that about. You're not going to turn it into a status symbol overnight.'

After a silence, Crossan said, 'Tell me, J.J. when you think of Irish culture, do you think immediately of the Irish language?'

'My definition of culture would run along the lines of Eliot's.'

'Eliot's definition implied a common language. Don't evade the question. Am I as much an Irishman as the native Irish speaker from Connemara?'

'Of course you are.'

'To whom?'

'To everyone.'

'There's some would say that the native speaker is a truer Irishman than I am, whatever "truer" may mean.'

'The traditions in which he grew up may go further back than yours.'

'To hell with that,' Crossan said. 'Ellen told me a few days ago that she always thought of Ireland as a place of culture. Why did she think that?'

'You can ask the girl yourself.' He turned to Ellen.

Crossan did not allow her to answer. 'I'll tell you why she thought that. Because it was a place that had produced Swift and Goldsmith and Shaw and O'Casey and Joyce and Yeats and Synge and Wilde and Beckett. That's what she meant. That's *all* she meant. How many of them had a word of Irish, or cared tuppence for it? Listen, as far as the rest of the world is concerned, Irish culture is an English-language culture. *My* culture is an English-language culture. It doesn't prevent me from loving the Irish language, which God knows I do, or from using it when the opportunity presents itself. But *my* language, my *native* language, is English, and I will not be held below any other Irishman for that.'

Haslam smiled an impish smile at the young man. 'By God, Stephen, who'd have thought you had all that inside your striped waistcoat.'

Crossan looked out over the sea. The crowd was at the end of the beach and the boats, now tiny, their occupants almost invisible, were about to make the run around the buoy. They were strung out now, the leader thirty yards ahead of the second, which was ten yards or more in front of the third. The fourth boat was far behind and well out of the contest.

Haslam was still smiling. 'I'd never have taken you for an Anglophile.'

'I am not an Anglophile,' Crossan said, slowly but reluctantly, for he knew the writer wished merely to draw him out. 'I'm confident of my Irishness, and I resent that tribe who tell me that I'm less of an Irishman for not being as fluent in Irish as in English. For being born in English-speaking Dublin and not in Irish-speaking Carraroe. For working in a centrally heated government office and not behind the oars of a currach. For liking Bach or Vivaldi as much as, or maybe more than, some singer of geriatric ditties.'

Haslam was almost whooping. 'Oh, by God, you have all the chips and no mistake about it. And we're all the same, aren't we? All driven demented about being Irish. And nobody in the wide earthly world gives a tinker's curse about it except ourselves. And they're right. What are we, my boy? Eh? A nation of roistering, belligerent poets? Or a nation of jumped-up, black-minded, devious peasants? Or both?'

He leaned back on the grass, resting on his elbow, looking out over the Atlantic. 'What was the greatest gift ever given this nation?'

'Tell me,' Crossan said, annoyed at the rhetorical tone.

'The English language, my boy. The greatest language in the world. And we got it for nothing. And instead of being grateful, we want to throw it back at them.'

'Who wants to throw it back at them?'

'The tribe you were talking about. The "true Irishmen".'

'To hell with them.'

'Or to Connaught.'

'Come off it, J.J.'

'It's true, isn't it? That's where most of them are. You said so yourself.' Haslam was laughing.

The boats were coming nearer, a thousand harbingers on the beach screaming support. The second boat had now cut the distance from the leader to about ten yards, with a quarter of a mile still to go. It would be a close finish.

Maynard, from a high rock to the north, had his camera pointed at the boats, Ober by his side.

'Jesus, Pete, I wish we were shooting this on the east coast. I'm getting so much goddamn sun.'

160

'That bad?'

'Nothing but flare.'

'I don't mind a bit of flare. It will have a good effect. Can you use a filter?'

Maynard clicked his tongue dubiously, but he did as he was asked. Questions from the producer, he well knew, were orders.

Ellen, who had left Haslam and Crossan and was now working again, sat on the rock, dark glasses on, pad and pen held sharp. 'We're on shot twenty. The last shot was that boy kissing the girl on the rocks.'

'One long cool kiss on the rocks, please,' Maynard mumbled.

Out on the sea the oars flashed and ploughed in perfect unison, shooting the little black boats over the water in great surges, and the sweating backs of the oarsmen glistened in the sun.

Crossan said, 'Would you say that any of those oarsmen ever wonders about the depths of his Irishness?'

The young man's casual tone belied the seriousness of his question. He found the whole business of being Irish at once boring and fascinating. *Odi atque amo*. Nationalist, Catholic patriotism was anathema to him, but the fashionable secular internationalism was such a vapid alternative, and he found himself constantly treading water between the two poles, putting a carapace of flippancy over his doubts in public. While feeling that nationalism was a thing of the past – and a dangerous, myopic disease of the past – he sometimes had a rushing insight that it was the only hope for the future, too. For Haslam, the question did not seem to have much moment: he appeared to have closed down the shutters on any ideas which might make him alter his attitudes.

Now Haslam said, 'I talked to two of them coming down here. One of them had hair and eyebrows as black as the hobs of hell. A Spaniard off the Armada set him in motion a few hundred years ago, no doubt about it. The other fellow has been sixteen years in London, in Cricklewood where the crack was good. What does that make the two of them? Irish?'

Crossan shook his head. 'I don't know.'

The second boat, with three hundred yards to go, had drawn abreast of the leader, and both prows now alternated in leading by the two or three feet that each surge gave them. The oars-men's mouths were wide open, making as much room as possible for the air to get into their lungs. Their faces were constricted in pain, their eyes half-shut against the streaming perspiration on their foreheads.

In the last fifty yards the second boat pulled in front, to a frenzied roar, and held the lead to Joyce's Rock, passing the point to a great cheer and much jumping about on the beach.

Immediately they passed the rock, the men fell exhausted on their oars, muscles slackening, backs bent double, their heads between their knees, their bodies heaving. One by one the other boats passed the point, the crews collapsing helplessly as the first. When they had recovered, they rowed slowly to the beach, coming near enough to each other to shake hands.

18

Later that afternoon they drove along the coast road overlooking Galway Bay towards Spiddal, so called because it had been the site of a famine hospital during those appalling years when the country's population was almost halved.

There was no sign of the hospital or its remains, and the whole road on either side was covered in modern bungalows, ribbon-built and raucous against the simple background. What had once been a country road with breathtaking views on either side was now nothing more than a continuous suburban pike all the way into Galway City.

They ordered food in The Wagon Wheel, a flat, grey modern pub with a very large car park which was littered with empty beer barrels. The building was done in imitation stone – while hundreds of square miles around were covered in the real thing – and a neon light over the door portrayed a bright yellow wagon wheel.

Liam Kerins, the owner, cut a cottage loaf of bread on the Formica counter, covering the slices with butter and making a mound of sandwiches from tomatoes and lettuce which his daughter Mairead, had just brought from a shop down the road. Kerins was dark and handsome. His wife was a slatternly, sullen bottle blonde with ill-fitting dentures and a perpetual cigarette.

Mairead, who was eleven, had rust-red, shoulder-length hair, and her face was soft and clear, with two almost perfect circles of pink on her cheeks. Her eyes were deep blue, and she was a bright, unselfconscious counterpoint to her mother's slovenly charmlessness, but she had no forwardness in her manner, and her fascination at Virginia's presence expressed itself in covert glances.

There was nothing covert about the interest of the others in the pub. Young men and old, with little to say to each other, sat at the other end of the bar from the group, staring at the Americans, particularly Virginia, and when she returned the stares, they transferred their eyes to the television set perched high above the counter.

Some of the young men were playing pool, hitting the balls with great strength and minimal accuracy, and saluting bad shots with cries of 'Well, fuck it, anyway.' The more loquacious would say, 'You fucking ape, Seamus, why didn't you hit the fucking thing the fucking way I fucking told you, for fuck sake.' While no sentence was complete without one 'fuck', the measure of a boy's ability seemed to be the number of them he could squeeze into any single statement.

Their elders, all of whom spoke natural Irish, sat unhearing and uncaring: Irish was a language which lent itself to massive understatement, and the man who made his point with a litany of profanities was nothing more or less than a fool.

Kerins came up and rubbed the crumbs and stout stains on the counter with a dirty grey rag. He nodded to the young men at the other end and said to Virginia, 'Would you think of taking a few of them back with you?'

'You trying to get rid of them?'

He blew his nose into a soiled green handkerchief and indicated a boy of about twenty, sitting on a stool staring at the television set, a half-pint of ale in front of him and a cigarette burning between his fingers. 'Five hours that fellow is sitting there. He done nothing today except drink and smoke and play pool and watch the TV.'

Ober said, 'Can't he get a job?'

'No jobs. Twenty years ago, even ten years ago, he'd a' been on the boat to Holyhead, or on the plane over to your place. But there's no work there now either, I hear tell.'

Virginia said, 'And how does the kid live?'

'The dole,' Kerins said. 'An' he'll do one or two days' work as well.'

'Isn't that illegal?'

'Who's going to do anything about it?'

'Well, if the guy who employs him for those few days . . .'

'Sure the man knows very well that the lad is on the dole. But it suits him fine. He don't have to take in a body full time, do you see? No cards or insurance. That kind of thing. So he gets the work done on the cheap and keeps his mouth shut.' He rubbed the counter again. 'There's a fellow down the road a bit drives his own Volvo, his own shagging Volvo, down for the dole money.'

Ellen said, 'What about the boy's family?'

'One of them has a job in Galway. The other two are the same as himself. Their father has about ten acres out there beyant Inveran, ye'd have passed it on the way. Not the best land, God knows, but there's the feeding of three cows in it. They don't even want it. They hates work like the devil hates holy water. Why should they work? Can't they live off the likes of me, the taxpayer? And amn't I worse to be going on about it.' He threw the rag to the far end of the bar to express his disgust.

Mulligan, who had said nothing all evening, placed his pint on the counter, at great peril to his balance on the stool. Alice held his arm protectively. He said, 'Yes, yes, yes, yes. But there's something that must be said. We all remember the West – you remember it, J.J. – when there was, with respect to the ladies, sweet fuck-all here. *Nobody* had any money. Nobody had anything. There *was* no money.There were no jobs and no prospects of jobs. Children were reared for the boat or the plane, same as you would fatten cattle for export. I'd swear to God half the Irish population of Boston and New York is from Galway and Mayo. And from Roscommon, too,' he said, looking at Dinneen. 'All right. So there are cases, plenty of them, like the young lad down there. But at least he's at home. He's not stripped to the waist in Dagenham or Düsseldorf! It won't be like this for ever, you know. The government is doing things for the West . . .'

Kerins, who had been giving Mulligan half an ear, looked up sharply at the last statement. 'Tell me what they're doing,' he demanded, with the eagerness of the knowing native.

'They're doing their best to attract factories to the West. Look at Fujikawa up there in Killala.'

'They speak English up there. This is a Gaeltacht. We have the mark on us, by Jayses.'

'And what about tourism? The Board of Welcomes pushes the West . . .'

'By Christ, don't talk to me about tourism and the Board of Welcomes. I know all about *them*.'

Kerins did not know who Mulligan was, and Mulligan did not apprise him, but asked, impatiently, 'What's your complaint about them?'

'My complaint about them? It's their complaint about me that's the problem. They won't leave me alone. A young whippersnapper walks in here, has his sandwich and his glass of lager.' He has told the story many times before. 'Then he goes in there' – he pointed to the men's room at the back of the bar – 'and he comes out after a minute and straight up to me. I want to make a complaint, sez he. No paper, sez he. No paper! All the little fucker had to do was ask for it! Anyway, there *was* paper there. I checked that after he was gone, only it got a bit wet. And then he sez there's no place to wash his hands. Is it a dee luxe hotel you think I am running here? sez I. This place is good enough for the customers who come in here every day, the people who give me and my family our bread and butter, and if it's not good enough for you, well. . . . You can imagine what I told him to do. You know, I never had a complaint from any tourist, not one. Finish their snack, in there, and straight out the door without a word of complaint.'

Mulligan looked down at his belly, his hands on his knees, shaking his head. He had no answer for Kerins. Mulligan had already been in the men's room: tiles broken, no washbasin, old copies of the *Western People* lying sopping beside the lavatory bowl, which was a Jackson Pollock of cloacal spatters. The smell of urine was overpowering, and the gutter was stopped with tobacco and cigarette paper. Mulligan had had the momentary thought that maybe the Irish got drunk to make the smell of pub lavatories bearable. But he banished the thought. It was a source of constant pain to him that almost every public house in Ireland had a lavatory which was an assault on the senses, and many hotels had an almost equally purblind attitude to basic hygiene. Once, reading about a pub bombing in the North, when the bomb had been planted in the toilet, he had the crazy notion of hiring the bomber to travel with him all round the South with small bombs, leaving a package in every smelly, shitty, filthy lavatory in pubs and guesthouses and hotels. In a fortnight, working night and day, he thought they might blow every foul cubicle into the skies.

He banished that thought too.

Kerins was gone to the other end of the bar, having left an invitation for them all to go to the dance free of charge. The dance took place in The Extension, which was what Kerins had called the large room which he had built onto The Wagon Wheel.

'What a wonderful name,' Mulligan said.

Alice laughed, and put her arm around him, and said, 'The Irish have words at will.'

Maynard said to Ober, 'Whaddya say we shoot this hop in here?'

The producer wrinkled his nose. 'Let's have a look first. Mains okay?'

Maynard nodded.

Crossan said, 'It probably won't be much of a scene in there.'

Virginia said, 'You don't think we should shoot it?'

'Whatever you wish,' Crossan said.

Virginia, with brittle vehemence said, 'I think we should shoot it. I think it would make a great scene.'

Crossan looked down at the floor. All present could feel the static between the reporter and himself.

The music had begun in The Extension, and the noise filtered through the doors.

'Come on,' Virginia said. 'Let's have a look inside.'

When they were gone, Crossan said, 'Why did I open my mouth?'

Mulligan patted him on the back. 'They'd have probably filmed it anyway.'

Haslam said, 'You mustn't carry the nation's woes on your shoulders. That place in there is as much a part of Ireland now as *The Book of Kells*, and there's nothing you can do about it.'

'Don't be so protective, Stephen,' Alice said softly.

Crossan was only partly buoyed by the comradeship. 'We could have found a ceili somewhere.'

'Why should you?' Haslam said. 'What the hell has a ceili to do with how the young disport themselves in Ireland nowadays? I seem to remember your saying in the Shelbourne that all you could ask of these people was that they show Ireland as it is. Well, this is it. An Extension built for maybe twenty thousand pounds and a lavatory that stinks to high heaven and hasn't had a penny spent on it since the famine. Think yourself lucky they didn't bring a camera into the john.'

They went into The Extension, reflexively squinting their eyes when the music hit them.

The room was larger than it seemed from the outside.

At the top was a small alcove for the band, and at the other end was a bar which backed on to the bar proper. Liam Kerins was on the bandstand, holding an electric guitar and singing into a microphone. Behind him was a young man with hair to his waist and sunglasses, playing a shining three-piece set of drums. And to Kerins's left was his eleven-year-old daughter, Mairead, hair aglow in the harsh lighting, face unsmiling, microphone in her right hand, the left holding the lead.

Her father was singing a song called 'Things My Maw in Tallahassee Told Me Not To Do'. Each time he reached the chorus, Mairead, in spangled bolero and Dale Evans hat, sang with him, an unfocused, childish wail which smote the ears.

Two couples were dancing on the floor, a strange, formless hopping dance wherein the couple neither touched nor looked at each other, but bounced around in tight jeans and plodding shoes. All four wore sunglasses, and all four were girls.

The boys milled about the bar aperture, where their needs were ministered to with sour-faced impatience by Kerins's wife. Some of them had a bottle in one hand and a glass in the other; others drank from the bottle. They nudged and pulled at each other, laughing and slugging back the beer and ale by the neck, while the girls stood or sat in the opposite corner, skittish and selfconscious, their mouths moved by rhythmic gum chewing.

Virginia Green, standing in a corner by the door, was as ever the cynosure. After a brief lull, Kerins began another song 'Don't Put the Nails in My Coffin Till I Kiss Momma Good-bye'. Maynard and Ober had decided to shoot after all. The producer asked Kerins to request that everyone get on the floor, and when the next song started – 'Show Me Your Yo-yo Tonight' – the youths answered the call of fame and thronged onto the floor, throwing up their hands and illustrating the lyrics with physical obscenities.

Little Mairead came in like a wound-up doll on chorus.

Virginia was sitting down, talking to Ellen. She was being eyed with sniggering speculation by a group of boys at the bar. One of them was being pushed forward by the others, who were laughing and downing their bottles of beer. Several times they pushed him forward and he sank back into them again. Finally, the boy put his bottle purposefully on a table, buttoned his jacket, pulled down the hems, and walked towards Virginia while his companions stopped laughing in disbelief. He came within a yard of his quarry and then at the last moment turned and made for the door, bursting into such hilarious laughter that a tadpole of green mucus shot from his nostrils. His friends roared. Mairead sang 'Show Me Your Yo-yo Tonight'. Her father twanged and smiled.

Out in the bar later, when the group left, the men young and old were sitting silent, watching the American movie on television.

19

In the breakfast room of the Great Southern Hotel the following morning, Virginia Green sat alone, mooning over the lavish Irish breakfast of eggs and rashers and sausages and tomatoes and black-and-white pudding which was before her. She reckoned it a tolerable indulgence, and had been eating hearty breakfasts since she arrived, except for the morning after the ball, when she had had a spartan American juice and coffee.

Five minutes before, Frank Dinneen had come into the empty breakfast room, walked right past her table with a throttled 'Hi', and seated himself in the far corner, spreading three newspapers on the table before him. She had not bothered to return his salute, and gulped down her anger with the bacon. The man was impossible, a cactus presence, and she tried to tell herself that he needed sympathy more than anger. But that was an uphill battle. He had made himself unpopular with every member of the group, all of whom, with the exception of Maynard, had their feelings boxed in by the exigencies of their various jobs. Ober was mindful of Halstead's warning, Crossan and Mulligan were paid to be pliant. Alice Foley maintained a cool confidence. Only Haslam was free to berate, and he seemed to manage what Virginia could not: a kind of understanding of Dinneen's warped mind.

The columnist had made a noisy fuss in Sligo when his call to New York was lost by a sweet but scatterbrained receptionist. Virginia had watched Crossan's intervention be greeted by a fusillade of rudeness. She later had, against her better judgement, confronted the columnist, only to find that he had turned his boorishness into a virtue: 'Those guys are always running for mayor. They need people like myself to keep them running. Make good buglers outta them.'

But what chiefly affected Virginia was Crossan's po-faced amiability in the face of such insulting words. She felt moved to commiserate and to praise, but he was smilingly dismissive about it: 'If Dinneen were the worst of my problems I'd be well off.'

Now he came into the breakfast room and spotted her. He came over to her table, the *Irish Times* under his arm, and pulled back the chair opposite her, saying 'May I?'

She motioned him to sit down, her mouth full.

He said, very deliberately, his chin in his hands, 'Good morning, sweet Virginia.'

'Good morning, sweet Stephen.' She nodded towards Dinneen. 'Bad vibes in the dining room this morning.'

Impulsively, Crossan shed a little more of his professional mask. 'Francis Dinneen is the greatest shit in five continents.'

'And so say all of us.'

It was a constant wonder to Crossan how two people were always brought closer to each other by the mutual denigration of a third. He said, 'He manages to shame both of us. You as an American and me as an Irishman, having the faults of both and the virtues of neither.'

He drank tea while she told him of Dinneen's earlier behaviour.

'Maybe the poor man is a bit afraid of you,' he said.

'Why should he be?'

'You're a formidable woman.'

'In what way?'

'You weren't averse to giving me a smack on the knuckles out there at Kerins's yesterday, were you now?'

Virginia's small smile of triumph was fleeting. 'I guess I wanted to see what way you would react.'

Crossan leaned forward. 'Why don't we leave that kind of thing to the porcupine in the corner, aye?'

'I'm sorry.' She continued eating, and then she said. 'You're too together, you know?'

'I'm falling apart, dear. I'm ...'

'Why can't you just be yourself?' She cut across his flippancy.

'There's nothing I'd like more, if I could discover which was the real one.' He paused. 'Or if there is one.'

171

'Why did you not want us to shoot in the dance hall?'

The question was academic: she knew very well why he did not want the cameras to roll in The Extension.

He did not answer, merely raising his eyebrows.

'You were ashamed of that place, Stephen.'

'Ashamed? Ashamed?' he said, playing for time.

'Yes, ashamed,' she said evenly. 'You stepped out of line by suggesting to us that it wouldn't be much of a scene, no?'

Crossan grasped this. 'Yes, I did. It was a professional lapse. In future I'll know that if I want you people to film something I just let on that I'd prefer you didn't.'

Virginia shook her head impatiently. 'Why were you ashamed?' she almost whispered.

He put down his cup and looked at her, his face genuinely worried. 'You're not going to let this go, are you?'

'I'm not going to let it go.'

'It's very difficult . . .'

'I know.'

'You're a stranger . . .'

She leaned across to him, shaking her head and tapping her index finger on his hand for emphasis. 'Uh, huh, Stephen. A few nights ago you were in my bedroom in the Shelbourne with your poetry and your wet trousers, right?'

Crossan nodded, perplexed.

'I was a complete stranger then, right? But you were ready to lay me there and then, right?'

He nodded again.

'So what's all this shit about being a stranger, Stephen? You can lay a stranger but you can't tell her why you're ashamed of your own people enjoying themselves?'

He sat back and said, 'Jayses, Virginia.'

But she continued to smile and said, 'Come on, Stephen. Let me hear you say it. You were ashamed of your own people.'

He said nervously, 'Aren't you sometimes ashamed of your own people?'

'I used to be,' she said, 'when I was *young*.' Her words cut Crossan to the quick. 'But I grew out of it when I learned to love them.'

'I love my people,' he said very quickly.

'Not half as much as you love yourself. You didn't want us to shoot that dreck out there, not because of what people might

172

think of those scruffy kids, but because of what they might think of *you*. Because the whole thing rubs off on *you*, Stephen. It's your dignity that's involved, not theirs. It's your image that's involved, not theirs.'

He sat silent for a moment, his eyes lowered, and then he said, 'Tell me, Virginia, how do you know all of this?' His voice was keyed to sarcasm and coolness, but all of this she quickly shattered.

'I know it because I've been through it many times. And it was much worse than anything you've ever been through. I've been ashamed before, oh, Jesus, have I been ashamed, but now I'm ashamed that I *was* ashamed. I was condescending, superior, a bitch. But not any more. And you're just the same. It was plain as hell that you were ashamed out there yesterday. The rest of them could see it, but I could feel it more than any of them, and that's why I said what I did.' She tapped the back of his hand again, but more gently. 'Somewhere inside that supercilious asshole before me is a nice guy trying to get out.' Her voice lowered to a whisper. 'And before this trip is over I'll have that nice guy out there and dancing.'

He sat quiet, a frown on his face. He was almost in shock, and for a few minutes, for the first time in many years, he had no words. Virginia, watching his face, knew she had struck home. She cleaned her mouth with her napkin and said, briskly, 'Well, that's enough of the lecturing for this morning.'

But he did not join her on the lighter plane.

He looked up and said, 'Are you really serious about what you said?'

'Of course.'

'You're not trying to make me drop my guard, or any of that nonsense?'

She leaned across and whispered, 'Why are you so fucking nervous?'

'It's not nervousness,' he said quickly. 'Well, not the way you think it is.'

'There you go, condescending to me again.'

'No, no, please,' Crossan said, and Virginia barely held back a triumphant smile at the unconsidered sincerity in his voice. 'It's just . . . well . . . what you're asking is an awful lot. It's taken me years . . .'

'I know all about that,' she said, nodding vigorously. 'Years and years of building up protection against people getting inside you. *I* know all about that. I don't need any lessons from anyone.' Her voice softened again. 'Tell me, Stephen, who hurt you?'

'What!' Crossan almost shouted.

'You heard me. Who hurt you? Nobody goes to all that trouble without a good reason. Was it a woman?'

'For God's sake, Virginia, it's only ten o'clock in the morning. Why are we going through this . . . this . . .'

'I'll tell you why we're going through it, kid. We're going through it because I want to clear the air. Since I arrived in this country you haven't spoken a single sincere word to me.' She held up her hand to staunch his protest. 'No bullshit, please. In the last few minutes you've said the first few honest words that I've heard. You came into my bedroom in the Shelbourne with your prick and your poetry, looking for a good fast lay, no strings. It sure as hell was a new approach. But you know what it was? It was patronizing, Stephen. It was insulting, Stephen. See that guy over there? The greatest shit in five continents? I know exactly where I stand with him. I know he means what he says, and says what he means. Now you can carry on your act with Pete or Ellen or Max or anyone else. But not with me. Not from now on. Straight up or not at all. Okay?'

She laid her elbow on the table and stretched her open hand to him, fingers together, thumb to the ceiling. He put his hand in it, and she squeezed very tightly.

He was thoroughly deflated, and thoroughly confused.

They drove out of Galway and on to Kilcolgan, turning down the side road to Moran's of the Weir. The sun was bright, though small clouds were rising before a westerly, and it was warm enough for them to sit outside the little pub to have smoked salmon and crab and several bottles of Chablis. They sat and watched the tide rise the river in front of them. The Irish were silent. The Americans indulged in the obligatory detailed discussion of the meal, and the Irish listened in awe, once again astonished that grown mature people could spend so much time talking about something so simple and basic as food.

Halfway through lunch a healthy young Dutch foursome arrived in a yellow Volkswagen, thirsty and famished. When they had eaten, the two young men took a guitar and a banjo from the car and strummed life into the afternoon. They were not very talented musicians and they had very few songs, and Haslam berated them for their lack, telling them that Ireland had more songs than all of Europe put together. It was good-humoured and taken as such, and in half an hour they were all singing, and Maynard set his camera rolling and Ober was delighted, and Haslam said that all of America would soon know how the Irish spent every day.

Then they went off down the coast road, round by Black Head at the top of the Burren, a hundred square miles of limestone desert pitted and pockmarked with gullies and tiny ravines which gave cover and comfort to a thousand rare plants and orchids.

They were now well and truly in County Clare, the great stronghold of traditional Irish music. Twenty years before, the music had been under sentence of death, but now it was alive again. The Clancy Brothers had started the Irish thing on the campuses in the US, floating into the Irish consciousness on the new wave of the worldwide folk boom. The Clancys were daintily packaged in their Aran sweaters, and were nowadays sneered at, inevitably, for their hucksterism. But the debt owed them could never be paid, certainly not by the purists who nowadays denigrated them. They had opened the doors and the young flooded in to taste the fruit that had hung before their eyes, badly packaged and free, from their birth. The groups sprang up in dozens, the fiddle was suddenly heard all over, and the *uillean* pipe, and the flute and the shy concertina.

These were the instruments that had been under sentence, and County Clare had been their fast-diminishing redoubt. But now they were everywhere, and the young fiddlers and pipers and whistlers came as pilgrims to sit at the feet of men who had never had an audience larger than would fit round a fireside.

The Russell brothers of Doolin were such men, and O'Connor's of Doolin was their local, and sure enough, when the group entered, Pakie Russell was sitting in a corner with the concertina on his knee, squeezing the music from the little box with a minimum of movement.

Pakie was a desiccated pixie, his eyes permanently weary, the face immobile under a cap that was surely never off his head. It was not only his cap that stayed with him night and day, and more sensitive souls were often seen to shuffle carefully upwind of the musician on warm evenings.

He did not acknowledge the arrival of the group with their camera and their lights. He sat, a little yellow sphinx, a sad half-smile playing on his face, as though he were remembering some dim and distant lost opportunity, and his drinking needs – a steady stream of pints of Guinness – were attended to by an adoring claque of young American girls, uniformly lovely in that clean American way, sitting in an idolatrous circle around their indifferent hero as he played and drank and drank and played.

When he had finished a set, Haslam sat down beside him, and the two old friends talked a little of bygone days, though talking, for Pakie, seemed an effortful waste of time and energy.

Haslam inquired after the musician's brother, Miko, who played the whistle with the same diffident genius as Pakie did the box.

'He's not around today?' Haslam said.

'He's in Stockholm, faith.'

Well, from Doolin in West Clare all the way to Stockholm was nowadays a short hop what with the folk halls of Europe crying out for Irish music, and Miko Russell, who had played all his life to a small and knowledgeable little group in this pub, was now top of the bill in halls from London to Munich to Zürich.

Haslam made a last effort to rise the musician to speech. 'It's well for you, Pakie, to have all those American girls like nurses around you. I'm dolled up to the nines and not one of them gives me the time of day. You don't even give your hair a lick and they're around you like flies.'

Pakie finished another pint and took up the box, drawing a sad, plangent note from it as he pulled it out. 'J.J., you'll never have a minute's comfort in this life until the caper with the women is dead in you.'

Down the coast road they came, through Miltown Malbay and Quilty and Doonbeg and Bealaha, and then in over the horseshoe bay of Kilkee, Victorian watering place, now the summer holiday resort for almost the whole population of Limerick, and this year the location chosen for the annual Merriman Summer School.

The group checked in at the Hydro Hotel on the West End, and they all went immediately to bed to sleep off the effects of the hours in Moran's and O'Connor's, and to prepare themselves for that evening, when Freddy Barton, Minister for Posts and Telegraphs, would give the opening lecture of the Summer School.

It was entitled, '1916 – A Reappraisal'.

20

The objects of the Merriman Society are twofold: to honour the memory of Brian Merriman the poet, and to promote interest in the history, literature, archaeology, folklore and traditional music of Ireland, and especially in the historic area of Thomond, which comprises the County of Clare and parts of Limerick and Tipperary, the area in which Brian Merriman lived and died.

One of the principal functions of the Merriman Society is the promotion and organisation of a Summer School of Irish literature, history, archaeology, folklore and folk music. The Summer School has been extremely successful, attracting students and scholars not only from Ireland, but also from Europe and the United States. Apart from the lectures and seminars, the school provides a unique opportunity for social and educational intercourse among students and scholars from different countries and different traditions, and also for visiting places of historic and archaeological interest.

'It was here the first meeting was held, exactly one hundred and thirty years ago this year,' Mulligan said.

They were walking along the beach in Kilkee, having slithered down the smooth brown rock at the East End – Haslam, Mulligan, Dinneen, Crossan and Virginia. The others had gone ahead. Virginia wore a light mackintosh against the Atlantic breeze.

Haslam had charted the beginning of the Great Famine of 1846–8, giving the causes in a neutral tone which chafed against Mulligan's desire for passion and commitment in any discussion of the momentous happenings of Irish history.

'Here,' Mulligan continued, with rhetorical affectation, 'the local landlords came together and announced that they hadn't a penny to spare for the starving thousands around them.'

'Nor had they, in all probability,' Haslam said. 'Half the landlords in the country were stony broke.'

'Like poor Mrs Gerrard,' Mulligan said.

'Who was Mrs Gerrard?' Virginia said.

'She was a dear kindly landowner who threw seventy-six families out of their homes and razed every dwelling to the ground.'

'Why did she do that?'

'She needed their land for cattle, the poor hoor.'

'They probably missed a week's rent,' Dinneen said, with a spitting bitterness which was meant to place him firmly in Mulligan's sympathy. But his attempt to step into the Irish camp was, as usual, doomed.

'They were not behind in the rent,' Mulligan said forcefully. 'Not by an hour. They were decent people, hard workers who had reclaimed most of their land, and paid the rent on the nail. Oh, no. Not that nonpayment would in any case have been justification for throwing them out, and then having her lackeys follow them wherever they went and then throwing them out of the very ditches they used for shelter.'

Haslam dipped his ashplant in the sand. 'Landlords are not emotional people. The evictions made economic sense.'

'The whole bloody famine made economic sense,' Mulligan shouted. 'Two million people died and the population of the country was halved because the great Trevelyan was moved by economic logic. Does it make it more acceptable?'

Haslam sometimes wearied of Mulligan's easily aroused emotions, yet he was attracted by them as targets for his own splenetic shafts. He did not believe that Mulligan's perpetual concern, whether expressed as humanitarianism, Christian feeling or – his favourite – 'common decency', ran deep and true. It seemed to the writer that his friend's passion was reflexive and superficial, yet he could neither ignore nor placate it.

So he goaded.

'The country couldn't support eight million people anyway,' he said. 'Most of them were living in misery. They were better off dead.'

'Oh, God.'

'Exactly,' Haslam said. 'Trevelyan, methinks, was an agent of God, who works, as you keep telling us, in mysterious ways.

Ireland, remember, is not in line for earthquakes, flooding is unknown, and there isn't a volcano anywhere on the island. It had to be famine. An act of God, I tell you.'

The tide was out, and the beige sand was hard under their feet, which left five perfect sets of footprints across the beach, with the imprint of Haslam's ashplant a recurring period mark. The sun was down over the bay, casting into perfect relief the point known as George's Head, the limestone cliff sculptured to the monarch's likeness by wind and rain and spume.

'British pig,' Mulligan muttered, staring at the profile.

'Which George was it, anyway?' Crossan asked.

'It doesn't matter. One was worse than the other.'

'Charity,' Haslam counselled.

'I've none to spare,' Mulligan said. 'You and Freddy Barton should be put in a sack and dropped in the Pollock Holes. Fifth columnists.'

'Rationalists.'

'Shoneens.'

'Men of reason.'

'Barton is too clever by half,' Mulligan said.

Haslam shook his head and dug his stick into the sand as he walked. 'What you mean is that he's a genuine scholar, a man of wide reading, witty, erudite and stimulating. In short, an intellectual, and therefore an object of hatred and suspicion to the peasant mind.'

Mulligan almost sniffed. 'I don't mind being called a peasant, if that's what you're implying. There's a nobility in the peasant, a simplicity, which I thought you, as a writer, would appreciate.'

The haughty tone sat uncomfortably on Mulligan: it was against his grain.

Haslam looked up from the sand and into the sky. 'I'll tell you what the word "peasant" evokes for me. Poverty, illiteracy, slyness, dishonesty, hopelessness. Only nonpeasants see nobility in the peasant's life. And as for simplicity, there was plenty of that, to be sure. He ate the same rotten food, he wore the same rotten clothes, he lived in the same rotten hovel, he did the same rotten work, day after day, week after week, year in, year out. If that's simplicity, then the peasant had plenty of it, and he could have done without it.'

Haslam was acutely aware of his status among the group as a man apart. Crossan was a civil servant, Dinneen a mere journalist. Virginia was a show woman and Mulligan's job, even by his own reckoning, was beneath him.

The writer, good or bad, who had spent the long solitary hours stitching his thoughts and inspirations into narrative, and who had done it as consistently and conscientiously as J. J. Haslam, was as distanced as the priest. His words were freighted, as the priest's were, with the mystic and the arcane, and he could seem immune to the mundane confusions of his fellows.

Haslam, too, took pleasure in undermining the most conventional assumptions of his friends, those props which enabled them to manage their lives, the stanchions of their sanity. It was a trick for which he needed no connivance: the hardiest intellects foundered when basic premises were lightly dismissed. It was a trick which the novelist had learned from Shaw, whose audacious talent was for stating the obvious in terms of the scandalous. After Shaw, this simple prestige hardly needed refinement, but Haslam had made an art of it. He well knew the fear men had of their deepest feelings, their unwillingness to probe to the pith, and their horror of being seen to step outside the corral of common opinion.

Freddy Barton had the same gadfly urges, tempered though they were by the exigencies of party politics.

But the two were aligned in more than intellectual impishness. Both were of educated middle-class stock for generations, and their social and spiritual comforts were replete without need of zealous nationalism or religion to support them. With their social and moral self-sufficiency went solid intellects and an innate scepticism: common opinions must be rigorously scrutinized for cant.

They had both deferred to these intellectual imperatives in their own ways and in their respective fields. Haslam's contribution to the laying away of old truths was more circumspect than Barton's, who, as Government Minister, had a constant pulpit and ready audience on radio and television and in the newspapers and who exploited them, his enemies avowed, unscrupulously.

Haslam, in his weekly 'Polonius' column in the *Irish Times*, used his talent for light ridicule as a constant chisel.

They were, in truth, a lonely pair, though the Irish people never thought of them as being united, politics and literature being oil and water.

They climbed the steep steps from the beach and crossed the square to the Sweeney Memorial Library. The others had arrived before them, and Maynard was on the stage, standing behind his camera, talking to Ober and Ellen.

Alice Foley was in a far corner of the hall, talking to Dermot Kirwan, the high priest of the Merriman Society. His big head was forward, his face to the floor, as though in deep concentration on what Alice was saying. His right arm was around her, his hand resting lightly on her buttocks.

The hall was full, and the party advanced to the front seats.

The conversation around them moved from English to Irish with that absence of strain and selfconsciousness which was Haslam's ideal; Crossan's too. But there were only about three hundred people in the hall, same faces every year, with the Scandinavian and American students adding international Tabasco.

The school was dedicated to booze and scholarship and good talk, their proper order never established, and prone to change from day to day. It was also dedicated to bilingualism, and its officers were proud of their efforts, even in such a small way, to undo the damage wrought by successive Irish governments, who had thrown constant sops to the Irish-language lobby. There had never been the mixture of mailed fist and bright initiative which might have brought about a bilingual nation. Most of the population oozed good-natured indifference – as they did to the North – and too many of the committed few let off a pong of superiority that drove away those who might be interested.

There was a commotion at the entrance.

The glass doors opened and a small crowd parted to admit Freddy Barton, and the murmur in the hall died.

This was a man who silenced people, who set them on edge with his sharp words and unwelcome logic. He was perpetually above them, for his efforts to place himself at a common level were patchy and inadequate: his heart was not in it. He was an intellectual and a politician, irreconcilable avocations, the conceits of the former in continuing triumph over the demands of the latter. Try as he might – and he did try – he could not train himself to enjoy the acclaim of hoi polloi as much as he did an appreciative chuckle over one of his bons mots from any of his few intellectual peers.

While his political colleagues' eyes were transfixed by the tiny navel of Irish politics, Barton's were always cast further, historically and geographically, setting Europe and its history as a cyclorama against which he tried to see the minutest movements in his own country.

And yet his cosmic view sometimes became wondrously narrowed.

'We will not provide a platform for murderers,' he announced, in an instant banishing the whole block of Republican opinion from the airwaves. It was his ministerial prerogative. They were thugs and terrorists. They were narrow, they were sectarian. Bloodshed was their game. He would have no truck with them, and the government would not talk to them. Nor should anyone else.

It was a simple thought. But coming from a man who professed the scepticism of the historian, it denied or ignored the indelible facts of history. How many times had the world heard that this or that government would not talk to terrorists, to murderers, to rebels? How many times had they ended up talking to them, pleading with them, bargaining with them, taking them into government, licking their murderous boots?

But this time it would be different. Ireland would not be dragged back into the mire of bloodshed and hatred from which she had barely emerged. Reason would have its day. And reason would prevail.

The Minister's tall form moved up the aisle. At his right arm was the young professor from Buffalo, New York, Brian Darcy, who came each year to the Merriman School. Barton looked neither right nor left, his lips shut tight. His bow tie, a godsend to cartoonists, was askew, and his collar jutted over the lapel of his jacket.

They went up to the stage and the Minister moved slowly across to the rostrum.

Soon there was total silence in the hall but for the Minister's sharp, confident, English-trained voice, which did not once falter. He stood beside the simple wooden rostrum, leaning on it with his right elbow, moving only to turn the pages of his prepared script. His phraseology, as usual, was pluperfect. The talk was syllogistic and concise, with the spare, pared terms of the schooled writer.

He was ten minutes into his paper, setting the charges around the plinth of Irish Republicanism with such professional delicacy that a stranger could have been excused for having no suspicion of the demolition to come. Each pellet of scepticism was sugared with bland praise for the integrity of the men of 1916. No criticism was stated, though much was implied, and when he homed on any aspect of the rebellion with which he found himself out of sympathy, his demurral was posed as a question. The master was at work.

'. . . If I were asked, then, whether the action of the men of 1916 was imbued with nobility, I would say without hesitation that it was. If I were asked whether the integrity of these men could be impugned, I would answer that it could not. But these questions beg others which have become, for us, momentous. And it is these questions which should be asked. It is these questions which are not asked. It is these questions, and the answers to them, which pose the greatest problems for us as a republic.'

Restlessness, anticipation, antipathy ran like static around the hall. People shifted in their chairs, others sat on the edges, gripping the backs of the chairs in front.

'The most important of these questions, for me, is whether the action of the men of 1916 was, in itself, a good thing. Years of painful reflection have led me to conclude that the action of the men of 1916 was a sad and mistaken thing.'

The first shout came from the middle of the hall, but it was difficult to make out its import, and Barton seemed not to hear it, for he continued without hesitation.

'We have taught our young men to honour the men of 1916, to honour their cause, to honour their motives, and most of all to honour their methods.'

There was another shout, from nearer the stage, and this time the Minister heard it, but he acknowledged it only by raising his voice.

'We now purport to deny and decry the actions of the Provisional IRA. I say that we cannot honour the actions of the men of 1916 and decry the methods of the IRA. *We have produced the thinking that produced the IRA.*'

The shouts came again, but this time they were not scattered heckling. They were concerted, and above the general din a clear chant made itself heard: 'British agent! British agent! British agent!'

Barton continued to speak, almost shouting, until the words of the chant became clear to him. Then he stopped in mid-sentence, shock and fury transfixing his features. He picked up his script and pointed it at the group of chanters. 'This is the truth,' he shouted. 'You cannot bear the truth!'

'British agent!' they continued to chant.

Dermot Kirwan's large head and shoulders rose from the front row. He waved his arms, gesturing silence, but he was ignored. It was a cornerstone of the school's existence that every man should have his say, a policy that in the past had produced lectures of stupefying pretentiousness masquerading as revisionism. But Barton was no ambitious young university lecturer desperate for headlines. Now he would not be allowed to have his say, for it was obvious that the audience had been infiltrated by a group whose beliefs were in direct confrontation with Barton's, and whose only object in attending the lecture was to deny him his platform.

The chant diminished, and one of the group, in forced English accent, shouted, 'Have another drink, Mr Minister, have another pink gin, old boy.' His friends laughed.

Barton folded his notes and moved from the rostrum.

The noise subsided, and Dermot Kirwan made his ungainly way up the steps and onto the stage. He turned and addressed the audience. 'As president of the Summer School, I plead with those who disagree with Minister Barton's views at least to let him finish . . .'

'Why should we?' A young man was on his feet, his voice high. 'Why should we let him finish? He's a lackey for the British. Why should he be allowed to throw dirt on the memory of Patrick Pearse and the men of 1916?'

'He is not throwing dirt on anyone . . .' Kirwan began.

'Where in the name of Jayses were you for the last quarter of an hour? Are you deaf or something?'

'A man is entitled to be heard.'

'Well, you fucking well tell that to *him*,' the young man

shouted. 'He won't give *us* a voice, will he?'

Kirwan found himself impaled on a political argument, and the injustice of it creased his forehead. 'We are here to listen . . .' he began again.

'You are here to give a platform to a man who laughs at everything Irish and belittles great men. And you want us to be quiet while he does it!' His colleagues cheered every sentence. 'We'll be quiet if you guarantee us the platform when he's finished.'

'There will be ten minutes for questions when the Minister is finished.'

'Give us the platform, same as him.'

'We cannot do that,' Kirwan said.

'Give us the platform! Give us the platform!' the chant began, and Kirwan stood behind the rostrum, his glasses off, rubbing his eyes, helpless. This had nothing to do with scholarship and chat and booze and feeling up winsome foreign students. Those wild-eyed young men and women had no place at a civilized gathering such as this. But he could not requite their demands. They were implacable.

'I have no option but to close the lecture, and hope that we can hear it at a later time.'

'We'll be here,' the young man shouted, and his colleagues chorused agreement. Barton left the stage with the help of young Darcy, to the continuing taunts of the hecklers. They followed him to the door, urging him to have a drink, to call in the British army, to have them all put in jail, to cut out their tongues.

Dermot Kirwan opened the door of the ministerial Mercedes and Barton fell into the back seat. They drove off to the Hydro Hotel.

From that hotel, when Crossan and his group later reached it, came the sound of the Shannon Sweet Band, four young men and a tiny girl. They were playing Irish music of the centuries on guitar, fiddle, bazooki, *uillean* pipes and dulcimer. They had superimposed their own idiosyncratic arrangements, for the most part enhancing the music's individuality. The sounds were sharp and frenetic, thoroughly Irish even to the alien ear, but with an unmistakable contemporary patina: a successful marriage of old tunes and new ideas.

186

Their grandfathers had played the same tunes half-hidden by turf smoke in front of a fire, fortified by porter and *poitín*. After the gig, the Shannon Sweet Band would roll their own joints, and their cheque would go to their manager in Dublin.

Their grandfathers had loved and enjoyed the music they played; so did the members of the Shannon Sweet Band.

That much was constant.

On the tennis court in front of the hotel, on this balmy August night, the management had thoughtfully set out plain white iron tables and chairs, so that visitors could enjoy the rare treat in Ireland of an alfresco evening drink.

On one side of the net, Freddy Barton was the centre of a group of sitting people. He was listening to their questions, which were slowly and carefully enunciated, as though his questioners feared that his answers might impugn their syntax. Mulligan had earlier helplessly noted that the danger with questioning Barton was not that you might suffer intellectual defeat – that was all but axiomatic – but that you might get a metaphorical clip on the ear for impudence and bad grammar.

But now, though the threat of acid was ever in the air, Barton's mien was pleasant, attentive and almost good-natured. He was nursing a lifeless glass of Paddy, sitting far back on the white seat, his right ankle resting on his knee.

There were about fifteen people present, and all of them could be counted among Barton's admirers. One, a smartly tailored young academic who had recently been elevated to what Haslam called 'that refuse dump for political hacks, ambitious academics and failed parliamentarians', the Irish Senate, sought to create a difference of opinion between himself and Barton by pointing up what he described as a 'piquant' inconsistency between Barton's present attitude to the IRA and his oft-quoted admiration for revolutions and revolutionaries of times past. Barton began to question the very nervous Senator in phrases that were almost insultingly deferential, and the young man was slowly strangled by his own 'yes, buts'. He ended up admitting that there was 'no fundamental difference between us, but I still find it piquant that . . .'

Barton looked around for another soul to stumble into his briar patch, but the group around him were not the stuff of confrontation. They were almost all academics, and their intellects, their scholarship, their reading in history forced them, Haslam had earlier insisted, to see 'all seventy-four sides of every question in Irish history'. They could not speak from their hearts, or their bellies, or from whatever organ of the body extreme Republicanism was thought to spring. For surely extreme Republicanism – that thinking that nowadays placed bombs in restaurants, shot husbands in front of wives and fathers in front of children, and forced milk roundsmen to deliver proxy bombs to market towns – surely that thinking did not originate in the head?

Barton did not think so, and those around him did not think so.

But those who did now made their ominously silent appearance.

Barton's tormentors from the hall filed onto the tennis court from the far end, seating themselves at the tables on the other side of the net. Their arrival brought silence to the group, who looked across at them with a mixture of nervousness and anticipation.

There were about a dozen men and three women, all of them in their twenties, though a few could have been younger. Their clothing was cheap and haphazard, a statement of their indifference to these things. They all had drinks, some with two bottles, which they placed noisily on the tables. They looked across at the Barton group without speaking. The sun was long gone, but the night was bright enough to make clear the features of everyone on both sides of the net.

Every member of Barton's group was aware that he was staring into the sharp-edged face of extreme Republicanism, the 'boys'. They knew that among the group opposite there were one or two – maybe more – who had killed, or who had made and planted bombs which had killed and maimed, and this knowledge set up uncomfortable stirrings in their stomachs.

It was not possible to dismiss these young people as common criminals, for common criminals would have no time for the exalted motives which these people would profess: love of country, a noble tradition, the right of the Irish people to rule themselves. But neither was it possible, for Freddy Barton and those with him, to admire them as revolutionary heroes.

They began to sing.

'In Mountjoy Jail one Monday morning,
   High upon the gallows tree
   Kevin Barry gave his young life
   For the cause of liberty.'

Barton did not move, and they finished the song, every verse.

In the following silence, he said, 'You have driven me out of one place tonight. You are not going to drive me out of here.'

The young man who had challenged Dermot Kirwan in the hall stood up. He was stringy and furry-haired, his dark eyebrows jutting over brown-rimmed glasses. 'We do not want to drive you out of here. We want you to stay and talk to us.'

The ameliorative note caused a shuffle on Barton's side.

'I have nothing to say to murderers.'

'How do you know we are murderers?'

'Are you members of the Provisional I R A?'

'That's a very disingenuous question, Freddy.'

The mixture of the adjective and the familiar gave the Minister pause. He said to the young man, 'Do you support the aims of the Provisional I R A?'

'We support the idea of a united Ireland.'

'What means would you support to gain this end?'

'Whatever means we felt were necessary.'

'Would that include killing and maiming innocent people?'

'How would you define an innocent person?'

'I will not bandy definitions with you. You know very well what I mean by an innocent person.'

'I would still like to hear you define it, Freddy.' The young man's use of Barton's first name was strange. The anger he had shown in the hall was gone, and his voice was soft and reasoning. There was no trace of irony in his familiarity, and his pronounced Belfast accent was without harshness. 'Would you have described George Collaghy as an innocent person?'

Among the Northern death news that morning, the newspapers reported the finding of George Collaghy's body in a Belfast cemetery. He had been shot through the head.

'My information is that he was an ordinary decent workingman who harmed nobody.'

'Would you like to hear a story?'

The young man did not expect a reply, and got none.

'I used to know a man who believed all his life in a united Ireland, and did everything he could, within the law, to bring

189

that about. He was a Republican, and he lived in the Falls Road. He never had a job. Every time a job came up, he found that a Protestant had got there before him, even though he was first at the site the morning the job became available. He believed that a united Ireland would end that kind of thing. He had a family of six children to support. He didn't drink, and he didn't smoke. And every Christmas he did his best to see that every child had a present. But every Christmas morning there was a knock on the door and four B-specials would come into the house. You remember the B-Specials, Freddy?'

'I remember them.'

'A fine body of men. They would take this man from his home and bring him to the police station and put him in a cell. And then for all of Christmas Day, while his family cried by the empty fireplace, they would kick and beat this dirty Papisher, this fucking Fenian bastard, until he was unconscious. They would in the meantime get themselves pissed drunk on Bushmills whiskey, and when their Christmas celebrations were over, they would put him in a van and dump him outside the city. And he would find his own way back, and his eldest son would meet him at the door and clean off his face.'

There was complete silence as the man talked, except for the soft soughing of the waves down on the beach. His glasses glinted in the moonlight. He did not rant. No emotion whatever manifested itself as he laid out the facts.

'You know who that eldest son was?'

Again the question was rhetorical.

'Me. I was the one that cleaned the blood and spittle off his face. That was my job every Christmas night for years. And do you know who led the B-Specials on their annual Christmas bash? Our decent, hardworking friend who harmed nobody, George Collaghy. You see, when the B-Specials were disbanded Collaghy faded from view. He became what you call an ordinary workingman. But only because he was no longer allowed, legally, to do what he enjoyed doing more than anything else in the world. Stamping on Catholics. Now I don't know who killed Collaghy, and I don't care. But tell me this. Do you expect me to think of him as an innocent person? Do you expect me to weep at the news of his death?'

Barton sighed and shook his head. 'Obviously I could expect you to do neither.'

'My father killed himself on Christmas Eve twelve years ago. He couldn't face another Christmas.'

Barton looked down at the black macadam and shook his head. 'What can I say?'

'You could say that men like Collaghy should not be allowed to live.'

'I will not condone the killing of any man.'

'A pacifist, are you?'

'I am not a philosophical pacifist . . .'

'Now it's my turn to refuse to bandy phrases with you.' His voice rang out in the clear moonlit night. 'Unlike most of the people around me' – he nodded to the others in his group – 'I don't hate you personally. But I'll tell you one thing.' He stood and leaned on the table in front of him. 'You don't know what happened to the Catholics in Northern Ireland.'

Barton straightened up in anger. 'That is not true. Nobody knows better than I do what the Catholics went through –'

'You have been *told* what they went through' – the young man cut him off coolly – 'but you don't *know*. You don't know what it is like to live in fear. You have had everything you ever wanted. You still have it. And you don't know what it is like to live without hope. I tell you, Freddy, if a maggot were eating your prize garden plant at the root you would kneel down and try to reason with that maggot. And even if that maggot could hear and understand you, he would still eat your plant. Because it is in his nature.'

'Maggots eat plants to survive,' Barton said brusquely.

'Protestants feel the same way about Catholics in the North.'

Barton's face clearly expressed his disdain for the young man's metaphor. 'You are saying that it is impossible to find a political solution?'

'If a political solution involves persuading Northern Protestants to consider Catholics their equals, then I *know* there cannot be a political solution.'

'I cannot agree with you.'

'I wish I could say that it didn't matter whether you agreed with me or not. Unfortunately, you have great influence on a lot of people, young people, in the Republic.'

'I try to be an influence for good.'

'I will even grant you that. But the problem is, Freddy, that you have never for a moment considered that you might be an influence for evil. You have never even thought that you might be *wrong*. I *know* you are wrong. We all know.' He waved his arm to cover his group, but clearly he felt that he was speaking for every Catholic in Northern Ireland. 'We will teach the Protestants of Northern Ireland that Catholics are not garbage.'

'How will you teach them?'

'I will not spell that out.'

'You are a foolish and misguided young man. You are not just dealing with Northern Protestants, you know. Northern Ireland is part of a sovereign state.'

'You don't seriously think the British give a tuppenny damn about the North, do you, Freddy? It's the worst pain in the ass she's ever had to suffer. You think the Queen gives a shit about her "loyal subjects"? Her government and herself and most of her subjects wish the whole lot, Catholic and Protestant, could vanish up their own arseholes, and they'd be rid of the problem. Britain, Freddy, will be gone the minute she sees an opportunity, and she'll pass no apology to anyone, any more than she did anywhere else in the world. And we'll help her to get out.'

'And suppose Britain did leave? What then? How will you avoid civil war?'

'What's so good about avoiding civil war?'

'Don't be a fool,' Barton said. 'Thousands of people will be killed. Civil war leaves scars that take generations to heal, as we in the Republic know too well.'

'Do you think that Northern Catholics would even *notice* a few new scars?' The young man's voice rose. 'They have so many already there isn't room for any more.'

'You cannot talk so flippantly about people's lives.'

'Lives? What lives? What kind of life is it to wake up every morning knowing that there's no job, and no chance of a job, just because your parents had the wrong religion? Do you call that a life?'

'Violence will not solve that.'

'My arse, Freddy. *Only* violence will solve it. Only violence solves anything. Remember your Machiavelli: the prophets with the guns always beat the prophets without the guns.'

'What Machiavelli actually said was . . .'

'There you go. More interested in showing everyone how clever you are than in learning from what the man said.'

'This conversation is getting nowhere.'

'What you mean is not that the conversation is getting nowhere, but that I am not even beginning to agree with you. I am not falling for your humanistic, philosophical, gin-and-tonic rationalism. To me, all those words mean just one thing. Bullshit. Because I hate. Do you understand, Freddy? I *hate*. It's thick in my blood and it runs in my mind. It is not an intellectual thing, and therefore you cannot understand it. It is an emotional thing, and you would have nothing to do with the emotions, would you? They are not good. But I think they are good. And my ruling emotion is a hatred for all those people who stood on the Catholics of Northern Ireland for all those years, and those people who, if they didn't do it, didn't protest that it shouldn't be done. So much for your innocent people, Freddy. For me, there's no such thing as an innocent Protestant. They are all guilty. And if they are not willing to face up to the consequences of their cruelty and savagery and bigotry, let them all fuck off to the Britain they love so much. The Protestants of Northern Ireland hate Catholics, they despise them and belittle them and treat them as dirt. They have had fifty years to prove otherwise and all they did was to stamp their faces further in the dungheap. And now you tell us to listen to them, to be patient with them, to reason with them, to compromise with them. Are you listening to me?'

'I hear you.'

'How *dare* you ask me to listen to them! Why should I listen to them? These people are primitives, real fucking primitives. Why the hell should we listen to them? Or reason with them? They've made our lives misery and hell for as long as we can remember and now you have the gall to tell us to reason with them.'

His voice dropped, and he drew his hand across his forehead. 'The time for reasoning is past, Freddy. It's all over for them. Now it's our turn. And we'll finish the business.'

He leaned over the net. 'Have you anything to say?'

'I have said it. Violence is not the solution.'

The young man shook his head in wonder, and then stood up straight. 'All we ever wanted was respect. *Respect*, Freddy. We never got it from the British. And we never got it from the Protestants. The Brits will run out, or be run out. And then we'll take care of those Protestants who think we are inferior human beings. And if that means civil war, so be it. If it means thousands dead, so be it. We have been stamped on for long enough.'

He turned from the net and walked slowly out of the court. His group followed him and they all went into the hotel.

The young Brian Darcy from Buffalo said to Barton, 'You can't talk rationally with these people.'

Haslam said, 'Oh, for God's sake be quiet.' He walked over and took the arm of Virginia Green, who was sitting in the moonlight, her eyes wet and glistening. He walked her into the hotel, and one by one the Minister's group followed.

When Barton came into the bar, the young man was there before him. He turned with two glasses of Paddy in his hand, and he offered one to the Minister. Barton looked at the drink, his face haggard and glum. He took the drink.

The young man said, 'You must respect me.'

Barton nodded.

His terms of reference were irrevocably different from the young man's, but knowing this did not dilute the grey feeling in his heart. In spite of his natural aversion to everything the young man stood for and believed in, he would happily have engaged him in a heady dialectic on the sources of and solutions to the problems of Northern Ireland. Instead of which they had that crude antiphony, leading nowhere.

He did not want to accept the drink. But to refuse would have been melodramatic, a fussy gesture. At all costs he must avoid a scene, and the cost for him was high.

He bought the young man a drink.

They talked for two hours, while the others listened, mostly about literature. Politics was not mentioned again. The young man said that Borges was the greatest living writer. Barton said that such a judgement was impossible to make: there were so many things to be taken into account.

They got drunk, and they both agreed, before going to bed at four o'clock in the morning, that Seamus Heaney was the best poet that Ireland had produced since Yeats.

'Funny,' the young man said, 'how the mantle should pass from a Southern Protestant to a Northern Catholic.'

21

The note read: 'Oliver. Jawballs said boo to your pageant at Dublin Castle. Please ring me as soon as you reach Limerick. Daithi Halley.'

Mulligan read the note for the fifth time, sitting on the edge of his bed in the Pery Grand Hotel in Limerick, the receiver cradled under his chin. He looked miserably out of the bedroom window.

The weather, so benign through Connemara and Clare, had grown dark and angry on the road in from Ennis, and within a few miles from Limerick City the rain was a steady downpour, washing the fields and trees. It was no surprise to Haslam. 'Every time I come back to this poxy kip it's pissing,' he said, but with resignation. Limerick was his hometown and he always spoke of it with an exalted dislike whose very intensity seemed to belie the feeling expressed.

The city did, indeed, have the sullen heartbroken air of a town forgotten, its few Georgian buildings augmented by patchy glass and concrete blocks, but with great holes everywhere, where untenable buildings had been razed without heed of replacement. The inhabitants were in tune with their surroundings, exuding a glum and philistine provincialism.

'It's the Redemptorists,' Haslam had insisted, while the minibus halted outside Cranmore Castle, a few miles from the city, to drop off the camera team for an hour while they set up the scene for that evening. 'They've had their thick evangelists' brogues on the necks of these people for too long. There hasn't been a man who thought for himself in this city for half a century.' And the city, when they reached it, threw back his gloom, myopically indifferent to the rest of the country, the rest of the world.

Arthur Whelan, whose advertising proclaimed him 'Ireland's leading hotelier', had chosen it as the site of his first hotel, the Pery Grand, impressing the local burghers with his seeming altruism. But he knew that labour was cheap. There was money to be made in the midst of the prevailing apathy, and the city was only fifteen miles from Shannon Airport, stepping-off place for thousands of touring Americans and Continentals. His hotel took its invariable shape – a flat grey box indistinguishable from any of his other hotels, indistinguishable from any motel in Smalltown, USA – cheap, functional, impersonal.

'And totally inefficient,' Mulligan said furiously, as he banged again on the receiver buttons.

He hung up and turned to Crossan, who was sprawled on the opposite bed, flicking quietly through the *Irish Times*.

'Every time there's a drop of rain in the Midlands, you can't make a call to Dublin. The Post Office engineers don't know that it sometimes rains in Ireland.'

'Maybe they're all from Florida,' Crossan said.

'Probably sweet shag all wrong with the lines. She just thinks it's too much trouble. Ah,' – he moved from the phone towards the mirror – 'the Irish don't know the first thing about service. Very strange, that.'

'The problem is an inability to distinguish between service and servility.'

'Colonial scars.'

'Like everything else.'

'The Brits have a lot to answer for.'

'The scapegoat holdall.'

The men spoke in affectedly Oirish banter, leaving much unsaid. They were both long accustomed to the strange friction that any kind of service set up in the Irish mind. The Irish did not mind being waiters or barmen, but it was a piece of crushing humiliation to *address* them as 'barman' or 'waiter'. So there was a whole unspoken language of nods and winks and gestures and murmurs by which Irish people communicated with their fellows in service. 'Er' and 'Excuse me' and 'Ahem' and simple 'Ah' were the mainstays, and one grovelled like a whipped mongrel for attention. And the service, when it came, was decent and mannerly and conscientious.

'But the price one has to pay,' Mulligan said, looking out the window of the bedroom. The rain had stopped, and the grass outside had a clean, silvery sheen. He watched a lone songthrush pull a worm from the reluctant earth.

The telephone rang. It was his assistant, Daithi Halley, ringing from his office in Dublin.

The young man said, 'I was expecting a call from you. Did you not get my note?'

'Yes, I did, but there's been a shower of rain. So all the lines from here are out of order.'

'How come I got through to you?'

Halley's gift for the obvious drew the worst out of Mulligan. 'It's only the Limerick–Dublin lines that are out of order, young fella me lad. The Dublin–Limerick lines are perfect.'

He said nothing into the silence that followed, returning Crossan's smile.

Halley eventually said, 'Well, anyway, as I said in the note, Jawballs won't allow the play to go on in Dublin Castle.'

Jawballs was Halley's – and Mulligan's – name for the Taoiseach, the Prime Minister of the Irish government. On the following Friday, the Taoiseach was to play host to a visiting party of governors from the United States of America. It was Gogarty's idea to invite them and their wives to Ireland. Entertainment had been a problem. Mulligan, as chairman of the Organizing Committee, had proposed the commissioning of a playlet. The play was written, the music chosen and arranged, the costumes were on their way from London. The play was timed to take place after the dinner at Dublin Castle, which was the highlight of the visit.

'And now you say he won't have it?'

'Not a bit of it.'

'That's over a thousand pounds down the drain.'

'So I told his secretary.'

'Did he give a reason?'

'Jawballs give a reason?'

The Taoiseach's philistinism was matched only by his arrogance, a purblind belief in his own rightness which differed from Freddy Barton's only in its anti-intellectualism. He was a constant embarrassment to the Department of Foreign Affairs, refusing to give his name or presence to any project or event which smacked of the artistic. He was a devotionally unread man; he had once boasted that he had never been inside the National Gallery of Art, and his appreciation of music was expressed in – and confined to – a deep love of the sound of the horn of the master of the hounds, to which he regularly rode. Horses were his passion, and the sole subject of all his leisure thoughts and conversation.

'Actually,' Halley said, 'he did give his secretary a kind of reason.'

'What was that?'

'He said the governors wouldn't understand the play.'

'Why not?'

'Because he said they were only a bunch of Wops and Polacks.'

Mulligan put his hand to his forehead. 'Oh, my great suffering Jesus.' Crossan looked up from his paper.

Mulligan said into the phone, 'Well, forget it. Pay everyone off. There's nothing we can do. He's the Taoiseach, God help us all.'

He hung up. 'Did you hear that?'

Crossan nodded. 'I got the gist.'

'God be with De Valera.'

'Jawballs is more pragmatic, my dear Oliver.'

Mulligan looked down on the young man on the bed, ignoring his tone. 'You know, I feel genuine shame when I think that we allowed that man to become our Taoiseach.'

'The people's choice. What do you expect?'

'The people have chosen well before, my boy.'

'Indeed. And they have a habit of producing the right men for the times that are in it. And for the times we are in now, I cannot think of anyone more suitable than Jawballs.'

Meanwhile, in Cranmore Castle, the camera crew were in the hands of Austin Buggy, who would be their host at the medieval banquet that evening and who was now answering Maynard's and Ober's questions about lighting and other problems with a canny perception.

He told them what the banquet routine was. 'You assemble downstairs, get a potted history and a few jars of mead. Then upstairs for the food, which is spareribs and veg, eaten without cutlery and served by the castle ladies – not wenches, mark you.'

He continued at a pattering speed, with sufficient topical and personal interpolations to make it all sound spontaneous.

Buggy had been born in Kilmihill, County Clare, and like thousands of other youngsters around, had had to emigrate to England in his teens, working his way up to several jobs as manager of east-coast amusement parks and arcades before returning to Ireland. He had been given complete control of tourism development for County Clare, and he had come in like a tornado, spewing out ideas, some of them useless and without future, others, like Cranmore, hugely successful. He worked incessantly, goading and cajoling. He persuaded the American-Irish millionaire Paul Grey to sink half a million pounds in the restoration of Cranmore and the erection of a model Irish village, which served as a shopping centre for the goods handcrafted in the various village cooperatives which Buggy had initiated. The nightly hundreds of tourists on their way into the Cranmore banquet were trapped in a brightly lit village of shops, the little thatched cottages bursting with tweeds, rugs, sweaters, ashplants, porcelain, linens and crystal and hundreds of less viable artifacts. Buggy was blithe about the entrapment: he said that a night watching tourists shopping was better than a night's drinking, an extraordinary statement from a man who loved a pint beyond words.

But the work had taken its toll, and early in the year he had suffered two heart attacks. He was to retire in a few months.

Yet the work – his work, his life – was a disease, and the arrival of a television group as important as the NBS team was an opportunity not to be missed, or mishandled.

He showed them through the castle, advised on light placings, pointed out the dungeon, the lord's banquet table, gave them a potted history, and buzzed about the stone floors with a verve that gave no countenance to his ailing heart. He was a small man, almost completely bald, with a little jet-black moustache propping up his tiny nose, and fitting perfectly his black eyes, which were the most obscenely lascivious in Ireland.

When business was finished, he brought the four Americans into the pub by the castle gates and regaled them with stories that made Maynard immediately want to put his camera in action.

But Buggy shook his head. 'The camera is for business, my

dear fellow. We're at play now. Best thing you can do for me is to show a few hundred Americans enjoying themselves. They are a much better advertisement than an old fogy like me telling yarns.'

His hard-nosed modesty charmed them, and they spoke about him on the way into Limerick.

'Haslam told me that that guy was a heavy drinker,' Ober said. 'He didn't show any signs of it.'

'You notice that?' Maynard said. 'So did I. But not just about him. They all drink all day. Mulligan, Haslam, Crossan, even Alice Foley. And they never get drunk. I thought this country would be crawling with drunks, but none of these guys has got soused since the trip started.'

'They're working,' Ober said.

'Yes, but they don't let you know they're working. Except for Stephen Crossan. He watches his words.'

'I don't like that guy,' Ober said.

Ellen said to Virginia, 'I don't agree with you. I think they're much more open than any government types I've ever met. And they're opening up more all the time. You can talk to them.'

'Especially J.J.' Maynard grinned.

'He's a nice man, Max.'

'Jeez, Ellen, I was kidding, honey. He's a great guy. I love him. What the hell, I love 'em all. Even Crossan. What you got against him, Pete?'

'He's too cool.'

'That's a fault?'

'Maybe he's just happily married,' Ellen said.

'He's not married,' Virginia said, more quickly than she would have liked.

'Well' – Ellen smiled – 'that's his problem, same as mine.'

'You're not easy to catch, Ellen,' Ober said.

'I'm not even flying, Pete.'

Maynard said, 'Lies. You're just waiting for Frank Dinneen.'

There were great groans from the others.

'Poor Frank,' Ellen said.

'Ellen, do me a favour, will you?' Maynard leaned across and took her hand in his. 'Just one favour?'

'What's that, Max?' Ellen said, smiling into his face. She loved the man.

'Say something nasty about someone.'

'About whom?'

'Anyone, anyone at all. About me! No, no, no, no. No use asking for the impossible. Let's see. Well. What *about* Dinneen anyway? Jeez, he's the easiest man in the world to say nasty things about.'

'My daddy taught me to be a nice girl, Max.'

'And my mummy taught me to be nasty. And I'm gonna be nasty tonight. Oh, my dears, am I gonna be nasty tonight.'

Later that evening, showered and dressed, they arrived back at Cranmore, and though it was still daylight, the castle was brightly lit and magnificent, over the slow green river. They clomped over the drawbridge, acknowledging the greeting of the first of the castle ladies, a young, dark-eyed girl with glowing cheeks who handed them each a jar of mead.

Crossan said to Virginia, 'In keeping with our policy of mutual honesty, I must warn you that mead can make you sick. And it's not easily washed out of trousers.'

He smiled at her, and she smiled back.

The great hall was crowded, and the late arrivals got a muzzy image of hundreds of silver-haired men and blue-haired women. Here, in this ancient castle of the O'Briens, the sounds were from Boston and Philadelphia and Chicago and New York, alien vowels echoing from the untouched stone walls which had for hundreds of years thrown back the raucous vulgarities, the poems and brazen songs, of feudal lords and minions.

Austin Buggy's voice blasted through the foreign accents.

'My dear fellow!' He took Mulligan's hand in a firm, two-handed grip, smiling, and bade him welcome with the group. 'Upstairs, dear hearts. This place down here is for hoi polloi.'

He led the way up the steep spiral stone staircase into a small room hung with tapestries and old portraits. In the centre was a big oak table. Two girls in green poplin dresses were standing at one end, hovering over a tray of champagne bottles and glasses.

'Marie, Dolores! A thirsty group approaches. Champagne for our friends of the all-powerful medium. Or should I say media, yes? We do have a newspaperman, do we not?'

Dinneen, who had stood glowering at the scene downstairs,

and still had his face fixed in a rictus of disapproval, was introduced by Mulligan.

'Delighted to meet you, my dear fellow, I've heard a lot about you,' Buggy said.

The others had moved on up the table and were taking the glasses of champagne.

Buggy lightly caught Virginia's arm as she made to follow them, and, in a voice that could be heard only by the three of them, said to Crossan, 'Stephen, for God's sake hold this stunning woman down here. My God!'

Crossan said, 'Now, now, Austin. I've told her all about you.'

Buggy said to a greatly amused Virginia, 'What did he tell you, my dear? About my heart attack? That I'm a cripple? Lies, every bit of it. I'm as vigorous as a young foal, by God.' He looked into Virginia's eyes. 'What a remarkably beautiful woman. Don't move a muscle till I return, bearing a modest glass of the most delicious Épernay.'

He slowly backed away from her and then momentarily immersed himself in the group at the top.

Virginia said, 'Did he mean all that?'

Crossan said, 'Does it matter?'

'No.'

After a pause, Crossan said, 'I love that man.'

'And you love J.J.'

'That's right.'

'You seem to confine your love to men.'

Buggy was back, bearing champagne. 'Actually, you people think this bubbly is for you. Truth is, it's for me. No more liquor. What a pain, eh, Stephen?' His eyes shone. 'I *have* to drink champagne. Well' – he raised his glass – 'here's to the exquisite Virginia Green.'

They drank. He said, 'Well, my dear, don't you love the timid, sober Irish?'

'Some of them don't like to be loved.'

'I've never met an Irish man or woman who didn't want to be loved.'

'I have.'

He turned and tapped the table, unaware of the import of Virginia's words.

'Ladies and gentlemen. You are all most welcome. Some of

you I know of old. J. J. Haslam, my old friend, who has given me hours of pleasure. The lovely Alice Foley, who has steadfastly refused to do so.' He bobbed delicately to the laughter. 'The majestic Oliver, and of course our teen-age Turk, Stephen Crossan. I hope you will all have a pleasant evening. I further hope that when your film is shown in the US, it will persuade thousands of your countrymen to visit our little parish. We need their money, bluntly, and we try to part them from it as pleasantly as possible.'

The mixture of grit and fanciful phrase had long been Buggy's hallmark.

'Isn't there any better way of getting money into the area than this?'

Dinneen's question sounded louder and more brash than he had intended. He was a visitor and a guest, and he knew that his question would cause embarrassment. But he was driven by a need to show that he was of a tough breed, unimpressed by the frippery around him.

Buggy smiled serenely and placed his glass on the table. 'I am sure, Mr Dinneen, that there are a thousand better ways of getting money into the place than this. I have tried a few dozen of them in my time, and they all failed, for one reason or another. This one works.'

'Don't you think the whole thing is kinda false? I mean all those kids dressed up, that kind of thing?'

'I would have thought that all entertainment is false, if I take your meaning correctly . . .'

'But this is supposed to be authentic. You call this a medieval banquet. The real Irish never had anything like this.'

Buggy placed his thumbs inside his vest, and spoke with relish – and not for the first time. 'Mr Dinneen, in the heyday of this castle the people you insist on calling the real Irish lived in wattle huts, wore goatskin knickers, and passed their days hunting and eating gruel. We could have built a few wattle huts and dressed people up in goatskin knickers and hoped that tourists would flock to them and enjoy the smelly discomforts. But tourists, particularly from *your* country, while they love to think of themselves as going native, actually like to go native with central heating, air conditioning and showers. Very difficult in wattle huts. So we renovated the castle. The people who owned and inhabited this place from its earliest days were just as Irish as the real Irish you are so anxious about. Now we have no solid documentation as to how they behaved themselves while they were eating, but from what we do know, it seemed hardly desirable to reproduce *exactly* the conditions which prevailed at the time.'

'You're saying it's not authentic, then?'

'It brings badly needed money into my parish, Mr Dinneen. For me it's very authentic.'

'Crap,' Dinneen said, and replaced his glass.

'And now folks, if you would like to file down the way you came, your first remove awaits you.'

They went out, and Buggy watched them go.

When they had gone, he turned to Mulligan. 'Another Brooklyn patriot, Oliver?'

'Why do we always have to go to New York to find out who the real Irish are?'

Crossan said, 'I think we three fakes should amble down with heads bowed.'

In the large dining room the girls were already serving. The hall was alive with conversation and laughter, the Lord and Lady of the Castle, from Pittsburgh, sat proudly on their thrones, and Maynard recorded the happy scene.

Ober watched the girls go about their work briskly and cheerily, and said to Virginia, 'They seem to be enjoying themselves.'

'Maybe they are.'

'I'll fry that bastard Dinneen.'

'Don't let him get to you. He's not worth it.'

'He's part of the group. They might think . . .'

Crossan interrupted. 'We don't think any such thing.'

Ober let himself go, in his dislike for the columnist. 'He's what I thought all Irishmen were like.'

'Our faults are different,' the young man said, with that air that so annoyed the producer. 'Think of what it's like for us. He thinks he's on our side.'

The first remove was taken away, and the second put in its place without fuss. Buggy's brainchild had been in operation for fifteen years, and year after year the management recruited young women who were attractive, thoroughly Irish with fine singing voices. And they were very efficient. Every night they served spareribs and passable wine, every night they were confronted with the same painted American faces, suffused with innocent enjoyment. And every night they maintained an even temper in the face of the monotony, hanging bibs on the hundreds of guests with a snappy 'Your napkin, my lord', serving, clearing away, refilling, assembling in a statuesque group on the podium to sing in perfect harmony and seeming enjoyment.

The master of ceremonies, a young man dressed in doublet and hose, drew stentorian attention to himself.

Haslam was sitting next to Ellen when the young man began to speak. 'My lords, ladies and gentlemen!' The author looked up, stared, and then his eyes grew large with shock. He reached out and gripped Ellen's forearm very tightly, never taking his eyes from the young man. The young man called the guests to order and Haslam finally turned to Ellen and said, 'It's Peter. Merciful hour, it's my son.'

Ellen turned quickly to look at Peter Haslam. She smiled and turned back and put the writer's hands in both of hers and said, 'You've got a famous son.'

Haslam shook his head in wonder.

So this was where he had ended up.

Peter stood on the podium, looking faintly ridiculous to his father, but perfectly at ease in himself. The author was suddenly overwhelmed by a sense of his own inadequacy while his son was growing up; a sense of his own lack of caring, his own irresponsibility. For all the sympathy which he had garnered for rearing his son on his own, in a closet of his mind he was aware that he had been too preoccupied with his own writing and radio programmes to care much how his son grew to manhood. Writing, drinking, talking with friends, travelling the country, preparing his series – these had all been diverting and pleasurable. But Peter had been a tiresome chore, and it was only the most profane sense of guilt that had occasionally caused him to inquire into his son's progress. He knew the boy was lonely – he had often watched him as he played frantically with half-a-dozen 'friends', battled with 'monsters', stumbled through 'woods', all of them having existence only in the child's mind – but to sit down with him and give him time was so wearisome. And the child had no interest in the written word, a profound disappointment to his father.

Thus they had drifted apart, even before young Peter went

off to boarding school. The distance between them became abysmal, until by his final year Peter talked to his father as though to a stranger. So he drifted, and changed his name – how he had hated it at school when he was asked to read his father's curricular essays – and now he was head of entertainment and chief barker at Cranmore.

The writer forgot his food, to the clucking disapproval of the serving lady, and kept trying to catch his son's eye. Later, as Peter passed him, the father caught his arm. Peter stopped, momentarily nonplussed, and then he said, 'Jayses, J.J.' and put his arms around his father's neck, hugging him.

The tears welling in Haslam's eyes were quickly brushed away with a napkin. The rest of the company – except Ellen, who smiled enigmatically through it – looked on bemused, never having seen the writer behave in such an ostentatiously human manner before. In the castle hall, surrounded by noisy Americans, father and son came together, the years of attrition dissolved. The son exuded a spiritual freedom and happiness in his job that made it an easy meeting.

Minutes later, after a word with Maynard, Peter Haslam went to the podium and announced, 'My lord! We have a traitor among us!'

Laughter.

'My lord! We beg to know your punishment for the said traitor!'

More laughter.

'The dungeon,' Pittsburgh shouted hoarsely.

Two young men in doublet and hose lifted Dinneen from his seat and dragged him across the hall, his eyes bulging with shock and humiliation. The crowd roared, the dungeon gates rattled open, and the fearless spectator was flung in, to land on the foam-rubber mattresses hidden out of sight behind the doors.

Maynard did a tiny dance behind his camera. Ober smiled.

'My lord!' the young Haslam cried after a moment or two. 'The prisoner begs for mercy.'

'I guess we'd better let him out,' Pittsburgh said.

The gates were opened, Dinneen was helped out, and he walked straight across the hall, his red and bulbous face made even redder by the light of the log fire, his black eyes insensate with anger.

206

Austin Buggy slipped out the door after him, and Crossan and Mulligan followed, too, leaving word with the others that they would be at the pub.

Outside, Crossan said, 'That Maynard's the very devil.'

'Thanks be to God for that.'

Buggy already had Dinneen sitting on a stool in the pub upstairs, having put a large Paddy in his hand.

Dinneen looked up as they approached.

Buggy ordered drinks and said, 'I'm trying to convince this man that we are not the con men that he makes us out to be. Tell me, Frank – may I call you Frank?'

Dinneen nodded.

'What's so awful about the spectacle of five hundred people enjoying themselves?'

'I told you.'

'Not good enough. Look, I'm retiring in a few months, so you can hear what I have to say . . .'

'You mean I can quote you?'

'You can fucking well quote me till the cows come home. What do you think, I'm afraid of you or something? I was afraid for long enough. Frankie, my boy, in my years here I've dealt with every kind of newspaperman and – with a few marvellous exceptions, for whom God be praised – you're all the same. The first chance you get to put the screws on someone like myself or the boys here – people who can't fight back – you lay it on. You all think you're the greatest. And columnists are the worst of all because the American people let them do their thinking for them. Walter Winchells all.'

Dinneen said, 'What's so Walter Winchell about saying that you're running an ersatz operation here?'

'Ersatz! Ersatz!' Buggy almost shouted. 'How dare you come over here and tell me what ersatz is. You, an *American*, telling me what's *ersatz*!'

The other two listened as Buggy continued, both of them deeply envying the freedom of speech that Buggy's impending retirement gave him. His diatribe was merely the explosion that had been simmering for all those years of bowing and scraping to people like Dinneen.

'Listen, Frankie, me lad,' he said, leaning forward, his mouth tightening, 'this entertainment, this castle, is *my* doing. The castle and the village give direct employment to nearly fifty people, and the cooperatives and craft centres a few hundred more. That's *my* contribution.'

'I'm not denying your contribution. I'm just . . .'

'Whisht, boy!' Buggy's voice cracked around the empty bar. '*My* contribution has been to bring about employment for several hundred people. What has yours been? Don't bother to answer. I'll tell you. Your bullshit has persuaded people to send hundreds of thousands of dollars to a crowd of murdering gangsters who want to drag us back a hundred years or more. That's what your contribution has been. I help people to live. You help them to get shot or bombed.'

'That's a load of crap and you know it.'

'I'll ignore that,' Buggy said, suddenly quiet. 'I'm used to ignoring things. When I came here first and got Cranmore going, I used to wait in terror to see what you and your smart-ass colleagues would say about the venture. There were some decent ones, God knows, and we are forever in their debt. But then there was your type, Frankie, my lad, and I'd bring them along here and feed them and pour booze into them – and Jesus, what booze, because one thing people like you are pathologically incapable of doing is putting your hands in your pockets and buying a drink – and they would wallow in the hospitality and then go back and trot out their puerile snideries. It could have meant my job, you know that? And the jobs of hundreds of others. Much you give a fuck, though, because all you and your type understand is shafting, especially people like me, who have no redress. There is another difference, of course, between you and me, and it is very important and it explains a lot.' He leaned forward under Dinneen's face, his bald head shining in the lamplight. 'I, Frankie, am an Irishman. You're just a Mick.'

He leaned back and smiled broadly to draw the poison. Crossan and Mulligan looked at the floor. The big American stared at the counter. He was growing totally dispirited with the Irish, but then these were not the true Irish, the real Irish.

'I guess I'd better go.'

'Stay awhile, Frankie boy.' Buggy put his hand on Dinneen's arm. 'I want you to take a message back to New York for me. I know you won't write what I've just told you, but you might get drunk some night – some night when someone else is paying – and pass on the word to the other Mick know-alls in the

Big Apple, the posturing half-Paddies who turn the Lion's Head into a sheep's arse. But before I give you the message, maybe you'd buy a drop for three impoverished lackeys?'

Dinneen bought and paid.

'Tell them to stay in New York, Frankie. We don't want them over here. Unless, that is, they are prepared to return and tell their fellow New Yorkers that what we are doing here is beautiful and good and true. *Ersatz!* Merciful Jayses. They sit over there in their dark bars drinking that horsepiss they call beer and they bewail the disappearance of the true Ireland. They bemoan the ersatz entertainment that we put on for their gullible countrymen. They sneer at people like myself who try to bring money into the country. We're shallow, we're false, we're frauds. And we have to sit back and take it all. But it's easy for me to do that now. When I was growing up the people ran out of Clare in droves, young people. Not any more. It hasn't all been my doing, not by a long chalk. But there's no emigration from here now. No desperate, disillusioned young men and women taking the boat for Holyhead or the plane for New York to rear a generation of pups like yourself. And we brought that about. Do you understand that? *We* did it. And I don't give two knobs of goat's shite what you think of the *ways* in which we did it. If those girls in the castle had to eat shamrock from the arse of a West Clare jennet, I wouldn't care, if it kept them in Ireland, in employment, in hope. Do you understand me? You wanted to go off and find the real Ireland. Well, look at me, Frankie boy. Look at me! I am the real Ireland, and if you don't like it you can fuck off back to New York and drink yourself to death, dreaming of thatched cottages and shawls and petticoats and donkeys. That's what drove your parents out of this country, and by Jayses we won't let it happen again.'

He leaned back and drank again, letting his words sink in to Dinneen's resistant mind and soul. But only for a minute. Then he said, 'Well, amn't I the terror, surely,' in a broad West Clare accent, 'to be goin' on the like o' that at ye. An' ye only a poor innocent Yank avisitin'. There's no stoppin' us Oirish when we gets goin', don't ye know. We're the devil's own talkers.'

Dinneen said nothing. Buggy ordered more drink, And more. He kept trying to bring Dinneen into the conversation – 'You're among friends, my dear fellow. No grudges allowed in this house' – but it was in vain. The columnist had no ability to let bygones be bygones, to shrug off Buggy's high-flown insults.

All three Irishmen, though, felt a certain sympathy for the man, if only he could know it. While his rudeness, his arrogance his contempt for their work made him an impossible man to be friendly with, his ignorance about Ireland was something which all three had to live with.

Most Irish-Americans – there were nearly twenty million of them – had no interest in Ireland and knew little or nothing about it. But even among the small group who were interested, there was an appalling ignorance. Their concern was patent, but it continually lurched in the wrong direction, and their misunderstanding of the true value of an operation like Buggy's was only a minor and unimportant part of a far greater misunderstanding.

A great number of them, decent people for the most part, simply could not grasp that the government of the Republic was a freely elected government, not a front for British interests. It was a source of constant horror to people such as Crossan, Mulligan and Buggy, that certain Irish-Americans supported groups whose aim, as much as any other, was to bring down the democratically elected government of the Republic. These very same Irish-Americans were the most frighteningly right-wing and reactionary people in America, stamping viciously on any form of radicalism, screaming blue murder at the first rebel whimper.

But they saw in the Irish government a vehicle for Britain, and they held to this view even in spite of visits to the Republic, where the state of the country could be seen to be less than perfect, but could not be reprehended as a democracy, or as near a democracy as one could hope for. They were not helped towards a rational view by the constant strident haranguing of people like Freddy Barton, who told them to give ear to a gang of Northern Protestants who for half a century had run a regime which was rank with corruption, bigotry and sectarianism. And Freddy Barton was a member of the government of the Republic. So the government of the Republic was on the side of the Northern bigots. Who were on the side of Britain. So the government of the Republic was on the side of Britain.

So the government should be brought down.

It was a neat circle of folly. It gave comfort to thousands of Dinneens in New York and Boston and Chicago. It gave great pain to Buggy and Crossan and Mulligan and others like them.

The door opened and in came Haslam, his son on one arm, Ellen on the other. The rest followed, and then came the ladies from the castle.

They sang into the late hours, good songs, happy faces.

22

Tony O'Riordan, the bard of Cahirciveen, sat behind the microphone, bubbles of saliva and stout at the corners of his mouth, singing the local anthem. The large platform was set up in the town square and his thin, amplified voice rang out over the slate roofs.

> 'You may travel from Boston to Ballinaglen,
> From London to Ballaghadereen,
> But no girls will you find
> That would put you in mind
> Of the colleens of Cahirciveen.
>
> 'They are stately and fair
> With the grandest of hair
> And their cheeks are the fairest you've seen.
> For twelve months of the year
> There's none can compare
> With our beautiful dear Carrot Queen.'

The throng in the square took up the chorus, arms linked. The pubs of Cahirciveen were full.

Tonight, the Carrot Queen would be chosen and would wear the crown for twelve months, taking with her 'a splendid cash prize of £1000 and the much coveted Golden Carrot Award', according to the brochure issued by the Cahirciveen Carrot Queen Festival Committee.

Forty-five Carrot Princesses had arrived in the town from all over the world, and after preliminary 'meetings' – after the first Festival the word *heats* had been dropped – the judges had chosen twelve to go through to tonight's final, basing their choice on 'uprightness, intelligence and personality', for the virtues of a good Carrot Queen were those not of the professional beauty, but of the good housewife.

The competitors were from New Jersey, Limerick, Los Angeles, Bristol, Frankfurt, Dublin, London, Belfast, South Boston, Cahirciveen itself, Brussels, and Martinique. The various centres each year chose a Princess under franchise from the Festival Committee, which was run by a third-generation returned Yank named Mrs Amelia Line, known to the locals as the Widdah Line.

Forty-five young men were selected from Cahirciveen and the surrounding areas to act as 'Bucks' to the Carrot Princesses from the time they arrived to departure, and these young men, also, were chosen for their uprightness, intelligence and personality. One Buck, some years back, had impulsively followed his charge to Philadelphia, only to be sent packing back to Cahirciveen by the girl's amused parents. Otherwise, as far as anyone knew, there had never been any untowardness in the Bucks' behaviour.

The day had started late.

Haslam could not be awoken in the Pery Grand in Limerick, and Ellen was not in her room. The rest of the party walked around the hotel, bumping into each other all over the place and pointedly saying nothing about the reason for the delay. Towards midday, Haslam and Ellen had come into the hotel together, Ellen calmly telling a diffident Ober that departure time on her schedule was twelve o'clock. 'And here I am.' She was beaming.

In fact Ellen had risen early, awakened by Haslam's telephone call.

'I'm sorry for waking you, but I can't sleep and I was wondering if you would care to ramble with me through my hometown?'

'I'd love to.' She did not need to force any enthusiasm in her acceptance of his invitation. With each day that passed, she sensed herself coming closer to the lonely, often acerbic novelist. She felt that there was a deep scar in the man which was not entirely attributable to being deserted by a beautiful young wife. He seemed reconciled to that. She knew that even the greatest bitterness became tempered by the years; she also knew that the writer's public persona, both his frequent bile and his infrequent compassion, were salient marks of a deep and troubled and lonely soul. She felt the sense of a man who had failed at trying not to be good.

Most of all, she felt that he understood her, the self that she carefully and nervously guarded. She felt that she could trust J. J. Haslam.

So she showered and dressed and made herself beautiful, and exulted in an almost forgotten sense of anticipation. They breakfasted alone in the empty dining room and sallied forth onto Sarsfield Bridge, where they paused for a while, looking down on the swift Shannon river.

Haslam pointed to the greensward on the bank.

'That used to be called the poor man's Kilkee. Every summer Saturday and Sunday it was full of old men and women, too poor to give themselves a seaside holiday. But they'd get the sun there and the river flowed past them, and they could use their imaginations. I used to be given to the theory that you get more writers from the poorer classes because they have to use their imaginations more. The rich can purchase their fantasies. But the theory doesn't really hold up, what? Mr Tolstoy was no pauper.'

They crossed the road to the other side of the bridge and he pointed up the river to Thomond Bridge and the Treaty Stone. 'Limerick is called the city of the broken treaty. But God knows every city in Ireland could be so called. There's King John's Castle down there on your right. A noble remnant. But you'll notice that the local Corporation has built public housing in it. That's the respect these people have for the past.' He turned around and pointed downriver to a green-and-white concrete office block. 'And that's the respect they have for the future. Worse than Dublin. But not much. There used to be an Irish parliamentarian named Boyle Roche,' he said, as they walked off the bridge into Sarsfield Street, 'who was famous for his bulls.'

'His bulls?'

'Not the four-legged kind, but rather an obvious contradiction that points up the Irishman's boneheadedness.'

'Can you give me an example?'

'Well, Boyle Roche's most notorious one was uttered when someone questioned the rightness of something on behalf of posterity, and he gave his immortal riposte, "Why should we do anything for posterity? What has posterity ever done for us?" '

Ellen laughed, but her companion did not. 'Boyle Roche wasn't half the fool he's made out to be,' he said, as they walked up William Street, the main shopping street. 'He was probably speaking for most Irish people when he said what he said. And he would be speaking for most of them if he said it today. Other nations are spurred by responsibility to their descendants. The Irish find perpetual impulse in the past. It is more real than the present or the future. The whole island is one large commemoration.'

'I like that, in a kind of a way.'

'Sure you do. It's quaint.'

'I don't mean that, J.J. That was hurtful.'

Haslam squeezed her hand in sincere contrition. 'My sweet girl, you mustn't take a blind bit of notice of the things that I say.'

They reached the Christian Brothers School in Sexton Street and Haslam stood before it, his face to the iron bars, holding tight to Ellen's arm, silent.

She said, 'Happy memories?'

'Mostly. The mind is a merciful editor.'

Down Sexton Street he led her and quickly past Parnell Street, a barren waste worse than any in bombarded Belfast, past Matterson's bacon factory, now an empty shell, a car park. 'My late brother used to work there once. But he left it. He was a Catholic, of course, and there was no future for a Catholic in Matterson's office at that time.'

'Down here?' She was shocked.

'Oh, yes, my girl. Down here. Sometimes I get a bit bothered when I hear Northern Catholics talking as if they suffered all the discrimination in this country. There was plenty of it down here, too, and even up to the fifties there wasn't much future for a Catholic in this firm. Oh the fools, the fools, There was a time when the Czar of all the Russias used to get Limerick bacon from within those walls there. Now look at it.'

He took her into Tom Collins's cosy snug in Cecil Street, remarking the painting hanging on the wall. 'How many publicans' sons become artists, do you think?'

Tom Collins brought a pint for the writer, and Ellen, wild, had a gin and tonic.

Haslam said to the owner, 'This wouldn't be the first today, would it?'

'A few before you this morning.'

'Good.'

Haslam drank and pointed out to Ellen, in the event that she ever became a pint drinker, that she should never take the first-poured pint in the morning. 'It could ruin your whole day.'

'I must say I find this whole pint ritual very amusing.'

'There's nothing amusing about a bad pint of stout, dearest Ellen. Drinking is a serious business, and pint drinking is a very serious business indeed. I know a man who drank twenty-two pints one Saturday in Dublin and when he got sick at two o'clock that morning he insisted that there must have been one bad pint among them.' He smiled at the thought. 'But then you don't have to worry about these things. In a few days you'll be back in New York, never to return again.'

He looked at her, a beige beauty, one leg draped over the other, her hands stretched forward, the thin tapering fingers folding gently down on her knee. She was infinitely graceful, and she had infinite repose, and Haslam was entranced.

'I shall be back.'

He quivered on the edge of word play that he had not used for a long time.

'And what would bring you back to this benighted isle?'

'The beauty of the country. The people. The surprises.'

'The surprises?'

'Every day, there's a surprise.'

'What was today's?'

'Your call this morning.'

'It was a nice surprise?'

'It was a lovely surprise.'

'Would you like another call in the morning?'

She looked at his sad eyes, full of knowledge, and, now, love. 'I'd prefer if you didn't have to call.'

He leaned over and took her face in his hands and kissed her softly, and they drew apart and looked into each other's eyes for a long time in silence.

At the reception to meet the twelve finalists in the Carrot Queen Festival, the group mixed with the contestants, and

Virginia said, 'It'd be cute if the kid from Martinique won it.'

The twelve young girls had smiled for an hour in the small room, fielding the questions of locals and visitors with varying degrees of confidence. 'New Jersey looks promising.' 'Frankfurt has a great chance.' 'I'll put me money on Brussels, by Jayses.'

The Widdah Line brought diminutive Martinique across the room to meet them. She ushered her little charge up before Virginia's tall figure, saying, 'I thought you two might like to meet each other.' She gabbled on in a Florida-garnished Brooklyn accent, her face heavily painted, the makeup pointing up her facial hair in small, sticky clusters.

She stood admiringly while the two black women swopped banalities, failing to achieve the immediate racial rapport that the Widdah wished on them. Virginia did her best, and Martinique tried to respond through a brilliant smile, her words hesitant, careful and heavy with responsibility. She did not know who was judging her. None of the contestants did. Every conversation was a confrontation, fraught with the threat of failure and low marks. Uprightness, intelligence and personality must imbue every sentence, every movement, every reaction. Not for them the blitzing, fraudulent charm of the beauty queen.

The Widdah Line led her charge away, saying again. 'I just thought you two should meet each other,' and Martinique was hawked along to meet another possible judge, her smile set and unwavering.

Around the room the other contestants were engaged in earnest bobbing and bowing and smiling and talking, never interrupting, rarely laughing, their Bucks in rented tuxedoes hovering at their shoulders, muscular Kerry duennas.

In Moriarty's Select Lounge and Bar, a man stood up and waved a wad of notes. 'Four to one Frankfurt! Sixes Kingston and Bristol! Eights Limerick! Ten to one bar!'

He shuffled around the pub, collecting money from the punters. 'I see de little darky is de favourite.' 'An' shur de best of luck to her.' 'Jayses, I'd say she have a lovely little cunth.'

Nobody in Cahirciveen had any idea where Martinique was. There had never before been an entrant from that country, and when the letter had come from Fort-de-France, the Committee had happily accepted the nomination of Ilona O'Neill, 'who is eighteen, and whose great-grandfather, Captain Patrick O'Neill, is believed to have come from Ireland in 1852. Ilona is very interested in Ireland, and has written an essay on London which her teachers admired much.'

Now she was sitting among eleven others on the platform in the square, while the Widdah Line told of the Festival history.

'. . . In those twelve years it has gone from strength to strength . . .'

Crossan said to Virginia, 'This takes half an hour. And there are more to come.'

She followed him into the pub, and the Widdah's Brooklyn vowels came through the open window. 'And last year's Carrot Queen, I know you will all be very happy to know, 'cause she was a very popular Queen, has become betrothed to a very fine young man who is a doctor in her native Pocatello, Idaho. They are both with us here tonight, and I know you all want to give them a big hand.'

Applause and shouts.

Crossan brought a pint and a Daiquiri. Virginia smoked her pipe

He said, 'I've been thinking about what you said to me.'

'Good boy.'

'I'd like to try it, but it's probably impossible.'

'To be honest with me?'

'Yes.'

'Why?'

'I've grown out of the habit. If indeed I ever had it.'

He could still, she thought, sound exasperatingly didactic and pompous.

'Why don't you like honesty?'

'I've seen it do too much damage. I've met a few young people' – he said the word 'young' with distaste – 'who believe in this total honesty nonsense. Tell it like it is. Let it all hang out. So they go around telling ugly people they're ugly, and stupid people that they're stupid. "I'm only telling you that you're plain and ignorant because I know you want me to be honest with you," ' he mimicked. 'I've seen the *pain* these honest people cause. They would be better off lying.'

Virginia said, 'You're just afraid to let yourself go.'

'That's a typical American woman's interpretation.'

'A façade.'

'I thought we had agreed on that a long time ago.'

'Why don't you do something about it?'

'Why should I?'

'It would make you human.'

'Nothing could be more human than pretence. The world runs on it.'

From outside came the Widdah's drone. '. . . to repeat that the judges have made their choice based on uprightness, intelligence and personality. I would also like to assure those who have not made it that in the opinion of many people they are fine girls and would make fine wives for any man.'

'Maybe you need a shrink,' Virginia said.

Crossan blanched. 'Not me. I'm Irish.'

'And the Irish don't need analysis?'

He laughed. 'Not this one.'

'What are you afraid of?'

'I think,' he said slowly, 'that I'm afraid of nothing and of nobody.'

'Then why are you so uptight, for Chrissakes? Let it all hang out, man!'

'I don't *want* to let it all hang out. Don't you understand that?' His eyes were alight, his voice low and urgent. 'You . . . you *modern* person. I want privacy for things. I want it all *inside*. I *like* my inhibitions. Letting it all hang out is a load of rubbish. I don't want any neurotic clomping around my mind with a torch, pretending to understand me, telling me to shed my inhibitions. Inhibitions are the root and glory of civilization, and I *love* inhibitions. If I didn't have inhibitions, Virginia, if I weren't weighed down with all kinds of guilts and complexes, I'd be a very unhappy man indeed.'

'You know,' she said slowly, 'I almost believe you would.'

'I'm just being honest.'

'Would you say you're a typical Irishman?'

'I wouldn't say I'm a typical anything.'

'How about J.J.?'

'Maybe. Maybe not. He's not like a lot of Irishmen that I know.'

'You all have two things you love to do.'

'What?'

'Talking and singing.'

'Where are you leaving drinking?'

'You drink to keep you talking and singing.'

He mused on the lurking truth.

The Irish queer was cynically defined as a man who preferred women to drink. It might be redefined as a man who preferred women to talking. He remembered being in Las Vegas some years before with a group of Irishmen on their way to a meeting in San Francisco. The hookers lined the hotel bar like moss, faces pert, or worn, or sad, or exhausted. One of the Irishmen had taken pity on a lonely young woman. 'Come on up and have a jar at the bar, not to be sitting on your own down there.' She came up, and she drank two drinks, and after half an hour of earnest one-sided conversation the young whore realized that the Irishman really did want to talk to her, was interested in her, wanted to make her happy, would give an ear to her problems and try to allay them with drinks. She slid from the stool, muttering about freaks, and stumbled away from the group, leaving a hurt and unhappy Irishman at the bar.

Later that evening the Irish contingent had held a singsong in one of the hotel rooms. At three o'clock in the morning, Crossan opened the door to an angry security man.

'What the hell's going on here?'

'Nothing. We're just having a singsong.'

'A what?' He peered into the room, noting the dozen men sprawled on beds and settees, singing.

'A singsong,' Crossan repeated. 'We're just singing.'

'Jesus Christ,' the man said hoarsely, 'you know who's downstairs? Perry Como. And Mel Tormé is next door. And Dean Martin and Liza Minnelli. And you guys are singing *to each other?*'

Crossan remembered the sheer disbelief in the man's face.

'Fucking ding-a-lings,' he said, and walked away.

Talk, talk, talk and sing, sing, sing. All in the blood.

There was a loud roar in the square.

He said, 'Somebody has won a coveted Golden Carrot.'

From the platform, a voice said, 'Ah am prahd to hab de honna to be Irish,' and Virginia threw her arms around Crossan and said, 'She's won it!'

Crossan smiled wearily and said, 'We're a great people, no doubt about it,' and she went off to do an interview.

Twenty minutes later, in the door came Tony O'Riordan and the Widdah Line, the new Carrot Queen radiant between them. The television crew followed them in, work done, and the group became large.

Champagne flowed, a fiddle started. Out in the square, the music blared from the platform, which had now been taken over by middle-aged people vigorously dancing sets. The people down in the square laughed and tooted and swung in and out, slipping, falling, clapping backs, grabbing behinds, their faces alight with an inebriation that was only minimally alcoholic.

They had a new Queen – 'our first little nigger Queen', as one of them happily remarked. The evening was warm, the bars were open wide, and they set about enjoying themselves without worry.

Mulligan's shoulder was tapped by Arthur Whelan, 'Ireland's leading hotelier', a powerful voice in tourism. Mulligan rose out of his seat as though it were a bed of nettles. 'Arthur! What a pleasant surprise! And Alison, too. This is wonderful!'

Alison Whelan was on her father's arm, smiling and looking round the group. Her father stood beside her, waiting for Mulligan to arrange seats for them. There could not have been a more incongruous pair. She was tall to almost six feet while he was little over five. She was blonde, and he was jet-black and oleaginous. His skin was yellow and desiccated, where hers was pink and healthy.

Mulligan introduced the couple with bellowing first-name familiarity: he loathed Whelan with his every fibre. He hated his philistinism – 'the man's soul is in his trousers pocket' – he hated his mercantile success, his semiliteracy, his total lack of charm, wit or originality.

But now he was an engine of industry, seeking after everyone's comfort, ostentatiously paying for the drink.

Pete Ober had not taken his eyes off Alison from the moment she entered the bar. When he discovered that she was to join them he was happy, and much happier when she sat beside him, smiling all over him and saying, 'Hello, I'm Alison. Are you the cameraman?'

'No. I'm the director.'

'I should have guessed. You have that look of authority.'

He drank in her openness and gaiety, as well as the compliment in her remark. 'What do you do?' he asked.

'I'm an accountant.'

'An accountant!'

She laughed. 'Look at your face. Yes. An accountant, Peter. Sounds dreary, doesn't it? And I'll let you in on a secret. It is dreary. But daddy says I must know how to handle the books if I'm ever to do anything in business.'

'And you're going into your father's business?'

'Peter, I've been in daddy's business since the day I was born.'

'That's not really answering my question.'

She looked rueful. 'You know what I'd really like to be?'

He shook his head.

She pointed to Virginia. 'I'd like to be doing that girl's job.'

'You certainly have the looks.'

'Ooh, I knew today was my lucky day. Have you got a contract with you?'

And when Ober looked up, mouth open, she laughed again and he laughed with her, and she told him that she had been Carrot Queen three years before, and she asked him if he had seen Dingle and he said no, and she said he should see it before he returned to the US and he said he'd love to. So she said she would call for him the following morning and take him back along the Ring and out on the Dingle Peninsula, 'and bring your swimming things and we'll go right out to the end of Inch Strand – you know where they made *Ryan's Daughter*? – and there are great breakers there and we'll have a terrific time. Would anyone else want to come?' she asked him.

'They might. If we asked them.'

'Shall we ask them?'

'No way.'

Meanwhile the blithe girl's father had just said to Ellen that he went to Las Vegas every year, and when she asked in reflective surprise why he went there, he said that Ireland had a lot to learn from Las Vegas.

Then he turned to Ilona O'Neill and asked about Martinique. 'I was never there. I'd like to see it sometime. Where is it exactly?'

She explained the geographical position of her island, and immediately went on to tell him of the population, the main industries, the principal exports. It came out pat, the result of many hours of rehearsal, and Whelan looked at her as one would at a pickled insect in a museum.

The room was now filled to overflowing. Outside, the music and singing and dancing continued, musicians taking up perches in the street and starting impromptu sessions, groups of young men prowling in search of partners, who were easy to find.

Whelan made motions to leave, looking over at his daughter. But she had no eyes for him tonight, immersed as she was in Pete Ober and his stories of his visits to the White House, and the Democratic Convention in Chicago in '68, his problems with people as diverse as Tallulah Bankhead, Lyndon Johnson, Jimi Hendrix and John Steinbeck.

The producer was metamorphosed. He nodded and blinked and smiled and laughed with a naturalness that up to now had been unmercifully battened. Alison's face was close to his, her eyes bright with interest, one long leg over the other, a glass of whiskey in her left hand while she gesticulated gracefully with her right. The whiskey was unusual. Not many young women drank it. Her blonde good looks were unusual. But most unusual of all was an almost frantically genuine presence, as though every moment of her life were precious and must be filled.

She waved to her father. 'I'll be along later,' and he said to Virginia, 'Well, I hope your programme is a success for CBS.'

Mulligan chuckled with embarrassment. 'It's NBS, actually.'

'Well, whichever one it is, I hope it makes a lot of money for you. And a lot of dollars for us. Plenty of dollars, that's the name of the game.'

He went off, and Mulligan mopped his brow.

'Relax, Oliver,' Haslam said. 'I was going to suggest that you make friends with the man's daughter, but she seems to be spoken for now.'

They all looked down to the chatting couple at the end.

'A beautiful girl, a beautiful girl,' Mulligan said, almost in disbelief.

Ellen said, 'A beautiful name, too. Is Alison an Irish name?'

'Not *exactly*,' Mulligan said, with heavy sarcasm. 'But who's to say what is, nowadays?' he added in lighter tones. 'New names for the new Ireland.'

It was happening all over the country.

Patrick and Nuala brought forth not a Kevin or a Sean, nor a Mary or a Bridget, but a Derek or a Jason or a Mark, an Alison or a Joyce or a Wendy. 'Would you not think of giving the child a saint's name?' the priests whimpered.

'That's the name we've chosen, father.' Sometimes they said more.

Haslam sang, 'I oft times think of home, De Oley Aye,' and Alice joined in. Crossan and Mulligan began to sing, too, and the song spread in waves across the pub.

> 'And when at last my journey here is o'er,
> Twill ring more joyfully than e'er before,
> Far up to heaven I will take my lay,
> The angels too will sing Dee Oley Aye.'

When the applause died, Tony O'Riordan called for order for a song from Martinique. 'Come on now, by Jayses, any Carrot Queen that's halfway dacent should be able to give us a few bars.'

Ilona smiled nervously, and when O'Riordan's request had been translated into plain language, she sang a small song in a sad, light voice, and when she had finished O'Riordan shouted, 'Sure that's "The Cobbler's Lament for His Lost Tool".'

As people everywhere had Irish grandmothers, so did songs.

Haslam turned to Ellen. She was sweetly inebriated.

They left through the din and went back to their hotel. They made gentle, undemanding love in Ellen's bed; she came quickly, and he sighed with internal relief, for he had felt the first pang of the familiar crush inside his chest. He rolled off and put his hand over his heart, and when she opened her eyes and saw how he lay and where his hand was, she slid down his body and in a few minutes she drank in his essence. He thanked her quietly, and they went to sleep.

23

To everyone's relief, Pete Ober declared the following day a day of rest.

The group was tired, the day was fine. Maynard went off with Larry the driver, carrying a Hasselblad and a variety of lenses. 'For my bathroom wall,' he said.

Alison Whelan, healthy and wholesome and dressed all in blue with a blue Jacqmar scarf tied gypsy-style around her blonde hair, called for the producer at eleven o'clock. She was no less effervescent than on the previous evening, and Ober called her 'my blue angel'.

On the road, which she drove carefully in her Sunbeam Alpine, she kept up a steady stream of information and anecdotes.

'I adore Kerry, especially the Ring. Although some people prefer the Dingle Peninsula. You can make up your own mind. I wish my father had never moved to Dublin. But Dublin's the place to be.'

She told him about Irish place names. She told him that *Kil* meant a church; *Ath* meant a river ford; *Bally* was from the Irish word *baile*, which meant home or town.

Ober said, 'They didn't always use the Irish word, though, did they? I mean, why is it Wexford, and not Wexath, for instance.'

'Oh, aren't you the bright one. 'Tis a pleasure to teach you. You see, Wexford is not an Irish name. It's Norse.'

'Oh.'

'Yes. And the word "ford" is really "fjord". The whole name means the ford of the mud. I think.'

They stopped at Glenbeigh and had a drink and collected

fresh-salmon sandwiches at the Towers Hotel, deciding to return there for dinner.

They drove through Killorglin and she told him about the annual Puck Fair. 'They go off up the mountains and catch the biggest puck goat they can find, and they bring him down and crown him King Puck and stand him in the town square.'

'Jeez. Who started all that. The Board of Welcomes?'

'Not at all. To the best of my knowledge it was started by the Normans. But everyone here thinks it's a pagan custom.'

'Didn't Christianity do away with all pagan customs?'

'Not a bit of it. There's still a strong streak of paganism in the people. Well, in the country people, anyway.'

At Castlemaine they turned out on to the long finger of the Dingle Peninsula, driving under the high blue Slieve Mish Mountains with the sea unruffled to the left, and then they came into Inch – 'which is not a measurement by the way; it's from the Irish word for headland' – and Alison drove on to the beach. Four miles of golden sand stretching out into Dingle Bay. Ober was overwhelmed by the absence of people.

'I suppose if the Board of Welcomes did their job properly this place would be full,' Alison said. 'I've often said that they're always advertising the empty roads and beaches. If their advertising were really successful, it would be self-defeating.'

They walked along the beach, hand in hand in the sunshine, not another human being in sight. She said, 'Let's walk right out to the end, and then we'll have a swim, and then we'll have those lovely fresh-salmon sandwiches. Do you have salmon sandwiches in New York?'

He shook his head. 'Not fresh-salmon sandwiches. Smoked salmon is very popular. And very expensive. It's a kind of Jewish luxury dish. We call it lox.'

'Lox?'

'L-O-X.' Ober nodded. 'But it's much more salty than the smoked salmon you have here. Jews usually serve it on a bagel.'

'This is a great day for words! What's a bagel?'

'It's a kind of doughnut made from white flour. It used to be a great delicacy among poor European Jews, who could only afford black bread.'

Alison shook her head in wonderment. 'Lox and bagel.'

'No. Bagel and lox. If you ever get to New York – what the

226

hell, *when* you get to New York – we'll have Sunday-morning brunch in my apartment. Bagel and lox with cream cheese and butter. Delicious.'

'How about bagel and cabbage?' she said, and laid her head into his shoulder, laughing.

He told her a story about a poor Jewish beggarman who tapped a rich man for a dollar and then immediately popped into the delicatessen and blew it on lox. The rich man followed him in and berated him for spending the money on a luxury. And the beggarman said, 'When I have no money, I can't buy lox. When I have money, you won't let me buy lox. So tell me. When can I buy lox?'

She clapped her hands and they laughed together. He introduced her to Yiddish, delighted to find someone who had never heard a single Yiddish word before, and she repeated the words after him like a child: *kvetch* and *yenta*, *chutzpah* and *mazel tov*, *shmuck*, *shmo* and *schlemiel*. She learned them all.

And then she told him Irish stories, or Kerry jokes, as she called them, and Ober recognized them as the Polish jokes of his own city, and he was fascinated at the changes wrought to suit locale.

When they talked about music he told her that he was a jazz man – 'Everyone I know who is in his forties is a jazz fan,' Alison said – and his most treasured hours were those spent in a bar on Twelfth Street, drinking beer and listening to a three-piece section, all blacks. 'Just drummer, bass and piano. Great.'

Alison told him she spent her music hours listening to the Brandenburg Concertos. 'But I always end up with Mozart. And recently, it's his flute concertos. I used to be in love with Andreas Blau. But now we have a great flautist of our very own, cuddly James Galway. Imagine it! An Irish flautist, or flute player.' She looked up at him. 'Is there a difference between a flautist and a flute player?'

'There is.'

'Oh, dear. What is it?'

'About a hundred dollars a week.'

They stripped on the empty beach and ran into the surf, plunging straight into the water and surfacing with shouts and screams. Ober swam away from her with powerful strokes, and she lay on her back in the water, her hair flowing down from her head like delicate white ferns in the sea, and he came back to her and lifted her and ducked her amid much laughter, and then he kissed her and she responded generously to him. She stood up and untied the knot in her blue bikini top and pressed herself to his large body. He held his hand under her buttocks, lifting her, and they floated in embrace, their feet barely touching the soft sand, their mouths tangy with brine. Then he lifted her and brought her ashore, and they made love on the tartan rug in the dunes behind the beach, and Ober could not remember when he had been happier.

Haslam looked at Ellen's face for a long time before he kissed her awake. In his writer's reflexive search for a word to describe her, he kept coming back to a word which as a writer he hated, and had never once used in all of his books: Ellen was lovely.

When she woke, they stayed together in silence for a long while, and Ellen said, 'I wish I could have stayed in that reverie.'

'Are you having regrets.'

'Not right now.'

'But later?'

'Who knows?'

'Do you usually have regrets?'

She looked at him for a long time before answering, and he knew he had said a silly and hurtful thing.

She turned away from him and lay on her back. 'Do you think I sleep with every man I meet?'

'I could cut my tongue out.'

'I haven't been to bed with a man for two years.' She spoke absently, the hurt gone from her voice, and he lay on his side and drew his finger gently down her cheek. 'I was thirty before I lost my virginity.' He said nothing in the long following silence. 'I guess there aren't many of my kind around today. Not deliberately, anyway. He was a golf professional from Rye. I didn't like him at all. But I was crazy about him.' She turned to him. 'You know what I mean?'

'I know.'

'And I was drunk. And we made love at midnight on the fourth green of the Lone Eagle golf course.' She spoke in a low monotone. A casual exorcism. 'I became pregnant. I told him about it. That he was the first. He laughed. No woman was going to catch him like that. "Not very subtle, Ellen," he said.

So I had the baby with cousins in New London. My parents never found out. It was a girl and I had her adopted. I never even saw her, except for a few minutes. She will be ten on the fourteenth of May next year.'

'Would you like to see her?'

'Sometimes. Yearn, I think, is the proper word. But it might set up things I couldn't control. I can't have that now.' She turned slowly round to him, her voice gone very soft, her eyes on his. Then her repose left her, the placid calmness and self-control that made her so attractive fell away. The tears formed and flowed from the sides of her eyes, but she stared at him unblinking, letting them fall. 'There are many things that I can't have now.'

He drew her to him and held her, having no words for her sadness, the tears forming in his own eyes. This strong and confident woman was no different. Everyone was lonely. Everyone was disappointed. Everyone was vulnerable.

He drew back his head and looked at her face, soft, unmasked, naked. Her eyes were closed and he kissed her lids and stroked away the tears from the cheeks.

She opened her eyes and smiled weakly. 'I'm sorry.'

'Don't be sorry, my love.' After a while, he whispered, 'Why did you tell me?'

'I don't know. I *do* know.' She put her hand on his face. 'I told you because we have slept together and made love together. It is a big thing. I *cannot* be casual about it. I told you because I wanted to tell you. And I want to tell you more. I want the time to tell you more. I told you because I have fallen in love with you.'

The writer said softly, 'An old man like me?'

She gripped him tightly, 'Please, J.J. Please be serious. Just for a few minutes. I want . . .'

'I know. Weep not. I am serious. I am in love with you.'

She said, 'Oh,' and held him, her forehead to his, her eyes wide open.

And then he said, 'But we should know better, shouldn't we?'

She nodded, but said nothing.

He said, 'You know, I wasn't really being flippant that time. I'm almost sixty years old. I'm set in my ways. I'm not rich. And unless I have a best-selling book, I never will be. And that is unlikely to happen, for I seem to be one of those writers who have a small but devoted following.'

He smiled at that.

She said, 'I know all that.'

'You're a beautiful woman. There are twenty years between us. I suppose I could forgive you that,' he said, smiling again. 'But you have a grand job which you seem to love . . .'

'I don't love it that much.'

'. . . and I honestly couldn't live in a place like New York. It would suffocate me.'

'But I could very happily live in Ireland.'

He looked hard at her. 'We're not mad young lovers, now are we, Ellen?'

'We're not mad. And we're not young.'

'This is very serious.'

'I know.'

'You would give up your job and come to Ireland to live?'

'I could get a job here. I'm a very competent woman,' she said, tapping him on the nose.

'I live in a squalid little bed-sitter that I'd be ashamed for you to see. I am crotchety and vain, and I get drunk often, and when I'm drunk I'm impossible to live with.'

'My, you really are running after me.'

He said tentatively, 'Listen, pet. You're not a little bit in love with J. J. Haslam the writer, rather than with pernickety old me?'

'I'm not differentiating. I want them both.'

Haslam sat up. 'I don't know what in the world to say.'

'Just say yes, J.J.'

'To what, pet?'

'I live alone in New York. I want to be with a man whom I can love and trust. I never met one until now.'

'Trust is at a premium nowadays.'

'I know.'

'What makes you think you can trust me?'

'I *know*!'

'Ellen, we've only known each other . . .'

'J.J., I lived with a man in New York for two years. I thought I was the only woman in his life. He cheated every single week of those two years. With my best friend.'

'You learned nothing from it, my love.'

'Every bachelor girl in New York has a dog. Or a cat. Or a bird. A friend of mine has a Pekingese. She's a teacher of English at CUNY, and she talks to that dog as if he were her lover.'

'Harmless.'

She shook her head. 'It's disgusting, J.J. The only being she can trust is that dog. She fondles him and kisses him and sings to him. She does everything to him that she wants to do to a man.'

'You'd like me to be your Pekingese?'

She brought him back down beside her on the pillow. 'You're making it very hard.'

'I don't mean to. That's the God's honest truth. But I don't know what to say to you. I was married once before, and it was a mistake. And it hurt me badly. But that's not all. Marriage as far as I'm concerned, Ellen, is a *sacramental* thing. Even though there's no church involved. It brings responsibility. It *means* responsibility. Even if there are no children. And that's another thing.'

'You don't have to say it. If I didn't feel exactly as you do about marriage, I would have been married long ago. We don't have to get married. Though I want to.'

'Merciful hour,' he said softly. 'There is nothing I would like more than to have you with me for the rest of my life, to wake up to your face in the mornings. But is that what you want? I'll be seventy in ten years' time. A really old man.'

'You'll be young to me.'

'This is a wonderful thing.'

'Well, then, say something, J.J., for God's sake.'

He kissed her and said, 'I love you, Ellen. And I want you to be with me. I surely won't change much, but I'll try to make you happy.'

'I love you, too. And don't you dare change.'

Oliver Mulligan sat on the bed looking at the telephone, wanting to pick it up, hating to pick it up. He was in a wash of self-pity. Arthur Whelan had called him at cockcrow to say that he would be happy to give an interview to the NBS people on tourism. 'Get the message across hard, you know?'

'Yes, I know exactly what you mean.'

'I presume you've been pointing them in the right places?'

'Oh, you needn't worry about that. They've got some really marvellous stuff. Donegal, all through Mayo and Connemara, the Burren and of course the Ring of Kerry itself . . .'

'These people like to make controversies, you know.'

'Oh, I know.'

'They didn't look for any trouble anywhere?'

'Well, at the Fujikawa factory . . .'

'What was that?'

'There was a strike on there.'

'I know. The bloody fellows are still out. They didn't film the pickets, did they?'

'No. Maggie Porter was out there, and she managed to get rid of the pickets for a while.'

'Who's Maggie Porter?'

'She's the PR woman for the IDB.'

'Good for her. It's more of her kind that we need. I must send a note to Phil about her.'

'Yes.'

'Well, let me know if they want the interview. I'll be here until tomorrow. Bit of a break.'

Mulligan had almost slammed down the phone. People thought his job was to get the message of tourism before the public. Mulligan knew better. Half his time was spent trying to keep the morons of the tourism industry off the television screen, off the airwaves, as far away as possible from news people of any kind. Mulligan knew his news people. He knew to his cost that they would lap up the most jejune tripe if it were delivered to them by a man who was witty, erudite, educated, nimble and seemingly forthright. Look at Freddy Barton. On the other hand, the most vital and important facts could have their import killed by bad packaging. And Arthur Whelan was as exciting as an old handkerchief. The biggest problem was, Mulligan had decided many years before, that Whelan simply did not know what being Irish meant. He had no idea of history, tradition or culture: if it could not be priced, it did not exist.

And now he wanted to go on television as a representative of Ireland. Oh, God.

Luckily, though, Ober had taken a day off. But unfortunately he had departed with Whelan's daughter. Had she told her father that she was taking the producer on a tour of the Dingle Peninsula? If she hadn't, was it because she didn't want him to know? If I don't mention it to him, Mulligan thought, she might mention it to him tomorrow. Then he will know that I knew, and he'll think . . . Merciful Jesus, what a life.

And Angela, what did she want?

'Please ring your wife immediately,' said the note at the desk when he arrived back in the early hours of the morning, Alice Foley on his arm. Alice had looked at the note and said, 'Oh, good night, Oliver,' and had gone off to bed. And she had been nicely drunk, and so had he, and it had all looked so likely.

Now he picked up the phone and a few minutes later his wife came on the line.

'Is something wrong?' he said, with by now habitual irritation.

'Siobhan is sick.'

'What's the matter with her?'

'It looks like appendicitis.'

'Well, that's all right, isn't it, I mean . . .'

'She has to go into hospital, and you know how terrified she is of hospitals.'

'Yes.'

'She wants you to take her there.'

'Me?'

'Yes. She says she'll go if you take her.'

'Jesus, Angela, that's ridiculous. I can't just gallop back to Dublin to take the child on a five-minute jaunt to hospital.'

'I'll tell her that.'

'Don't tell her that, for God's sake, woman.'

'What'll I tell her then?'

'*Explain* to the girl that I'm very busy, up to my ears in work, and just cannot make it back in time. But that I said she was to go with you, and I'll bring her back a doll on the week-end.'

'She stopped playing with dolls six years ago.'

'Well, whatever she wants, then.'

'She won't go, you know.'

'*Make* her go.'

'What do you want me to do? Beat her all the way to St Vincent's? I'd be a nice sight . . .'

'The girl is sixteen years old. She's acting like a baby.'

'She's just afraid of hospitals, that's all.'

'She's never even *been* in one.'

'You don't have to get burnt to be afraid of fire, you know.'

'Jesus, you're a genius.'

'So you're always telling me.'

'Look, we're at a critical stage of this trip. If the child were seriously ill I'd be back in a flash. I can't walk out on this group just like that. I'm a professional at my job, Angela.'

'You take it very seriously, and that's a fact.'

'Don't start that again.'

'More seriously than you take your family anyway.'

'God, as if I didn't have enough on my plate already.'

'You poor man.'

'Are you going to take her to hospital?'

'I'll have to, won't I? If I was to wait for you to come back she could be dead on the floor with peritonitis.'

When she hung up, he had a flashing vision of the three of them, mother and twins, dying quickly and painlessly of peritonitis, and the funeral, and the lovely sympathy from everyone, and the wonderful freedom for ever. Ooh.

He walked out the door and down the corridor to Alice Foley's room.

She let him in. She was in a dressing gown. He said, 'Have you any such thing as a drink here?'

'Now, Oliver, what do you think I am?'

'You are a lovely, desirable woman and I want to make love to you but I need a drink to pluck up the courage to ask you.'

'Well, give me a few minutes and we'll go down to the bar and you can have as many as you like. It's a free day.'

'And then what?'

'What what?'

'Alice, take pity on me.'

'Now, Oliver, you know that is no basis for an affair. All the textbooks say so.'

'Fuck the textbooks.'

'I dare say it's been tried.'

'I'm serious, Alice.'

'Indeed you're not.'

'What have you got against me?'

'Not a thing!' she said, going into the bathroom with her clothes.

'I wish you had.'

'Oliver!'

'Can I come in and watch you?'

'My God, you're turning into a dirty old man.'

'I'm forty-eight, for Jayses' sake. I can't help it. I have a wife who hates my guts, and two of the worst children in the world. And I spend most of my time arse-licking a lot of Johnny-jump-ups from all over the world. It's beneath me.'

'You love it.'

'I do not!'

'Yes, you do. And they all love you. And you love that more than anything.'

'By Christ, when I get back I'll write a book, I swear it.'

'That's another shilling you owe me.'

'Alice, why are you so cruel to me? You know I love you.'

'You wouldn't want me to be hypocritical with you, would you.'

He sat on the bed, head in hands. 'I wouldn't care. Just stop saying those nasty things.'

'They're true.'

'Of course they're true! Why else would I object to hearing them?'

She came out of the bathroom, brushing her hair, dressed. She went over and kissed him on the head and sat down in front of him.

He looked up at her. 'You know what everyone used to say about me?'

She shook her head.

'They used to say I could do anything. "There's a young man that could do anything", they used to say. And they were right. I could do anything. So I end up doing nothing.'

'What do you want?'

'You know what I want. Love. Pity. Cuddling.'

'There are plenty of girls around who would . . .'

'There aren't, Alice. There aren't. Not any more.' The bantering tone was gone from his voice.

'So now you are reduced to me?'

'That's not what I meant.'

'What else am I to believe? Oliver, this is the first time you've ever asked me to go to bed with you when you were sober. At least you don't have your hand down the back of my skirt this time.'

'I know, I know, I know. I get romantic when I have a few jars . . .'

'You get sloppy and messy and offensive. But I'll agree that a lot of Irishmen think they're being romantic when they have their sticky paws on your blouse.'

'Oh, God, Alice, why are you so cruel? Why can't we have a simple affair?'

'Because there's no such thing, Oliver.' She listed some of their mutual friends. 'All moving around from one to the other. The whole world thinks Dublin is a nice Catholic city. It's worse than Paris. I don't want to join that merry-go-round.'

He looked up. 'It's nothing personal then?'

'Of course not, dear Oliver. You know how much I like you.'

'Well, then, just this once . . .'

'No.'

His eyes narrowed. 'Is it someone else? It can't be J.J. He's gone head over heels for Ellen. And Ober's gone off with . . . is it Crossan? It *is* Crossan. By God, I thought you said . . .'

'Stephen Crossan isn't interested in me,' she said, turning away from him.

'No,' he mused. 'He's too busy trying for Virginia.'

'Good luck to him,' she said lightly.

'Alice, my dear, beloved Alice . . .'

'Please, Oliver. Let's go down and have that drink.' And then she said the sentence that Mulligan heard increasingly lately, and had grown to hate more than any in the language. 'Let's just be good friends.'

Later that evening, Stephen Crossan sat alone in the bar and wondered whether he should ring Virginia Green.

But then she stomped into the empty bar in high-heeled brown boots, her denim slacks rolled up to under her knees, her shirt open, as usual, to the third button. She came and sat beside him and lit her pipe.

'Guess what?' she said, when they both had a drink.

'What?'

'We've turned into a nest of lovebirds.'

'Oh?'

'Ellen and J.J. Pete and Alison. Oliver and Alice I passed on the street holding hands, and who knows what Max has found. Not bad, eh?'

'One big happy family.'

'Not quite.'

'No. Not quite.'

She said, 'I mean there's Frank Dinneen.'

'Oh. Yes.'

'He shouldn't be left out, now should he? I mean he's a handsome guy . . .'

'Handsome!' Crossan said, before he could stop himself.

'Waal, not in a conventional way, you know. But he's got character in that face, eh?'

'Yes, he's got character in his face.'

'You know something? I really kinda find him attractive, in a funny kind of way.'

'Why the hell don't you tell him, then?' Crossan muttered.

'I might.'

She stared at him across the table, her right hand holding the pipe by her ear, its stem pointing backwards, the smoke insinuating itself in her tight curls. Her head was slightly forward and he could see her breasts. But denim, at least, was opaque. Not quite jersey or cheesecloth, or those new flimsy materials which covered without hiding, so that a man's eyes were transfixed by the strawberry peepers. Did women find men's crotches as alluring? he wondered. How much more 'equal' would the sexes be if men had breasts, or some male equivalent which could be flaunted in the same provocative manner? Some women were ashamed of their breasts because they were too small, others because they were too big. They were driven to dementia – and anorexia – by savants who laid down the standards of beauty. All the savants were men. Most of them were homosexual. Fashion was a queer world surely. A tyranny, too.

'Why are you staring at me like that?'

'Because you are the most beautiful woman I have ever seen. And you will be gone in a few days and I may never see you again, and that's a painful thought, but if I look at you for long enough I should be able to remember every bit of you, and that will be better than any picture in my wallet.'

'Whew!'

'There you are now. You asked the question.'

'You meant all that?'

'Every word.'

'That's very nice.'

'It's not very nice at all.'

'Why not?'

'Because there are certain things I want to say to you, certain things I want to ask you, and I can't do it.'

'Try. Jesus, what an exasperating young man.'

'I can't. I'd need your help.'

'Just tell me what to do or say. I'll help.'

'We're too far apart, you know?' he said, sitting on his hands.

'I'll move nearer . . .'

'I don't mean physically,' he said, laughing, not knowing whether she had deliberately misunderstood. 'You and I, Stephen Crossan and Virginia Green, are too far apart for me to be able to say the things I want to say.'

'Well, we have all night.'

'I don't think time is the problem.'

'Well, what is the goddamn problem, Stephen? What's the matter with you?'

'Nothing is the matter with me. I am myself. Private, pedantic, predatory. How's that for alliteration? Do you like alliteration? How do you feel about the various poetic prestiges? You like a little dash of zeugma? Or good old synecdoche? Lots of people like a little bit of synecdoche now and then. The part for the hole, as it were. Or chiasmus? Too arcane? You don't need them if you're Irish, of course. Hyperbole and allegory are your essential Irish weapons . . .'

'Stephen.' She put the pipe on the table and looked at him. 'What is this all about?'

'I don't know,' he said glumly.

'You're running away again.'

'I suppose so.'

'What happened?'

'You keep asking that. As though there were a simple answer. There isn't one. If you like I'll try one. I fell in love when I was twenty. A wonderful, passionate redhead, marvellous dancer. We were pure as the driven snow. She was wild in my arms, but we promised to remain clean until after marriage. And then I found out she was having it off with two or three other fellows. Oh, the pain, the pain, the pain. Never again.'

'It happens to everyone.'

'I suppose you mean that to be consoling.'

She felt a terrible frustration in the young man's company. She was more attracted to him than she would ever tell him, but it had to remain physical, for every time she tried to introduce another dimension – of sympathy, understanding, simple liking – he dodged away through a thicket of words. He was patently afraid of her. But was it just her? She could not break down his fear. And she knew he wanted her.

It should be easier than this.

They talked on for several hours as the night closed in, with occasional long silences as between good friends or people who are determined not to be the first to give up. Sometimes he was lighthearted and very amusing in a self-depreciating way – this she was beginning to think of as typically Irish – but other times he was grandiloquently caustic and vicious, especially when the conversation touched on aspects of life which he considered 'modern'. Before she met him, the word had had a very simple meaning for her. But on Crossan's tongue it was a monstrous adjective, gathering into itself all that he considered vile and specious. It was astonishing to hear a young man being vitriolic about modern art, about what he termed 'denim literature', about loss of faith, loss of certainty, loss of a centre.

His mind and words dodged and darted and she gave up trying to stay abreast of his thoughts. She could not anyway, for while the drink made him even more pedantic and precise, it simply made Virginia very drunk, and by late evening her head was spinning as it had been in the Shelbourne on the night of the ball. She stumbled to the ladies' room and threw up as though she had been doing it all her life.

She spent a long time in front of the mirror afterwards, having one of those hilarious conversations with herself which she always had with ladies' mirrors when she was drunk.

When she came out, she was beautifully high, as though after a good joint, and Crossan was in full poetic flight with Frank Dinneen. But Crossan, too, had gone over the edge, and though he was as pedantic as ever, he was now gesturing broadly, and his voice had risen somewhat.

He looked up as Virginia sat down, and he said, 'And she's a perfect example of it, Frankie, my boy. A perfect example of it. This beautiful, beautiful woman. You do agree that she is beautiful, do you not?'

'Sure,' Dinneen said, laughing. He was delighted to see the government man drunk at last.

'I cannot talk to her on her own terms, snap for snap, you see, my dear scrivener? I do not have the talent for it. I do not have the patience for it. I long for the old days. Curious that, what? I wasn't even *around* in the old days. But I long for them. My terms of reference are different. My standards are different. My priorities are violently opposed to Virginia's. Would you not agree? And I'm the last! You hear me? I'm the last of them all. The present young generation, Oh, Jesus, spare us, those youngsters filling the bars every night, their sticky hair on their shoulders, buying vodkas and oranges for their tufty, foulmouthed girlfriends, they're the people who can talk to this gorgeous, *modern* woman here. They have the vocabulary. Or rather the lack of it. They have that grunting, philistine, colourless, pseudo-pragmatic personality' – the words gave him difficulty – 'that comes from living life vicariously, having one's fantasies worked out by television and the films. Having them *invented* by those media. You know how it goes, Frank? You know how it goes, Virginia? "Look, man, who gives a shit", right? "Let it all hang out, man". "Fuck you, baby".'

Dinneen looked at Virginia and threw his eyes up to heaven, laughing silently. Virginia laughed, too.

'Laugh, laugh, laugh. Oh, my God. Tell me, when Yeats feared the rough beast slouching towards Bethlehem to be born, tell me, reassure me, that he had something more substantial, more gritty, in mind than the mess we have all about us today? Eh? How can there ever be another revolution? Where will it find its impulse? What shape could it possibly take? Eh? You know, Catholicism may be a terrible thing, but at least it gave one something big and noble and majestic and tangible to go with or kick against. Now I kicked against it, God knows. Well, I didn't so much kick against it as slink away from it. Or, let us be nothing if not precise, it slunk – slank? slinked? fuck it – away from *me*. A spiritual tabes. But by Christ, if I didn't know what I was going into, I sure as hell knew what I was leaving. But now? What now? And forever more? How can anyone be certain? Every tenet has been undermined, every certainty destroyed. California. That's the name of the game now, my friends. Califuckingfornia. That's the future. And my friends, if California is the future, the world is finished. Finished. Dead. Gone. Destroyed. Lost. Irretrievably. Down the fucking plughole. And this innocent little island, my beloved Ireland, Europe's ancient baby, down the with rest. Aah, for shame, my friends, for shame.'

The other two were in paroxysms, mitigated by the delicious shock they both felt at the spectacle of Crossan without his government cap on. He looked up at them, smiling drunkenly, knowing in his inebriation the reasons for their mirth.

'A most unusual sight, what?' he said, in a terrible English drawl. 'The real Crossan. *In vino veritas*. And another little bit of *veritas*, dear Frank' – he took the columnist by the arm, and leaned over to him – 'another little surprise. Guess who's got the hots for you, Frankie boy?'

Dinneen looked reflexively at Virginia, and she was smiling a who cares smile of drunkery.

'See, see, Frankie? She thinks you're a veritable Adonis, a face with *character*, my friend.'

Virginia laughed, on the edge of hysteria, her handkerchief to her eyes.

Dinneen took her arm. 'You okay?'

She didn't answer him, but looked at Crossan, who was still smiling, his eyes half closed. 'He's a better goddamn man than you are. He's a fucking *man*, for Chrissakes, not a goddamn talking machine.'

'You're absolutely right, my dear, absolutely right.'

Dinneen said, 'Come on, I'll take you to your room.'

She rose, swaying, and glared at Crossan, who smiled back.

They got to her room and she leaned against the doorjamb while he fumbled with nervous fingers for her key. He put it in the lock and opened the door and brought her in and she immediately fell on her back on the bed. He jerked off her boots and pulled down her denims, throwing them behind him, and then he pulled down her white panties. He was sweating and his heart was pumping as he pushed down his own trousers and underpants, kicked off his shoes toe-on-heel, and then he was on top of her, his mouth on hers, his fingers desperately searching for her entry.

She stiffened and straightened up, screaming. She pushed him violently off the bed and backed into a corner, grabbing the light stand, crying. 'Get out!' she screamed. 'Get out!'

'Don't throw that goddamn thing.'

'Get out!'

'I'm getting out, for Chrissakes. Let me . . .' He pushed his legs into his trousers and pulled them up, stuffing his green-silk underpants into his pocket and picking up his shoes.

He was at the door when the light stand hit it, and he ran stumbling down the corridor to his room.

24

Haslam it was now who saw the destruction first, and his 'Merciful God!' rang out in the minibus.

They were on the road overlooking Bantry Bay, vast under a blue sky that should have been reflected in the sea. But the face that the sea presented as far as the horizon was a thick impenetrable black. Gradually it dawned on all that the whole of Bantry Bay was carpeted with still, black crude oil.

The shapes of small boats became evident in the bay, fussing around a huge silent tanker tethered to the island in the middle of the bay, from their prows little jets of foam spouting on the sea. Mulligan had his head in his hands.

They stopped and alighted, and the producer and camera-man looked at the scene with critical eyes, while Mulligan paced nervously up and down the road, hoping they would not take out their cameras.

On the island, squat and grey, stood the vast storage tanks. The huge tankers filled their bellies in the Middle East, plough-ed across the ocean and emptied themselves into the tanks, whence other, smaller tankers took the oil for further distribution in Europe.

Only Bantry Bay, of all the bays in Europe, was deep enough for the big ones, and the promise of employment had persuaded the Irish government that the risks were worthwhile. Leaks were impossible and even if one did occur – and of course it could not occur – it was automatically monitored and cut off before it could do any serious damage. The Irish people were told that there would be employment for five hundred people, and were given a cast-iron guarantee that the environmenta-lists' fears were unfounded, their screams mere hysterics. The tanks were built, giving the promised employment; at their completion, if was found that a dozen men, more or less, could adequately service them.

But the tankers stayed for three or four days at a time, and their hungry, thirsty, randy crews spent their money with great intensity, the benefits of their presence permeating the whole areas so munificently that environmentalists, still waging their futile little war, could find no toehold of understanding. 'Doomsayers', 'alarmists', they folded their tents and left weeping.

Ober said, 'What do you think?'

Maynard shook his head. 'Not enough light,' he said.

Ober said, 'You could use a sun gun.'

Maynard looked at him as though he had been struck. Ober laughed. He was in high good humour this day. 'We'll go into town, hire a boat and get out to the tanker. Then we'll get everything.'

They drove into a silent, indifferent Bantry and Ober and Maynard went in search of a boat. After an hour they rejoined the group in the lobby of Vickery's Hotel, dispirited.

'We can't even find a boat. Nobody wants to talk to us.'

'They're nervous,' Haslam said. 'You can't blame them.'

But his analysis was wide. A little man came tripping into the room and approached the sullen Ober. 'You were looking for a boat were you?'

'That's right.'

'How long do you want it for?'

'For as long as it takes to get out to the tanker and back again.'

'Say about two hours?'

'Sure.'

'And how much will ye pay?'

'Whatever the going rate is.'

'Well, now,' the little man said, 'the going rate is a hundred pounds an hour.'

Everyone looked up. Ober almost shouted. 'A hundred pounds!'

'That's what we're getting from the company.'

'What company?'

'The oil company. They're hiring us to spread that detergent stuff. If you can top the hundred I'll take ye out.'

'That's a rip-off. I can't pay that kind of money.'

244

'I'd like to help you, like, you know? But you couldn't expect me to pass up a chance like that.'

'What kind of boat is it?' Haslam said.

'A fishing boat.'

'You're a fisherman?'

'All my life. I never thought I'd land a windfall like this, though. There's may be a fortnight's work out there, or more. A few more spillages and I could retire for life. Send my children to the university. Well, we can only hope for the best.'

That night, in his room, Haslam sat reading, and writing his perpetual journal.

Ellen lay behind him in the bed, staring at the ceiling, occasionally looking with contentment at the writer as he bent over the table, his pen scratching lightly across the pages.

'I am trying not to think of the fisherman,' he wrote. 'I fear his simple words speak the bible of the new Ireland. Expediency is all. But I may be wrong. We have always had our share of mercenaries. Yet I feel that the share in the last two decades his grown monstrously. The people have taken such a pounding, from all of the media, but mostly from television, that they are losing the ability to appreciate the things that are *truly* good – and free – and to eschew those things which are expedient, transient, chimerical. The birds are already flapping into black death in the bay, and all the fisherman can see is a hundred pounds an hour and hope of further spillages.'

He flipped through the book beside him, stopping at an excerpt from Wolfe Tone's *Journal*, written out on Bantry Bay aboard the luckless *Indomptable* on Christmas Day 180 years before, when yet another French fleet was on the point of freeing Ireland from the English yoke.

'We have now been six days in Bantry Bay,' he read, 'within five hundred yards of the shore, without being able to effectuate a landing; we have been dispersed four times in four days; and at this moment, of forty-three sail, we can muster of all sizes but fourteen. . . . Notwithstanding all our blunders it is the dreadful stormy weather and Easterly winds which have been blowing furiously and without intermission since we made Bantry Bay that ruined us. Well, England has not had such an escape since the Spanish Armada . . .'

Poor Wolfe Tone, Haslam thought, the Protestant who

became beloved of the Catholics and was now the centrepiece of Republican thought, the singular godhead of the Provisional IRA. What would he think if he came into the bay today? The English have gone, but what has replaced them? How perplexed and appalled would he be by the tanker and the millions of gallons of oil? What would he have to say to proxy bombs, and children blinded, crippled and crushed to death by young freedom fighters?

'Oh, my life and soul,' Haslam read, 'my darling babies, shall I ever see you again?'

And Wolfe Tone never did see his children again, betrayed by a school friend and shut up for the hangman, whom he deprived of historical notoriety by cutting his own young throat with a penknife.

Haslam closed the book, unwilling to pursue the thoughts that it provoked.

Wolfe Tone was a hero. And winsome Robert Emmet seven years later. And Lord Edward Fitzgerald. O'Connell, Parnell, Pearse, and even De Valera. All singular men. More or less heroic, more or less pragmatic.

But where were the heroes now?

The time of heroes was past and gone. Their simple world was gone, taking with it their simple choices. It was no longer possible to define goodness, heroism. There was too much knowledge. There were too many contradictions. There was no hierarchy. There was no order. It was foolish and fruitless to invoke the names of those men of times past as inspiration for present action: their worlds were small, and their words – honour, justice, valour – had become tainted and unusable except on the tongues of hypocrites and buffoons. The truly great men now, the contemporary heroes, did not lead armies, sway millions; they started small cooperatives in areas of poverty; they prevented strikes; they taught hundreds of disaffected slum children. Or they merely fought silent, lifelong battles against mortgages, school fees, sons and daughters on drugs.

He put the book away and undressed, falling asleep almost immediately in Ellen's arms.

25

'I'm a lover, man, not a goddamn Shakespeare,' Franklin Heller said, sitting back behind his large white writing desk.

Around the room were his best-selling novels, in hard-cover and paperback, including the three which were to be found in every railway and airport shop in the world: *I, Ada Subin, The Subin Inheritance* and *Ada Subin's Revenge*, the torrid accounts of the life and couplings of Heller's most enduring heroine.

The author's blonde wife, her twenty-five-year-old figure encased in pink velvet pants and white sweater, served Dom Perignon to the nine guests, who were strewn around the full-sized billiard table which took up the centre of the room.

'One a year,' her husband said, waving his glass to the books. 'Six months writing, three months resting, and three months playing.' He drank, and smacked his lips, and looked at his wife. ''Course there are certain things that go on all year round.'

'Oh, Hell,' she said.

'Bit of an asshole, huh? No goddamn manners.'

Haslam looked at the floor, his face tormented, the glass hanging lightly in his fingers. On the desk were several photographs of Heller – in open-necked shirt, padded jacket and elevator shoes – smiling at the camera, his arm around one or another movie star who had been made famous in the movie adaptations of his books.

'Whaddya think of our little cottage, huh?'

The house, which had forty rooms, had been built in 1810, and had been the family home of Lord Beltown. The last Beltown, a morose drunk and pathological gambler, had bankrupted the huge estate in twenty prodigious years on the

Riviera. The land had been sold off piecemeal, and the house was in a sad disrepair in 1969, when the Irish government passed legislation making artists, writers, composers and sculptors free of income tax on their earnings from their work.

Six months later, Heller arrived from Barbados. He moved in a team of architects, masons, electricians and painters, and they worked for fifteen months under the stewardship of Andries 'Beebee' Pellegrini, the interior designer, who commuted between East Hampton and Beltown House – or Hellerville, as it had been renamed.

The stolid Georgian mansion, while retaining its outward symmetry, was inwardly transformed into a modern architectural soufflé which smote the eye with pinks and blacks and swirling turquoises, the original predictability of its layout giving way to a twisting, split-level mélange of shocking chambers.

Heller had taken them on a tour. He brought them to view the pride of the house. It was an incredibly large round bed: twenty people could lie comfortably in its pinkness. Above it, on the ceiling, was a huge mirror. 'Mirror, mirror on the ceiling,' Heller said with a smirk, 'how'm I doin'?'

Then he brought them to the pool. It was inside a glass house, and it was shaped like a shamrock. 'Nobody can say we're not Irish, huh?' In a second he was out of his sweater and slacks and he dived to the bottom of the centre petal of the pool, which was decorated with a large nude mosaic of his wife. He kissed the nude breasts and pubis, causing them to light up and start blinking like tiny underwater lighthouses.

He surfaced, and they all saw that he was naked. He nodded down to the blinking underwater mosaic. 'Had to get a guy over from Italy to do that. Locals wouldn't touch it. Prudes.'

He pulled down a senatorial towel robe and put it on. 'Sausage will be along in a few minutes and she'll know I've been thinking of her. Get it?' he laughed his rib-nudging laugh. 'We can all have a swim tonight, if you folks wish. Only one condition. In my pool, everyone swims in the raw.'

Everyone looked at the floor.

'You can all boast that you dived on Frank Heller's wife.'

Crossan wandered back into the house. In one room, four large paintings of Mayan women were hanging, Virginia Green standing before one of them.

He went silently up behind her and whispered, 'What do you think?'

'Beautiful taste.'

He sat down and she sat beside him. He said, 'I hope I wasn't offensive the other night?'

'I don't remember.'

'You don't remember anything?'

'I remember leaving on Frank Dinneen's arm.'

'I remember that, too, very clearly.'

'I also remember him running down the corridor with his shoes in his hand when I threw him out.'

'Thanks be to God for that.'

'Were you worried?'

'You were very drunk and . . .'

'You didn't look very worried when I left.'

'You had already told me you found him attractive.'

'Oh, God, Stephen. You're a hopeless case.'

He nodded. 'I know.'

'Still, you're cute when you're drunk.'

'Be kind.'

'You wouldn't really like that.'

'There you go, analysing me again.'

After a moment, she said, 'Weren't you even the tiniest bit jealous when I went off with Dinneen?'

'Very.'

'Why?'

'Because I wanted to go off with you myself.'

She took his hand in both of hers, and he was shocked and thrilled by the naturalness of it. 'I can't just jump into bed with you,' she whispered. 'You know that? It has to mean something. To both of us. I'll talk to you all night and tell you everything you want to know about me, but you won't tell me anything. You must hate me . . .'

'Good God, no!' She was looking at him almost plaintively, and he could hardly match her gaze.

'Well, then, show me some little regard, some affection. I don't know what to make of you.'

'I want to, Virginia, I really want to. You're beautiful and you're exciting. You're like nobody I've ever met. But I'm . . . I'm . . .'

'You're afraid. Jesus,' she whispered, 'you have everything

going for you and you're afraid. A little pussycat.' She kissed him on the lips, as she had done in the Shelbourne. 'Why don't I come to your room tonight and we can talk the night away?' she whispered.

'I'm sharing with Oliver.'

'The world is against us.'

'And I'm sharing tomorrow night again in Tinahely.'

They sat in silence and barely heard J. J. Haslam come in. He had been drinking champagne zealously and his eyes had that impish gleam with which Crossan was so familiar.

'Two little lovebirds.' He looked up at the Mayan women. 'Don't you wish now,' he said to Crossan, 'that you could be moved by them?'

'I don't know the first thing about painting.'

'Nor myself and that's a fact. But then sure the whole Irish nation is profoundly ignorant of visual art. An aural culture. We never produced a single painter or artist of world renown.'

'What about Hone, Osborne, Jack Yeats . . .'

Haslam made a terrible face. 'Small talents, my boy. Where is your Irish Caravaggio? Or your Irish Rubens or Turner or Velasquez? Ne'er a one. Words, words, words. That's all we're good for.'

'What about *The Book of Kells*?'

'More words, dear boy. If a few dozen monks spend their whole lives fashioning one capital letter, you're not going to accuse them of being great artists now, are you? No. We have not produced a great artist. And we can blame that on the British too, can't we, same as we blame everything on them? If you make a nation so poor that they cannot even afford brush and oils, chisel and stone, paper and pencil, you are not going to produce a nation of Renoirs, now, are you?'

'I don't suppose you are,' Crossan said, absently, still thinking of Virginia's words.

'If only the rest of the world would leave us alone,' Haslam said. 'But of course we don't want to be left alone. We want to be thought about, cared about, loved and admired, roguish but lovable little brats, always scrapping but with kind hearts. If only the rest of them would leave us alone, we pray. First the Vikings, then the Normans, then the ineffable English, the cause of all our woes, robbing us of our dignity, stamping us into subjection, turning us from the proud noble and high-minded race of scholars and saints and warriors that we all know we were into a nation of cowards and flunkeys, doffing our caps, tipping our forelocks, singing our sad songs, getting drunk to banish our melancholy, spouting our poetry, dancing our hornpipes, a mad, childlike, innocent race that needs guidance and indulgence and the occasional cuff on the ear when our ambitions outstrip our abilities.'

Mulligan had slipped in on the last note. He nodded towards Haslam and winked at Crossan and Virginia.

'At it again, is he? He'll have us all in tears before we reach Dublin.'

'It was very interesting,' Virginia said, looking at Haslam's quiet, hunched figure.

'It is indeed. First time you hear it.' He sat down. 'Well, what do you think of our Heller in pink tights?'

Crossan said, 'She doesn't say very much, does she?'

'Has anyone ever read his stuff?'

They shook their heads.

'Wait there,' Mulligan said, and went out of the room. When he returned, he had a copy of *I, Ada Subin* in his hand, and he opened it. It was obvious that he had been reading it already, for he went straight to the page he sought. He stood in the middle of the room, surrounded by the passive, impervious Mayan women, and began to declaim from the book in a voice that he made heavy with lubriciousness.

'Ada stood at the door, unseen, and looked in at Mark's bronzed body. She saw his athlete's biceps and his well-muscled thighs. She saw his strong nose and square jaw. She saw his sea-deep blue-eyes. She saw the thick black hair on his fine hands. And then her temples began to throb and her knees became weak. Her eyes travelled down his lean brown body, seeing his chest with its mat of curly black hair. And his flat stomach. And then her eyes moved downwards and suddenly she was weak. Very weak. Her eyes stopped moving, riveted in her head. Suddenly he was looking at her. But before he had time to exclaim, she was across the room, tearing off her clothes and throwing herself upon him, bringing him to the floor, moaning her love. Ada Subin knew then, as she had never known before, that she had found her man.'

He stopped reading with a flourish, snapped the book shut

and held it to his chest with mock affection, waiting for their guffaws.

But the other three were staring past him to the door, where Franklin Heller had been standing for the last three or four sentences of the reading.

Haslam said, 'Mr Heller, Oliver has been giving us a private reading of your work.'

Crossan said, 'It certainly gets across the message.'

'Yah think so?' Heller advanced into the room. 'Here,' he said to the stricken, speechless Mulligan, taking a large felt-tipped pen from inside his yellow jacket and opening the book at the title page. He wrote, 'This is for my good friend . . . ' He looked up. 'What's your name again?'

Mulligan told him.

'. . . Oliver Mulligan. Signed, your old pal, Hell,' he said slowly, as he wrote each word in the book. 'Let me get you the other two. You'll love 'em.' He went out. Mulligan sat down in misery, Haslam's shoulders were pumping with silent laughter.

'You know,' Heller said, returning, 'I've never heard my work read by an Irishman before, and man, it sounds better than when I read it myself. You were terrific. Let's hear more of it.' He went to the door and shouted. 'Sausage? Get your ass in the Mayan room. You guys! In here.'

The others trailed in, questioning.

'Ollie here has been reading my work out loud, and he makes a better job of it than I do myself. Listen to this, Sausage.' He put his wife sitting between his legs on the floor, his hand resting on her breast. He nodded to Mulligan, who stood in the middle, looking helplessly at Crossan and Haslam in turn. He coughed twice, and then began to read in a tired monotone.

Heller interrupted after one sentence. 'Christ, man, put some life into it! That's not how you sounded when I was standing behind you. I know what's the matter. You don't like an audience, right? I understand. Just forget we're here.'

And Mulligan began to read again, in the same monotone, but suddenly, turning humiliation into triumph, he launched into an even more lubricious rendition than the first.

Heller sat on the edge of the sofa, fondling his wife's breasts. She gazed at Mulligan in dreamy awe, shaking her head and smiling like a simpleton. The others sat in silence. Ellen looking as though she was listening out of politeness to a talk on marmalade.

Haslam looked at the floor and thought of his own innocent stabs at writing about sex, and the fate he suffered for it. Irish literature, for the most part, avoided the subject, or treated it with all the louche camouflage of *The Scarlet Letter* or *Tess of the D'Urbervilles*. There was old Shem the Penman Joyce, of course, lyrical in the *Portrait*, coprophilous in *Ulysses*, for ever a victim of the po-faced intensity of American scholarship. And nowadays dear Edna, the rustic coquette, the words flowing out between her legs, spatchcocked with harsh, bucolic memories. The heavy prudence of the Church, augmented by the grim reality of censorship, had forced himself and others like him – those who allowed the merest tincture of sexual reality to give authenticity to their stories – to earn their living from inadequate sources.

But that was all gone now, almost. The list of banned books grew smaller by the week and the titles were *Leather Lady*, by Jack Boots, and *Lesbian Positions VI*, by Dr Hilda Wolitzer. Haslam felt no deprivation in the loss of these.

Mulligan had finished, and after a second's silence Sausage sighed and said, 'Nearly made me cream my pants.'

A small, sad-eyed woman appeared at the door and announced that dinner was ready.

'Right on, Mrs Clancy,' Heller said, rising.

The woman went out and he said, 'There's one helluva woman. Seven kids, one after the other. Never knew coal mining made men horny.'

In the dining room, he seated himself at the head of the table and told his wife where to seat the others. 'Not there, dummy. Jeez, where did I pick you up!' She smiled the smile of a patient whore.

He talked throughout the meal, describing its virtues. The vegetables were from his own garden. He had a great guy. The Irish could produce the best vegetables in the world, but then they boiled the shit out of them. No meal was complete without a bucket of potatoes. They were the best-fed people in the world, caloriewise, but they couldn't cook for nuts. They had to teach Mrs Clancy everything she knew. *He* had to teach her everything she knew: Sausage couldn't boil an egg. But she could do other things, heh heh. If Mrs Clancy had her way they would get potatoes and cabbage every day of the week. That's probably what she served up to the children. And still they looked so goddamn healthy. And that husband of hers, filling her up with babies every year. Of course the priests wouldn't allow them to use the pill, and the husbands were too lazy to use rubbers. Couldn't get the damn things anyway. Illegal. The priests still ran the country, no matter what they said. No divorce, no contraception, no abortion. The place was still uncivilized. That's why we loved it.

Haslam, who had fambled his dinner, said, 'Do I take it, Mr Heller, that you judge divorce and contraception and abortion as true marks of civilization?'

'They're facts of life, man.'

'I must say we have reached a pretty pass when contraception and abortion are considered facts of *life*.'

'Listen, you know I'm telling it straight. Don't give me any of your ironic bullshit. I've been around here too long to fall for it. There's a couple of thousand girls taking the boat from Ireland every year to have abortions in England, and you know it.'

'We should make it legal to save them the journey?'

'You should make it legal because it would prove that the Irish are facing up to the truth. 'Course, that's what the Irish never do. They run away from it. Or leave it for others to face. They blame everyone but themselves for their own faults.'

'There is something in what you say, o Laelius, but not everything.'

'More crap. You know, I used to think that the Jews were the most fucked-up race in the world, and Jeez, we *are* fucked up. But the Irish are worse.'

'It's not a bad way to be, I sometimes think.'

'Listen, I know what you're at, and I'm not falling for it. I never met an Irishman yet who couldn't talk his way into a blue twist trying to prove one thing, and the second you agree with him, he's off again trying to prove the opposite. All he wants is argument, chat, talk.' He lit a cigar and waved the smoke away impatiently. 'Mind, I don't give a shit. I like all that crap. Give an Irishman a choice between talking and working and he'll talk any day. Talking is a disease.'

'Contagious, obviously,' Haslam said.

Heller waved his arm generously. 'Okay man, we don't

agree. What the hell. We understand each other.' He sucked on the thick cigar and said, 'We're both writers after all.'

After some moments of silence, Alice Foley said, 'Have you been out to see the High Cross at Direnny?'

'Parish priest dragged us out there first week we arrived. I guess it's the only thing they have to show off around here.'

'What do you think of it?'

'It's a cross, man. You seen one, you seen 'em all.'

Ober said, 'It's supposed to be one of the oldest in the country.'

'Don't you believe it. These locals will tell you anything. Visit any cross or tower and they'll tell you that it's the oldest or the tallest or some other goddamn thing. You need an archaeologist to tell you the facts.'

'Miss Foley is an archaeologist,' Ober said.

'Oh, yeah? Well, I guess you know what you're talking about.'

'We're going to see it in the morning,' Virginia said.

'Enjoy yourselves. Watch out for the guy with the key. Went for his mother with an axe. And he's still running loose.' He turned to Haslam. 'In the States that guy would be in the slammer. Here they let him walk around.'

'We are a very tolerant race, as you must have noticed.'

The conversation lurched on, the lines drawn between Haslam and his host. But they were not truly deep lines, or clearly marked. Aside from the fact that much of what Heller said was true – it was his way of saying it that riled – there was the more potent fact that he was inviolable in his eyrie, and indifferent to Haslam's small gobbets of poison. He was insulated by a carapace of massive popular success, material aggrandizement, and a bullish insensitivity which he had built up over years of savagely critical and dismissive notices in those places where it was deemed to matter. It did not matter to him, he insisted. 'I'm a lover, man, not a goddamn Shakespeare,' he had said, and perhaps he believed it. 'So a dozen snot-nosed critics say I'm a lousy writer. So fucking what? Three million people think the opposite. Fuck the critics.'

The brandy was finished.

'Okay, folks. Who's for skinny-dipping?'

Crossan watched for Virginia's reaction. There was none. It was, he thought, a curious reversal of practice to swim *after* a meal, but Heller made the rules in Hellerville. Silence greeted his question. It was, of course, unmannerly to refuse a man's food. It might even be thought rude to refuse a man's drink. But was it part of a guest's obligations to swim in a host's pool?

Haslam said, 'Tell me, Mr Heller, why does everyone have to swim naked?'

'Freedom, man, freedom.'

'We're free to swim naked or clothed?'

'No way. People are afraid of their bodies, man. They needn't be in my pool. No one gives a shit here.'

'It seems to me that a freedom that is compulsory is a strange freedom indeed.'

'There you go, Irish prude. Why don't you 'fess up, man? You're ashamed.'

'True, true, but not in the way that you mean. Isn't it a funny thing how people who break away from old customs and conventions always replace them with others more tyrannical?'

'More Irish horseshit,' Heller said, rising from the table. 'You can't get a simple answer to a simple question in this country. You wanna have a swim, have a swim. Raw. You don't wanna have a swim, don't bother me none.'

He pushed back his chair and said, 'Sausage, I'm going to the pool. I need a button on the cuff of this shirt. I want you to sew it on *right now.*'

He went out of the room, taking his shirt off. His wife said, 'Sure, Hell,' and tripped out after him.

Later, Haslam and Ellen walked hand in hand in the clear starry night toward a distant wooden gazebo. With each hour in his company Ellen became more certain of the rightness of her decision, and of the folly of passing up an opportunity which would never present itself again. She had been shocked at the way she had laid herself bare before him, but was at once reassured by his sympathy and understanding. She had never before felt so comfortable in the presence of a man: there were no small battles being fought, there was neither jealousy nor envy; there was complete ease.

He saw the gazebo and said, 'I suppose a hundred years ago a lovely Beltown daughter would sit there on an evening such as this and write impassioned billets-doux to her gallant captain. Now, our friend the *writer* sits there from time to time, naked, no doubt, and writes his randy twaddle for the shopgirl in Kalamazoo. *O tempora!*'

'There aren't three million shopgirls in Kalamazoo, J.J.'

They sat in the gazebo and he crossed his legs and looked up at the stars through the wooden slats, and she laid her head into his shoulder.

'For thirty-odd years I wrote my books,' he said slowly. '*No Tears for Kathleen.* Banned. *Swan of Bright Plumage.* Banned. *Sage and Fool.* Banned. *The Hour of Gentleness.* Banned. They even scrutinized my life of Father Luke Wadding in case I'd have him touch some maiden's feathered nest. Thirty years. And nine books. And all I ever made from them was three hundred and eighty-five pounds. Not a single one of them in print now, and a whole generation of youngsters who haven't read one of my novels. Of course they all read *Percussion Section* and *Linnet's Song*: they're on the syllabus.'

His eyes were brimming in the silent darkness, and he stared back at the big house. 'I tried to do some good. Maybe mine is not a great talent. But it is a good talent. It would have been enough to give me a living. And they deprived me of that. My own people. They made me sell myself for buttons, and they said they were protecting decent people from my evil mind. And now they boast to the world that Ireland is the new Athens, a haven for – for *artists* like our friend, splashing about in his shamrock pool with his little pink tart. By Christ, we are a strange people. In that much he was right.'

After a while, Ellen said, 'Are all of your books still banned?'

He shook his head wearily. 'They're all off the list now. But it's too late. They're all out of print. Nobody knows about them. Nobody can see them in the bookshops. So nobody asks for them. So nobody will publish them. In ten or twenty years' time, when I'm in the clay, no doubt I'll enjoy a revival, and my son will be able to cast off his doublet and hose and live off my work.'

26

The following morning Mulligan rang his assistant Daithi Halley and told him that Ober had been unable to get out to the tanker. 'But it's still bad. They've got film of the bay which makes it look like an ocean of slurry.'

'Nothing we can do?'

'Maybe. I want you to find out for me, as discreetly as possible, what Alison Whelan's number is in Dublin. I know she has a flat somewhere in the Elgin Road, but I've never had reason to find out her number.'

'And you have reason now?'

'I'm not sure. We'll see.'

'Isn't she a bit young for you?'

'I told you before, I like them young. Ring me at Murphy's of Tinahely tonight and give me the information.'

'Consider it done.'

'Anything else I should know?'

'The governors are here. Arrived this morning. All but one of them.'

'What happened to him?'

'He's in jail for embezzling. Maryland, I think.'

'I'd never have guessed,' Mulligan said. 'Any problems?'

'The governor of Massachusetts went off to Rathkeale straight from the airport.'

'That's the woman?'

'Right. Bella Fiori. Apparently one of her constituents has a cousin there and she wants to shake his hand.'

'She's going all the way to Rathkeale to shake the hand of a constituent's cousin?'

'That's right. And a photographer with her.'

'Dear God.'

'Different place over there, isn't it, Oliver? Real politics.' Mulligan sighed. 'Anything else?'

'The governors are going to the Abbey Tavern on Sunday night, as you know. Every pop-up fart in Dublin who has been invited has accepted. The singers have been instructed to learn the American anthem. Will your crowd make it?'

'We'll be there.'

The telephone rang as soon as he replaced it. It was for Crossan, and he called him out of the bathroom.

It was Heller.

'Hi, Steve. There's a call in my study for you. I think it's your driver.'

In the study, Crossan took the receiver from Heller.

'Mr C.? This is Larry the driver. We have a problem, Mr C.'

'What's that, Larry?'

'The big end is gone on the bus.'

'What does that mean?'

'Well, Mr C., I'm afraid it means that we can't move without a new big end or a new bus.'

'Can we get a new big end?'

'It would take two days. But it's all right. I got on to our office in Dublin and they told me that the Mercedes bus came back last night. So that's available. Only thing is it will take about four hours to get down to Kilkenny. How does that strike you?'

'It's the only thing we can do.'

'Would we have time to do the Cross then, Mr C.?'

'Afraid not. We'll have to forget about the Cross.'

He hung up.

Heller said, 'Whatsa matter?'

Crossan told him.

Heller said, 'I can drive you out.'

'I don't want to impose . . .'

'You're not imposing, man. Least I can do. I got a new Dodge truck out there. Open back. Only one in the country.'

Ober to Crossan's surprise, was delighted. 'I saw that truck as we came in. If there is any kind of flat ground out there . . .'

At noon they arrived at the field where the Cross of Direnny stood, and Crossan collected the key from Ritchie Condon, the caretaker who had gone for his mother with an axe. He seemed an amiable enough fellow to Crossan.

They drove smoothly down to the Cross and Ober said that the flat ground was perfect for a slow zoom, and when everything had been set up, Alice said her piece to Virginia, the twenty-foot high Cross of Direnny standing magnificently between them.

'. . . It is best, I think, to think of these crosses as sort of picture Bibles, with the panels on the stones representing scenes from the Bible. . . . We think of the Vikings, I suppose, primarily as marauders and invaders. But this is to overlook their positive contributions, which are substantial. They may have been responsible for reawakening Irish interest in stonework, and indeed it may have been their influence which prompted the building of the first real stone churches in Ireland. . . . The best-known high crosses have a ring surrounding the junction between stem and arms, but the first crosses had neither ring nor scenes from the Bible. They were probably built in the seventh century. The Cross behind me here, at Direnny, in County Kilkenny, is an example of what might loosely be called the second wave. It is probably eighth century. It is possible that this cross is exactly twelve hundred years old this year.'

This last piece was a result of Virginia's prompting. Alice had been reluctant to include it, her academic scepticism recoiling from such glibness. But she had relented.

She stood back from the Cross, and Ober got his slow zoom as Heller backed the truck slowly up to the Cross.

'Perfect,' Ober said, and Maynard dismantled and dismounted, and Ober told Heller to drive out.

Heller started up in gear, forgetting that he was still in reverse. The truck shot back and slammed into the Cross of Direnny, breaking it into several pieces which scattered over the grass.

The truck lurched forward again, and Heller drove it a few yards.

He cut the engine and came out.

Everyone stood around, silently looking at the remains of the work of artists of 1200 years before.

Heller said, 'I bet the goddamn thing isn't even insured.'

27

So it was a subdued group that arrived in Tinahely that evening and checked into Murphy's Hotel in the village square.

Ober went for a walk, attracted by the imposing but derelict stone building in the middle of the square, once obviously a fine centrepiece for the village, now a dilapidated repository of secondhand beds, chipped gas cookers and cheap chairs and tallboys that stood in confusion inside the dirty display windows.

Ober had been pained by the sometimes appalling dirt and untidiness of some of the towns that they had passed through. Ennis had been awash with litter of all kinds, and everywhere there seemed a complete indifference to the most elementary kind of neatness.

Later that evening, in Murphy's lounge around the fire, after a meal and several hours of sullen drinking, he passed his thoughts to Mulligan, risking his displeasure.

But he found no disagreement, and was surprised at the vehemence with which Mulligan underlined his remarks.

'The problem, my dear Peter, is not just to *eradicate* the dirt and litter and untidiness. It's to get the Irish to actually *notice* them.'

'Can't you do anything about it?'

'We try. God knows we try. But it's a hard road. Mind you, I have my own little theory. You take Switzerland, for instance. Cleanest place on earth. But did you ever hear anyone praise Swiss hospitality? And what's the common chant of praise from anyone who has ever visited Ireland? The friendliness of the people, right? They will chat to you, help you, go a bit of the road with you, and they'll give you more of their time than any other people on earth. But if they have all that time to talk to you, where are they going to find the time to clean the toilets, wash the floors, empty the ashtrays, pick up the old cans and papers and plastic wrappers that litter their towns and villages and countryside? The question is whether you can be hospitable and clean at the same time.'

Crossan said, 'I must say that the most hospitable people I have ever met in my life were Americans on their home ground. It's embarrassing. And they never get any credit for it.'

'Mind you,' Mulligan said, ignoring Crossan's comment, 'we have as much xenophobia as the next, though we think of ourselves as the most tolerant people on earth. We don't even have to go outside our own country for it. We have cute Corkmen and deep Kerrymen and Dublin Jackeens and culchies and bogtrotters and turnip-snaggers and all the rest.'

Crossan said, 'And, of course, we have the people in the North.'

Ellen said, 'What is the difference between a Northerner and a Southerner?'

'There are more sudden deaths among Northerners,' Maynard said.

'Well,' Mulligan said, smiling bleakly at the cameraman's interjection, 'you couldn't exactly accuse the Northerners of being as *talkative* as us.' He affected a Northern accent, drawing out the vowels, saying the words very softly. 'A quieter type, like, y'know, inclined to let you say your say, judging you while you say it, summing you up, assessing you, like, y'know? And the less they say, the more you feel obliged to say, because, being a Southerner, you abominate a conversational vacuum. They are definitely not hail-fellow-well-met, no, sir, and if you construe their long silences as rudeness, that's just another typical Southern misapprehension. Shrewd they are, surely, and shrewdness does not advertise itself in long discourses.'

The accurate perfection of content and accent drew applause from the Irish, but it was mostly lost to the Americans.

Virginia said, 'But isn't there a difference even within Northern Ireland itself? I mean between Catholics and Protestants. Isn't that the whole problem?'

Haslam said, 'Differences, differences, differences. Putting people at each other's throats, causing pain and hatred and murder. We are all the same under the skin. We should bury our differences.'

'The differences are buried all over the North, J.J.,' Mulligan said. 'We are *not* all the same under the skin. You know that better than anyone here. And the difference in the North is that the Protestants have one allegiance and the Catholics another, and *for no other reason*. All this talk about an economic base is rubbish.'

On any question concerning Britain and Ireland, Mulligan's professional prudence and Christian forbearance took flight.

He stood up, the pint in his hand, and his stance was that of the nineteenth-century fit-up lead actor playing to the back of the hall, as he delineated the Northern dilemma.

'It is a fact, is it not, Mr George Jenkins of Belfast, that you acknowledge the Queen of Great Britain and Northern Ireland as your Queen?' he said, and then he turned to face where he had been standing and said,

'That's most certainly a fact.'

Then he stood back where he had been, and he kept changing thereafter for questions and answers, while the whole lounge looked on in admiring silence.

'And you will not change that allegiance?'

'Not me, nor any member of my family, nor any of our descendants. Ever.'

'And how many people think like you in Northern Ireland?'

'Over one million people.'

'It is a fact, is it not, Mr P. O'Neill of Belfast, that you do not acknowledge the Queen of Great Britain and Northern Ireland as your Queen?'

'She is not my Queen. She never was my Queen.'

'And your allegiance is to a Southern government?'

'My allegiance is to an all-Ireland government of the thirty-two counties.'

'And you will not change that allegiance?'

'I will never falter from striving for that ideal. Not me, nor any member of my family. Ever.'

'And how many people think like you in Northern Ireland?'

'Over half a million people.'

Mulligan sat down, and there was applause, and he looked at Haslam, but the writer did not return his gaze.

'Refute that, J.J.'

Haslam shook his head. 'A fine performance, Oliver. But a bit too simple for my tastes.'

'I didn't even mention bigotry.'

'The Northerners didn't monopolize bigotry.'

'You had only the tiniest taste of it in Limerick, J.J. It doesn't compare with the legally sanctified bigotry of the last half-century up there. And your beloved British turned a blind eye to it.'

'We'd be badly off without Britain for a whipping boy.'

'They made that bed up there. And even to this day their leaders don't know the first thing about it, and couldn't care less. It's a handy distraction from the godawful economic mess their country is in.'

'The world loves to eat the dead lion.'

'The lion, unfortunately, is not thoroughly dead yet. Did you read the paper this morning? Another letter from Lord Bowrawn himself, giving out about the despoliation of the countryside with signs advising people not to drink and drive.'

'Sure it's nice the man cares about something.'

'I don't give a shit about that. What I want to know is why, in this day and age, this whippersnapper should sign himself "Bowrawn" and the papers of the Republic print it. Same bloody thing with Lord Wicklow.'

It was a fact of Irish life that a number of peers – most of whom did not have a whole county to speak for – still signed themselves, with episcopal hubris, by the name of the area they purported to represent, that is, if they had an area name, which men like Bowrawn did not.'

'It's all very anachronistic, to be sure,' Haslam said.

'It's bloody pathetic,' Mulligan said. 'Of course, Dicky Alliss doesn't sound half as impressive as Lord Hogpuss. That other turd, Lord Lucan, you'd think he'd be ashamed to use the title after what that lunatic forebear of his did to those unfortunate men in the Light Brigade. The bastard is now slinking around the world funking a murder charge, and he owns nearly all of Castlebar, a place he has probably never seen. Merciful God, it makes my blood boil.'

'That's a foolish thing now,' Haslam said. 'The trappings of Empire. Harmless.'

'Harmless, my arse. I don't mind the empire dying – bloody good riddance, I say – but why are we all forced to sit around the deathbed?'

'Nobody is forcing you to do anything.'

'Every week, every bloody week, we have to read thousands of words of nostalgia. That's the order of the day. Bloomsbury. Jesus, if I read another word about Bloomsbury or the Mitfords I'll have a seizure.'

'Nobody makes you read it.'

'You can't avoid the stuff! There's nothing else the British are interested in. It clogs every bloody paper. All those awful Evelyn Waugh babies spluttering and farting and belching into senility. What a bloody boring crowd. And what do they call them? Eccentric! My God! All their insufferable insolence, all their self-indulgence, all their abysmal, drunken fooolishness is called eccentricity. And of course the Irish, ever the servants, play up to these eccentricities for as long as they last.'

'They won't last long more,' Alice said.

'They've lasted too damn long already?'

'They civilized half the world.'

'That's a handy word for it.'

'And what's so wrong about the trappings that remain? Surely you wouldn't begrudge them their Queen and . . .'

'Don't talk to me about that woman!'

'What have you got against *her*?'

'She's such a boring little woman. Her whole family, from the very beginning, boring, boring, boring. Middle class. The house of Windsor never managed to produce one single monarch of talent. Isn't that a wonderful record? You know how you can tell which English King is the intellectual?'

'How?' Crossan said.

'He's the one who collects stamps.'

Haslam did not join in the laughter. Mulligan's wild words in front of the Americans had taken him off guard. He was well used to Mulligan's rantings on the Empire, and once they had almost come to blows when Mulligan had said that Lord Kitchener and Field-Marshal Montgomery were paradigms of English arrogance and stupidity. Haslam had pointed out that both men were Irish born, and the old problem of definition once again reared its hydra head.

Now Haslam said, 'That woman gives the British people

265

something to look up to, something tangible. She stands for something.'

'If that woman is the realization of the highest British aspirations, then I pity the British. Dogs and horses and respectability. Not an ounce of intellect in the whole dumpy little package. And her rude consort is just as stupefyingly boring as she is.'

'I suppose you think we are better off with Jawballs?'

Mulligan was silenced. Haslam, enjoying the numbing effect of his shaft, said, 'He is your idea of the perfect leader, Oliver? Listen, my dear fellow, any king, any queen is better than that. But then that's what the times are all about isn't it? Nobody wants to look up to anyone any more. Nobody is his own man either. Nobody is responsible for anything. Responsibility is society's, and the buck passes from hand to hand and *never* stops. Responsibility. That's what the Queen stands for. Hierarchy. Order. Responsibility. We can't manage our own lives any more. And how could we, when we are no longer responsible for our own actions? Vandalism, madness, fanaticism, anarchy, murder, thievery, bed-wetting, warts, nose-drip. What causes them all? Society.'

'You'll be bringing back the gibbet next.'

'Oh, *I* won't. But it will come back. And do you know who will bring it back? Society. The very society that your so-called sociologists blame for all these ills will throw up the only answer it can think of. Give me the old order any day.'

'And what was the old order, J.J.?'

'A pint of Guinness and a large Paddy, please, Oliver.'

Ellen and Max walked down by the small river, leaving the others to pursue the problems of an arrogantly secular age.

They leaned over the parapet of the granite bridge below the village and looked down into the slow-moving waters. The night was comfortably cool. A late-roving thrush flew under the bridge from the riverside undergrowth.

'It's hard to keep up with them,' Ellen said.

'I've never met anything like it. I can't make up my mind whether they are totally crazy or totally sane.'

'And we've got none of it on film.'

'I know. Jeez, I'd love to have an invisible camera and mike.

The things they say! And right in front of us. You notice how they've changed? Oliver was really at it back there.'

'I think that's very complimentary to us.'

'Sure. But how long do you think you could take it?'

'For the rest of my life, I hope.'

Maynard looked quickly at her. 'You're not serious, Ellen!'

'Absolutely.'

He put his arm around her. 'Come on now, my dear. We can't have you losing your head. I know you find J.J. interesting but . . .'

'He's not just interesting, Max. He's in love with me. And I'm in love with him.'

'Ellen!'

She continued as though she hadn't heard him. 'He's the most fascinating man I have ever met. He is also gentle and kind and considerate. And he is well past any hang-ups.'

'But you've only known him for a fortnight.'

'How long did I know Tony?'

The cameraman looked down into the water. His objections were almost totally protective. He loved Ellen, and they had been close friends for many years, visiting each other's apartments, dining out, going to the ballet and to parties, and generally enjoying themselves together with that absence of jealousy there can be when one of the partners is a homosexual. She told him everything, or almost everything, and they spent many long nights in his apartment over bottles of wine, while she stared at his collections of horse brasses and duck decoys and miniature nineteenth-century American portraits, pouring out her heart to him as she did to no one else. He followed her affairs with an avuncular eye and ear and affected disdain for all her beaux. 'You're a sucker for these tragic types,' he told her. But even he had liked Tony Ferrante. So had everyone else, including all those women with whom he cheated on Ellen. It was Maynard who had found out about it, seeing Ferrante one evening in P. J. Clarke's with Ellen's best friend. 'The sonovabitch didn't even have the decency to do it in private.' So Ellen lost lover and friend at once, and almost fell apart, and for a while had actually gone to live in Maynard's apartment, causing all kind of talk among their colleagues.

'Still,' he said now, 'Tony loved you in his own way, Ellen.'

'He loved me so much he had some left over for my friends.'

267

He threw a pebble into the water. 'What are you going to do?'

'Come and live with J.J. And marry him, if it's possible.'

'Live *here*?'

'Why not?'

'They're different people, Ellen. You love New York. These people are . . .'

'Are what, Max?'

'Jesus, I don't want to offend anyone but I mean, you know, Dublin isn't New York, Ellen.'

'I'm well aware of that, Max.'

'There's this big Catholic thing.'

'I'm aware of that, too.'

Maynard, desperate, said, 'You have a beautiful apartment, you have a great job, everybody loves you . . .'

'Oh, Max, for Christ's sake don't say that!' she said, with uncharacteristic bitterness and lack of restraint. 'The problem is that *nobody* loves me.'

'*I* love you,' he said loudly.

'You're the only one. And Max, dearest Max, you're no good to me,' He pulled away reflexively, but she drew him back and kissed him on the cheek. 'You know what I mean, my love. I want a man who wants me, every bit of me. I want to go to bed with him and wake up with him, and give him everything that I have to give.'

'But you're leaving so much.'

'What am I leaving? The apartment? The apartment is where I sit alone and cry night after night. Everyone else has someone to go to. I have no one to go to. And people are stupid enough to envy me my freedom. I don't *want* that kind of freedom, Max. And they envy me my job, too. It's a good job and it gives me enough to live on. But that's all it is. A job.' She shook her head. 'I know you'll find it hard to believe. But I won't miss the apartment or the job. I'm a lonely woman and I'm forty years of age and the older I get the more cruel I feel America becomes to me. And don't tell me it's the same for you. It's *not* the same for you. Oh, I know it is cruel to you, too. But you're a man, Max' – he smiled grimly – 'and I'm a woman. And what have I got to look forward to? Old age, alone.'

'He's sixty years old, Ellen,' Maynard said quietly.

'I don't see it. I know it but I don't see it. I hear his voice

268

and I see his eyes, and I have never been happier than I have been for the past few days. I've been careful all my life and where has it got me? You have to risk all to gain all, Max. I know I can trust this man. I know it. He is not trying to get anything from me. He tried very hard to put me off. And he painted as bad a picture as he could of what life would be like with him. So I trust him.' She looked down into the stream. 'He's no film star either, but, to be perfectly honest, I think he's beautiful.'

'I don't know what to say.'

'You could at least wish me luck.'

'Oh, you know I do, my lovely Ellen.' He put his arms around her. 'I'll miss you,' he whispered, 'I'll miss you horribly.'

She felt his tears on her neck, and she said, 'You'll get over it, Max. Before I leave you can give one of those wonderful parties of yours. And when I come here I'll send you some horse brasses. I'm sure they have plenty in Ireland. And we'll write and tell each other all the news. And maybe you will come and visit.'

'Maybe I will.'

28

'Ladies and gentlemen,' the voice came over the loudspeaker, 'I would like to remind you that the judging of Shorthorns and Herefords is now commencing in rings two and three. Competition C in the pony-jumping contest is now beginning in the first jumping arena. This competition is for unregistered ponies, twelve-point-two hands high and under, to be ridden by children who have not attained their fourteenth birthday. The prizes are generously sponsored by Mr Goodwin Furlong of Rossnastraw. Will entrants for Competition C please assemble just below the bar tent.'

Behind the bar tent, the group sat on the grass in the sunshine.

The Wicklow County Show was in full swing. The show programme thanked Lord Bowrawn 'for the generous loan of the two north fields as the show grounds'.

Over five thousand people milled under the clear blue sky on the side of Coolafancy Hill, which stretched down in a great green sweep into the Maddenvalley and up again in green, brown and distant blue degrees to the far-off Wicklow Hills. This was South Wicklow, on the Wexford border, where the prospects were not as spectacular as in the northern part of the county. But the fields were beautiful – bright gold where the hay had been recently cut, light green where the second cut of silage had been taken the day before. There were no corncrakes to be heard in Wicklow any more: intensive farming had done for them. The sun was high and hot, and small white clouds threw running shadows across the valley and along the distant hills.

The children on their ponies pranced and shuffled at the entrance to the jumping arena. Their faces were calm. They had jumped before. It was their world. Their names were Leslie and Warren and Mervyn and Sarah and Vanessa. Their ponies were called Velvetine and Dolomite and Pennycress. They were the horse people, 'the other Irish', as Haslam called them.

Across the field were the marquees housing the various other competitions.

'*Farm & Garden*: best three stump-footed carrots, best six potatoes (kidney), best three sections of honey (not to be frilled).'

'*Country Crafts*: best Lumrha rug (in unspun wool, hooked through canvas, unlined, synthetic dyes, bound all round and sewn), best homemade frock for adult, best garments in Fair Isle.'

They were also looking for the best poultry and eggs and butter, brown bread, and the best tart (filling optional), the best jams, the best salads, the best fruits and flowers and photographs and dogs of all kinds.

And of course the best hunters.

For this was hunting country. Horse country. Protestant country. Behan had defined an Anglo-Irishman as a Protestant on a horse. The Republic of Ireland was 95 per cent Catholic. The Protestants had ruled the country for hundreds of years, and when the new State was born, with a Catholic government for a Catholic people, it might have been explainable if the Catholics had turned bloodily on the ascendancy to wipe out them and their memory.

But nothing of the kind had happened.

The Catholics, showing that kind of tolerance and open-mindedness which the Protestants could never manage, elected a Protestant as first president. The Protestants were left to themselves. There was no bloodbath. There were no recriminations. And if the Protestants kept themselves to themselves, well, it was no more than they had ever done. If they felt themselves besieged, they had built the wall themselves. Their heyday had been chronicled by the gifted Lesbians Somerville and Ross; their demise was now being delineated with fluent compassion by John Banville and Jennifer Johnston.

But today, on the side of Coolafancy Hill, the Protestants were still on the horses, though there were a sturdy number of Kevins and Sheilas and Brians among them, one of them actually wearing a lapel pin proclaiming himself a teetotaller,

271

the only possible way nowadays overtly to proclaim oneself a Catholic.

Maynard, as ever, bobbed and weaved among the marquees, accompanied by Virginia and Ellen and Ober.

The jumping was over.

Bowrawn, in twill trousers and tweed jacket, wearing a huge straw hat, presented the Coolafancy Trophy to the owner of the best hunter. His voice needed no amplification as he gabbled out the bland congratulations.

Mulligan said, 'That's how you get to rule the world?'

'Don't be too hard on them,' Alice said. 'They're English to the Irish and Irish to the English.'

'Still, there'd be no show today if it weren't for the British,' Haslam said. 'You'll have to admit that, Oliver. This show is a verse from one of the Empire's oldest songs, even if the words have changed. What's it all about? Good husbandry. And sure what else was the Empire made of?'

The horses had been boxed, the sheep and cows and bulls entrailered, and the large cars and their complements bumped across the grass towards home. Bottles littered the ground around the bar tent. Children with burnt noses whimpered with tiredness. The heavy heat of the day had gone out of the sun.

Everyone went back into Tinahely Village and into Murphy's lounge, finding seats before the big crowd came in. Des and Pat and Jimmy kept the drink flowing to the thirsty customers, and Mona kept an unobtrusive and mistressly eye on the affairs of her hotel.

Maynard, sitting on a small stool, had got to talking to two local farmers, Joe Doyle and Bertie Cleary, and he was now listening to Doyle, who needed no prompting.

Crossan leaned in from his stool at the corner of the bar, where he had been studying the strange floral pattern of the wallpaper for a while before he realized that it was hung upside down. Virginia sat beside him, but she was taken up, to his chagrin, with Bowrawn.

'. . . one hundred and seventy acres,' Joe Doyle was saying. 'Mind you, that wouldn't be all the best land, not by a long chalk. But most of it is good now. I worked myself to the bone to make it that way, and even if I say so myself, 'tis a far cry from the land that I took over twelve years ago.'

272

Bertie Cleary said, 'By Christ and that's a fact.'

Even over the din in the bar, Bowrawn's voice could be heard like that of a schoolteacher addressing a noisy class. 'Could someone kindly lend me some coins for the telephone? I have no money on me.'

'Ah, go and fuck yourself. Couldn't you buy and sell the lot of us ten times over.'

This brought immediate silence.

Bowrawn's family had once owned the village, and many another village adjacent to it. For hundreds of years they had employed every able-bodied man for miles around on their massive estate. They had been truly lords of all they surveyed.

Coins were proffered, and Bowrawn, unfazed, vanished into the back room. Virginia turned to Crossan. 'Does that kind of thing happen often?'

'I don't know. I spend as much time in the company of lords as you do with George Wallace.'

'You don't like them?'

'I don't suffer from that peculiar American malady.'

'I guess you suffer from enough already.'

'I'm suffering now.'

'Why?'

'Because I want to lie with you and I'm afraid to ask you.'

'Lie with me? For Chrissakes, Stephen, where did you get that! Why can't you say that you want to fuck me, ball me, lay me, screw me . . .'

His face showed pain. 'Please, Virginia. I hate those words.'

'You don't mind doing them.'

Below them, Joe Doyle continued, '. . . incidentally, don't mind Johnny there. He's pissed. And what's more, we have a lot to be grateful to Lord Bowrawn's old man for. Oh, by God I could tell you a few things. The Bowrawns were decent, you understand. Decent people and good landlords. But there was a quare lot of hoors running the place for them. The worst out. And they were *our own* if you know what I mean. Now my land isn't Coolafancy land, you know, never was. 'Twas my uncle's land, and I came in twelve years ago and we made a deal that I would work the land for him, clear out the furze, lay on the fertilizer, turn it into a good decent farm, like, you know? And the deal was that I would inherit the land when he died. And be Jayses we even drew up the will in black and white. Well, after four years of breaking my back, and I didn't stint myself, Bertie there will tell you. Isn't that right, Bertie?'

'By Christ that's a fact,' Bertie said.

'I had the place going like nobody's business, when didn't the ould uncle fall straight down on the kitchen floor one morning with the heart going in him. And he says to me, "Go out quick, Joe," says he, "and get the priest." The priest! I don't mind telling you that that took a skelp out of me, for he hadn't been near church chapel or service for twenty years. Go out and get the priest, says he, "and then get the solicitor." The solicitor? says I. Yes, says he, for the will *is not signed*. Well, as the lord is my judge . . . what's your name again?'

'Max. Max Maynard.'

'As the lord is my judge, Max, I nearly joined the ould hoor on the floor with the shock of it. But be Jayses, I says to myself, it's time you looked after yourself. So off I go to the solicitor's office in Arklow and I park the tractor outside his door on the main street, a Fordson Major it was, they don't make them like that any more, and I tell your man my story and I say come on back with me now and witness that will. I'll follow you in my own car says the solicitor. You'll do the other thing, says I. Do you want to have him dead before you get there? You'll come back with me on the back of that tractor, else I'll not stir. What could he do? Up he gets on the back of the tractor, with his briefcase and all, Jayses, 'twas a rare sight, and we drove all the way back. In we go and the uncle is still lying there where I left him. Oh, thanks be to God you got there, Father, he says. He was a bit gone like, you know? Your man gets out the will, the uncle signs it, and *then* I go for the priest.'

He leaned back and enjoyed the laughter.

Ellen said, 'And did the priest get to him before he died?'

'Didn't he live on for six months afterwards?'

'But you got the farm?'

'Every inch. But wasn't I the lucky man didn't lose it all? After all the work I put into it? And there was plenty would have had claims on it. I was one of six children, d'you see, and not one of them would lift a spade to save his life. But they'd all have a claim on the money from the sale of the land. *My* land. My work, and my farm.'

'And it's all yours now?' Alice said.

'All mine now.'

'And what about your children?'

'No children at all. I didn't get time to get married yet.'

Bertie said, 'He took a lep at a woman last September and broke three ribs, and that's a fact.'

Doyle took all of this in good heart. He was a small stringy man with a shock of grey hair and a very mobile face.

'Now that's not the way it was at all, Bertie.'

'Four days in hospital he spent, and didn't he make another lep at one of the nurses and had to spend another week there.'

Bowrawn returned to the bar and said, 'They're getting impatient back at the house.'

The drunk who had previously spoken lurched again out of the corner. 'Well, did ye sell the place yet?'

Bowrawn looked past him. 'Not in my hands, old chap. You'll have to talk to the agents.'

'The fucking agents is in London. How can I talk to them there?'

'Who said the place is being sold?'

'Everyone.'

'I'm not responsible for what everyone says.'

'You're going to sell the place to some fucking Arab, and by Jayses we won't take it lying down. Irish land for the Irish people, is what I say, and that's the way it's going to be.'

Bowrawn looked at the ground dismissively and the drunk lurched away.

Then in the door came a radiant Alison Whelan, going straight to Ober and taking his astonished face in her hands and kissing him. Then she gave everyone in the company a free smile. She sat and asked for a large whiskey and a little water, and half an hour later they left the hotel for Bowrawn's house, Bertie Cleary and Joe Doyle accompanying them at Bowrawn's invitation.

Crossan said to Mulligan, 'That Alison surely is throwing her cap at Ober.'

Mulligan patted him on the back, beaming. 'She's a grand sweet girl, Stephen. And don't you worry. There won't a a a single drop of oil to be seen in "The Whole Story".'

In the minibus, Ellen Harbo asked Joe Doyle, 'Why was that man so angry?'

Joe took the corncob out of his mouth. 'Because he wants one of the Coolafancy farms.'

'*One* of the farms?'

'That's right. There's twenty-nine farms on the Coolafancy estate and every one of them has a grand stone house and outhouses to beat the band. There's one of them farms, over five hundred acres, and I tell you 'tis the best land in Europe, nearly five feet of topsoil on most of it. The rest of them isn't as big, mind you, but there isn't an acre of bad land in the whole place. And the rumour is that they're selling the place. And between ourselves, the rumour is true. I know for a fact that Lord Bowrawn signed the papers this morning.'

'How do you feel about having Arabs for neighbours?' Virginia said.

''Tis no Arab at all but an Irishman he sold it to.'

'An Irishman?'

'Aye. By the name of Brian Carroll. A self-made millionaire, the same fellow. Intervention beef. The E E C. Made a fortune.'

'And he's going to run that whole estate?'

'Divil a bit of it. He bought it for three million pounds, *cash down*. The Bowrawns needed the money, d'you see. And he'll sell it off piecemeal and my own personal guess is that he will make another three million on it.'

Maynard said, 'Why can't the guy back in the pub just buy the damn farm from him?'

'Well, now, there's lots of reasons for that,' Bertie Cleary came in. 'First of all, he hasn't the money.'

'Jeez, if he hasn't the money, why . . .'

'*He* doesn't want to pay for it. He wants the Land Commission to buy it and then give it to him, and he would pay them back over twenty-five years.'

'And will they do that?'

''Tis the great fools they'd be if they did. You see, what we are talking about? We're talking about interest of maybe a hundred and fifty pounds an acre for twenty-five years. Say your man back there got even fifty acres. You see what I'm coming at? The Land Commission would want to know that their money was going into good hands. It's taxpayers' money after all, and as you know the farmers pay almost no tax at all. They'd want to be sure that whoever got the land would work it properly. So whoever got it would want to be a farmer already, a fellow that had proved himself. Now that fellow in the pub back there. Jayses, I have to laugh when I hear him yelling about Irish

276

land for the Irish people. Do you know how many acres he has?'

'How many?'

'Four and a half! Four and a half! And half of that is covered this minute with lamb's-quarter.'

'That's a kind of weed,' Joe Doyle said.

'He works full time at the nitrate factory and he can't manage his few miserable acres, and he wants the Land Commission to buy him some of the best land in Ireland. So that he can let it go to rack and ruin. Do you get me, now?'

'I think so,' Ellen said.

Joe Doyle continued. ''Tisn't the good farmers who are screaming and shouting for that land. Because if they are good farmers they are working like n . . . working themselves to the knuckle to keep their own farms going. This is my first day off for three weeks, three solid weeks. And this morning I had to do the milking, and that makes three hours by the time you've finished the cleaning out, and only I have a milking man, I'd be back there now doing the same thing. Of course, there are some farmers as won't go near dairy cows.'

'Why not?'

'Because, ma'am, it would interfere with their social life,' Joe said, very dramatically. 'By Jayses, I don't like admitting it, being a farmer myself, but this country is rotten with lazy farmers. Lazy! That's what they are. I have a fellow up there next door to me and by Christ he has nearly twenty acres in ragwort. Twenty acres!'

'That's another weed,' Bertie said.

'And the worst of it is, that bloody weed is illegal, and I can't do nothing about it.'

'Why can't you?'

'You don't want to be falling out with your neighbours. If the shagger would give me the land I'd have it tip-top in two years. Less. But he won't do a blessed thing. And he's not the only one. There's a factory over there in Tuam, ye might have passed it on the way, a sugar factory. Now that factory can take ten thousand acres of beet. And do you know how much they get? Four thousand acres. That's all.'

'Why is that?'

'Because the buggers won't grow the beet.'

'Is there not enough dough in it?'

'Isn't it the best tillage crop there is, for God's sake. Nothing to do with that. They're just bone lazy, that's all. Store cattle, that's all they're interested in. No problems, no worries, You can get pissed out of your mind every second day and never mind. And on top of that you can draw the dole.'

'How can you draw the dole if . . .'

'No need to go into that. It's being done. All over the place. And the thing is, the money for that dole comes out of the pockets of those very workers in that sugar factory, sooner or later. The next thing that'll happen now is that factory will close down, and that's more dole. Ah, Jayses, 'tis only idle.'

He stuck the corncob back in his mouth. 'Am I boring ye?'

'No way,' Maynard said. 'If we came to interview you in the morning, could we have all that?'

'Oh, begod no. You don't spit on your own for others to laugh at. But you're welcome to come out and see the milking. I've a grand new parlour and I don't mind showing it off. I'm fairly proud of that.'

29

The minibus drew into the courtyard. The house was unremarkable, sprawling and grey, with a dull Victorian aspect. A silver-and-blue helicopter stood on the lawn. Joe Doyle said, 'That belongs to the new owner.'

'I'd like to talk to that guy,' Ober said.

Inside, Bowrawn led them down a long hallway to the Pewter Room. 'Ah, yes, here they are,' he said, and the group filed in, looking and being looked at.

There were about a dozen people scattered about a very large room, some standing, some folded into settees, others sitting on the floor.

In the corner, the Minister for Livestock, Paddy Cusack, watched Virginia. Bowrawn did not bother with introductions – 'They're so boring' – and summoned champagne.

Joe Doyle said, 'First time I was ever in this place.'

'Me, too,' Bertie said. 'And I worked for the old man for twenty-eight years.'

Joe said, 'There's the new lord and master.' He pointed to a tall young man in a blue suit, sipping an orange juice. 'Mr Brian Carroll, millionaire.'

Haslam took a bottle of champagne from the proffered tray, saying, 'This will do me for a while,' and walked across the room to where Dinneen was talking with Paddy Cusack.

'Well, Frankie, how about this for the real Ireland?'

'Some very pretty girls here.'

'True, true, I didn't know you were interested.'

'I like the company of attractive people.'

'Aren't you lucky others don't feel the same?'

Crossan, at Haslam's side, could hear in the writer's voice

a familiar seismic rumble, and he searched for a distraction.

In one corner, sitting softly on a sofa, was Romana Clay, 'the Irish short-story writer', who had scandalized the country fifteen years before with her first book of spicy vignettes, *A Plicket, A Placket*. There had been a public burning of the book in her native Limerick, it was reported, but then that kind of story was always being bruited about Limerick. She had taken the high road to London and fame, gathered to the collective bosom of that coterie of English critics for whom anything written in Ireland was touched by genius, any work which smelled of hearths and booze and ashplants and country fairs. Romana provided all of these in her stories, which were unvarying in their temper, style and content. Never more than twenty pages long, with a beginning, a middle and an end, they reeked of grass and trees and pubs and dung and Mass, with a sprinkling of rustic scatology and, invariably, a dash of antique sex: 'a dark-eyed handsome brute of a man'; 'a delicate, forgiving creature'.

She was smoking a cheroot and her body, now flaccid and overripe, was swathed in a long, filmy dress. She showed a small ankle and made the most of her cleavage, and her blonde hair fell in natural waves to her shoulders. Her face was still lovely, soft and creamy and slightly weatherworn, her beautiful eyes were almost authentically wistful, and she seemed to float in a perpetual aureole of bog mist and the memories of a thousand orgasms.

Crossan said to Haslam, 'Would you say that Romana's hair is natural blonde?'

'No gentleman would ask that question,' Cusack said.

'Anyone can ask it,' Haslam said, 'but no gentleman would answer it.' He slugged from the bottle and said, 'But then I'm no gentleman. Her hair *is* natural blonde.'

Cusack said quickly, 'What is the black woman's name?'

'Like a blast of that, would you, Paddy?'

'She's a beautiful woman.'

'What do they call it? Poontang. Pooooontang,' he said loudly, increasing Cusack's discomfiture. But then he turned away and said, with wry remorse, 'To be honest I don't know if Romana's natural colour is blonde, yellow or green. But there is one way to find out.'

He walked across the room to where she was sitting, Crossan

following. When they reached her, and knowing that she had forgotten every word of the Irish language that she had ever learned, Haslam declaimed:

> '*A striopach na mbod n-iasachta*
> *O chathair na mbreall*
> *Ni lia poll i gcriathar*
> *Na rian fear ar do ghabhail.*'

She smiled, touched by the native greeting, and stretched out her hand to him.

'Darling J.J. It's been so long.'

'It has indeed, Romana. And it's longer now that I'm looking at you.'

'Still the same old J.J. And who is this handsome young man?'

Haslam introduced Crossan, and Romana stretched her hand out to him.

'Do I kiss it or shake it?' Crossan said.

Haslam said, 'Tell him what to do with it, Romana. He wants to know whether your hair is natural blonde.'

'Pity you couldn't tell him, J.J.'

'It is indeed. Still, it's never too late.'

'It is for you, dear.'

She looked at Crossan's hand, which she still held in hers. 'You have nice long fingers.'

'Thank you.'

Her own fingers were fleshy and nicotine-stained. There was about her a faint and attractive touch of the slattern.

She said, 'Would you like me to read your palm?'

'If you want to.'

'I won't do it if you don't want me to.'

'Can you read palms?'

'Oh, yes. Don't you believe in palm reading?'

'Certainly not,' he said, with mock bumptiousness.

'You're not a romantic,' she accused.

'Is that in my palm?'

'We shall see.'

Several people gathered round, as she had intended, among them the thin white-faced actress Deirdre Haran, beautiful in an empty, conventional way. She worked hard at being placid and dreamlike – an O'Phelia, Haslam called her – and thus did she pose now as Romana Clay deciphered Crossan's psyche and future from the pink lines across his hand.

'You may live a long time, but there is a break here which seems to indicate illness and long convalescence. You do not give your heart, and your love life seems to be bleak. You are a selfish and intolerant . . .'

'Whoa there. You're making a monster out of me.'

'I tell only what's in the palm.'

'I read palms,' Deirdre Haran said quietly.

'You do?' Romana said, hiding her annoyance at loss of uniqueness. 'Wonderful. Then you can tell him I'm right.'

'I'd like to read your palm.'

'Mine?'

'Yes.'

'Why?'

'Because I think it would be interesting.'

'Believe me, it's not. I've had it read before.'

'I'd still like to read it.'

'Don't funk it, Romana,' Haslam said.

She pushed her hand up to the girl, saying, 'I know very well what's in it.'

Deirdre Haran took the hand gently in hers and looked at it for a long time, slowly shaking her head. Then she placed it back in Romana's lap, saying softly, 'No, no, no,' the while.

This produced complete silence in the assembled group. Deirdre Haran's face was unchanging in its dreaminess, but Romana's grew black with offence and hurt.

Crossan took her arm and lifted her out of the chair. 'Your palm says you like walks in the garden,' he said, pulling her to the door. He glanced across the room and almost stumbled in his stride when he saw the look on Virginia's face.

They walked for a long time in silence, eventually stopping at the top of a grassy incline and sitting down. She did not look at him. She seemed to be almost unaware that he was there.

After a while, she said, 'I can't believe it.'

'You can't believe what?'

'She's better than I am.'

'At palm reading?'

'At acting.'

'Do you act a lot?'

'I haven't said a spontaneous word for twenty years.'

'Are you acting now?'

282

'I don't think so. But I can never be sure. I used to be fairly natural, unselfconscious. But it made me very vulnerable. I suffered a lot.'

'How?'

'Men.'

'All men?'

'Almost all. I always yearned for a mature man, with greying hair and oceans of experience. But they're all bantam cocks in the end. I don't want any more mature men. I want a young boy who knows nothing and will sit at my feet and bring me marmalade on toast in the mornings.'

The night was warm, and small patchy clouds moved across the white face of the moon. Romana's arms were around her upraised knees as she sat, but her head was back, the rich hair falling down almost to the grass, and her face in dark profile was that of a young girl.

'Do you really want to know if my hair is natural blonde?'

'Only if you want to tell me.'

After a minute she said, 'Jesus, I hate men. The more I need them, the more I hate them. And I need them, oh, my God, how I wish I didn't need them.'

She spoke to the moon of her hatred, and he listened and could not tell – and would never know – whether she really believed all or none of it, or whether any of it was true, for Romana's truths were in her stories, only her life was a fiction.

'I remember the first time, against the cold concrete wall of the Shamrock Dance Hall. The pain and the blood and the fear, and the smell of stout and the hard hairs at the back of his young stupid head. Every time I smell stout now . . . And the terror afterwards. And he never looked at me again. He was afraid too. But I was lucky. Mary Hannon and Sheila Conway and Olive Noonan all had to go to England. And Mary Hannon never came back. But she loved it. They said she became a prostitute, but prostitutes don't like it, do they? Maybe she did. All those thousands of little Irish fetuses being flushed down London lavatories while the priests preached sermons about pagan England and the purity of Irish girls.

'The second time it was beautiful, with a strong and mature and careful man in Dublin. At least, I thought he was mature until he found a pair of my soiled knickers in his bathroom and he told me if it ever happened again he would throw me out in the street. He couldn't stand the reality of womanhood. No man can. Beautiful bodies and nice faces and lovely smells. Oh, yes. But bloody knickers and shit and jam rags and snot and discharges. They mustn't see them. I should have met Joyce. He didn't mind those things. He *loved* those things. But then I wouldn't want a man who loved that kind of thing.

'I remember the first black man I had, and the disappointment. Not the first time, of course. It was all strange and wonderful the first time. That lovely shiny black body and that great big prick, as big lying down as it was standing up. But he was nothing special, and he always came too soon, and he would never stay in, no matter how much I begged him. Rolling off and sleeping and snoring. He was always half-pissed anyway. And so was I. I wonder how long it is since I had a sober lay? That should tell me a lot about myself, but I don't want to hear it. Drinking, thinking, reading, writing, and getting laid. That's all I live for. And I can do the first four on my own. They're all active verbs. Did you notice that? Only the last one is passive. And it has to be passive, no matter what they ever say or do. You can't legislate a man into you. It's impossible for me to rape a man who doesn't want to be raped. I hate that. Jesus, Mary and Joseph, I hate that. Once, just once, I'd like to have power, to have the upper hand. Not that I haven't had it. There's been many a man who would walk over hot coals for me. Crazy about me. But I can't stand that either. How can you respect a man who will do anything for you? You never know whether he means anything he says. And anyway they're always so weak when they're like that. And I *despise* weak men. I want them to be strong and quiet and totally in control at all times. But that means being in control of me. It means that they have the power. Because they can use the ultimate weapon in this war. The withdrawal of the prick. They can walk away and leave you with your empty, hungry hole and you sit in your room and fondle teddy bears or talk to your dog or just cry. And it is never any different.

'You could have a *nice* man, of course. I've had one or two. They were kind and gentle and thoughtful and understanding. They were wonderful, wonderful people. And they were so fucking *boring*. They were so predictable in their kindness, in their forgiveness, in their understanding. When you wanted rage and madness and excitement. So you went for those things again. And you had your months of madness, and you found again, inevitably, that it was all a cover for that one single ingredient in men who are exciting and stimulating and interesting – selfishness. Every man who has ever attracted me in an exciting way has turned out to be completely selfish, no matter how many tricks he had learned to cover it up. And many others I've been attracted to and never pursued. They've been unattainable. Or the pursuit would have been too painful and humiliating. Or they were married to my friends. I just walk away from them now. I can never look at a man without thinking of him in bed. And I have many friends, not that many, but a few, who are married to men I would like to know better. But I never invite them to my place now. When I'm at dinner with them I try to ignore the men and talk to the women. Because I know what would happen. I know the ritual. It would all end in misery for myself and the wife. The husband would emerge without a scar. I used to love the frisson. The look in the eyes. You always knew, just like they say queers know. But I've been through it all too many times now. And yet I can't stop it. I can't imagine what it will be like when there is no frisson any more. I can't bear to think of it. I wouldn't mind men losing interest in me or not finding me attractive any more. Provided I lost interest in men at the same time. But I know that's not going to happen. I'll never lose the interest. Never. It's a need. It's biological. I'm sure it is. It's more than wanting a body above you, beside you . . .'

That was the last that Crossan heard before falling asleep.

When he awoke, Romana was gone. He stood and stretched. He felt light-headed, powerful, and the memories of what she had said flooded into his mind. He walked quickly back into the house, remembering that Bowrawn had said Virginia was in the Mill Room tonight.

In the Pewter Room, everyone was grouped around Alison Whelan, who was singing a song in Irish.

Virginia was gone, and Paddy Cusack was gone.

He backed out of the room, closing the door. He ran down the hallway and up the far staircase, along the first corridor looking at the room names. Up the second staircase and along the corridor. The Mill Room. He turned the smooth ivory handle and the door opened immediately and crashed back against the inside wall.

Virginia was lying on the bed in a white caftan, her arms behind her head, pinioned by Cusack's hands. He was sitting by her side and looming over her. His jacket lay askew on the floor.

As they both looked round at him, Crossan moved quickly to the bed and grabbed Cusack's shirt by the back of the collar with his left hand, pushing his right under his buttocks and grabbing his crotch. He yanked him with all his strength off the bed, turned him round and ran him to the door, letting go when they reached the doorway.

'Hey!' he heard Virginia say, but he gave her no mind, remembering the look on her face when she saw him go out with Romana.

'What the fuck do you think you're doing!' Cusack shouted.

'How dare you!' Crossan shouted back. 'How dare you interfere with this woman!' His face was red. He could feel it. He was enjoying it.

'Interfere! What in Jayses' name are you talking about?' Cusack made to come back into the room, but Crossan picked up his jacket from the floor and flung it in his face. 'Get out of here, and stay out!'

'Listen, you civil servant. I'll have your job for this.'

'Don't threaten me, you hypocritical little shit,' Crossan said.

Virginia said, 'Hey, wait a minute.'

Cusack said, 'You're in trouble, Crossan,' but he did not move farther in, stopped by the look on Crossan's face.

'*You're* in trouble, Cusack. Open you're mouth about this and I'll send a memo to Jawballs describing in detail how his Minister for Livestock tried to rape a guest of the government. And I'll copy that memo to the New York press, who, as you know, are downstairs.' Crossan's pedantry in times of stress amazed even himself.

Cusack stood in the doorway, looking at Virginia, his eyes pleading with her to tell this upstart civil servant to get out.

Crossan turned quickly and sat on the bed before Virginia, his back to Cusack. 'Tell this man to go,' he said, very slowly and deliberately, his face within inches of hers, his breath fluttering her eyelids. And then, more slowly, more distinctly, he said, 'I will take care of you.'

286

She looked from one to the other, and then she said to Cusack, 'I guess you'd better go.'

Crossan got up from the bed and marched to the door.

'I'm staying right outside this door until you leave,' Cusack said, the full measure of Crossan's effrontery making his stomach churn.

Crossan caught him by the tie and smiled broadly into his concave face. Cusack was slightly taller, but less lithe, and the ministerial life had laid hedonistic inches on his body. Crossan whispered, 'You lost, cock. Why don't you go downstairs and dangle your micky in front of Romana? She won a prize at the show today. Best tart, filling optional.'

He pushed Cusack back and slammed the door shut, standing behind it until the Minister's sullen footsteps faded. Then he turned and saw Virginia's wide eyes. He beamed at her and she returned it. He shuffled off his clothes and said, 'He won't be back.' It was a moment of pure male glory such as he had never experienced. Fighting a man for a woman! How wonderful, in practice, the cliché was. It beat Yeats into a cocked hat. He was down to his small black briefs, flinging his socks across the room in exuberance.

He sat down on the bed, his eyes bright. 'Not a man? Not a man?' he said to her, and leaned over and brushed her full lips with his. 'Have you had a shower?'

She shook her head, still looking at him in awe.

'I think we need one after the long day.'

He pulled her up from the bed and lifted the caftan over her head. She was wearing tiny snow-white panties, a stark triangular contrast to her chocolate body. He pushed his tongue into her mouth, darting it quickly under and around her tongue and she shoved her groin into his, moving feverishly left and right as he became stiff against her belly. He went down her neck and onto her breasts, sucking hungrily on her small hard nipples so that she cried out in pain, and he knelt and pulled down her small white pants and pushed his face into the black nest, breathing deeply the strange and wonderful smell, exulting in the odour. She pulled him up and knelt before him, and rolled down his briefs over the tender bulb of his member, watching it entranced, then taking it in her mouth and sucking sucking, sucking.

He pulled away from her. 'Shower,' he said, and marched

her into the bathroom, his penis between her buttocks, his hands on her breasts, nuzzling her neck.

'Just a minute,' she said, and she bent over the washbasin. He watched her, his finger moving in her crotch, as she removed the tiny filaments from her eyes and placed them in their tiny capsule. She would be entirely naked for him.

He stepped under the shower and adjusted the ancient faucets until the water was almost too hot, and she stepped in beside him and joined herself to him, the water flowing over them and into their mouths as they kissed and fondled and rubbed against each other. He turned off the water and took the soap and rubbed her all over until her whole body was an oily abstract of black and white. She did the same for him, and when she reached his member she rubbed the soap into her own palms and then she knelt and took him in her hands and rolled him between them, her forehead against his navel, his hands in her damp, springy hair.

When they were both thus covered, they stood and locked into each other, moving their bodies with infinite languor, slippery and smooth and lubricious, their undulations making soft, sucking noises.

He turned the water on again, and they stood slightly apart, and it washed the soap from them. And then they stepped out and he pulled her to the bed and they probed and fondled and massaged each other, and she sat in his lap, and they sat on the chair, and they lay on the floor, and on the edge of the bed, and against the furry wallpaper, and he screwed her and balled her and fucked her and laid her and buggered her and rogered her and he choked in her red rank hollow and she gagged on his high purple knight as his seed spurted down her throat and into her hot cunt and up her tiny rectum, and there was no tiniest inch of one body that the other did not kiss and pinch and fondle and fuck and rub and lick and they stayed at it for ninety minutes while not one word was spoken. They spent the night as close together as two people could be, and towards the dawn they rolled away from each other in mute exhaustion, and they were as far from each other as two people could be.

It was the perfect modern coupling.

30

The following morning the crew visited Joe Doyle's farm, and followed him round as he proudly listed the improvements he had made since he took over. He showed them the two tractors, the milking parlour, the hundred milking cows, the fine new concrete outhouses.

They came back and interviewed Brian Carroll, the new millionaire owner of the great Coolafancy estate, whose pilot had brought him down that morning over the hills from the hotel which he had bought and used as a home in Greystones. He was composed and articulate under the lights. He told Virginia that he did not drink or smoke, and that his favourite way of spending his leisure time was sitting at home, watching television with his three children. 'But I don't have that much leisure time, as you call it. Work for me is the same as leisure. I enjoy working so much that I don't need a holiday. I haven't had one now for eight years. I enjoy doing deals, making money, working. I've always liked working. When I had nothing as a young man in Waterford I had three jobs, and my wife was also working, and it just became a habit. That's the way you build up the business. Now I don't need to work any more, but I wouldn't dream of stopping. That's the advice I'd give to any young man starting out in Ireland today. Don't worry about your education. Forget about those degrees, all that learning. Start working at something you like doing and never stop. Keep your eyes on the boss's desk, and one day you'll be sitting at it. Never tell anyone to do anything you couldn't do yourself. Never trust anyone, never depend on anyone. The only man who will get on in the new Ireland is the one who thinks for himself, depends on himself, works for himself.

Keeping those three in mind, any young man who is prepared to work hard will have a lot of money one day.'

They drove into Dublin and checked in once more to the Shelbourne. Alice Foley went home, saying that she might make the Abbey Tavern that night. Mulligan rang his home and Angela told him that his daughter had had her appendectomy and was fine. He said, 'You don't need me for anything, then?' and she said, 'I don't need you for anything.' Dinneen and Maynard went to their rooms. Ober took Alison to Doheny & Nesbitt's. Crossan took Virginia shopping. And Haslam took Ellen on a short tour of what he called 'your new hometown'.

He brought her to Dorset Street, shabby and squalid, the Georgian houses mostly gone, or standing frozen, red-bricked hulks awaiting demolition, their eyes buttoned by corrugated sheets, doors hanging drunkenly.

'I want you to see the bad as well as the good.'

'Poor old Dublin.'

'Aye. Jewel in the imperial crown two hundred years ago. Look at her now. A slatternly old woman. And look at those buildings they are putting up in her belly. Functional, functional, everything functional.'

He took her to the Phoenix Park. 'This was begun in 1662 as a deer park and it hasn't changed much since that day. It is the largest, enclosed urban park in the world. Or so we claim. We're always claiming something.'

'You've claimed me.'

'Sometimes our claims are inspired.'

They sat at the base of the Wellington Testimonial in the Park, and Haslam, looking up at it, ruefully admitted that there had been grossness in the past. 'But some fine things, too. You see, the words might be lost or changed or twisted, pages might be burnt, ideas forgotten. But buildings, my love, have an ineradicable honesty as testaments to their time.'

She looked back into the decaying city. She said, 'Ineradicable?' and he moaned and shook his head. 'I know.' The city was being demolished even as they sat there, buildings being bought up and allowed to wither, then torn down and replaced by the functional boxes he deplored.

She said, 'Can no one stop it?'

'Some try. But first you must find your villain. And nowadays it is not easy to find the villain. There probably is not even a villain,' he said. 'Vague ethos is the true villain of our times. And what man can do battle with that?'

Later, as they passed the Municipal Gallery, Ellen pulled him in to see the Cosc exhibition of modern art. Someone had left a heap of rubbish inside the door and Haslam kicked it into a corner in disgust at another example of Irish indifference to litter. But what he had kicked away was 'Vision III' by the German sculptor Joseph Goils, who had brought the bits of twine and paper and plastic wrappers and sausage skins from Bonn for the exhibition. The curator, already a worried-looking woman, had burst into tears when she saw Haslam kick the rubbish to the wall. It could not be reassembled, since the artist had returned to Germany. But she saved the day. Goils had given a lecture at the opening of the exhibition and he had illustrated the lecture with some squiggles on a blackboard. She would put the blackboard on view; it was after all, the artist's work. The board was brought out. There were three small squiggles on it. Haslam looked at it, and then at the rubbish by the wall. He walked slowly out of the hall, Ellen at his side, tears in his eyes.

Ober, in Doheny & Nesbitt's, was as animated in Alison's company as he had been generally taciturn among the group.

'So the stupid bastard starts her up in reverse gear and the next thing is the whole goddamn Cross is all over the place. Jesus! And you know what he says?'

She shook her head.

'He says, "I bet the goddamn thing isn't even insured"!'

This time Ober shook his head while Alison laughed.

'But there's so much more,' he said.

'Good for you. You got to like the Irish, then?'

Ober made a gesture with his right hand, indicating ambivalence, and he said, 'I'll tell you straight, you're the only really *open* Irish person I met. Jesus, I never knew where I was with that guy Haslam. Or Mulligan or Crossan or Alice Foley, for that matter. They weren't, like, *straight*, you know what I mean? You ask them a simple question and next thing is you're in this forest, you know what I mean? No such thing as yes or no.'

'Well, of course,' Alison said, smiling, 'there is no word in Irish for yes or no. That probably accounts for that.'

'But how come you're not like that? I mean you're honest and open . . .'

'Oh, they let things bother them. I don't. I just enjoy myself.'

'I wish I could help you.'

'We have all day.'

'Not long enough.'

'How much time do you want, Peter?'

'All you've got.'

She held up a chiding finger. 'Now, Peter, we went through all that last night. We've had a good time – I've had a *great* time – and you were wonderful. But you're going home tomorrow and I may never see you again.'

'You could come to New York.'

She shook her head. 'I swim better in small pools.'

He sighed melodramatically. 'You'll probably be married in a year.'

'Marry? Me? Peter, I'm only twenty-four years old. I'm just getting into my stride. And I like my freedom. Just think, honey, if I had been married we could not have had that great time together, could we?'

'We could have had an affair.'

'Not me. When I get married, I stay married, and there will be just one man for me. But that won't be for another good many years yet. I'm going to enjoy my freedom while I have it. Ten years' time I'll get married, have a couple of children, and settle into domestic bliss.'

Virginia woke Crossan that morning and, while he lay passive and moaning, worked on him from a vast and exotic thesaurus of sexual actions whose existence had never entered his mind. She was by turns gentle and savage, impulsive and careful, and all the while she murmured a litany of laudatory superlatives which made him momentarily think of his body as one of the great monuments of the Western world. No woman had ever spoken to him like that before, it was wilder and more wonderful than his wildest and most wonderful fantasies about her, and he felt that the gates of a great new experience were opened to him. He looked on in ecstatic wonder, his body seemingly detached from his head as she moved fingers and tongue over it with a suppleness and delicacy and intuition that he had thought should have been the reward for years of living with the same person. But it was as though she had known him all his life and was intimate with every smallest nuance of his sexual desires. And when she finally lay alongside him – and still her hands were gently working – he found all that speech, all those words, that had before lodged in his throat, and he poured it out all over her, and she smiled through it all and kissed him many times and told him over and over again that he was wonderful, virile, unusual, stimulating, that his timing was perfect, that she had come more often than ever before, and she wished they could do it all over again many times and he said, Why not? and she said she was going back to America, and he said that he would follow her and she smiled at that, but he insisted, and he pointed out that Ellen had the courage to leave her home and job to be with J.J., and why could he not do the same for her, and she smiled again, and the phone rang and it was Ober, saying that they were ready to leave for Joe Doyle's farm.

So they had come to Dublin, and Crossan's fine heady fancy ebbed and flowed, rose and fell, and he took her shopping in Brown, Thomas in Grafton Street. She bought him a woollen tie and wallowed for an hour among the knits and tweeds and jewellery and crystal. Then they went next door to the Bailey.

The bar was almost full of the usual early Saturday-morning crowd of what Haslam called the Baileywicks. Thin, prancing young men at the counter, shirt necks open, their little bottoms poured into tight blue denim, ugly slatternly young women and their slovenly young men, sitting around chewing gum and saying 'Hi' and 'Shit, man'.

There was also an old American couple, grey and blue-haired, sitting incongruous and vacant-faced in the corner. Someone had told them that the Bailey was a good pub to visit and they did not know that the information was out of date and they were too early for the beautiful people who still came in. So they sat there and waited for some famous Irish writer to make his appearance, and with any luck he might vomit or blaspheme, and they would have a story to bring back to Schenectady.

The famous Irish writers, meanwhile, were at home in their

studies working, or having a quiet gin and tonic in a small suburban bar, thinking – like all writers, everywhere, most of the time – about money.

Virginia's presence caused the by-now-familiar cessation of conversation, though it was not so noticeable in this bar, where it was untoward to be impressed by anything or anybody. The habitués worked themselves into a sweat trying to be cool, and Virginia sat among them surrounded by her purchases, dressed in denim, the contemporary uniform for the millions who wished to be different. She was not at all out of place among the frantically different denizens of the Bailey.

When she had sipped her Daiquiri, she turned to Crossan and said, 'Would you do me a favour?'

'Anything.'

'Put your arms around me and kiss me for a full minute, putting your tongue right down my throat.'

'Christ, Virginia . . .'

'You said anything.' She held her face up to him, her open mouth a great pink-and-white siren cavern.

'I can't. These people . . .'

'Any one of those guys would give ten dollars for it.'

'I am not any one of those guys.'

'That's right.' She ostentatiously closed her mouth and leaned back. She said, 'Do you still want to come to New York and move in with me.'

Crossan, who one minute wanted it more than anything and the next was petrified by the idea, nevertheless nodded his head vehemently and, as though to give substance to his intentions, started to speak in a rush. 'I have never met a woman like you. Just being in your company . . . ' but she silenced him, her long finger to his lips.

'You told me all of that this morning, Stephen. It was delicious, though I had to wait a long time to hear it. But you know? You are right. You have never met a woman like me. And that's the problem, Stephen.'

He looked questioningly at her.

She said, 'You know the word you use for everything you hate? *Modern*. That's the absolute rock-bottom zilch word in your vocabulary. Every time you talk of young Americans – of young anybody – your tongue nearly sticks to the roof of your mouth. Califuckingfornia, remember?'

294

He nodded, not looking at her.

She leaned over to him. 'What makes you hate all the perfectly wonderful people over there? It's not just Califuckingfornia, you know. New York, too. And everywhere else. Why do you hate them ? Tell me, Stephen.'

And after a while he told her, drinking and talking slowly and finally very quickly.

Those 'people' were shallow people, bright and brittle and unreflective people. There was a disease rampant among the American young and they had contaminated the whole West, even little Ireland. Those people were attracted by the jejune, they lived from fad to fad, from fashion to fashion. They were incapable of true repose, and were forever in pursuit of sensory satisfaction. They sat in their apartments with their beloved stereophonic machines and they listened in pathetic swoon to songs which, in their varicose cynicism and mordant wisdom, reached astral heights of sentimentality. When they spoke, they spoke only in superlatives, shades or gradations being foreign and complex. They read little, and only those books which would lift them out of the mess of reality, so their shelves held Hesse and Tolkien and Adams and Castaneda. They spoke admiringly of the superiority of armadillos – or llamas or turtles – over human beings as loyal mates, and of the fabulous organizational ability of ants. They dipped ignorantly and gullibly into sociology – the greatest nonscience of all – and psychology and psychiatry and they spattered their etiolated vocabularies with new-minted jargon, barely assimilated and wholly meaningless. They insisted on 'doing their own thing' and on 'being themselves', neither of which they could do, so they bought books which told them how to do their own thing, be themselves. Their industry involved preparing fun desserts and cute batiks and assembling funky collections of small furry toys. They longed for the world to be simple again, and they bawled out panegyrics to the Aborigines and South American Indians and other suitably primitive peoples. They blamed *society* for every ill, thus conveniently shifting personal responsibility into a collective, amorphous corral. When they got married – for the children's sake – they worked days and took night courses in fondue cookery, colour photography and transcendental meditation, while some absolutely fabulous slum girl looked after Adam and Carlotta. And Adam and

Carlotta grew up in a feathery cocoon of indulgence, never once hearing the word 'no', and some of the parents and children, gifted by providence with the proper admixture of faith, industry and perseverance, achieved eventual contemporary apotheosis – they became total macrobiotics.

He leaned back, spent.

Virginia said, 'And you still want to move in with me?'

He nodded. 'I'll have to scout for a transfer to New York. Or give a month's notice.'

She moved her face very close to his, and spoke with a harsh urgency. 'Do neither of those things, Stephen. Don't even think of moving to America. Because it would burn you up in a week. America is the future, boy. Califuckingfornia is the future. All those people you have been talking about are the future. All those people around you in this bar are the future. *I am the future*, Stephen! And you hate the future, the thought of the future, don't you?' Her huge eyes drove every sentence into his brain. 'You hate it. You're scared of it. Well, I'm not. I'm part of it. I love it. I *am* it. You and J.J. are the Ireland of the past. The only difference between you is that he's not ashamed to admit it. He hates the future and doesn't mind saying so. But you try to keep one foot in the past and the other dipping into the future when it suits you. And you'll fall on your ass. And you deserve to. And I won't be around to pick you up. I'll be out in Califuckingfornia smoking dope and listening to a stereo and being what I am and always will be – a good lay. You stay here, honeychile, and mourn for the past, and end up an alcoholic when you're forty. You'll have a great story to tell.'

And then she put her hand into his and kissed him and said, 'Let's get drunk.'

Max Maynard spent the afternoon in Rice's pub with Dick Townes and they talked for hours about the horse show and the ballet.

Frank Dinneen started his last column on Ireland, working alone in his room with just one note on a brown envelope: 'Brian Carroll, self-made mill.', it read.

His column opened, '*Ut quisque fortuna utitur ita praecellet, atque exinde sapere illum omnes dicimus*. That's what old Plautus

said, and he was no slouch. I translate for the dummies:
When a guy makes it we ding-a-lings think he has something
on top.

'Let me tell you about a young Irish springbutt I met the
other day. He proves old Plautus wasn't so far out after all. . .'

Many bottles of Bernkastel Green Label had been consumed
in celebratory spirit by the group in the restaurant of the
Abbey Tavern in Howth that night. Mulligan was drunk. He
said to Alice, 'Not another drop after tonight. Never again. I'm
on the wagon from tomorrow. And I'm going to write a book.'

Haslam said, 'What about?'

'This journey we all had.'

'Do you think there's a book in it?'

After Irish coffees they adjourned to the Barn, where the
twelve governors and Maryland's deputy had just arrived and
were being treated to what the compere described as 'a rousing
medley to get ye going'.

The management of the Abbey Tavern had laid on a waiter
to every table and the governors and their wives and children
and security men were plied with wine and stout and Irish and
Scotch. The room was full with faces, all familiar to each other
for the frequency with which they met wherever free drink was
flowing. Semi-state company executives, their wives and girlfriends were all on hand. Some of them had infiltrated the
governors' tables, to make them feel comfortable, to let them
meet the ordinary Irish: they jawed fiercely through the music,
which was contemptibly familiar to them.

At the back of the Barn the waiters stood in line, unable to
spread across the bar counter for the number of policemen,
inspectors and plainclothesmen of the Garda Siochana who
were there. There were twenty-three of them in all, and they
stayed at the bar all night, filling themselves with stout and ale
and large whiskeys.

Their presence was necessary to ensure the safety of the
governors.

Crossan looked at the governors as the band played 'We're
off to Dublin in the Green'.

O'Malley of New Jersey must have known that the song
would be played. He wore a bright-green suit, white shirt and
green tie, and his wife, the lacquer in her hair sparkling, was

dressed in gold. Their daughter sat between them, fat and disconsolate, sucking Coca-Cola through a straw.

Brodsky of Virginia, who had squandered ten million dollars of his personal fortune in vain pursuit of the Democratic Presidential nomination, was watching and listening, his eyes alight and eager.

Beside him, under a huge hat, sat the steatopygous Bella Fiori, the porcelain on her huge teeth gleaming.

Casey of New York was in a corner, drinking dry white wine with some Dublin friends. He was a quiet, buttoned-down presence, whose face expressed his distaste for the whole thing. He was a regular visitor to Ireland and was known to prefer dinners in the Royal Hibernian with people like Freddy Barton to singing pubs where you could not hear your own voice.

The noise was terrific. The party was high.

Brodsky of Virginia leaped on the stage, flung off his jacket and asked for a fiddle. Thorpe of South Carolina joined him, and the tavern came alive with hillbilly rhythms as the two governors belted out 'Turkey in the Straw'.

Haslam was at Crossan's side.

'There's the whole story for you now, my boy. A Polish-Jewish American playing a Scottish tune in an Irish tavern. The whole world is gone mad.'

Crossan slipped out of the tavern and walked up to the top of the hill to the minibus. Nobody was around. He opened the back door of the minibus with the duplicate key that he had had made that morning in Woolworth's, pulled away the rug and stared at the blue plastic cans of film.

There they were, in a neatly stacked pile.

'The Whole Story'.

Not that, Crossan thought. Not that at all. Just a tiny, inadequate sketch from the great confused tapestry of Ireland. For Ireland was dying, and nobody cared. Dying just when she was, at last, beginning to live. Just when she was flexing her muscles after centuries of misery. She was all dressed up with nowhere to go. The Western world was finished. The party was over. And Ireland had just arrived at the door.

It was all over.

He took from his pocket the small bottle of paraffin and the matches.

He looked once more at the cans.

But then suddenly he turned away and slammed the door shut, and with a terrible whimper he flung the bottle and matches far away into the black night.

He walked back down the hill and into the tavern, and joined hysterically in the chorus of the song 'A Nation Once Again'.